AUG 0 1 2017

P9-CEN-713

METAMORPHOSIS BY
DECREE

SPRINGDALE PUBLIC LIBRARY
405 S. PLEASANT
SPRINGDALE, AR 72764
479-750-8180

SPRINGDALE
2605 J
SPRINGDALE, AR 72
479-750-8180

METAMORPHOSIS BY DECREE

THE BEGINNING

BRIAN PIGG

iUniverse®

SPRINGDALE PUBLIC LIBRARY
405 S. PLEASANT
SPRINGDALE, AR 72764
479-750-8180

METAMORPHOSIS BY DECREE
THE BEGINNING

Copyright © 2016 Brian Pigg.

All rights reserved. No part of this book may be used or reproduced by any means, graphic, electronic, or mechanical, including photocopying, recording, taping or by any information storage retrieval system without the written permission of the author except in the case of brief quotations embodied in critical articles and reviews.

This is a work of fiction. All of the characters, names, incidents, organizations, and dialogue in this novel are either the products of the author's imagination or are used fictitiously.

iUniverse books may be ordered through booksellers or by contacting:

iUniverse
1663 Liberty Drive
Bloomington, IN 47403
www.iuniverse.com
1-800-Authors (1-800-288-4677)

Because of the dynamic nature of the Internet, any web addresses or links contained in this book may have changed since publication and may no longer be valid. The views expressed in this work are solely those of the author and do not necessarily reflect the views of the publisher, and the publisher hereby disclaims any responsibility for them.

Any people depicted in stock imagery provided by Thinkstock are models, and such images are being used for illustrative purposes only.
Certain stock imagery © Thinkstock.

ISBN: 978-1-4917-9948-2 (sc)
ISBN: 978-1-4917-9949-9 (e)

Library of Congress Control Number: 2016910803

Print information available on the last page.

iUniverse rev. date: 10/13/2016

SPRINGDALE PUBLIC LIBRARY
405 S. PLEASANT
SPRINGDALE, AR 72764
479-750-8180

ACKNOWLEDGMENTS

'd like to thank Heather for all her efforts in finishing this book and for being a lovely woman.

PROLOGUE

His ears popped and the black of the darkness wrapped his eyes. The darkness was palpable and alive. It defeated every attempt to see around it and it muffled every sound. The air smelled of dust and something like dry rotten straw.

The man took confidence in his own power. He could feel magic flowing through him like blood. His enslaved spirits enhanced his magic and he flexed his shoulders in response to the input.

His tingling ears picked up the sound of his mentor breathing nearby and the hesitant breathing of their sacrifice.

The faint orange glow of the smoking brazier he carried cast an odd light on the unfortunate man's head floating between the two mages. That's all it illuminated. The darkness gobbled up the light the brazier produced not far from the man's face.

The man looked useless. Possibly because he was upside down, unconscious, and unaware of his impending doom, but he seemed hardly capable of magic. The mage had doubts as he observed the sacrifice.

The man observed the floating victim with disdain. The curse required a man of magical talent. This victim was an idiot and his soul would be a burden after he died.

The sacrifice was nothing compared to the powerful mage as he reveled in the flow of his own power.

The mage's curiosity was strong. The Grand Master made the rules clear. This was serious business. The Order's continued survival depended on this annual event.

The mage scratched his smooth black beard and contemplated the darkness. He knew where he was. The horrors of this room were legendary in the gypsy circles in which he was raised. Blood running down the walls, moving headless corpses, spirits of the ancients - he had heard all the stories.

No story mentioned how it was so dark, you couldn't see any horror or even the hand in front of his face. His eyes watered as he tried to penetrate the darkness with the power of his gaze alone.

The morons he grew up with would piss themselves if they stood here.

The whole room seemed to hum - there was power here. He knew it was an immense room filled with treasures and many magnificent things, but no one had seen them for millennia.

It was nothing like he imagined. No light penetrated this dark and it stank like an old barn.

The rotten carpet revealed under the brazier showed the path he would take in the dust. That dust was so thick everywhere else, it appeared the carpet had carpet.

Suddenly, a change in the hum of power and a dim light ahead marked the exact moment to begin the ritual.

The two mages dutifully stepped off at a measured pace. Shadowy things appeared on the edge of the dim light they carried as they walked forward. Statues or ghosts, it was impossible to tell.

His curiosity itched to swing the brazier for a better look, but the Grand Master had been clear. Don't stray from the proscribed ceremony.

The tower of magic resided over the hall of the last emperor. It was a simple arrangement, they would sacrifice to the emperor for eternity, and he would allow them to live.

It has been this way forever. Which is why he was here now with a country magician floating next to him, as they headed towards the throne of an emperor long since dead.

He had asked the Grand Master last night if the emperor was still there. The Grand Master had just shrugged.

Something is still here, the mage could feel it, and the curse still holds. Weak evidence, but the sacrifices always died. Everything stayed the same. So the curse must hold.

The mantra for this room was: Don't touch anything, don't break the curse.

The golden throne on the dais came into view in front of them. It glowed with its own dim light. A yard in front was the point where the disturbance of the dust stopped. It was getting close.

Energy thrummed with anticipation.

The group stopped at the end of the dustless trail.

"We submit to the Emperor of all and hold up our end of the bargain for eternity," they said three times in the dead ancient language of the emperor.

They both bowed and back-peddled down the carpet - leaving the bumpkin alone in the dark.

The sacrifices were the only ones who knew what lived here and their souls never said.

There was something moving around them, but he couldn't see it. There was a sound, maybe a moan, and the bumpkin began screaming.

"That's it, let's go." His mentor said and disappeared with a pop.

Curiosity drove him to want to stay. He peered into the darkness towards the screaming, but he couldn't make out anything. Whatever was happening to the idiot - it would remain a mystery.

Getting through the initiations to be part of the tower of magic was a cruel process. He had done some horrible things for his ambition and he wasn't going to ruin it now by messing with a dead emperor - against master's explicit instructions.

There was nothing to see, but having completed the ritual, he felt enormous. *There was no power in the world like this,* he thought to himself. *It won't be long now.* Smiling, he thought about his study and translocated to it.

CHAPTER I

Kate woke up shivering and cold. She crouched in the corner of her cot with her back against the wall, the brown woolen blanket wrapped around her. The candle she used to time her sleep hadn't burned down far enough for dawn yet.

Kate's tiny body shivered more from the dream that woke her, than the cold of late winter. Being small was an advantage as the blanket wrapped nearly twice around her.

Kate pulled the blanket tight as she relived the dream.

"I was in his mind," Kate said. "He killed that man intentionally even though he didn't know what was in the dark."

It was a horrible escalation in the nightly dreams that were terrorizing her.

Kate stared at the dark of her room. It seemed like a living breathing thing that was slightly malicious. The candle cast odd shadows and the dancing shadow behind the tiny wardrobe that held her sky-blue trimmed grey robes, seemed alive.

She stared at the shadow and it beckoned her into the darkness.

Kate was tempted. Five years as a priestess had been a long slow descent into abject misery. Her wonderful childhood illusions of the magic world of priests lay shattered around her.

Outside her shuttered window, she heard the door of the cloister creak open and closed several times. Men always left the cloister before dawn to avoid being caught here. It wasn't only against the rules, it was against the laws of the Council.

Nothing here in Theopolis, City of Temples, was what she dreamed about as a child.

"We are supposed to be chaste!" Kate screamed at the closed shutters.

The dark shadow vibrated as it laughed at her outburst.

Every night for months Kate had been warned the Gods were coming. That meant punishment. Every night a beautiful woman requested Kate make changes, but Kate hadn't changed anything. She would be punished, but so would those priests that didn't maintain their vows.

"I'm going mad. No one listens to me and I talk to shadows," Kate said to the laughing spirit. "What can I change?"

The dreams were the same until last night. Last night was worse. She had to report it to the High Priest of Mirsha, but she dreaded the conversation.

The high priest was a wise and kindly old man, and he had been clear the last time. The determination of the Council was final - Kate's dreams were unsupported by other evidence. They were to be ignored.

Kate ran her fingers through her reddish brown hair and rested her head on her small palm facing the taunting shadow.

The shadow had been joined by another.

"It's easy for the men on the high and mighty Council," Kate said sarcastically to the shadows, "they haven't gone without this much sleep."

She closed her green eyes for a moment and felt the sultry lure of sleep. The absolute dark behind her eyelids was the same as the last dream.

The screams of the dying man returned. Whatever he saw was horrifying - those screams were animalistic and filled with terror.

Kate quickly opened her eyes and the screams faded. She didn't know how she was ever going to sleep again with that scream bouncing around in her head.

Dawn would be coming soon. She had a duty to perform, so Kate slid off her cot.

In the giant machinery of Theopolis, everyone had their place and function. There were rules that codified this, and those rules were called the Code.

Kate's part was simple. As a priestess, she supported her assigned temple by doing the duties assigned by her superiors and the rules of the Council.

Her religious duty was to be one of thousands of priests that welcomed Holy Mirsha to the new day with the dawn ritual. She was excused from other rituals because of her other duty.

That duty consisted of doing the temple books. It was menial and boring work. Kate had learned accounting as a small child on her merchant father's knee. It seemed trivial then.

Apparently, no one else thought it was easy. The High Priest had praised her for her work, and made a position in the Temple of Mirsha just for her, which at first was wonderful.

Now it was a cage.

Kate threw her night shift into the wardrobe as the shadows leered at her nakedness. She no longer felt self-conscious of her skinny, pale body in front of them. The shadows had been watching her for at least a month.

Kate pulled on clean under garments and her warmest wool robe with only a momentary shiver in the unheated cell.

It only took a moment to put on her silver wheat clasp that signified her status as a junior priest with five year's service. Just five more and she could have a stripe on her sleeve.

The shadows mocked her. They seemed to know what she was thinking. Kate hung her head, and a tear rolled down her nose.

"This can't be all there is," Kate said as she turned around.

The room wasn't twice her height in length and it was barely wide enough for her to lay down side to side.

She stepped over her things and climbed up on the little altar under the window to open the shutters. The room wasn't made for someone this short.

The eastern horizon was lightening. Dawn was coming fast.

Kate dropped back to the floor and knelt in front of the altar. Everything she needed was here, except patience. Kate watched her mirror. It would reveal the first break of day.

When it did, Kate began her ritual. Every ritual began with gratitude. Winter and fallow fields made for fertile ground in the spring. She said the words, poured the wine and grain, and repeated the winter prayer.

Kate lingered on the last line of the benediction.

"Thank you bringer of light and life, bless us with land ready for seed, and rejuvenation of new life ready to spring forth."

Begin and end with gratitude.

There had been horrible wars. The gods brought the Code, and the Code brought peace and fulfillment with its regularity. She had no right to question it.

Kate poured out the ritual wine and tossed the grain through the window for the birds. She sat on her cot and blew out the candles. Her religious duty for the day was complete.

Light started to fill the room. The shadows behind the wardrobe were gone. They fled from the sun every morning, but they would be back to tempt her again tonight.

"If I've done my duty, why do I feel so empty?" Kate asked her empty room.

Distracted, Kate picked wax off her little traveling altar. She never broke it down. Priestesses didn't travel. It was rare for her to even get outside the walls of the temple compound and into the city.

She rubbed her thumb along a name carved into the raw wood.

It was her father's name. Kate had carved it in honor of her father. He allowed her to attend seminary thirteen years ago after much begging. It was a loss for him. She would give him no grandchildren as a priest.

She would be married with kids by now - if she had stayed in her forest home. That was a dream she'd never wanted, but neither was this, exactly.

Kate wondered if she'd been wrong as she got up and headed to the staircase. She had to see the High Priest before starting another day of her other duty - deciphering hundreds of nearly illegible receipts.

The hall was filled with the smell of breakfast being made in the cloister's kitchen. That would be where the other priestesses were, but Kate didn't get along with them. She ate in the common facility.

Kate never fit in here and she didn't even know why. On the long wagon ride from the seminary, she dreamed of a sisterhood - supporting each other in faith, but that's not how it was.

It was like the seminary - competing groups of women vying for status and position. The women had been vicious to her.

Kate turned left toward the exit.

"Was it you who yelled at my senior priest?" A blonde woman, named Gracell, with perfect hair, and a single stripe on her robe blocked Kate's path.

"Yes," Kate said. "Did you report me for yelling through a closed window at a man leaving the cloister that is restricted to chaste women?"

"You are so arrogant. You will not be tolerated much longer," Gracell hissed. "A lot of people here hate your self-righteous prudishness."

Kate shrugged. "I thought I was just following the rules."

"Then follow the rules. I'm senior in this cloister," Gracell shouted. "You yelled something offensive at a senior priest of Radan. Submit yourself for punishment."

Kate humbled herself before the tall blonde. "I did it, I'm sorry."

"Your apology is not accepted. Someone is going to do something about you," Gracell said as she stormed off.

Kate watched her leave and then hurried past the gate, through the entry, past the matron guarding the door, and outside.

Kate didn't know what she meant, but the blonde priestess wouldn't report Kate. She couldn't tell the authorities that Kate had disrespected a senior priest where no senior priest should be.

The sun was shining and Kate took a deep breath. This was the cleanest air she would get in a big city full of people and animals. Fortunately, there hadn't been any executions in months. Yet, the stink of burning people lingered.

Kate hurried past the prison and darted into the common dining facility. Kate snuck past the large, red leather armored, church soldiers - called Churlars - and grabbed a loaf of bread.

The men barely seemed to notice her.

The commons was full and a riot of color. Red leather, red robes of Radan, blue robes of Aknan, yellow robes of Drorsis, black robes of Val, the green of Talen - God of merchants, (her father's favorite), and the utilitarian brown of the workers.

Kate didn't want to search for a seat, so she left. She nibbled bread as she walked up the hill towards the temples. The High Priests' residences were close to the top.

She turned on the broad, elaborately decorated, residence street. Statues of the gods and statues honoring the priests that received the Code line the road. Everything here was kept with meticulous care.

At the end of the street, a runner was posted outside the High Priest of Mirsha residence, which meant he was inside.

Kate entered the yard and tossed the crusts of bread to the birds picking at the winter hard ground. Spring was coming and the rains would follow, but this was a lean time for birds.

"Thanks," they chirped.

Kate hadn't heard it with her ears, or at least she didn't think so. She watched the birds peck greedily at the crusts.

"Kate," the runner said nervously. "What are you doing here?"

"Hedlvin," Kate left the bird mystery and walked up the stairs to the brown haired young man with the slightly wild eyes. "I need to see the High Priest."

"Okay," Hedlvin said as he relaxed a bit. "Just knock on the door, the guy who will answer's name is Chiron - the High Priest's valet."

Kate paused at the door. "Do you like your job, Hedlvin?"

"Yes," Hedlvin said excitedly. "I never thought I'd be this close to a High Priest and I've been in the Council chambers. It's a prestigious position."

"It is. Thanks," Kate said and rang the bell on the door.

A neatly dressed, bald, older man opened the door. He wore a grey robe with the crest of Mirsha on it and had a kindly smile.

"Kate!" he said. "What brings you here, this morning?"

"I'm sorry," Kate said nervously. "You know my name?"

"Of course, I'm Chiron," he smiled, "And you are the only priestess in the Temple of Mirsha. Everyone knows you."

"Of course," Kate hesitated. It unsettled her, that everyone knew her name, but she knew very few people by name - she spent all of her time in the cloister or with the books in the library.

"Kate?" Chiron asked gently.

"Oh, I need to see the High Priest about the dreams. They've changed," Kate replied hastily.

"You're still having them?" Chiron asked. "The High Priest didn't tell me that. Come in."

"He probably doesn't know," Kate said as she entered.

She wasn't exactly sure what she expected of Haervan's house, but this wasn't it. The High Priest's home was full of books. There were books piled everywhere.

Like a library struck by a storm, books and papers were everywhere.

The dining room to her left had books scattered on the table and the room to the right was congested with shelves full of more books.

Chiron waved her to her right. "He's in here, reading by the fire."

Kate walked into the book lined room.

Behind a bookshelf, Kate found two large chairs in front of a fireplace. There was a cheery little fire burning and the room was warm. Only the crackle of the fire broke the silence.

An old man's face and wispy white hair, poked around the side of one of the large chairs. It was Haervan.

"Kate," he exclaimed. "I wonder why Chiron didn't announce you?"

Her heavy winter sandals rubbed on the thick carpeting as she walked in-between the High Priest and the fire to position herself correctly in front of him.

He was reclining with his feet towards the fire in his colorful nightshirt. A large book lay open on in his lap. A bright lamp next to him cast harsh shadows across the floor.

Kate didn't look at them.

"What's brought you here?" Haervan asked as he rubbed his thinning hair.

"The dreams, High Priest," Kate said quietly, "They've gotten worse."

Haervan's grey eyes narrowed. "Worse? I didn't know you were still having them."

"Yes," Kate said. "Nightly."

"How have they gotten worse?" Haervan asked.

7

"Last night, I was in someone else's mind and he led a man to be horribly killed by an unseen evil," Kate reported. "It was very dark, the man didn't know what lived in the dark, but the victim screamed and screamed. It was awful. I hear it every time I close my eyes."

"Kate, that's terrible." Chiron put a tray on the small table between the chairs. "Sit down and have tea."

Kate looked at the High Priest, but he was serving himself tea. It was strange for such an impossibly junior priest to be in this position. Kate couldn't sit.

Haervan waved at the chair as he sat back with his tea.

Kate sat and Chiron poured her a tea.

"So, not only are you getting dreams of warning, you are now dreaming about killing people," Haervan declared.

"I didn't kill him," Kate replied. "That's what's so weird. I was in the head of the man who left him in the dark. He had such disdain for his victim. He called the victim a sacrifice. I felt his feelings, his ambitions, his awful curiosity."

Haervan rubbed his clean shaven chin. "The rest is the same."

"Yes," Kate replied. "The gods are coming. They want something changed. I don't know what it is."

"You still feel they come from Mirsha," Haervan said. "Even though the Council has ruled and others have had similar dreams."

"Yes," Kate admitted. "But you said it stopped for them. It's been months and now I can hardly close my eyes."

Chiron pushed a jellied biscuit into her hand. "You do look pale, Kate. Please eat something."

Haervan spoke while she swallowed the biscuit. "There have been hundreds of auguries since the dreams started. There has been no evidence to support the assertion that changes must be made or that the gods are coming."

Kate took a quick sip of tea to wash down the biscuit. "Yes, High Priest."

Haervan nodded. "Avoid the sins of questioning. Be grateful, and I suggest you focus on your duties. You are making a difference and you have changed our temple."

Kate swallowed a sigh, "Yes, High Priest."

Haervan smiled at her. "So sad for one so young. If I remember correctly, you went to seminary because you loved the magic of the mid-winter festival."

Kate nodded, she had loved the all festivals at home.

"Now you don't see any magic," Haervan chuckled. "You don't see your worth, but you're the smartest priest to come to me in I don't know how many years. You have single handedly brought our finances out of chaos. That is magic."

Kate blushed at the compliment. "Thank you."

Haervan picked up his book. "I hope the dreams stop soon."

"I do too," Kate replied.

Chiron, who was standing behind them, nudged Haervan's chair. "It is unusual for such a young priest to be getting visions. Particularly a priestess."

"It is," Haervan agreed. "But woman have only been ordained for less than a century. That's a blink of an eye to the gods."

Kate stood. "High Priest, are you worried about all the warnings of the gods coming? I mean, other than dictating the Code, visitations have been disastrous."

Haervan stopped chuckling. "Kate, Mirsha may have a message for you. I can't judge the actions of the Holy Goddess, but we can't think or speak about end of times predictions. We are the shepherds, what would the sheep do?"

"Yes, High Priest." Kate bowed and turned to the door.

"Hold on a minute," Haervan said as he wobbled to his feet. "Chiron, where is all the stuff from my mother's house?"

Chiron smiled, "In your study, of course."

Haervan nodded and motioned Kate back to the chair. "Thank you. Wait a minute with Chiron, I think I have something that will put your fears to rest."

Haervan shuffled off and Chiron sat in his chair.

"This will take a while. Those boxes have been in his study for twenty years," Chiron smiled. "I think I know what he is looking for, but he hates it when I anticipate him too much."

Chiron made small talk while Kate sat nervously sipping her tea.

"There are a lot of books here," Kate said.

Chiron nodded. "The High Priest's biggest passion. He searches them endlessly to divine the nature of the gods."

Kate pointed to the book Haervan had left on the ottoman. "I can't read it. Can he?"

"Not yet," Chiron nodded. "He's deciphered half the books in this house."

"Are they legal?" Kate asked curiously.

Chiron nodded. "Yes, as long as he doesn't use them to subvert the Council."

"Oh." Kate felt the High Priest was walking a thin line.

There was an immense wealth of knowledge in this room alone. Kate wondered what Haervan knew, but was unable to say, because it was against the law.

Chiron stood up as Heaven shuffled back into the room. "Found it."

He handed Kate a dirty white stone, about an inch in diameter, hung on a long, corroded brass chain.

"What is it?" Kate asked.

"That," Haervan said as he resumed his place in the chair, "is a chip off the godstone in the Temple of Mirsha. It has been passed down forever in my mother's family."

Kate hadn't seen a special stone in the temple. "Okay."

Haervan picked up his tea. "It should glow if the gods are near or in your dreams. At least that's what legends say - no one has seen it."

"Thank you, High Priest." Kate said as she put the long chain over her head and pulled her long hair through it.

"Keep it hidden for now," Haervan said seriously. "I haven't researched if it is legal or not."

"Understood," Kate smiled and slid the stone under her robe.

It slid down between her breasts. The chain was covered by her robe and her hair. It effectively disappeared.

"Good," Haervan nodded. "Hopefully, that will prove they are just dreams."

Kate stood and turned to leave. "Thank you, High Priest."

Chiron escorted her to the door. Hedlvin was still seated outside.

When the door closed, Hedlvin spoke. "You were in there a long time. Something special?"

"No," Kate lied. "Just temple business."

A wispy white form was standing in the road looking at her. Hedlvin was speaking, but Kate stared at the spirit. It had a large axe and its hair blew sideways in a non-existent wind. The sunlight passed through it, and there was no shadow.

Kate interrupted Hedlvin. "What do you see where the garden path meets the road?"

Hedlvin stood up and got uncomfortably close to her to see what she was looking at.

"Nothing," he said but he didn't move away. "The High Priest of Drorsis went by not long ago with his retinue, but that's all."

The warrior spirit stared implacably at Kate.

"Okay, thanks," Kate walked down the garden path and stepped around the spirit to turn up the road towards the library.

The spirit followed her.

The sanctuary of the library beckoned her, but the spirit kept pace. Kate's head started to tingle. She didn't remember touching the library door, but it flew open as she approached anyway.

Kate spun and closed the door behind her. She waited at the librarian's desk watching the door for several minutes, but no spirit followed her. Kate breathed a sigh of relief.

She turned and nodded to the librarian at the check-in desk. All the librarians knew her by sight after five years of near daily use. She never signed in anymore and if the bald librarian was interested in her actions, he didn't say.

"The librarians don't speak," Kate whispered. "What can he say?"

Dust floated in the beams of light made by the sun shining through the windows up near the ceiling. It swirled as she passed by the rows and rows of neatly organized volumes.

Every piece of paper created in the complex ended up here. All of them, sorted, recorded, and put into labeled volumes for future reference.

Kate made her way through the shelves to her desk. It wasn't really her desk, but she had claimed the dark mahogany furniture for herself, and the librarians never challenged her.

She looked at how light landed on the desk. "Fourth day of Fal."

Kate had carved the months of the year into the surface. It marked where the light hit during that time and it was fairly accurate. The quill holder was placed so the shadow marked the hour of the day.

It was after mid-morning.

She had already missed hours of work.

Kate started on the piles of papers the librarians had laid out for her and began sorting them - finding it hard to focus on the paper. She was tired and her head kept buzzing.

Very little had been accomplished when Kate heard the library door open. The thought of the spirit that had followed her from the High Priest's residence came to mind immediately, but it turned out to be Hedlvin.

"Chiron sent lunch over," Hedlvin smiled as he put a small package and a jug on her desk.

"Shhh!" Kate hissed at him. "This is the library."

"Oh, right," he whispered as he looked over the desk. "Nice, you've got a sun dial and calendar on the desk. I wonder who did that?"

"I did." Kate grabbed the food and the jug. She was suddenly hungry.

"So the light hits differently every month?" he was moving papers to see all the labels. "You could have used their full names."

"Too much carving," Kate said around a mouthful of ham.

Hedlvin, put her papers back. "Yeah, but the months are named after the priests that received the Code. It seems disrespectful to use the common names."

He looked around for a moment. "You could throw a stone from here and hit the temples they founded."

He was irritating her. "Would you be quiet? The librarians are silent."

He grunted. "Technically, I outrank you."

He made a point of showing the stripe on his sleeve. What he actually said was curious.

"What do you mean, 'technically'? You do outrank me," Kate asked.

Hedlvan laughed nervously. "You're outside of rank. I'm just his runner and you're the 'great accountant'. That job isn't even defined in the Code. He talks about you all the time."

Kate waved at the small row of reconciled Temple of Mirsha account books behind her. "That's my magic. I keep the books. Same as I learned on my father's knee."

"Keep telling yourself that," Hedlvan smiled again. "Although it says a lot that you have both a way to keep time and a full calendar carved into the desk."

He paused. "About how interesting the work is, I mean."

"Yes." Kate had wolfed down the ham and finished the jug of water.

Hedlvan scooped up the packing and the jug. "I've got to get back. Can't have the High Priest screaming for me for long. May Mirsha grant you a good day."

"And you also," Kate said as she watched him leave. It was unusual to see anyone other than the librarians in the library.

Kate stared where Hedlvin had disappeared for a long time.

It was a particularly dark cloud blocking the sun from the windows above her that startled her out of her reverie. The library became dim.

The temperature dropped.

Kate stood up and paced back and forth in front of her desk to get the warmth back in her body. She tried to focus. She'd have to, if she was going to get anything done today.

Kate stopped pacing. She knew she was being watched.

Kate turned slowly to face the library. There were bald men in the dust floating around the room. They were like ghostly librarians and they were all looking at her. They filled the spaces between the shelves in front of her.

A swirl in the dust started at the end of a row, and it got closer and closer to her. A dark haired woman appeared out the dust. Her skin was grey and dark stains soaked the front of her ripped blouse.

The dark woman walked directly at Kate. Her colorless, cloudy eyes were locked on Kate's green eyes.

Kate stumbled back into her desk as the woman approached silently.

A sultry voice oozed out of the dark mouth. "Prepare yourself, She is here. You are chosen. Only you. Beware, many will try to stop you. Only you can do it."

Kate's knees buckled and she slid down the desk leg in front of the dark woman.

The dead woman leaned forward and her blouse fell open. The dark bloody clothing revealed the broken ends of ribs. Her chest had been ripped open.

Kate gasped and put her hands over her mouth. The dark woman's desiccated finger touched the stone under Kate's robe.

"Be strong," the dark woman whispered. "Only you can free us."

Kate blinked and the lady was gone, as were the ghost librarians. Kate was alone, frozen in shock.

The sunbeams moved across the room. Dust continued to float randomly throughout the day. Kate sat shivering on the floor and watched it all happen until the twilight of a winter evening settled the library into darkness.

When the library door opened again, she tried to get up, but her legs had fallen asleep. She hoped whoever had come to the library wasn't looking for her, she didn't want to found helplessly sprawled on the dusty floor.

A dark skinned hand grabbed her arm and pulled her to her feet. To her immense relief, it was her friend T'az. Kate grabbed the desk to keep from falling down. Pins and needles screamed down her legs.

"What is going on? Why were you on the floor?" T'az asked.

Kate turned to her strong and energetic friend, "Give me a minute - it's a long story."

T'az sat on the desk, "It'd better be, you missed our dinner at Tabbard's."

"Oh, god's blood, I forgot," Kate moaned. "I'm sorry. I hope I can explain. I'm not supposed to talk about it, but things are getting weird."

A bald, robed librarian brought a taper and lit the oil lamps around them. He smiled and walked away to continue his duties.

T'az pointed at the disappearing man, "Do they ever talk?"

"No," Kate replied. "By vow they are silent. Every piece of paper produced by the Council, Temples, or administrative offices ends up here. The library is meant to be neutral from all seven temples. It would be a difficult job."

"It would be a crappy job," T'az sneered.

"Did you eat?" Kate asked.

T'az shook her head, "Nope. I waited a bit and came looking for you."

Kate pushed off from the desk - her legs were still shaky, "Let's go to the commons, they should still be open. Besides, the library isn't a place you spend the night. I've got a lot to tell you."

Outside, the sun hadn't set and the soaring marble temples glowed in the sunset.

T'az paused to look at them. "Now that's something you don't see every day."

Kate was going to answer but she saw a knife coming at her from high to her right. The knife didn't appear to have a hand attached. The situation was completely unreal and it didn't make a sound. All she could think to do was drop to her knees.

Real or not, Kate surrendered to the will of Mirsha.

Kate heard the whisk of steel on leather and a muffled grunt. There were a few more unexplainable noises, before she opened her eyes.

T'az was wiping her hands in the grass nearby.

"That was real? What happened?" Kate asked.

"Somebody tried to stab you," T'az walked over calmly, but her brown eyes were searching the shadows. "Good thing you ducked."

"I didn't," Kate admitted as heart raced from sudden fear. "I didn't know if it was real."

"It was real," T'az said. "We need to move. What's close?"

Kate got to her feet and pointed at the blood on the ground. "I've been seeing so many things. What happened to the man?"

T'az shrugged. "He came out of the bushes and I put him back in the bushes. Kate, what's close?"

"We should report it to the Churlars," Kate said, but she didn't want to - she was afraid of them. "The temple - we can report it in the morning."

T'az grabbed a stunned Kate's arm, "Let's go."

Kate led her into the Temple of Mirsha and took a seat on the benches in the entry forum. Ta'z' short sword clunked on the armrest as she sat too.

"Someone tried to kill me," Kate said it more as a statement.

Ta'z nodded. "Who'd want to kill you?"

"I know I bother some people," Kate said, "But kill? Who was that man?"

"He looked like a regular street mugger to me," T'az shrugged. "I see them regularly in the market. Why don't you like Churlars?"

Kate knew her friend was patrolling the market for the merchant's guild, but, "You kill someone every day?"

"No," T'az smiled. "It's been months since there has been any fighting. How do you bother people? You seem nice and sincere."

Kate sighed. "That's a really long story, but I joined the clergy because of our town priests. We respected and revered them. They took their vows and duties seriously, but always had time to help and counsel people. It was like a magic power - comfort from the gods."

"You were around different priests than I was." Yaz watched the acolytes light the braziers in the sanctuary. "Where I'm from, most people are afraid of priests."

"See, I didn't get that. We were afraid of Churlars," Kate sniffed. "They only appeared to mete out punishment. Everything is different here. There's no magic in it. It's vanity and manipulation. I took a vow, just like everybody else, but it feels like mine was different. With the cloister full of men at night, it's like I work in a brothel."

T'az eyes narrowed. "You mean to say, someone tried to have you killed because you don't like them having sex?"

Kate shook her head. "It's just a symptom of a bigger problem. I think we've lost our way. I believe that is the reason for the dreams, but I don't know what I can do about it."

"Dreams?" T'az asked.

"It has been months since I've seen you," Kate said as she laid on the bench. Her heart rate was slowing from the fright. "I was getting dreams then, but the High Priest said a lot of people were and I was to keep it quiet."

"Now you can speak about it?" T'az said as she moved to the bench closer to Kate's head.

"No," Kate sighed, "but it's gotten serious and the dreams have stopped for everyone else."

"How serious?" T'az asked. "Like an armed man jumping out the bushes at you serious?"

"Like a dead woman with her chest ripped open saying that I'm the only one that can save her, serious," Kate said.

T'az nodded. "That's pretty serious."

Kate told her all about the dreams. How they had gotten more frequent and how last night she'd been in someone else's head when they killed a man as a sacrifice.

She also described the warrior that followed her and the encounter in the library. Kate only stopped when a more senior priest approached.

He seemed calm. "Will you be remaining in the temple long, priestess?"

"Yes, senior priest," Kate replied. "I'm counseling a friend."

"It is quite late," he responded.

"I'll restrict myself to the temple and perform my dawn ritual here," Kate said as he nodded. "Thank you, may Holy Mirsha grant you a night of peace."

"And you also." The man bowed and left.

T'az watched the priest leave. "So, a lot of people had these dreams?"

"That's what I'm told," Kate acknowledged.

"But they stopped," T'az continued. "Yours got more frequent and the one today was more specific."

Kate sat up, "That wasn't a dream. She touched me."

"That's creepy," T'az said. "What are you going to do?"

"I don't know," Kate admitted. "I'm so scared of them that an actual man stabbing me doesn't even cause alarm. The High Priest told me not to worry about it, but I think something is coming."

T'az sword scraped on the bench as she shrugged. "Talk to your God."

"I checked," Kate sighed as she squirmed to get more comfortable on her bench. "There's no ceremony or ritual for this, and no mention in the Code."

Ta'z looked over at her, "Don't you just ask them?"

"No," Kate said. "Not usually, we have books of rituals for most things, but nothing about getting answers from the gods. You're not supposed to even ask questions, just be grateful."

T'az pulled a cushion from a nearby chair and put it under her head. "I'd ask if I were in your position."

Kate got up and extinguished the oil lamp on their end of the entryway. Only the dim glow of the braziers pushed back on the darkness.

Kate pulled a chair cushion for her head and tried to get comfortable on the bench. She shivered in the cool darkness. It was mostly from the fear as the braziers were doing their job well.

T'az spoke quietly, "Why is your chest glowing?"

The godstone chip shone brightly under Kate's robe.

"No, no, no," Kate said as the stone started to fade.

"What is it?" T'az asked.

"A chip off the godstone in the temple," Kate said breathlessly. "It's supposed to glow in the presence of divinity. I'm not ready!"

"Shush!" T'az said forcefully. "It's faded again. Just relax and try and get some sleep. We'll deal with it in the morning."

Kate nodded, but was unable to sleep.

She decided to pray. Kate unburdened her heart. She was so afraid and now someone real had died. What could she do? What could she have possibly done to be murdered? It was just too much. The horrible dead woman laughed at her in her mind as she begged for answers.

No answers came. Kate closed her eyes and prayed to not hear the screams again.

CHAPTER 2

There was a noise like a chime, and Kate's eyes shot open.

A soft glow was coming from the darkened sanctuary of the temple. It was pervasive like the sun and it indicated to Kate that she'd failed in her duty.

"I've missed the dawn," Kate gasped as she rolled off the bench.

T'az snored softly nearby.

Kate hurried to the altar. She had never missed a day in five years. Any other needs she had would have to wait. Duty to the goddess came first.

She never made it.

There was a tall, beautiful, white apparition standing in front of the altar. It was a woman in armor and she glowed brightly. Wisps of power snaked out from the apparition and one of them came down the side aisle and encircled a frozen Kate.

It wrapped around her before Kate could struggle or run. It was comfortably warm and snug.

Kate couldn't take her eyes off the figure at the altar, but she knew she was flying down the aisle towards the altar. The movement ended with her standing less than yard from the apparition that was at least twice as tall as she was.

Kate was frozen in shock. This was no ghost. The power and presence revealed it as a god. Gods brought punishment. Training took over and Kate dropped to her knees.

At that moment Kate knew fear - cold, raw, fear.

Kate couldn't think of anything but her failures. Images from her life flashed before her eyes as she stared at the carpet. It was a sad procession.

Kate started to cry. "Holy Mirsha, I'm sorry. I have failed in so many ways. I'm sorry I begged for answers for all my doubts. I haven't changed anything. I'm so sorry."

The white light picked Kate up off the floor.

This was it, she was going to be punished. Kate could only cry. She felt so unworthy of this being and a complete an utter failure.

She was brought to eye level with the apparition. It had the most beautiful grey eyes Kate had ever seen. She felt comforted because they weren't angry eyes. They were sad eyes.

A voice spoke in Kate's head.

Don't be sorry, my child. It is not sin to ask and the answer is yes. There is something wrong with the way things are. Your steadfast belief and gentle queries have brought you to me. Your learning and your devotion make you the perfect instrument for my Purpose. I have tasks for you, and you will bring about Change.

Kate could only think of her feeling of helplessness. No one but T'az and Haervan listened to her.

"I'm not worthy, I've haven't been able to change anything," Kate sobbed. "Even after I was warned."

You have changed. Each little thing you have done is adding up to a Greater Change. You are Changing the way things Are.

The beautiful voice got more formal and grew hard.

Katelarin, Mirsha's daughter, I charge you with a Mission. Recover the lost Tablets of Markinet. Return them to me. The Temples will bend their will to support you, even if they don't know why. This task is dangerous and strewn with magic, take only those that will help you. You must go to Chryselles. There is a thief there who knows the way. He will guide you, although he serves a separate Purpose.

There was a sound like a bell and then the voice and the light were gone. The silence remained and Kate was on her knees in front of two giant boot prints burned into the marble step in front of the altar.

T'az ran down the aisle. "What was that? There was a noise, a gong, and light."

Kate couldn't take her eyes off the prints.

A priest ran out of the administrative offices yelling, "the godstone glowed, oh my god, the godstone glowed!"

He ran down the length of the sanctuary and out into the dark.

"Kate?" T'az said softly.

Kate swallowed hard. "She was here. Right here. These are the prints of her boots. She was beautiful."

"A God. Mirsha. Stood right there," T'az said in disbelief.

"Yes," Kate nodded. "She spoke to me. She was kind."

Men were running down the aisles to quickly do their altar ritual before heading back to see the godstone, but they couldn't get to the altar.

T'az drew her short sword and her dagger. She bared her teeth at the hustling crowd of men.

"Stay back!" She shouted.

A tall, strong, leather armored, southern woman promising violence kept them at bay. Until a priest with four stripes on his sleeve walked to the front.

"What are you doing? We are obligated by a god to do an altar ritual upon entering the sanctuary." The other men nodded.

T'az just smiled at them. "She has been visited by your god and I'm her protector, so stay back until she says so - or die."

"What's going on?" An old man tottered in his nightshirt to the front of the crowd. "Quiet!" He yelled in a voice much larger than the man.

Kate recognized the voice and tore her eyes from the prints. One of the most powerful men in the world stood there in his striped nightshirt. "Haervan!"

"Kate," Haervan said as he carefully moved forward. "What's happened?"

"Haervan, She was here. These are her prints," Kate whispered.

The High Priest's eyes were big with shock. "It has melted the stone."

"She melted the stone," Kate smiled through her tears.

Kate pulled the godstone chip out of her robe and held it up to him. It glowed dimly, but perceptibly.

Haervan took it in his hand, "No one alive has seen one glow."

He dropped the stone and it fell back to her chest, glowing a little more as it did so. Haervan straightened up.

"Adnan," Haervan spoke to the four striped priest. "Get rope and block access to this area. Station four priests here day and night for now. Kate, come with me."

Kate took his hand. He was surprisingly strong for his age and Kate needed the help getting to her feet.

An aisle cleared as Haervan led Kate back into the chancellory.

Kate looked over her shoulder and T'az was following. "Why did you say you were my protector?"

T'az sheathed her sword and dagger. "I woke to a very clear voice telling me to keep you alive. I saw the light and heard the chime or whatever it was. That's when I ran to you."

Haervan answered, "So you are not a guest, what is your name?"

"T'azula," T'az responded, "but most people call me T'az."

Haervan led them past a large open area and only paused to see the same small glow in a large stone carved into the shape of a women.

He smiled, "Thank you. So you are a fighter? Are you good?"

"Yes," T'az replied simply.

Kate was envious of how calm T'az was. She was so confident. Kate was struggling and now she was envious of her friend.

Haervan was still talking. "That's good, actually it is perfect."

"Why perfect?" Kate asked.

Haervan chuckled as he held a door to the restricted part of the temple open. "Most fighters are allied with the knights, the dukes, or the Council. Which means any hired sword could be influenced by money or patronage. Your protector is allied to you alone, which is perfect."

The High Priest muttered to himself as he led them farther down the hall.

Kate had never been in this part of the temple. The carpet was thick and sky blue. The walls were grey and trimmed in a beautiful dark wood. This was more what she had expected at Haervan's house.

He led them to a large office full of books. He put the contents of two chairs on the floor and had them sit down.

"Now, tell me everything," he said.

Kate told him everything. Every word Mirsha had said, the apparitions, the assassin, the dead woman, her questions-everything.

Haervan immediately sent for the Churlars to investigate last night's attack, then sat down and held his head in his hands in silence.

Kate worried he was considering punishment.

"What is Markinet?" T'az asked.

Haervan lifted his head scratched his chin. "I don't know everything, but Markinet was a town. After the war that felled the empire, it is said that the gods first appeared there and handed down laws to prevent a war like that from ever happening again."

"Okay, so we go there and get them," T'az said smoothly.

"I don't think so," Haervan chuckled as T'az bristled. "I'm sorry, I'm not laughing at you."

Haervan was still chuckling as he pulled out a big book full of maps. "A couple of problems. First, Markinet was swallowed by the western desert hundreds of years ago."

He was pointing at a map. "Secondly, they weren't last seen there. They were actually here, but I don't remember what happened to them. I'm not that old."

He rooted through a shelf, found what he wanted, and pulled down another book. He sat and flipped through it.

Kate waited in silence.

Haervan finally spoke. "Here it is. They were stolen. Yes, stolen from the Council chamber."

"That's bold," T'az said.

"Yes indeed," Haervan agreed. "A powerful thief, certainly."

"Powerful?" Kate whispered.

"Yes, I expect so." Haervan was still reading. "There isn't much written about it, but there were two large stones set on a large stone base. I can't see how anyone could sneak that out. It would be hard to get more than a few people in."

Something about that statement was bothersome to Kate.

Kate looked over at T'az. "Which begs the question how you got in last night and how did the assassin get in."

"I didn't sneak, honestly." T'az seemed embarrassed. "I just walked through the gate and asked directions to the library."

"Really?" Haervan's brow crinkled. "Huh. I've been under the impression for longer than both of you have lived that no one could just walk into the complex."

There was a knock on the door. Kate stood as Chiron hustled in with his master's robe.

"Haervan, you left in such a hurry." Chiron fussed over the High Priest as he donned his robe over the night shirt.

Haervan's voice was muffled by fabric, but he said, "Important things are afoot today, Chiron."

Chiron straightened the large embroidered hood. "So, it's true?"

Haervan nodded. "She appeared to Kate."

"That's wonderful," Chiron said. "You must be so excited."

Kate thanked him but she was more worried at the moment than excited. She was watching the High Priest as he searched through volumes of the Code.

He looked up to see her staring at him. "I don't know if it's wonderful. There is absolutely nothing in the Code for this. A woman. Maybe you should tell someone else. Hedlvin maybe, could go. He's stout hearted."

Kate was almost instantly angry and her head started tingling, but it was Chiron that spoke.

"Haervan, be serious. A god picked her," Chiron said. "You're a powerful man, but that's not something you can change."

Haervan argued with Chiron. "Chiron, the Council isn't going to go for it. They haven't let women into voting positions yet and what about the Dukes or the knights? Do you think the Temple of Val will submit to Kate?"

Chiron raised his finger. "I don't think they have a choice. Her holiness burned her foot prints into marble. I think She's serious."

"There are rules, Chiron," Haervan said seriously. "The Council acts on behalf of all the gods. They will rule on this and I don't see them ruling for a woman to go."

Chiron stood in front of Kate, "I know the Code, Haervan. I don't think they have a choice!"

Kate held her hand open and let the tingles go all the way to her fingers. She had intended a different target, but Chiron rose in front of her - effectively putting an end to the argument.

T'az stood in surprise and Haervan's eyes goggled at his floating valet.

Kate stopped Chiron before he got to the ceiling and dangled him in front of the stained glass window depicting Mirsha blessing a sown field. She let Chiron float gently back to the floor behind Haervan's large desk.

All eyes turned to her.

Haervan whispered, "What was that?"

Kate started to cry, "Can Hedlvin do that? Can you? Can anyone else?

"When?" Haervan asked.

"When? I don't know." Kate collapsed into her chair. "I've been able to do things like that for weeks."

Haervan continued to stare, his books forgotten in front of him. "I guess that's settled."

He seemed to wake from a dream. "Kate this will not be easy. The Council will be tough, and the knights will be worse. You cannot demonstrate power in front of them. They will probably react badly and you may be burned. They will see it as a threat. It's been centuries since a priest with power existed."

There was a knock at the door. A Churlar officer stepped in.

"Ah, Captain Ringold," Haervan said. "What did you find?"

The Captain stood to attention. "High Priest, we found the body. Stabbed through the heart. Looks like a street thug. We have not ascertained how he entered yet, or who stabbed him. He did have a gold Talen on him - unusual for someone of his ilk."

Kate knew a gold Talen was more than a month's wages for the Captain.

T'az whistled, "I stabbed him."

"Yes, this woman is Kate's protector - decreed by Mirsha herself," Haervan said. "I'm disturbed that he found entry so easy."

"Yes, High Priest," the Captain said. "The general will be here within the hour to apologize, and he will submit new security plans to the Council this afternoon. It won't happen again."

Haervan walked over and shook the man's hand. "Thank you, Captain. Do you have a reliable sergeant and few men to escort Kate today?"

The Captain seem shocked at the contact. "Yes, sir. Immediately. They'll be outside waiting."

He saluted and left the office in silence as Haervan sat back down to his books.

T'az broke the silence, "Knights?"

Haervan swallowed and nodded. "Of course, any quest with even a hint of danger will be attractive to knights and it sounds like they might be a good idea."

T'az shrugged. "Couldn't you just order a troop of Churlars to go with us to Chryselles? She's already in charge of them."

Haervan laughed again and held a hand up.

Haervan's humor had returned after his shock. "Don't be offended. Mirsha help me, but I probably shouldn't even think these things. The Churlars were formed as armed monks to defend the temples. In the beginning, people were resisting being ruled by clergy."

Kate sat up, she already knew the story.

"The rebellions were put down and the will of the gods was universally accepted," Haervan continued with a cough. "The Churlars stopped being monks, but continued in the role of religious protectors. They never built a solid training program like the knights and have a much less militant role now."

Haervan shrugged and smiled at them. "Mirsha told you this would be dangerous. And as last night's demonstration proved they aren't notably effective as a protective force. The question is: are the knights going to be any better?"

Kate wasn't sure what he meant. "Aren't they the armies of the Dukes and defenders of the land?"

"They are," Haervan said as he put his book down. "They are, but there has been no real fighting in a long time. It is very expensive to be a knight, so there aren't that many of them, and they are allied with the Temple of Val. As a matter of fact, you have to bow to Val to be a knight."

Haervan turned to search for another book.

"Val is a problem?" T'az asked.

"Val," Kate answered as she pushed her unruly hair back. "The Warrior God, keeper of strength and valor - defender of stiff protocol, order, and rigidity."

Haervan looked up from the book shelf. "Don't be so critical. They are stiff and they will certainly see any quest as theirs to perform, but from what little we know - you will need them."

Ta'z rubbed her braided black hair, "I don't know, Kate didn't mention them. We could hop a barge and be on the way to Chryselles by noon."

"Whoa! Nothing happens this quickly," Haervan said as he stood with another book to add to the pile on his desk. "I'll take it to the Council today."

He turned to the still slightly stunned Chiron, "Send a runner to find the, you know, magic people. They have a representative lobbying to get them recognized as a guild every year. He must be around."

Kate frowned. "I didn't know they existed."

Chiron bowed and left.

T'az had deflated. "Why do we need the Council at all?"

"No one does," Haervan chuckled at his joke at the Council's expense.

"What?" Kate said astonished. Haervan had just committed blasphemy.

"I meant the magic people," Haervan said quickly. "Without a precedent, a ruling will be necessary. The Council gives you authority to handle knights, request services, travel, and more. We must do this within the confines of the Code - at least as much as possible."

Haervan sat back down. "You need to have patience. This will not be as easy as it sounds."

Kate sighed at the thought of quibbling with the Council. This morning had been a stupendous event. It changed her.

"I did not change you." A voice said clearly as it resonated around the room. Kate's stone glowed.

Haervan froze.

"Yup," T'az nodded. "That's the voice I heard."

Kate sat up. She hadn't changed. The way she was - was enough.

Haervan yelled, "runner," and Hedlvin entered.

"Go to Adnan. Celebratory Gratitude ritual - now," Haervan said. "All priests, send word out everywhere. Mirsha has blessed us with a visitation. Celebratory Gratitude ritual - seven days. Now boy, move!"

Hedlvin bolted.

Haervan bent over his personal altar in front of the stained glass and conducted a quick gratitude ritual. He sang it in a beautifully gruff bass voice.

Kate wondered if she should be doing the same thing, but she was so warm and comfortable in the fading glow of the stone.

Haervan broke her reverie. "You are blessed, but be wary of pride."

He sat back down. "This will be difficult, but She lays the challenges before us, it is our duty to deal with them. Go with T'az. The Churlars will escort you. Be here an hour after midday for the Council meeting. There is much to do."

Kate blindly followed T'az out of the temple. Five Churlars were waiting. The one with the stripe on his armor gave a grumbled order and the others stood to attention.

"We're going into the city," T'az said.

"Yes, ma'am. You heard the lady, form up," Stripe ordered.

T'az giggled, "I've been in the army sergeant. I want a loose formation so you can look where I can't see."

T'az pointed at the back of her head.

"Oh, yes ma'am," the sergeant replied. "Open formation."

The men spread out.

Kate walked to the gate with her guard in open order around her. T'az apparently needed to talk to the sergeant and Kate was left alone as they crossed the wide stone bridge and into the city of Theopolis proper.

Normally, Kate enjoyed the market. It was bustling. She loved the new things and wonderful smells. It was nothing like her sleepy little forest hometown.

Even at this early hour, everyone was busy here. It was a constant flow of people. Kate didn't even mind the smell of sweaty humanity mixed with various animals and dust. She loved the purposefulness of it.

Today was different.

"What's got into you?" T'az asked as she caught up.

"Everything is different," Kate said. "All the color is washed out and there are things in the shadows I can't quite see."

"I don't see anything different," T'az replied as she swiveled her head back and forth. "Same brick and tan stucco as always."

"It's different," Kate declared.

T'az stopped them, "Ok, I'll take your word for it. Stay here. I'll be right back".

T'az darted into a lodging house.

Kate was completely preoccupied with the shadows and distracted by the annoying buzzing in her head. Her guards stared outward menacingly and Kate retreated to the tan brick wall of the building T'az had entered.

The feeling of thirst overbore Kate's wandering mind.

Kate wasn't sure if she'd been asked something. It felt like someone asked her for water.

She spun around and looked at everyone nearby, but no one was looking at her. It could be said that they were all studiously ignoring her. The Churlars continued to face away.

There was a gentle nuzzle of something furry against her hand.

There was a grey donkey staring up at her with its brown eyes and big ears. It was tied to a post near the door T'az entered.

The donkey dropped its ears.

That was a 'please' if Kate had ever seen one.

She filled a bucket from the half empty rain barrel. The donkey was drinking from the bucket before Kate could set it down.

The donkey didn't thank her.

"You're welcome," Kate said to it.

The donkey continued to drink, but its ears were still pointed at Kate. So Kate knelt down and whispered her doubts to the donkey. At least it would listen.

The donkey seemed sympathetic and nuzzled her again.

"Hey Southern!" A man yelled. "I don't pay you to work on your own time. Why aren't you patrolling?"

Kate turned around and T'az, who had been watching her, turned to the angry merchant.

T'az smiled and shouted. "I quit, Jarius. Complain to the priest!"

The man saw Kate as she stood up from behind the donkey and the Churlars leveled their spears halting any chance for him to approach.

The man's angry expression turned to fear. He put his hand on his heart and walked quickly away.

"I've wanted to do that for a while," T'az sighed. "You do realize you were talking to a donkey?"

T'az was now in full kit: brown leather pants, green brigandine armor over a white shirt, and a small pack. She looked ready for travel, but what really caught Kate's eye was the sword. The hilt and scabbard were beautifully made.

"Yes. He was thirsty," Kate mumbled embarrassed. "Where did you get such a fine sword?"

"It was my father's." T'az' face darkened for a moment. "It's all I have left of him."

"I'm sorry," Kate said.

"No time for a story, we've got more to do. Sergeant, we're going to Cloth Road," T'az started out into the market traffic and the Churlars cleared the way.

"What else do we need?" Kate was confused.

"You're not traveling in that thin robe and flimsy sandals," T'az said.

"But this is what priests wear." Kate plucked at the front of her robe. She was struggling to keep up with the pace the sergeant was setting. "We're just going to Chryselles."

"And then where?" T'az asked over her shoulder.

"I don't know," Kate admitted.

"Exactly. We have access to good clothes and boots here." They turned up Cloth Road. "We get them here and we're ready for whatever comes next."

"I don't have any money." Kate had not brought her small purse.

"Gods, you worry. Chiron gave us money," T'az picked a shop and pushed her in.

What followed was an uncomfortable hour. Kate was useless in selecting appropriate clothes. Her mother had made her clothes as a child and she'd worn robes ever since.

Soon enough it was over and Kate now had pants, shirts, and boots - along with other things. Kate went outside with her packages, while T'az argued with the vendors.

The Churlars formed back up around her.

Kate ignored them and stood in the early afternoon sun. It was still weak this time of year, but she wasn't cold. Her new clothes felt like armor. The things in the shadows didn't seem so threatening now.

A strange man walked through the crowd, past the row of Churlars, and stood in front of her. He was huge. Powerful muscles bulged under his furs. Kate stared at the man's eyes, sunken in his dirty bearded face. They were black and burned intensely as he stared.

Kate was caught by those eyes; she couldn't look away.

He moved so swiftly Kate didn't have time to take in a breath. It looked and felt like he cut her throat and Kate fell backwards.

T'az caught her. "What are you doing?"

Kate was grasping her bare neck. "He cut my throat."

T'az leaned over her as she set her down. "Let me see. You look fine."

Kate looked around, there was no wild man. There was no cut and no blood.

"I saw someone," Kate whispered.

"Okay, I don't see anything." T'az looked at Kate with concern on her dark face. "You're all flush. Did you eat anything this morning?"

"No," Kate admitted. "I'm not hungry."

"Too bad," T'az smiled. "You've got to eat. Then we'll talk about what we do next."

Tabbard's was a windowless tavern on the west side of the market. Kate's father would have called it a den of thieves, but Kate liked it. The scarred black wooden tables, white stucco walls, and rush strewn floor felt safe and familiar.

This was where Kate ate with T'az on their infrequent visits together. Tabbard's sunless interior was cool in the summer and the great fireplaces made it warm in the winter.

It wasn't the neatest place. Boys were moving around as they tried to stay ahead of the mess. Except for a few men at the bar, the tavern was empty.

"Can we get seats with a lot of light?" Kate asked as they walked toward the bar. "I don't need shadows right now."

T'az looked for Tabbard and Kate eyed the few men at the long wooden bar. The men ignored her, but they didn't ignore the Churlars. When the sergeant entered, the men at the bar hustled out another door.

Kate ran her hands on the dark wood of the long, now empty bar. It was pleasing to the eye in the oil lamps overhead and felt alive.

Tabbard seemed angry. "We don't serve them here."

T'az leaned on a brass fixture at the bar and pointed toward the back of the tavern. "You do today Tabbard, and I'll make it worth your time."

T'az showed her an empty table with two lamps overhead. No one else was in this part of the tavern. T'az convinced the sergeant to split his men between the other two tables.

"Does this cost extra?" Kate plopped into a solid wooden chair and leaned heavily on her hands.

"Worrier," T'az waved away her concern. "When I tell you I know people; it means I know people. Tabbard fought with my father for years. He was there when my father died."

"Oh," Kate struggled to find words. "Were you always planning to grow up like him?"

T'az leaned back in her chair. "My mother sent me to seminary while dad was out fighting."

Kate gasped. "You went to seminary? How? Why aren't you in the priesthood?"

Kate knew nothing of T'az' history. Mostly, they had always talked about Kate.

"Through no fault of my own. When I was thrown out - my father was the only one there." T'az was distant and seemed sad.

"Thrown out? For what?" Kate was outraged. There were southern priests. Bigotry existed, but it wasn't rampant in the priesthood.

"Purity," T'az said darkly. "Dad knew I'd be thrown out. He'd killed the man. After that, I learned to fight."

T'az had admitted to being raped as a child and Kate didn't know what to say. It was too horrible a crime. It was punished by death in the city, but raped girls rarely married. Most of the beggar women were rape victims.

Kate fidgeted. "I'm sorry, I had no idea. Um. You've been training to fight since you were eight?"

T'az nodded and seemed relieved at the subject change. "And I've made good money doing it."

Tabbard returned and dropped food on the table with wine and mugs. Kate liked the food here, it was hearty, and the pot roast was delicious.

Kate frowned, today was pork.

Boys brought food and beer for the Churlars.

"I never asked you how you ended up here?" Kate spooned the gravy covered pork.

"I'd been speared in the lungs." T'az poured the wine and took a big gulp. "Ambushed down on the Vistula river patrol. I thought I was going to die. That motivated me to see more of the world. Tabbard was here, so I came here."

T'az was just what Kate needed in more ways than one.

"Mirsha works in mysterious ways," Kate said to herself as she began to eat.

T'az left a generous amount of money on the table, but Tabbard intercepted them as they passed the bar. Kate walked with the Churlars to the door.

Kate could tell when T'az rejoined the group, that the discussion with Tabbard hadn't been about money. T'az looked serious.

"Back to the temple sergeant," T'az said curtly.

"Why?" Kate was alarmed.

"The word is out. Rumors are flying in the market about a priestess with a glowing godstone," T'az said grimly. "I didn't think anybody would know what it was."

The walk was uneventful. Nobody would challenge a squad of Churlars and T'az' face probably made that impossibility even less likely.

The sergeant held up at the front stairs to the temple. The temple itself was a flurry of activity. Celebratory decorations were being placed and hung. Priests sang as they worked. The joy was palpable.

Kate still had doubts. She walked in and up to the altar. There was now a velvet rope around the three stairs up to the altar.

Mirsha's boot prints were still melted into the stone. Kate knelt and did her own devotion in front of the four young priests attending the rope.

Hedlvan entered and knelt for his own devotion.

Kate wanted to be alone, but Hedlvin sat in the first row of pews with T'az. There would be no privacy.

Holy Mirsha, Kate thought, *I will not question why you chose me. I want to, but I also want to be chosen. I need your help, my head is buzzing and I can't concentrate.*

It is power, learn to use it, you will need it. Was the response.

Kate shuddered at the voice in her head. It took a moment for Kate to compose herself. This wasn't a ritual; she was in conversation with one of the gods.

Kate tempted fate to ask another question. *What about the shadows, Holy Mirsha?*

All things that have ever existed, still exist and things you can't imagine exist also. The voice responded.

The response was a bit confusing to Kate. The voice seemed to chuckle. It wasn't a sound, it was just a feeling.

Then the voice spoke without prompting. **My daughter, you are perfect for your task. There will come a time when all your questions are answered.**

The presence of the voice left Kate's head. Kate started to cry with joy. Holy Mirsha had answered her question and seemed pleased.

Kate rose and turned to T'az and Hedlvan. T'az started to rise, but a priest burst into the sanctuary.

"The godstone just glowed as bright as the sun!" He yelled as he ran down the side aisle and out the front door.

T'az was still looking at Kate. "Something you want to tell us?"

Kate smiled, "Nothing can stop us."

"Well maybe," Hedlvan said. "The High Priest is having a difficult time with the Council. He sent me to tell you to be at his house tomorrow morning. You are going to appear before the Council then."

"Well then maybe we don't need them. Holy Mirsha and T'az are all the support I need," Kate said drawing her sleeve across her face.

Hedlvan seemed hurt. "Hey, that doesn't mean other people aren't behind you."

"I'm sorry," Kate smiled at him. "I didn't mean it that way, Hedlvan."

He shuffled to his feet. "I'm putting together something that may help. I'll see you tomorrow."

Hedlvan left them alone in the brightly decorated sanctuary.

T'az snickered. "I think he likes you."

That took Kate aback. "Who? Hedlvan?"

"Never mind," T'az smiled knowingly. "Where to now?"

"The Commons?" Kate asked without any serious conviction.

T'az shook her head. "I don't think so, I don't like the way everyone watched you walk up here. Let's avoid crowds for now."

"That just leaves here and the cloister." Kate really didn't want to spend a lot of time in the cloister, but T'az picked it anyway.

"The cloister then," T'az said as she led Kate down the aisle. "Can you get me set up there?"

"I think so, I mean yes." Kate was still trying on her new confidence.

Churlars in tow, they walked down the hill to the cloister. Kate pushed the door open and walked up to the matron on duty.

"T'az is my protector. I need the room across from mine cleaned out for her," Kate said as confidently as she could.

"But she isn't part of this cloister." The older woman protested.

Kate took a deep breath. "That doesn't matter. I've been charged with a quest. She has the blessing of the High Priest of Mirsha. You can confirm it. Please get the room ready."

The woman seemed stunned, but she got up and left.

Kate turned to T'az. "Come on, let's put your stuff in my room."

They headed up the stairs and crossed to the east side of the building. Kate opened her door. The room was exactly as she'd left it and it was a mess.

"This is tiny," T'az said as she dropped her pack.

"I believe that's why they're called cells," Kate replied as she turned around.

Kate and T'az spent the afternoon discussing what Kate could do with the tingling power and they experimented with it in the confines of the darkening grey stone cell.

They ate and bathed in the cloister's facilities. The other priestesses avoided them. Kate wasn't sure if this was the normal discrimination or if the women were intimidated by T'az.

There was a three striped priest of Radan in the hall when Kate returned from the bath and dinner. It shocked her to see him standing so blatantly outside her door.

"What are you doing here? This is a cloister," Kate said.

"Do you not recognize your superior?" The man said haughtily. "I can go wherever I want. I can do what I want, and I what I want to do is educate you."

"Educate?" Kate asked, "Is that a euphemism for sex?"

T'az chuckled.

"How dare you disrespect your senior," The man howled. "Do you think I'm intimidated by your sell-sword?"

Kate was not intimidated either. "I didn't know the Code was different for each rank. This is for women only, by Code."

He smiled. "I can enter in the course of my religious duty and it is my duty to re-educate you in how the temples and the Code work. You seem confused about the role of a junior priest. You will be sent back to seminary as a bonded penitent until you learn."

"A slave," Kate said. "I will not. I have been picked by Holy Mirsha to retrieve a relic."

That made the priest chuckle. "You. A priestess, and the worst one at that. I'd heard Haervan brought it up to the Council. That doddering old man isn't convincing anyone of your subterfuge."

"You mean the High Priest of Mirsha," Kate growled.

"Bumbling fool, more like," the man smiled. "He has long outlived his usefulness in your minor deity's service."

Kate shook her head in disbelief. "You wouldn't say that if you'd met her."

The man rose to his full height. "Holy Radan is the father of the Gods. Val is his right hand, and Talen his left. Mirsha does little more than tend His garden. You will recognize the hierarchy - the lash will ensure that."

"Over my dead body," T'az said calmly.

Stomping boots reverberated on the stairs behind Kate. Churlars marched into the hallway, led by Gracell the smug blonde one striped priestess that was always angry at Kate.

Gracell had an evil smile as she led the Churlars forward.

"Arrest them," the man said loudly. "The priestess for questioning the Gods, and the southern for not understanding her place and for not staying in it."

T'az started to draw her sword, but Kate put her hand on her arm.

"I can take them," T'az said confidently.

"No," Kate whispered as she pointed with her chin at the window in her room. "Go to Haervan. I'll provide a distraction. It will be alright."

"I have to protect you," T'az said earnestly.

Kate smiled, "I won't be hurt by these people."

Kate turned back to the priest and silently prayed to Mirsha for darkness. Her head tingled and the oil lamps blew out in an odd gust of wind.

T'az grabbed her pack and leapt from the open window into the late winter night.

"Lights," the priest yelled, outraged at the turn of events.

Light was quickly restored and Kate laughed as she stood alone outside her cell. Mostly, because of the look on the priest's face, but partly because the power responded to her need. That was a relief.

There was a brief search for T'az, but the tall priest of Radan never stopped staring at Kate. His dislike was palpable.

"We will hunt her down." The priest hissed.

Kate smiled and turned to walk down the stairwell in front of the Churlars. "Good luck."

CHAPTER 3

Kate listened to the rain pattering on her canvas hood. It was a grey and dreary morning, the seventh since she had been thrown in jail. The arrest was only a formality, but the one night in prison had scarred her.

The inquisition priests worked late into the evening. The screaming had almost been better than the silence. The silence meant you didn't know where the inquisitors were or what they were doing.

The shadow creatures were ever present. There was a grey apparition of a man that haunted one shadow in particular. Something about him was terribly cold and malevolent.

He seemed to walk endlessly through the unadorned hallways.

After a while, Kate stared at the wall to avoid shadows. It took effort to ignore them. To distract herself, she had scratched 'the gods are coming' over the other graffiti on the wall with her silver wheat clasp.

The clasp was ruined by the work.

The High Priest had secured her release the next morning. T'az had found him. He was both angry at Kate and outraged by the priest of Radan.

He had lectured her endlessly, "I told you about the dangers of pride."

He couldn't ignore that the godstone statue of Mirsha glowed every time Kate was near it. Haervan had swallowed his anger and his desire to replace her with someone more suitably humble.

In the end, he let Chiron outfit her expedition with temple funds.

Now she sat on the back of her horse on a rainy road, surrounded by grey, unplowed fields, and felt relief. The contrast-less days had kept the shadows at bay, she was away from the routine and the stress of her daily life.

Kate rubbed the neck of the horse who had picked her. His name was Zhost and he was a leader. He kept the other horses in line. As only T'az was an experienced rider, the other horses looked to Zhost for guidance.

Kate and Zhost now stood on the damp road, not far from the trees where they had camped the night before. The two of them were willing T'az and Hestal, the mage, to get Bernard, the healer, on his horse in the slippery grass.

Bernard was a balding, fat man, who had seemed eager to come. That was before three solid days of rain revealed a lifetime of comfort didn't lead to a stout heart.

At their initial meeting in Haervan's dining room, Bernard had introduced himself. He stood before them like an actor taking the stage in his brown healer's robe.

"I am as you see me. As for my story, there really isn't that much to tell. I was born here and went to school here. I've been working here as a Healer for just over ten years. I have had no wild adventures and I have done nothing of any importance, just like my father, and his father before him. I am very good at my job and I volunteered to go."

With a flourish and bow, he sat down to drink the wine Chiron had offered.

At the beginning of the journey, Bernard had been full of jests and jibes. The continuous rain changed that to grumbling about the horses or the rain, or the lack of hot food. The journey north was a trial, but Kate took it as a good sign that Bernard was determined to pass this test.

Zhost broke her train of thought when he nudged her mind. The rider was on the other horse.

Bernard was finally in the saddle and moving to the road. Hestal was brushing off his dark red robe with a bitter look on his face and caught Kate watching him.

"Why don't you ask Mirsha to stop all this rain?" he sneered.

"Why didn't you just levitate Bernard onto the horse?" Kate retorted.

Hestal quickly mounted. "Magic doesn't work like that."

T'az had already ridden onto the road. "Nothing ever does. I don't think we've seen any magic from you yet."

T'az was irrepressible. It was T'az who had outfitted the group and bought the supplies. It was T'az who knew how to camp and stay dry. It was T'az who knew how to feed and care for the horses.

Nothing bothered her and Kate thanked Mirsha, for possibly the thousandth time, for her friend.

Hestal wasn't as fond of her.

His thin, black bearded face grimaced as his horse cleared the ditch next to the road. "I haven't seen you kill anyone yet and I don't need to hear about the Vistula river again."

T'az blocked his approach to the group, "I got all day, volunteer when you're ready."

Hestal turned his horse and rode ahead without a word.

It was no secret where they were going. Nordsvard, the capitol of the North and a frustration for Kate. Nordsvard was the opposite direction from Chryselles, which was the only place Mirsha had told them to go.

Bernard's horse finally reached them and they all started forward.

Kate looked at T'az, who wore no hood. "You seem to enjoy the rain."

T'az smiled at her. "I could say that it makes me feel alive, but I think I'm mostly doing it to annoy him." T'az pointed at Hestal's back several hundred yards ahead. "It's fun and passes the time."

Kate stared at Hestal for a while. He hadn't been eager to go. His actual title was senior apprentice to the grand master. He had demanded to see the Letter of Mark from the Council and confirmed that his expenses would be covered before he would say anything.

"Magic, magic, magic," T'az sneered. "The tablets are magic. Only magic could whoosh them out of the Council chamber. Magic can do anything it wants."

Bernard chuckled. "I wish magic would make me dry. Alternatively, it could fill my jug with something warm. That would be nice, too."

"Give him a break," Kate said. "Both of you were volunteers."

T'az groaned, "No, I don't think I will, if he doesn't get better, they're going to have to send us another one."

"You may not like what you get in exchange," Bernard said as he wiped rain off his bald forehead. "Could be another whiner like me."

"I never said that there'd be anything to exchange," T'az smiled.

Kate shook her head.

In spite of that and the gloomy morning, Kate was reasonably happy. Hestal was sour and had a prickly demeanor, but he was smart and noticed things Kate missed and that would be an advantage. Kate just wished he was more agreeable.

Bernard, on the other hand, would be fine. He was obviously scared and out of his element, but Kate had faith he'd come around.

T'az stared up at the heavily laden clouds. "I'm so glad the Council chose Norseland Knights. This is much better than riding South into warmer weather."

"I think the rain is following us," Bernard whined. "Stalking us, you might say."

T'az laughed. "I'm pretty sure it is."

The discussion of weather was a daily occurrence and Zhost knew where to go without any input from her. There was nothing to look at, the scenery was pretty bland. Kate's tired mind drifted.

They had met almost no traffic on the road, just the constant rain and the damp, fallow fields. The only break in the scenery was the grey leafless trees waiting for the warmth of spring.

As they moved north, spring was being delayed for them. They rode deeper back into late winter.

The few people they'd met were pilgrims happily heading south to warmer weather. It was a cold reminder of their detour to appease the Council.

Kate looked at T'az. "Norseland Knights are reputed to be the best."

T'az nodded. "So they say, and the High Priest also said they were the most religious. Which is going to be a lot of fun."

The Council had decided, that made it law. The compromise had been part of the agreement to get the Letter of Mark.

That memory stung Kate.

The Council had argued about the veracity of the visitation. They doubted the godstones, and they doubted her. Her reputation preceded her and the rumors were vile.

Haervan maintained confidence throughout the process.

The High Priest of Val was their foil. He was adamantly against a woman led operation and refused to offer any support from his temple. He had even threatened votes on Haervan's competence as High Priest of Mirsha.

In the end, Kate took the podium to make her remarks. She had no idea what to say, and as it turned out, she didn't have to. White sparkles drifted down on the Council as she watched from the podium.

No one else noticed them, but the men stared blankly as the sparkles drifted over them like glowing snow. They didn't react to anything she said and agreed with her presentation blindly.

They voted her way on the letter, but the details were still outside the Code. Many votes followed on the wording of the letter, on what would constitute a holy mission, and who could go.

Haervan worked tirelessly to win votes, but even that seemed to irritate the other High Priests.

The resistance was appeased by her acceptance of Val's own knights - The Knights of Norseland. It was a political move that now had Kate riding weeks out of her way. Mirsha had to know, there had to be a reason.

Kate sighed. "It's in the hands of Mirsha."

Kate drooped in the saddle. They had won a marginal victory with the help of a goddess. Haervan had accepted this ridiculous demand to get the Letter of Mark from the Council.

T'az poked her arm, "Don't tell me you're thinking about the Council again."

"I can't help it," Kate replied. "It was humiliating. Dangling in front of those old men while they quibbled over gender roles in society."

It made Kate angry. "I used to want to serve on the Council. Now I wish to never set foot in that place again."

"Be careful what you wish for," Bernard said behind her.

Bernard looked pathetic. The rain seemed to suck the life out of him and droplets were hanging from his three-day old beard.

"Why couldn't we use Chrysellian Knights?" Bernard moaned. "They're religious and somewhere warm."

"The Council has had trouble with Chryselles. It has something to do with piracy," Kate repeated. "The High Priest thinks the Lord of Chryselles would negotiate for using his knights."

T'az blew water off of her nose. "I think we should have argued that point more. Who cares if they can or can't trade with Eorsians."

"What's an Eorsian?" Bernard asked.

Kate ignored the question. She really didn't know the answer.

"You saw Haervan," Kate shivered. "I wasn't going to push him very hard after getting me out of jail. He could stop us, or send me home, or confirm the penitent's bond. I'd be a slave for life."

T'az smiled at her. "He wouldn't do that to you. He loves you."

Kate wasn't so sure. "He could."

T'az nodded and stared at the clouds again. "I wonder how these knights keep from rusting up in all of this."

"We needed the Letter," Kate said with finality.

They did need the Letter. It gave Kate the right to requisition anything or anyone and it was backed up by the unquestionable Council of the Gods.

It was also the only thing keeping Hestal around.

For that, they were riding north in a cold rain to gather knights.

"I've never seen a knight," Bernard said.

"Me either," Kate added. "I only saw Churlars a couple of times as a child. The priest was our authority."

"I've seen them," T'az said. "Dad and I went to tournament once. All I really remember was a lot of metal crashing into each other, but I was pretty young."

Kate was an indifferent student of history and now they were riding into the stories of her childhood. She had difficulty remembering the children's books.

"We'll be meeting dukes and lords and other parts of the aristocracy too," Kate smiled.

"Yay?" T'az cheered sarcastically. "I doubt they'll be as friendly as Haervan. I never thought a High Priest would be so helpful or talkative."

Kate had no experience with dukes either. "Fortunately, Chiron coached me. You two just have to keep your mouths closed and look dangerous."

That made Bernard chuckle. "There might always be a first time."

Chiron had been very kind and generous. He sat with Kate in front of the fire while the High Priest had napped and taught her what he knew.

Haervan's mansion wasn't like the exquisite home of one of the leaders of the world. Kate was distracted by all the books and it was an odd household. Chiron was the only servant and the second chair in the library was obviously for him.

Zhost flicked his ears and Kate glanced back at the pack horses trailing T'az. Her ability to communicate with horses was limited. It was more feelings and passing thoughts than actual conversation.

The pack horses seemed content and not overly burdened. Zhost nickered as she looked back at their baggage.

"I know they're fine," Kate told him.

Bernard thought she was talking to him. "I think this nag isn't fine. At least I'm pretty sure she doesn't like me."

"She doesn't," Kate acknowledged. "She thinks you should lose some weight."

"Everybody wants that: my wife, my father, and now my horse," Bernard sighed.

Kate opened her mouth to reply, but T'az was staring at her.

Bernard started to talk to his horse and T'az rode closer. "I thought we agreed to not talk about that?"

Kate shrugged. "I know you and Haervan have concerns, but he's going to find out."

"True, but not yet." T'az gave her the serious eye--the look where she stared sideways with one eyebrow raised.

Haervan said it had been five hundred years since priests had magic power and he was concerned for her safety. T'az had agreed with him. They had made her promise to keep it quiet.

Hestal was living evidence of the secretive mages. The public didn't react well to them since they were the villains in the downfall of the Emperor.

Magic had gone underground - away from the eyes of the public and from the Code. No one had seen magic or anything like it in centuries.

No one knew how it would be received and none of her friends wanted to find out.

Keeping it quiet seemed like a good idea, but that was harder to do than it sounded. She couldn't help understanding their horses and the buzzing came and went, but every time she had needed it, it was there.

The group slowly caught up to Hestal.

He was as tall as T'az and skinny. Kate wanted to know why he was still an apprentice, but his brooding face didn't invite open conversation. Kate would have to wait to learn more.

"Another week?" Hestal asked as he rejoined the group.

"Yes," T'az answered the mage. "Unless you've been holding back some sort of magic thing."

The insults began immediately. Kate tired of it, but when she tried to stop them, she saw Hestal was smiling. He was enjoying it as much as T'az was.

That buoyed Kate's confidence. It might be annoying her, but her team was coming together.

Bernard asked miserably, "Do they even know we're coming?"

"Yes," Kate replied. "Messengers left days before us to alert the Duke and have him gather his knights."

"Oh, good," Bernard sniffed. "I'd hate to spend all this time soaked to the skin just to beg for bread when we get there."

T'az threw the miserable healer a look of disdain, but Kate ignored the complaint.

Kate nudged Zhost and he picked up the pace enough for her to be in the lead. Somewhere up ahead was Nordsvard. Holy Mirsha had said that she would get help - even if the helpers didn't know why.

She hoped that someone up ahead wanted to help her. More importantly, she hoped they were capable of helping her. She didn't know there was a great muster of knights, and she didn't know her prayers were being answered.

Another week and she would get her first experience with knights. They and the life they lived were a complete mystery to her. Kate sighed again as the rain continued to patter around her.

CHAPTER 4

The second evening after the great muster of knights, a watchman saw seven horses and four riders top the distant ridge and turn toward the castle.

No one was alarmed by the small group - any number of people could have the misfortune of riding north through the rain. An alert was sent to sergeant of the watch, and a messenger was dispatched to the officer of the watch.

The officer did nothing. The delegation from the Council wasn't due yet and the Council would send more than seven horses. The insignificant number meant it was nothing. No force that small could challenge the main gate.

The castle of Nordsvard was imposing structure. Water streamed off the darkened grey stone of the outer bailey as Kate rode up to the closed gate.

"Halt!" was shouted at her from the northern bastion. "Who approaches the Duke of Norseland at sunset?"

Weary from more than a week of rainy travel, Kate shouted back, "I am Katelarin, Priestess of Mirsha. I am charged with a mission given unto me by Mirsha herself. The Council sent the duke notice that we were coming. Surely it has already arrived?"

There was silence from the bastion, and the gate started to open. Kate was relieved, it had been a long trip. She was soaked through and had been for days.

Now, Kate was annoyed. This wasn't how she had imagined meeting the aristocracy and she felt like a beggar. Bernard's misery was spreading.

A man in armor with the dark blue and grey surcoat of Norseland ran out of the opening gate, "Your Holiness! We didn't expect, er, we expected..."

Kate stared at the indecisive man until he recovered and put his hand over his heart.

"Please follow me," he said. "I've sent runners for the duke and the priest." He turned and trotted with his armor jingling, across the bridge into the inner fortifications.

T'az drove her horse forward and led the group across the bridge after the man with a hissed curse.

Kate watched Hestal and Bernard follow the pack horses into the turreted mountain of stone. It was like watching her friends enter the mouth of some great beast.

Kate followed and the gate closed solidly behind her.

Inside, they were led to an enormous stable complex. You could house a thousand horses here. Zhost showed his approval by picking up his feet and prancing into the dry, well-appointed quarters.

"They like their horses," Kate quipped. "That speaks well for them."

Hestal dismounted as she pulled Zhost to a stop. "They like their horses big."

"What's a knight without a horse?" Bernard offered cheerfully, but no one else needed a joke.

Stable boys took their reins. The sleepy stable had become a flurry of activity. Grooms and servants removed the gear. Servants stood by for a reason Kate couldn't fathom.

Before Kate would be hustled into the castle though, she spoke to Zhost. She embarrassed him by kissing his nose in front of the young man that was standing by to brush him.

"Thank you Zhost for the haste getting here. Enjoy your rest." He whinnied in response and pounded his hoof.

He was ready to go now.

"Soon," Kate smiled at the eager stallion.

T'az was waiting behind her. "It's unnerving the way you talk to that beast."

Kate shrugged. "I believe he selected me, not the other way around, and he's influencing the others."

Kate watched the horses disappear. "Zhost is why we made such good time."

"Just don't start having conversations with donkeys where other people can hear," T'az warned.

"Donkeys? What about them?" Bernard said trying to herd everyone to the door that promised warm food and ale.

Hestal picked up his bag. "Isn't it obvious? She speaks to animals and they respond. A priest with real power like that hasn't been seen in a long time."

"Power?" Bernard hadn't connected anything. "I thought we were talking about donkeys. I think I might like a donkey better. They are easier to get on."

"Never mind, Bernard." Kate led them into the castle.

They were led to a large room with a large table and an abundance of comfortable chairs. Heat wafted out of the enormous stone fireplace and it drew Kate straight to the fire.

A well-dressed man in blue and grey silk, Duke Comerant, awaited them and did the introductions himself.

"I apologize for the welcome, your Holiness, noble questers." He bowed deeply. "We were expecting something completely different."

Kate turned in front of the fireplace, letting the heat penetrate her cold, wet clothing. "Thank you, my lord, but what were you expecting?"

He smiled and rubbed his brown beard. "Well. I expected a full procession. Wagons. A guard of church soldiers. And to be honest, about three more days."

He waved them to the chairs.

Kate left the fire reluctantly and didn't mention that she thought slipping out of Theopolis quietly was the safest option. The two dark things capering in the shadows on either side of the hearth seemed to know what Kate left out. They always knew.

Servants brought wine and Kate accepted a large glass from a young, freckled blonde girl, and got right to the point. "My Lord, how long will it take to assemble the knights?"

The Duke laughed. "You have made a nearly record passage to the north in bad weather. Are you really that eager to leave again, my lady?"

Kate kept the sarcasm out her voice, "My destination is Chryselles. It will be a long journey, my lord."

"Yes, of course," the Duke smiled. "Fortunately, I assembled them just the day before yesterday."

Food arrived and there was the momentary distraction of trays, settings, and the smell of hot meat. The servants were quick and efficient, leaving them with a mouthwatering assortment of dishes.

Bernard had the decency to wait for a sign from the Duke before he ate. Kate filled a modest plate.

"My Lady, what exactly are your expectations?" the Duke asked politely.

Kate told the Duke of their mission while she enjoyed roast turkey and bread. "I don't think very many knights are necessary. Holy Mirsha said to take only what I needed."

The Duke seemed relieved. His face and demeanor relaxed, "An interesting phrase, that one. To a knight, that would mean, take everything. Never regret leaving a weapon behind."

The Duke swirled his wine. "In spite of the rarity of a quest, I think you can only expect a few knights to volunteer. This will be too unusual for most of them. Knights here tend to be quite conservative in their thinking and completely devoted to their families."

T'az looked up from her dinner. "How many is a few," and after a pause, "My, Lord?"

The duke thought for a second. "I am nearly certain you will get one. Possibly as many as two."

The door banged open and the Grand Priest of Val and his retinue swept in to fill one side of the room, cutting off the explanation from the Duke.

The Grand Priest cleared his throat. "That seems generous, my lord. Mighty Val has remained silent on the subject."

He turned to Kate. "Priestess of Mirsha. Noble Val has not championed this quest. He has not imbued you with the Right of Leadership. There is no precedent for this. Why should any knights join you?"

"Because they are commanded to?" Kate lost her appetite and pushed away her plate.

She caught the Duke's eye, "The knights aren't Churlars. They are under your command. Do you accept the decision and leadership of the Council?"

"I said...," the Grand Priest began, but the Duke stood halting all conversation.

"You are dismissed, Vestral. You have said your piece." The Duke turned to the armored man behind him, "Eldin! Clear the room, please."

An older knight drew his sword and waved both priests and servants from the room. The Grand Priest appeared reluctant, but everyone else scurried out.

Eldin closed the door behind him and Kate used the opportunity to move back to stand in front of the warm fire. The warmth was worth tolerating the spirits.

"It is hard to have a private conversation in my position." The Duke paced from the door to the fire. "You touch on thorny subjects, my lady priestess."

He was serious and he held her gaze with his blue eyes. Only the crackling of the fire broke the silence as Kate waited for the explanation.

The Duke broke from her gaze and rubbed his neatly trimmed beard. "I am a knight and a Duke. As a knight, I bow only to Val. As a duke, I have to think of the needs of all my people."

He returned to pacing. "Politics and taxes run a duchy, not tournaments. Connections to the Council are crucial and the requirements you are setting are low. The burden will also be low."

Hestal leaned back in his chair with his wine. "What burden, my lord?"

The Duke turned to him. "To the treasury. My people won't be burdened to support you. Some of the older families could also handle the cost. As the Duke of Norseland, it is in my best interests to support you. As a knight, a servant of Val, supporting you is most unusual without the consent of Val."

SPRINGDALE PUBLIC LIBRARY
405 S. PLEASANT
SPRINGDALE, AR 72764
479-750-8180

The fire continued to crackle merrily.

Kate was actually getting tired as she dried. "The Council requires it. Does that ease your burden?"

The Duke nodded, "Officially, but only in the simplest sense. I will support you. But, the priests of Val have significant control over the knights. Without their blessing, it will be hard to convince knights to put aside their families and incomes to do so."

"But, you could order them," Kate said tiredly. The two imps in the shadows were laughing at her.

"I can," the Duke smiled. "The knights are sworn to me, and they would go if ordered, but I'm not sure that kind of knight would be useful to you."

The imps looked surprised as Kate mentally pushed them away. She sighed and sat back in the chair. The rivalries between priests were so tiresome and should be beside the point after convincing the Council.

"You might consider recruiting a priest of Val," The Duke offered. "That would simplify the arrangement."

"No, I don't think so," Kate smiled. "I will trust that Mirsha will provide."

The door opened and Eldin entered.

The Duke nodded to the knight. "Rest tonight. The willing knights will be gathered tomorrow afternoon. We shall see what Mirsha brings you."

The Duke left, leaving only Eldin with them in the room. The grey bearded knight stood respectfully by the door.

T'az eyed him suspiciously. "Haervan was right. Remember when I asked why we weren't using Churlars?"

Hestal couldn't know what T'az was talking about. "The Duke thinks we will get a few volunteers. I'd prefer a volunteer and we don't need much. An army would only be a hinderance."

Kate stared at Hestal for a moment - he wasn't a volunteer.

"We'll see." Kate got up and let Eldin lead her to her room.

Kate woke up the next morning lost. She had slept soundly and her worries and cares were forgotten for a night. No dream interrupted her, and it took a minute to remember where she was.

SPRINGDALE PUBLIC LIBRARY
405 S. PLEASANT
SPRINGDALE, AR 72764
479-750-8180

The room was opulent by any standards. The bed was large and comfortable. The carpet was thick, and all the furniture was nicer than anything Kate had experienced. It was a far cry from her messy little cell.

No duty changes had been made, so Kate pulled a candle and cornmeal out of her bag. The morning ritual was still her obligation and would remain so.

Kate watched the sunrise through the glass window. She had not missed a single morning since the adventure began without a candle to time her sleep. Not even in prison.

When the ritual was complete, Kate packed her ceremonial kit away. She wore only a shift and panicked when she realized her clothes weren't where she left them.

"That's just like a stubborn priest," Kate vented. "Remove my clothes so I attend breakfast in only my night shift."

The deep shadows were retreating across the room from the coming daylight, but they made an effort to conceal a chest on the far side of the room.

Kate followed them in their retreat and found her clothes folded on the chest the shadows were trying to hide. Her clothes smelled of flowers and not stale sweat and horses. Someone had cleaned them overnight.

"Being a guest of royalty had its advantages." Kate laughed as she moved to investigate what else was available.

The bath was warm and she enjoyed it, even though a servant stood in attendance to her needs. Months of being naked in front of spirits and shadows helped keep her embarrassment down.

Kate dressed and checked the mirror. Her red hair was unruly, but she brushed it into to a temporary truce. She would get T'az to tie it back up later. It was time for breakfast.

Another servant waited for her in the hall.

"This way, your Holiness," he gestured to the stairs.

No one else was physically present in the new room, but breakfast was laid out on a large table set for five. Candles lit the room with a warm glow, but they cast long shadows.

Kate acknowledged the spirits in the shadows and served herself. She was hungry and doubted they would be waiting on the Duke in this little room.

She had eggs, bread, and butter. Everything she enjoyed. Kate was uncomfortably full when she leaned back in her chair to enjoy a refreshing red drink. It smelled of fruit and was delightfully sweet.

The door opened and the Grand Priest of Val entered with his entourage. Kate couldn't understand why he needed so many people with him to speak to a visiting priestess.

From the look on his wrinkled, pinched face, Kate knew this wasn't going to go well. He looked like he was prepared for a crushing victory.

"Priestess," The Grand Priest said as he moved to the table.

He stayed standing, and he waited, but Kate didn't know what for. She looked at the parchment he held, but could glean nothing from what she saw. Vestral probably knew her need and had arranged this breakfast to negotiate with her alone.

Kate did not like to be manipulated.

Vestral smiled.

His aggressive and confident demeanor made her want to refuse anything he said. The Code didn't require her to acknowledge his rank - he wasn't in her hierarchy. So, Kate didn't stand for him.

There was some debate if he should recognize her authority as she was the one approved by the Council for a quest and had been visited by a god. If this were a traditional quest he would, but Kate was a woman and not recognized as a leader.

So Vestral wasn't going to bow either.

Kate could feel the shadows lining up behind her. It felt supportive and less scary than usual. There was a look on Vestral's face that made Kate think he sensed their presence.

"What do you want?" Kate asked.

"I have here a document that relinquishes control of this quest to more appropriate people." He slid the parchment towards her.

Kate ignored it.

"For obvious reasons, a dangerous quest cannot be led by a woman," Vestral smiled, "and it has no chance of success without knights, who also cannot be led by a woman. Or at least, not without instruction from Holy Val."

Kate thought it must all seem so logical to him. Vestral, like most men, was apparently against women having a role, particularly a leadership role. He wasn't against the quest itself.

Vestral continued, "Surely you can see that you are in no position to negotiate. What do you have? A questionable magician, a fat healer, and a southern woman. There will be no knights. I can guarantee it."

Kate continued to drink juice and waited.

"Well? What do you have to say?" Vestral pointed at the document. "This is the only appropriate action."

He was starting to anger and his entire retinue of priests showed an equal level of disdain.

Kate decided only the truth would do.

"I have exactly what I need," she replied. "I have the direction of a God and the support of the Council. Surely we, as priests, can trust the gods to provide."

That caused some of the retinue to show discomfort.

Kate put her juice down and sat up. "Let's be clear. You are saying that Holy Mirsha chose incorrectly. That I should rectify Her mistake, step aside, and put you in charge?"

"No," Vestral was placating. "I'm not arguing whether Mirsha chose you, however wrong I feel it is. We know there is limited evidence to support that claim and the Council may not be fully committed."

He continued to dismiss her argument. "I'm also not saying that you shouldn't go along to appease Mirsha. What I am saying is that you will not be a success without knights and you will not get knights unless you relinquish control to someone who has the Right of Leadership imbued by Val."

It was the same line of argument made by Deoshus, the High Priest of Val. Kate started twirling her hair. It had always worked with her father and she could see Vestral's anger rising as his face slowly reddened.

"I don't recall that section of the Code that gives priests of Val the right to control knights and quests, could you quote it?" Kate asked in her most winsome voice.

Vestral's eyes flashed, but he didn't say anything.

Kate was winning the long fight. She felt a surge of energy from the shadows behind her. "Mirsha picked you. Mirsha spoke to you," they said.

It was clear to Kate that Mirsha intended her to find the tablets. Kate no longer felt swayed by anyone's station. A god had picked her.

Vestral mistook her silence as deliberation.

"Trying to maintain control over that which you have no knowledge, is folly." He pointed at the document on the table. "That's why these rules exist. If you would look at this document, you will see it has the backing of many Council members."

Kate pulled out the Letter of Mark, which she had been keeping on her person at all times, and found her voice amid the chanting of the shadows.

"I have a document too, Vestral. My document is signed by all the Council members and it says that this quest has the full backing of the Council." Kate opened it to page after page of signatures. "All people, I believe that includes you, are required to assist in the successful completion of this mission."

Vestral's face reddened even more and his voice went up an octave. "I am trying to assist you, by putting someone competent in charge!"

Kate kept her cool. "That's absurd. Everyone knows I'm not capable of leading the fighting. Look at me, can you find a demon small enough for me? I would have to take the advice of fighters. That argument has no legs."

Kate stood. "What you are trying do is take control of this quest for your own purposes and to bring glory to Val. In defiance of both the Council and Holy Mirsha."

Vestral regained his composure after a moment. "I have Lord Val on my side and the other large temples agree." He emphasized his point by hammering the table. "I don't care about your little gardener goddess. A quest into the depths of evil is not like killing corndiggers. It requires a real leader and it will require knights. Reconsider or you will get no knights here."

As he turned to leave, Kate tossed another barb at him. "I'll write it down somewhere. I will get no knights here. Which can only mean I won't need knights. I'll need fighters who aren't afraid of women."

The Grand Priest chose not to acknowledge the statement as he and his entourage stormed out. T'az bumped the last two as she entered.

"It took a while to find this room," T'az said from the doorway. "What's got the rats all riled up? And what is that behind you?"

That surprised Kate, "You can see them?"

"Not really, but it's something." T'az walked behind Kate and the shadows seemed to fade.

"They were supporting me in the face of this." Kate slid the Grand Priest's document over to her and T'az scanned it.

T'az' eyes narrowed as she read. "So they thought they could bluff you into signing away a quest given to you by a god? That's an odd thing for a priest to do."

Kate sat back down. "I'm pretty sure they felt if they had me alone, I'd do anything. Besides, they don't care if I go, I just can't lead it. Vestral said they had little evidence to support my claim and he has backers at the Council."

Kate wondering what Vestral knew about the Tablets that she didn't know. He had said, "depths of evil." The image of the grey malicious spirit rose in her mind again.

T'az talked as she read. "This is serious. I don't understand all the words, but I'll have to step up security. From now on Kate, you eat or drink nothing here until I've checked it. You don't go anywhere without me."

T'az stared at the thoughtful priestess. She was quite fierce looking with her hair tied back and those emerald eyes boring into Kate.

"Poison?" Kate laughed. "That's preposterous. They'll yell and resist, but I don't think they'll do anything permanent. Poison is completely out of character."

"I think someone who wrote this," T'az waved the document at her, "would do anything to have you declared incompetent. Real or imagined - even temporarily. Nothing and nowhere Kate. I'm serious, this thing goes nowhere if you die."

Kate had been led down here alone. Which seemed like a coincidence, until the priests arrived. Maybe the Grand Priest had wanted her alone, but it could have been for a different reason.

Bernard and Hestal arrived and sat down for breakfast. T'az filled them in on the details.

Hestal shrugged as he served himself, "I was expecting something. I just didn't think he would play his hand so aggressively."

"What do you mean?" Kate asked.

Hestal looked at the letter again. "He is trying to wrest control of the local knights from the duke. It seems he may be close to doing it and that would give him a small but powerful army. I suspect that's why we were sent here for knights in the first place."

"Of course," said T'az. "This letter had to follow us here. He couldn't have sent for this since yesterday."

Hestal pulled on his thin beard for a moment. "The people that signed this letter probably hoped that if you weren't dissuaded here, your refusal and possibly the duke's support would allow Vestral to gain the upper hand. You're a sideshow in a much bigger power game to them."

T'az leapt on his train of thought. "Haervan said that Churlars aren't an army. The people that support this would carry more weight if the armies of the north were behind them."

Kate held up a hand. She didn't like where this was going. "That would be the end of the world as we know it. Chryselles, Tarh, Kohlgen, all the cities and peoples in the south, the army on the Wall, no one would back them. It would be war."

T'az raised an eyebrow. "Mirsha said you'd bring change."

"That would be change," Hestal nodded as he ate.

"No," Kate said loudly. "The Council is made up of an equal number of priests from each Temple. He, at best, has support of less than half. And not everyone from any temple is from the north. This is not going to lead to civil war."

Kate was against conspiracy for conspiracy's sake.

She stood up. "I'm going to go to the Temple of Mirsha here and attend the gathering this afternoon. I think we should plan on leaving with or without knights, first thing in the morning."

"Agreed," said the group.

Kate pointed at the letter. "Hestal, see if you can get a moment of the Duke's time, let him see this, and try to get a read off of him for me."

"No problem," Hestal said.

Bernard looked up from a large plate of breakfast, "What do you want me to do?"

Kate moved to the door. "Go with Hestal and keep your eyes open. Get the lay of the land. We'll stay in pairs. T'az is going to protect me. You two try and see if the Grand Priest is as influential as he thinks he is."

T'az insisted on donning her armor, so there was a small delay before leaving the castle, and heading into town. Kate asked the servant in the hall for directions and soon they were outside walking through the outer bailey they'd entered the night before.

It was a cool day and Kate found the walking to be invigorating. Her enjoyment of the bustle of town life was returning. The bright pre-spring day kept the shadows at bay all the way to the temple of Mirsha.

It was time to test Hedlvan's surprise and Kate wanted to see it in action.

In secret, Hedlvan had set up a network of fast horses and volunteers to get Kate what she needed. It was a wonderful surprise that was going to make the uncertainty of the logistics of the quest easier.

Haervan had been beside himself with his runner's ingenuity. The old High Priest had actually gushed with pleasure.

"Honestly, Mirsha forgive me, but I may have underestimated Hedlvan," the old man said. "The messenger network he is setting up is a stroke of genius and there is no shortage of young people willing to sign up. They want to be a part of a holy quest."

Haervan had been impressed, but it had only been in operation two weeks, and Kate wanted to see if it worked. If it did, she could get and send information, and it would be able to move money. That removed the need to carry large amounts of coins.

Haervan believed it was best to use the Council's authority sparingly. Beating everyone with the Letter of Mark was the surest way he could think of to lose support. Money was a good way to keep that support.

It was no surprise that the system worked. The priests at the temple already knew about her arrival and Kate was able to send a note to Haervan detailing her plans. It was a comfort to know she was supported.

The walk back to the castle was more relaxed until Kate spotted an odd shadow near the gatehouse, where the road curved around the fortress.

"That's not a normal shadow," Kate said.

T'az swiveled her head side to side. "Where?"

Kate was intrigued by this shadow. It wasn't malicious or tempting. It just was.

"Just a moment, I want to look over here." Kate said to T'az as she stepped off the road.

T'az paused. "Why? It's nothing but grass."

Kate couldn't answer that question. She was curious about the shadows and visions. Mirsha had said everything that had existed was still here and Kate wondered what that meant.

Kate stepped into the darkness and the grass was gone. In the darkness it seemed like a large room. There was something moving at far end where it was still dark.

Light at this end emanated from Kate herself, although dimly. The air was still, and the smell was worse than the prison. There was only one sound Kate could hear.

The sound of dry paper rubbing on stone. A raspy noise, but soft.

Kate pinched her nose and said, "I need to see."

The glow expanded and Kate screamed. Dead people were shuffling towards her and they were horribly disfigured. It was their desiccated feet inching towards her that was making the noise.

The scene, illuminated by her glow, was black and white. All color was gone and the dead kept coming. The few that had eyes were fixated on her.

Kate stepped back. She expected to step out of the shadow, but she ran into a wall. It was solid, black, and firm. The way out was blocked.

Kate felt fear rising and she froze.

There were two doors.

The corpses were already reaching out towards her with damaged and broken hands. She was going to have to decide quickly between the two, but she couldn't move.

The lightless, pale eyes never wavered as they held her gaze.

Something grabbed her from behind and Kate closed her eyes and screamed. Her knees gave out and Kate dropped to the ground expecting stone, yet finding grass. Kate felt her face warmed by the sun and opened her eyes.

T'az was angry. "What in the name of the seven gods was that?"

"I don't know," Kate whimpered. "I don't know."

"You disappeared into the shadow. You were just gone." T'az was poking around her with her sword.

Kate told her what happened. "How did you find me?"

"I didn't," T'az admitted. "I saw your hair where you disappeared. I grabbed it, and pulled. That's it."

"Oh," Kate said.

"I thought you said they couldn't hurt you?" T'az stood in front of her.

Kate shivered from the chill of the room. "They haven't before, but they are certainly capable of scaring me. Worse yet, these things were something no one should have to see."

T'az sheathed her sword. "New rule then, no going into the shadows without me."

"It isn't every shadow," Kate said defensively. "There was something about this one that was different."

"Don't get picky with me about how we define shadows," T'az said with deadly seriousness. "You know what I mean - the ones that are calling to you, the ones that aren't made by the sun, whatever you want to call them. Don't go into any more of them without me."

"Okay, but I have to know more. There's a reason for this," Kate said as she stood.

"It started in the library, right?" T'az said thoughtfully.

"That was before the visitation and it was like the dream so I chalked it up to that," Kate said thoughtfully, "But why before?"

"I don't know, what did you do right before?" T'az asked.

"Hedlvan brought me lunch. Before that, I was at Haervan's house. He gave me the stone." Kate pulled out her robe and looked under her shirt. The stone was still glowing softly against her chest.

The glow was the same light she'd seen in the dark.

"The stone." T'az rubbed her chin. "You think the stone is responsible? Take it off."

"No. I don't know, but I don't think it's hurting me. I think it's showing me things." Kate dropped her robe. "I just don't know why."

"Ugh!" T'az howled. "I really prefer a stand up fight. I hope the boys had better luck."

They hadn't.

Sir Eldin met Kate and T'az as they entered the castle and silently led them to the same parlor in which they had eaten breakfast. He left them at the door and T'az watched him go.

"He's like an armored librarian." T'az eyed the silent Eldin as he walked away.

Hestal and Bernard were there, and Hestal spoke first. "We saw the duke."

Kate looked at the door as she sat down. "What did you learn?"

Hestal spoke softly. "It was a very brief meeting. He didn't say anything about the document, but he seemed upset about it. I think he's on our side, but there is conflict there. He may not be in a position to help. Politically."

Bernard, who had waited his turn, jumped in. "We spent the rest of the morning in the market. The duke is popular amongst the average people. Most of them are tired of knights and priests. We..."

"Tell her all of it," Hestal said firmly.

"Well, I had some drinks at a pub in the market. I was telling people about the quest. No one has heard anything about it." He looked a little sheepish, "I may have said too much."

"May have?" Hestal countered. "We have no secrets now. It was a popular idea, though. People crowded in to hear."

Kate thought he looked sheepish too and Kate raised an eyebrow as she stared at him. She had counted on him to be more discreet.

"I'm sorry, I should have shut him down sooner," Hestal admitted. "The crowd got restless, since most people couldn't hear. There was some pushing and shoving."

Kate didn't know if she should be angry or just exasperated. "You started a disturbance? We are already pariahs with the priests here and possibly the knights too."

T'az shook her head, "I guess we do everything together from now on. Did you win?"

"Win?" Hestal was dismissive. "I'm not going to get involved in those kind of fights. No. Armed men showed up before things got out of hand. I think we were arrested, but Sir Eldin brought us back here."

"Mirsha protect us!" Kate exclaimed. "I hope this isn't trouble for Duke Comerant. We need him on our side."

Kate worried about the possible implications, but she couldn't change it. "If it's not big trouble, we'll smooth it over."

Bernard changed the subject, "What did you learn?"

"Not much," Kate said flatly, "The messenger service works."

"And weird disappearing dead shadow people," T'az said eyeing Kate.

Hestal perked up. "What? Tell me."

Kate let out a little groan. She didn't necessarily want to relive it, but her experience with the outer bailey shadow was a short story. Hestal questioned her closely and picked up that it started before the adventure.

At his urging, Kate showed them the glowing godstone.

Hestal held it in his hand for a moment, "That is very interesting."

"What's interesting," T'az asked, "Is it dangerous?"

"Well magical items often feel magical. It's hard to describe. Almost like they're vibrating. I've held a few." Hestal pointed at the stone. "That isn't magical from my perspective. But, that leaves the question - why does it glow? I know of no stone that glows on its own."

"It has to do with Holy Mirsha," Kate declared as she put the godstone away. "That can be the only explanation."

"Well it's one explanation anyway," Hestal smiled. "I can think of a few others maybe, but none of it explains anything."

"What do you mean?" Kate needed more clarity, not less.

Hestal shrugged, "Well, I would normally say it's giving you visions. Past or future? I don't know, but that would be my diagnosis." He leaned back in his chair, "The more important thing is what Mirsha said. 'All things in the future and in the past still exist.' That opens up a lot of possibilities."

Bernard looked confused. "What possibilities? Can she predict the future or not?"

"Bernard," Hestal said he shook his head. "You're so practical as to be painful. Do you know where we go when we die? Any of you? Imagine, if," Hestal hesitated. "What if we didn't go anywhere - everything that is past is still here. What if that's what she sees?"

T'az snorted, "You mean she sees dead people."

"Not exactly." Hestal's eyes were bright. "What if you were the woman the wild man was sacrificing to ancient gods? Or you saw it through her eyes. What if you were watching ancient librarians at work in the library?"

Bernard scratched his head. "So, she sees the past?"

"Oh, the Blood of Heros! NO." Hestal exclaimed. "We see time as linear - one long line from birth to death. Overlapping with other people born and dying in the same time period, you see? What if it isn't linear? What if time periods overlap?"

"Whoa," T'az held up a hand. "That's really over my head and it doesn't explain the room of dead people. What use is it?"

Hestal's expression went flat. "The best philosophical debate I've come upon in years and I'm surrounded by you people. To your point, I have no idea of any practical application. For all we know, the dead people are the future."

He laid back in his chair and closed his eyes. "Try and get a better look around next time. Something we can reference."

"Thanks, I'll try and draw a picture while scared out of my mind," Kate sighed.

Hestal just smiled.

The servants brought trays of food in and laid lunch out on the big table. No one leapt up for lunch, which was good, because the Duke swept in after the servants left. Sir Eldin closed the door behind him.

The Duke looked like he was about to say something, but he paused at the group's collective expression. "Did something happen I am unaware of?"

"No, my lord," Kate said as the group stood.

Only Hestal seemed happy.

"Well, My Lady, the rumors are flying." He smiled knowingly at Bernard.

Kate apologized. "My comrades were instructed to find the lay of the land, not start a disturbance."

"Pah!" He waved them to chairs around the table. He was going to lunch with them. "That was no disturbance. There was almost no blood."

They all sat and served themselves.

Kate was relieved, "I don't understand, my lord. I was afraid this disturbance might hinder the gathering."

"Nothing of the kind, Kate," he said as he served himself. "It was quickly sorted out, and it solidifies what I know about my people. I found it significant that when my men showed up, it stopped. They still respect the authority of my house."

"I didn't think of it that way," Kate said as she took bread.

That kind of fight would have been a big deal in her home town. Kate was caught up in how things affected her and she only had the lens of her own experience to look through. She hadn't even considered that others wouldn't be impacted in the same way.

CHAPTER 5

Berigral stood in the room of his humiliation. It was here his father had berated him and declared his punishment publicly. It was here the Duke had turned him down and sent him back to his family.

Here, in the audience chamber of the Duke of Norseland, the laughter of the assembled nobles and knights still rang in his head and he felt the unbearable pain of the shame in his stomach.

"Sir Berigral," Berigral said to himself. "There is nothing to a title. Knighthood is meaningless."

He was standing under the championship banners won by the Norseland knights - hundreds of them. Two of them were won by Berigral single-handedly, but he didn't look up at them. It would just make the shame more real.

Sir Berigral had never lost. Five years of tournaments. Five years a knight and it all boiled down to profit and loss. Everything he wanted was deemed a loss.

"Bear!" Thervan yelled through his bascinet. "You're early."

Thervan clanked across the dark stone floor to where Bear stood. Everyone called him Bear except his family. With every exception there was an exception. Thervan was brother three and he used nicknames.

"I didn't want to enter with father and the lick spittles." Bear moved out from under the banners to the columned, raised area the knights stood in for presentations.

Thervan clanked after him. "It has been six months. The shunning has stopped. You should probably get over that - they'll still be your family in six more months."

That was true. Bear needed to change the subject.

"Why are you wearing that? You hate ceremonial armor," Bear asked as he picked a place up front.

"You know who suggested it," Thervan said as he removed his helmet. "The same person that suggested you wear all your honors."

"Mother," Bear grinned.

"You need a wife and your squire doesn't count," Thervan said in the best imitation of their mother.

"Me?" Bear asked. "You're four years older - you'd best get to it."

"Right," Thervan sneered. "Mother put me in armor so people would at least see me as a knight. Maybe they won't think of the losses."

"Girls like a shiny suit of armor," Bear grinned.

"Not on me they don't," Thervan smiled. "But you've changed the subject."

"It runs deeper than the shunning," Bear grunted.

"So you asked the Duke to lead forces to the watchtowers. It wasn't a bad idea." Thervan settled his helmet on his pommel. "Father was mad about how you did it at your awards ceremony."

"You're pretty bright, Thervan," Bear whispered. "Do you think I thought of the idea?"

Thervan turned slowly, "What are you saying?"

"Daerval," Bear grunted. "I was his test mouse. There's a rumor he and father are already turning that idea into a reality, but Daerval will lead."

"Wow," Thervan whistled. "They sacrificed you to see how the Duke responded. I always thought you were going to be Daerval's man."

"You were wrong," Bear said. "As first son, he gets everything, I'll forge my own path." Bear closed his mouth quickly before he said too much.

"You're not planning on volunteering for this, are you?" Thervan inquired. "Father has expressly forbidden it."

"I'm twenty-one," Bear said.

"Oh boy, have you even thought this through?" Thervan whispered. "Have you shared your plan with your squire? You won't be the only one put out."

"Foester's on board," Bear said.

"He's as crazy as you." Thervan's coif creaked as he shook his head. "You're made for each other."

Bear laughed, "You're just jealous."

Thervan chuckled as he nodded. "A little."

More men were filing in. The last time Bear was here, they all paraded into the castle in the pouring rain to hear that the priestess was coming. Every knight was eager then, but things had changed.

Priests had made it clear to all the families - there would be no support of the quest. Documents had been circulated showing her claims to divine visitation were false.

Bear didn't care. It was clear. A life serving a brother who betrayed him, or leave. Fighting was his only skill. There was no way to afford the armor he wore, let alone the full interlocking plate Thervan was wearing.

Breaking free of his family and supporting himself would take something special - a quest might do it.

Knighthood was an attractive trap for a young man - victory, knighthood, the glory of Val, and the adoration of the women. None of it was true. Bear's experience was different.

Knighthood was expensive. Bear's substantial winnings wouldn't cover his expenses and knights didn't win tournaments after thirty. Younger men were just faster and the rules favored them.

Bear started to tear up at his own helplessness. He forced his mind to remain calm and blinked away the tears. He'd spent every waking minute training to be the best, he had to use that training now to remain calm.

Bear saw the rest of his older brothers enter with their father. They ignored Bear and took positions in front - off to his right.

Bear didn't follow them. He kept his eyes on the door by the throne. That door opening would start a series of events, the outcome of which Bear couldn't predict.

"Looks like a lot of knights aren't coming," Thervan said casually.

It was true. Just days ago, this room had been full. There would only be a couple hundred nobles and knights total today. The Duke would see that as an affront, because it was.

Father walked over to them before taking his seat with the council members.

"Put your helmet on Thervan," Father hissed and Thervan did. "Where's your helmet Berigral?"

Bear kept his face calm. He'd been yelled at his whole life. "Foester has it."

"Such disrespect," Father fumed. "I know I didn't dictate what armor you wore, but fighting armor? At a ceremony. Don't you think that's what ceremonial armor is for?"

"Mother approved," Bear countered.

"Did she?" Father sneered. "What do women know? You are treading on thin ice. Your brother won't keep you with this kind of disrespect."

Bear nodded, "That's fair."

Father slapped him across his face. "Boy, you think those medals are good for anything? You better straighten up young man and start supporting your brother - he will be the General."

Bear's cheek stung from the metal studs in his father's gauntlet. "I know the medals are meaningless."

Father seemed to realize his mistake. "They aren't either! Val's blood, boy, they are the only thing you've got and you are throwing them away. Disrespecting your family and years of tradition. Now get in the back and stay out of sight."

Bear didn't move.

Father turned his wrath to Thervan. "What are you smiling at? You don't deserve the armor you're standing in. Make sure you stand in front of him."

"Yes, father," Thervan said even though it would be a useless gesture. Bear was a head taller and broader than Thervan.

"If either of you do something, anything, I'll strip both of you and put you out," Father snarled.

"Yes, father," The boys said in unison.

Father stormed off and sat with the Duke's council of advisors.

"There you go," Thervan said. "Stripped and put out."

"I'm going one way or the other," Bear said quietly.

He was convinced this was his chance. If he didn't he'd be in this summer's tournaments, married by next fall, and probably have children in the spring. All in his father's house.

At least until one of his older brothers inherited the family. He could easily be thrown out then. Brothers often didn't keep younger siblings around to challenge their authority.

Not siblings that won tournaments anyway.

Get thrown out now with a chance at fortune and glory, or get thrown out later with whatever he had plus a wife and children. That was his lot as the fifth son.

Bear chose now. If it worked out, he wouldn't need his father's approval anymore and his brothers, whichever outlived his father, could inherit the lot.

It was the perfect day to go into trouble. The hall was cool and less than half full. He was wearing his favorite armor - plates strapped over chain. His shield was over his back. The helmet he detested was tied to his horse.

Comfortable, he thought to himself.

Today, even his golden awards didn't feel heavy on his surcoat. He didn't move. He waited. This was the day.

The wait wasn't long. The door opened and four people entered in front of the Duke and he waved them to places on his right before taking his seat. Noise settled quickly as those in the half bare hall took seats.

Those that had seats. Knights stayed standing. Bear watched the newcomers closely.

Those four must be the delegation from the Council. They didn't look like much to Bear. They were just a tiny woman, a bookish man, and a man that obviously enjoyed his meals.

The last was a dark skinned woman. She looked formidable. Bear watched her exclusively. She wore her armor with comfort and a confidence he could appreciate. She looked strong, but moved smoothly.

He didn't know why, but he felt this woman had seen combat. Her eyes never stopped moving. She took in the whole room of knights and locked eyes with Bear for just a moment.

The southern woman did not take a seat but stood behind the first woman, who was mostly likely the priestess of Mirsha. The priestess wore no rank or insignia and she wore her robe over brown riding clothes. That was unusual for a priest.

She was tiny - even compared to the non-knights in the room. Her dark red hair was braided and tied back like she was ready for a fight in spite of her size. Her eyes were as quick as the dark woman behind her.

Bear judged them to be an unusual group.

The Duke stood and addressed the assembly. "A momentous day! Today Norseland is blessed. Today, some of us will join a Holy Quest and whoever goes takes the reputation and pride of this duchy with them. It is not known where this quest will lead, but danger and evil magic have been professed by the Goddess Mirsha."

Bear thought the Duke was trying to raise interest in a shameful display of knights.

"Before you sits Katelarin, the priestess who stood before Mirsha herself and accepted this quest. She has traveled here to seek our assistance."

The Duke walked out to the knights.

"The master mages have provided her with a magician, the healers have provided, the Council now asks us to provide. As you see her party is small and only lacks in solid force. She has not asked for anything, but very humbly she sits before you hoping some of you brave knights will choose to help her in this difficult endeavor."

That was well done, thought Bear.

The Duke knew what he was doing. He was playing on some of the core sympathies of all knights: duty, honor, and defenseless women. Bear thought a few might have been swayed.

Bear didn't disagree that the quest needed some strength, but he didn't feel she was defenseless. The warrior woman standing behind her seemed capable.

She had strong arms and she could have been a statue she was so perfect. She radiated strength and confidence and Bear couldn't stop watching her. She was nothing like the pale, mopey women his mother paraded in front of him.

There was a disturbance that caused many heads to turn, but the Duke didn't look, he seemed to know it was the Grand Priest of Val.

Vestral's voice boomed throughout the room. "My Lord, I apologize for my tardiness. I'm glad I got here in time. I feel it is my duty as Grand Priest to point out that Val is still silent on this subject."

Vestral strode to the middle of the room followed by eleven priests. All of them had sleeves full of stripes indicating their rank. That's more what Bear expected of priests.

Vestral addressed the knights directly. "Val has not seen fit to grant this poor woman with the Right of Leadership and she has this morning refused our generous offer to assist her. So, I am unsure why we are here."

He smiled over at the priestess. "Had she accepted, then a competent leader who has been imbued with the Right, would have been provided."

Bear had never had a good feeling about the Grand Priest. He was surprised when the duke walked out past the seated court and confronted Vestral.

"Vestral, I know of the offer you tendered this morning. A rat would have turned away from it. It is for your gain alone. You dishonor this hall by even mentioning it." He spun around to face the knights. "This morning the Grand Priest asked the Holy Priestess to give up her burden."

"A burden, I remind you all, that was placed on her small shoulders by a god!" The Duke's voice soared. "Who here would turn away if Val issued the same burden? None of you. Even if Val had asked you to walk into demon fire, you wouldn't turn away, or give that burden to another."

Vestral seemed a bit surprised at the reaction, "You compare this priestess to the Knights of Norseland?"

"Yes," the Duke nodded. "Yes I do. She has taken a holy vow. She struggles with the enemies her god places before her with every asset she is given."

The Duke spread his hands to the room. "That sounds a lot like us. Admittedly she does not possess the strength or martial skills of a knight, but the courage and commitment are there."

"That's absurd," Vestral spluttered. "Priests of Mirsha tend to farmers. They know nothing of courage and valor. Only priests of Val are suited for this."

He turned to the Priestess at the high table. "It is pride and folly for this person to continue to demand to lead with no skill and no right of leadership imbued."

The warrior woman put a hand on the priestess' shoulder.

"Val sees it," The Grand Priest continued. "He has remained silent because Val doesn't support this quest as it is currently configured."

The Duke lowered his voice as he walked up to the Grand Priest. Most likely the knights couldn't hear him, but the helmet-less Bear did.

"This Priest of Mirsha taught me a lesson about courage," the duke hissed. "As a boy, I was often cowed by your bombast. Alone, she faced you and your priests. She told you no."

The Grand Priest appeared confused by the whispered exchange.

"What does that matter?" he said. "Our past is not relevant. We are talking about how these great knights should not support this lowly quest. Not unless it is properly organized by our traditions."

The Duke walked away from Vestral and raised his voice. "You forget yourself Grand Priest. I support this quest and I am also a knight - which you are not." He waved his hand to the hanging flags above. "And we are surrounded by tradition."

The Duke turned back to the priest, "You are also quick to dismiss the farmers, but without them what would you eat?"

The Duke turned again to the knights. "Everyone serves in their capacity as directed by the gods, and should be respected for their successful fulfillment of the gods' plan. That is the essence of the Code."

As Bear understood it, Duke Comerant had gotten too close to being exactly right with the Code.

"There is no honor in this quest!" Vestral howled. "No glory for the Norseland Knights. No glory for Holy Val. None of the great knights throughout history stooped so low."

The Priestess jumped up and spoke in a much bigger voice than Bear expected from someone so small.

"History also shows us that not all victories are glorious, and honor is not found in self-promotion," she said. "It is more often found in quiet dedication and self-sacrifice."

Good point, thought Bear. The priestess was feisty, he had to give her that. To stand between those two men took some guts.

The whole room seemed to hold its collective breath. Everyone was looking at the priestess and she didn't sit.

"I continue my quest in the morning," she declared, "we head to Chryselles to pick up our guide. I would welcome the assistance of the Norseland Knights."

"There will be no knights for this quest, as I have said, and you have declined the one chance you had!" Vestral shouted. "No one will cave to this little girl's folly."

Bear grimaced. He now liked the Grand Priest even less. That statement was vile. No real man would attempt to humiliate a woman in public like that.

Bear would be happy to champion this woman against Vestral, and he wasn't the only one to take notice. The knights around him were whispering.

The Duke cut through noise with quiet words that still carried to Bear. "You forget your place, Vestral. This is my Hall. These are my knights. They will go if I say so."

Bear didn't feel that many knights had been swayed in spite of the outrageous behavior of the Grand Priest. He would bet his armor that every knight here had received the same warning he did that morning. The Grand Priest had won before the start with subterfuge.

There was no movement and only whispering for a moment. The two men standing in front of the crowd seemed to be wrestling with their eyes. Bear had to act now, before an edict was issued from the Temple to punish supporters.

Bear stepped out into the open space in front of the two men and and planted his sword in front of the Duke. "I'll go, my lord."

A deathly hush fell over the room as every eye stared at him. Bear could see his father turning red out of the corner of his eye.

The duke, on the other hand, smiled and let out a deep breath, "I give you Berigral Danagor."

The Grand Priest was flushed but didn't say anything.

A voice came from the other side of the room. "I believe this adventure will need some experience! Don't worry, I will ensure Val receives all just glory for our success."

Bear knew that superior voice. It was Sir Leoshus and he was rumored to be Grand Priest's employ. No one would say as much, since a challenge would ensue, but Bear thought it was true and this proved it.

Leoshus was an older knight, which would put him in charge. This was a chink in the armor of Bear's plan. Leoshus would claim any victory as his own and reap any benefits.

With a deep sigh, Bear resigned himself to it. He was committed.

There were no more volunteers.

The Grand Priest stormed out with his priests right behind him. Leoshus had swept across the room to shake Bear's hand and just as quickly exited.

Father had stormed out without acknowledging his son and Bear saw his brothers jogging to catch up. He sheathed his sword and stood in the middle of the hall watching everyone leave.

"Now you've done it," Thervan smiled as he clanked up. "It'll be more than shunning now."

"I'm ready," Bear smiled. "Foester has it covered."

"Good thing," Thervan said as he watched the room clear.

"Pack your things brother." Bear clapped Thervan on the shoulder. "And leave this behind. We leave before dawn."

"What?" Thervan was surprised.

"Are you going to get anything out of the youngest brother leaving?" Bear asked. "Will your life be better?"

"No," Thervan said carefully.

Bear smiled at his older brother and marched off.

Two of his brothers were waiting in the stable for him - Daerval the oldest, and Lachlan, the one between Thervan and Bear. Bear was expecting something like this.

Both of them seemed out of breath and must have hurried after receiving instructions from Father. It was a long run in full plate armor.

Now they were between Bear and his charger, Breyier.

So it begins, Bear thought as he walked up to them.

"What do you think you're doing Berigral? Father told us," Lachlan said in a harsh whisper. "Val is against this, you'll ruin him."

Bear just stared him down. Lachlan was a lackey, he did whatever Father and Daerval wanted. He was the perfect brother for Daerval.

Bear leaned down to Lachlan's height.

"The Grand Priest said they had no word from Val, so he couldn't be against it," Bear sneered.

Lachlan looked away.

"Are you happy in your place, Lachlan? Fourth son? You're not great at the tourneys and your wife's family can't support you. You are going to be forever at his beck and call." Bear pointed at Daerval.

Lachlan turned red, drew himself up, and stomped off.

Daerval put a hand on Bear's shoulder, "Bear, you can't do this. It is not your place. If Father was going to volunteer someone, it would have been me. Back out now."

Bear stared at him until he dropped his hand.

Daerval continued, "It will bring shame on the family. You will have nothing, you will end up like Thervan, outcast."

This was the first time Daerval had spoken to him since he'd convinced Bear to ask a boon of the Duke.

"Shame on the family, or on you and Father?" Bear turned away from his horse. "I'm not falling into that trap. I could keep winning tourneys and still never be free of you. You know very well I can't earn enough to support myself."

"That's why we have families and order," Daerval said. "We spread the cost and share the influence. This will only hurt us."

"Hurt us?" Bear laughed, "You mean hurt you. The world is centered on you as first son. I was your puppy for too long. Your lies last summer cured that."

Berigral turned back to his charger, "As for shame, helping the defenseless is part of our oath. You beat that into me. You've read the same stories I have. The knights of old didn't worry about status and their place at the high table."

"Bear, don't do this, you won't be able to come back," Daerval said harshly.

Bear mounted his charger as Daerval released the reins. "I'm not eight anymore, Daer. Your advice no longer sways me. Feel free to issue the challenge. We both know I'm better than you."

Bear had never considered that he wouldn't be able to come back home. His dream included coming home to glory, but as he thought about it he found the idea didn't bother him. He was excited, the world lay before him.

The next morning before dawn, Bear, Foester, and Foester's oldest son Brendan dismounted outside of the castle's stable. There was just a gloom of light in the east and the grooms were rousing the stable boys.

Bear looked over their pack horses. As usual Foester had picked well and the panniers were full.

He turned to the greying, red haired, squire "Is there any money left, Foester?"

"Yes. I got a pretty good deal and you're so big, any competent smith can make that armor smaller for someone else." Foester let out a little laugh. "And probably re-sell it for full price. There was plenty of money."

The formal plate and the formal mail had been sacrificed to fund this chance at a new life. Bear didn't really feel like he was stealing from his father. That armor was made to fit him.

Out of the gloom came another rider and Bear watched him approach as he finished his conversation with Foester. "You left the rest of the money with your wife?"

Foester seemed a little embarrassed, "I did exactly as you asked."

Bear nodded as he relaxed. The rider was Thervan. He raised his hand in welcome, "You got away?"

"The stable boy knows I left. We should be miles away when Father hears about it. I'm not sure he'll care either way," Thervan replied as he dismounted. "I couldn't get my squire up last night, I don't have much money."

"Don't worry, this is going to work," Bear grasped his brother's hand.

"You're taking a big chance," Thervan said.

"And you aren't?" Bear responded.

"You know I'm not," Thervan replied. "The only thing better would be if I died."

They both laughed.

"I guess that's still possible," Thervan smiled. "What do we do about Leoshus?"

"I don't know. Let's keep you hidden," Bear sighed.

"Hidden," Thervan laughed. "How long do you think that'll work?"

"I don't know. You're the smart one." Bear turned towards the stables. There was activity there.

The grooms were bringing out seven horses, three of which were pack animals. The priestess' party was traveling light, too. He watched Sir Eldin lead the party out of the castle.

The warrior woman immediately started checking the horses.

She's done this before, thought Bear.

The priestess' party was headed towards them and Bear started towards them when he was grabbed by the arm and turned around.

Thervan had a hood over his head and his bow and arrows slung across his back. If he kept his chainmail covered it might work as a disguise. No one would believe a hired fighter would have mail of that quality.

"Call me Tiril," Thervan whispered. "I'll stay in the back with the pack horses. Leoshus won't even notice me."

"Sounds good," Bear could hear Foester sending Brendan for the priestess' pack horses.

"It will be like riding with the family," Thervan chuckled.

Bear didn't get to reply. There was the whisk of steel on leather and both knights turned to the sound.

"Hold," yelled Foester. "Please, lady. He's my son and we are going with you. He's skilled and will handle the supplies honorably."

It was the southern woman with her sword out and she didn't put it away until the priestess waved at her. Bear got a good look at the sword and that was quality only a knight could appreciate.

Bear left Thervan behind and marched up to the priestess.

"Holy Priestess. I'm Berigral. Foester is my man and his son Brendan will also be joining us." He berated himself for not adding Thervan. "This is Tiril, he's also one of my men."

The priestess stared at him for a moment. He must look like a giant to her. The top of her red hair barely rose to his chest.

"Do knights normally have so many attendants?" Kate asked him.

Foester snorted, "Usually, there are a lot more. It takes two just to get them in their armor."

Bear blushed momentarily, "Thanks. That's the way to start a quest."

Foester laughed as he helped Brendan.

Bear smiled, "Please accept them as part of the group. You won't find two more dedicated men with their level of knowledge of warfare and horses."

"Three," The dark bearded man said staring at Thervan.

"Yes, I'm sorry. Three men." Bear was flustered.

"Sir Berigral," Kate said, "thank you for joining us. I welcome you and your men on our quest. You can call me Kate."

Kate made the rest of the introductions.

Brendan reported everything was set the way he liked it and there didn't appear to be any reason to wait. Bear secretly hoped Leoshus wouldn't show. Kate declared it was time to go and they all prepared to mount.

Duke Comerant ran out to them.

"I had this drawn up this morning." He said as he handed Kate an envelope. "I have as many supporters as detractors and not just in Norseland. This letter may help you."

"Thank you, sir. That is generous," Kate answered sincerely. "I can't tell you how much we appreciate your hospitality."

"It's a small thing," Comerant dismissed her gratitude. "I hope the letter helps."

The Duke turned to Bear. "Berigral! I knew I could count on you. This is your chance boy, make us proud."

Bear gave as deep a bow as he could with armor on, but the duke slapped him on the spaulder. He gave Bear a sly wink as he looked over at Thervan, but he didn't say anything.

The group mounted and walked the horses out of the gatehouse.

A trumpet blared causing everyone to look up.

There were at least twenty armed men on horseback and two heavily loaded wagons waiting for them. The leader rode towards them with his attendant, guidon unfurled, racing behind him. It was Leoshus.

"Hail and well met!" He hollered at them. "Sir Berigral, I'd expected more from such a wealthy family!"

His barb struck home and Bear stood in his stirrups. "I need nothing more."

"But surely, the family flag must fly," Leoshus sneered.

Leoshus knew why Bear was here and why he was without family trappings. He must be doing this to exert control - to shame him.

"No?" Leoshus said cheerfully. "Well if you don't plan to honor your family, I shall fly the single honor and you may ride at the back. You have the honor of guarding the pack train."

"I believe I'm still in charge, Sir Leoshus," Kate said.

"Yes, of course, Holy Priestess," Leoshus bowed. "I'm just ordering the disposition of the knights, which is my place by right. Now let's get started."

He turned his horse. "Chadrick, sound the forward! We lead the way!" He rode off to lead his retinue forward - with his attendant blowing his horn again.

Kate led her group forward and Bear led his group to the back.

Foester whistled as they passed the baggage train, "Two tandem wagons! I know knights like comfort but that seems unreasonable for one."

Thervan laughed. "Ah, the good old days. You've taken up with rogues, Foester."

"An even chance of that," Foester said. "I like my odds."

Bear still stung from the shame. Leoshus was going to be a problem. If he kept them at the back, then Bear would probably never know if anything happened, let alone what it was.

Bear thought back to the evening before. His father and mother had stormed into his room.

"You will not go. I forbid it," Father shouted but Bear hadn't been swayed.

His mother had cried, "You shame me. Who will you marry now?"

That had been too much for Bear.

"Shame you? You know what my lot is here. Fifth son," Bear shouted. "I'm a spare's spare. None of the ladies you've been trying to line up are going to marry the fifth son. There are still plenty of first and second sons. Sons that will inherit."

His father had kept his back turned, but his mother pressed on. "You'll miss the tournaments if you go. You always win, you're popular, that's how your father won me - he wasn't a first son."

Bear hated this argument, "Endless tournaments, that's what you want for me. That's what I mean to this family. Tournament glory for you and a well-heeled wife to pretty up the place until Daerval can take over."

Bear turned to speak at his father's back.

"You know," Bear said. "You know if I horde that money, curry favor, and get lucky investments - I might, I just might make it before Daerval throws me out."

"He won't," Mother cried.

"He will," Bear snarled. "He's already thrown me to the wolves when I out-achieved him. He'll do it again."

His mother may know more than he thought, because she didn't reply. Bear turned back to his father.

"And I'll be just like you," Bear said to his father's back. "Pandering to ensure my place at the table. That's not the life I want."

His father turned around, "You don't know what's good for you, and you don't have anything. The armor, horses, all of it belongs to me."

That made mother cry out. "No! Don't leave him naked, at least he'll be a knight in our memory."

She sobbed and left the room - she was already grieving him as if he'd died.

"Fine," Father said, "but I'm going to have that squire of yours watched. You'll take nothing with the name Danagor on it."

And with that he stormed down the hall.

The hurt of cutting ties with his family burned as he stared at the back of the pack train. He could see Kate and Leoshus at the front of the column. It looked like they were arguing. That was a small comfort to him as the dust from the wagons began to obscure his view.

Bear realized the Grand Priest had failed to wrest control of the quest from the priestess, but that wasn't the only way he could do it. It looked like the new tactic was to force her to accept military leadership of everything.

Bear hoped they misjudged their victim.

The pace of the wagons was slow. It was going to take more than a ten-day to reach the coast at this speed. Bear knew how this went. All knights were trained in the same school of warfare. It wouldn't be long before Leoshus called a halt and just over an hour later, the expected order was given.

It trickled down the line. Wagons halted in the road, and servants ran to the front - presumably for Leoshus' comfort.

"Stay on your horses," Bear called to his team.

He felt something was about to happen and he rode clear of the lingering dust. Kate was still on her horse and talking to a dismounted Leoshus. Bear couldn't hear the argument, but Leoshus accepted a glass from a servant as they talked.

Bear looked at his team, they were ready.

Kate rode back to the road and tore off at a gallop. Bear saw T'az wave. He didn't know if she was waving to him, but two others, probably the mage and the healer mounted, and rode into the dust too.

It was time for another decision.

"Let's go," Bear yelled at his team and took off at gallop.

They rode past the wagons and dismounted men. The wide eyed spearmen hurried out of the way as Bear thundered past.

"Berigral! Halt!" Leoshus was standing in the road.

"I'm sorry, Leoshus, but I have her pack animals tied in with mine. We must follow her," Bear shouted.

A smile crept across his face. He liked this priestess more and more every minute. Bear had already defied his family and was probably disowned. There was nothing more Leoshus could do to him.

Foester laughed at the disorganized mob behind them.

CHAPTER 6

Kate actually had to have a stern talk with Zhost. Now that he had been set free, he was determined to show his worth. Somebody had to be the adult and she pulled him up to a quick walk.

"We have to give the others a chance to catch up," she told him.

Zhost snorted, but he obeyed.

T'az thundered up. "Kate! Don't get so far out front!"

Her words were recriminations, but she and her horse seemed a lot happier now that they had, at least temporarily, changed the laboriously slow pace.

Kate heard more horses charging up behind them. Sir Berigral had caught up to Hestal and Bernard. He brought the pack horses with him. That was more what she wanted.

Knights to help and be available, not to slow her down.

The blonde knight rode right up to the front and pulled up next to Kate and T'az. Kate stared at him for a minute. He was huge. His grey horse was bigger than the others and was proud of its position.

Sir Berigral was grinning. His mailed hood was pushed back and he seemed to be enjoying himself. It irritated Kate.

"What is wrong with Leoshus?" Kate demanded and the knight's grin disappeared.

"I'm not sure what you mean, holy priestess," Sir Berigral responded. "I'm sure he's doing what he was instructed to do and his actions seem right out of the Book of Warfare. The chapter on movements of large bodies of troops."

T'az eyed him suspiciously. "You knights seem like a tedious bunch. We aren't a large body of troops and what's with all of that baggage?"

Berigral smiled at her. "You have no idea. The rules of movement are meant to keep your troops fresh for the fight. It is time tested wisdom."

T'az grinned, "We didn't have rules for such things patrolling the south jungles."

That caught the knight's attention. "You were on the border campaign? I've read about it. Small units fighting vicious hand to hand battles, night and day, in the thick forests. Tell me about it."

His attention seemed to annoy T'az. "Some other time. Why did Leoshus bring so much stuff?"

Berigral laughed and his squire laughed behind her.

"I'm sure Leoshus has at least three sets of armor in all of that gear," Bear laughed, "and the gods know what else for his comfort."

"It's the way of knights," Foester interjected. "Battle in lines with comfort before and after. It's very civilized."

The knight shook his head. "Thank you, Foester."

"No problem." Foester turned to T'az, "You want to have fun, put a mosquito in the full plate and watch 'em dance."

"Really not the first impression I wanted to make," Sir Berigral frowned.

T'az pointed to his armor. It was essentially a chain mail suit with plates over strategic areas. His grey surcoat was unadorned.

"Where's your plate suit?" T'az asked.

The knight coughed. "I don't like it - too restrictive. I think the improved mobility offsets the defensive advantages of the interlocking plates."

Foester chuckled, "Plus it would feed a dozen families for a year to make plate that would fit him as fast as he grows."

Berigral slumped a little. "That's true."

T'az smiled at Foester.

Kate looked at the knight quizzically and spread her hands. "Sir Berigral, why don't you have flags flying and trumpets blaring?"

T'az smiled. "You are a knight aren't you?"

"Oh yeah. Full belted," Berigral nodded. "I've studied since I was eight and I've never lost."

But Berigral's smile faded.

"Leoshus isn't wrong. My family doesn't approve of this quest because of politics—so no family honors, no pennons, no horns. Just us." He turned to Kate, "You can call me Bear, most people do."

Hestal had been listening. "Politics - as in priests taking over the knighthood?"

Bear turned in his saddle. "I don't know about that, but being a knight is expensive. Families have to make advantageous connections and investments to make it work. Priests are important connections to have."

"No offense, priestess, but the damn priests have their hands in everything," Foester growled.

Bear grinned at the women. "I'm good in a fight and Foester knows everything there is to know about campaigning. I think we'll be assets, but if you were hoping for long term support from the Court of Norseland, Leoshus is the better bet."

Kate was concerned by what she'd heard. "Are you saying you were disowned for helping us?"

"No, maybe yes," Bear smiled sadly, "let's just say they are less than pleased."

Foester laughed, "Humble to a fault. This will go in the book as the definition of disloyalty to family and god. He's disowned, and I was fired. You've picked up a rogue's gallery of knights, priestess."

"You can always go back, old man," Bear grinned.

Foester rubbed his greying beard. "I could. I don't want to. I think I'll check on the baggage, sir."

Foester turned his horse and rode back to his son.

"That's awful," Kate was appalled. "Why would you do it?"

Bear shrugged, "I'm fifth son. I won't inherit and I'm destined to fight and serve my brother for life. It's a long story, but I decided it was better to try something on my own. Foester agreed."

"You tolerate him with good humor," Kate said.

"Oh, he's the best. I love that man," Bear turned to look at the train following them. "He and his wife are more like family to me. They have always been there for me."

T'az turned back to the front. "He doesn't use your title? What kind of servant does that?"

"He's not a servant," Bear said confidently. "He's a professional."

Kate sensed there was more, "So no - Sir Berigral?"

Bear sighed. "That's part of the long story, but I learned last summer that titles are meaningless."

They rode for a few miles in silence.

"You've fought in tournaments," T'az said to the sullen knight. "Anybody die?"

"Not in years," Bear admitted. "They fashion the rules so that injuries are rare."

"So how do you know you're good?" T'az asked bluntly.

"Unlike most knights, I've spent every waking hour training with the last veterans in Norseland," Bear replied confidently. "They say so and they fought in the last pirate invasion."

T'az continued to needle him and he seemed to enjoy the attention.

Kate relaxed. She knew what T'az was up to - she'd done it to Hestal on the last journey.

The miles passed quickly, Kate looked back at her team. There was only one question she had left. It was time to ask about the story of the heavily cowled man that stayed with the pack horses.

"I understand Foester and his son - will you explain the other man," Kate asked. "I'd hate to start the journey with secrets, Sir Berigral."

"It's my brother Thervan," Bear said defensively. "We were only trying to keep his presence from Leoshus - not you."

"Why?" Kate asked.

"He's smart, good with a bow and an excellent hunter, but he has repetitively failed to win in the tournaments," Bear explained. "He has basically been disowned already. Please don't send him back."

"That wasn't in my mind at all," Kate smiled at the knight. "I just want to actually meet him."

"You're right," Bear looked back and waved to the cowled man, who quickly joined Bear at the front. "Holy Priestess, I present my brother, Sir Thervan."

Surprised, Thervan had only a moment of distraction before he threw the cowl back. "I'm honored to meet you, Holy Priestess. I apologize for the charade."

T'az eyed him boldly, "Bear's been trying to explain, what's your story?"

"I'm an outcast and an embarrassment to my family," Thervan said with a smile.

Bear snorted, "Our father would have tied him to tree to keep him from coming and in his opinion, shaming the family further. In the knightly families, only winning knights are rewarded."

Kate was confused, "Your father doesn't appreciate an archer or even intelligence?"

Thervan bowed his head, "Those are skills for the lower classes and priests. Not a knight. You have to understand as third son, I'm a spare. Father wanted me to take holy orders, but I failed the tests on purpose and passed my knightly challenge instead."

Bear seemed shocked, "I never knew you took the test!"

"You were four and only had eyes for Daerval," Thervan said. "Other than Bear, the rest would rather I disappeared."

"That's not true," Bear said. "To my shame, I was with the family on that until last summer."

"What happened last summer?" T'az asked.

The two knights shared a dark look, but Bear spoke.

"Last summer, I won," Bear smiled and patted his horses neck. "Best knight in the land at the great fair in Chryselles. My oldest brother convinced me to use that victory to ask a boon of the Duke."

"Sounds reasonable," Kate said.

Thervan chuckled. "You don't know this family. He was refused. Our father was outwardly humiliated. Bear was shunned for over six months."

"Outwardly?" Hestal asked.

Bear nodded, "Yeah. It was a ploy that Daerval and Father worked out. I was humiliated in front of the court and punished, but it gave my father an advantage. I was knocked out of any contention for leadership roles and it diminished my ability to make a living, which advances my brother. Father moved up in the Council and this summer, Daerval will be named General."

T'az said, "You were sacrificed."

Thervan smiled at her, "The fate of the fifth son."

"My heroes," Bear smiled sadly. "Important lesson learned, and I gained a brother out of the deal."

"Which isn't saying much," Foester chirped from behind them.

Thervan threw Foester a rude hand gesture and Foester laughed.

"Thank you Foester," Bear smiled. "I wasn't going to leave him to rot if I could help it."

"Or honorably kill myself?" Thervan added quietly.

"Certainly wasn't going to let that happen," Bear said darkly.

"If you're a knight," T'az inquired, "where's your squire and everything?"

"My father didn't pay for me to have a full-time squire," Thervan admitted, "I didn't win enough to pay for one either. The man that helped me is much too old and has no sons. I brought only what you see."

"So, why hide it from Leoshus?" T'az asked.

"He'll torture Thervan and the rules allow it," Bear said simply.

It was a convoluted tale, but Kate was actually pleased. She was certain she was hearing the truth, even if she didn't understand the knight's complicated family life.

"Well, I thank you for coming Sir Thervan," Kate smiled. "I suspect your skills will become more necessary as we may leave civilization behind."

Kate felt better knowing everyone and the day was turning out magnificent. The sun shone. The road was dry. The horses were at least as excited as their riders. None showed any sign of need.

The trip to Nordsvard had been rainy and wet. Conversations were minimal and misery was high. This was completely the opposite. Bear and his team were a welcome addition.

Midday found them near a bridge over a brook, a chance for the horses to drink and graze. Kate dismounted in a lovely clearing near the road and let Zhost choose where he wanted to go.

They made a small fire to cook with and soon the pot was boiling. Spring was coming and Kate looked forward to fresh greens, but the bread, cheese, and boiled meat tasted good.

Bear sat and accepted the bowl Kate offered him. "Shouldn't we at least tie up the horses?"

T'az shook her head, "They won't go anywhere."

"Why?" he asked. "You know our secrets, what's your secret?"

T'az looked at Kate who nodded.

"We have a priest with magic power," T'az said.

Bear looked at Kate, "Really? I've never even heard of that?"

Kate nodded her head, "It's true."

"It's true," T'az interrupted. "She talks to animals, maybe more, but take my word for it, the horses won't leave her."

Bear whispered, "How does it work?"

"A gift from Mirsha, but we don't want word to get out," Kate said fervently.

T'az slurped up the rest of her bowl. "It's a competition between her horse and I about which of us is most loyal."

"Ha," Bear laughed. "That's great!"

"You laugh at a lady, Sir Berigral?" T'az eyed him.

"You have my word, we won't share that information," Bear smiled at T'az' insinuation.

The horses started whinnying about the time they were wrapping up the meal. Kate looked at them, they could tell horses were coming and had all turned to look back up the road.

T'az followed Kate's gaze, "Are they ready to go already?"

"No, well yes... but that's not what this is about. Riders approaching behind us," Kate said.

The whole group rose to their feet. Bear seemed unconcerned and when Leoshus' banner topped the hill, Kate knew why. Bear stayed standing as did T'az. Kate walked in front of them to greet the newcomers.

Kate heard Bear whisper to T'az, "Leoshus will be angry."

Leoshus' horse was lathered as he and two of his men thundered to a stop. His face was stormy, and Kate waited for the storm to break.

There was a delay, as it took a moment to get a heavily armored Leoshus off his horse.

Leoshus stomped up to the group and angrily pointed at Bear, "I will deal with your insubordination in a moment Sir Berigral."

"I think not," Kate said placidly to the metal covered man in front of her.

"My Dear Lady, you cannot impose and take my responsibilities as commander of the knights on this quest," Leoshus said venomously.

"I think you're wrong," Kate said putting down her dishes.

"This is intolerable, Holy Priestess." He stamped his foot, "You are under my protection, you will do what I believe is necessary to protect you!"

"And for the success of the quest?" She said benignly.

"Yes, of course. I," Leoshus didn't finish his comment before Kate spoke.

"Have you ever met a god, Leoshus?" Kate asked.

"That's Sir Leoshus, and no I have not, Holy Priestess," he shifted uncomfortably making his armor creak. "I don't see how that's relevant. I have the Right of Command, blessed by Val."

"I have," Kate smiled at the older man. "In an instant you know. You don't have to be told, the power is immense, unfathomable."

Kate walked around behind him to hold his horse's head.

"I was lucky Leoshus, the god I met loved me. I could feel it, and yet I was driven to my knees by Her power."

Leoshus appeared unprepared for this conversation. "It sounds like you were lucky."

"You're right," Kate nodded. "No matter what, you know you are unworthy of their presence. It's like you're a bug, even lower maybe."

She waved Brendan over and he brought water and fruit for the tired, sweaty horses.

"So you see, since She very clearly put me in charge, I will not fail Her." Kate held his gaze, "You are also right that this is intolerable. I won't tolerate it."

Kate put her hand on his chest plate and he staggered a half step back like he'd been struck by the diminutive priestess.

"I went two weeks out of my way to get the best knights," Kate's voice grew stronger. "You volunteered, which means you are free to leave. If you stay, you will do what I say."

Kate took her hand off of him and turned to walk away, but Leoshus recovered quickly and leapt back into the argument.

"The goddess directed you to have knights," he argued. "She must have meant for us to protect you, military matters are my area and I think security dictates a slower pace."

Kate turned thoughtfully back to him.

"Actually She didn't say anything about knights," Kate said. "Holy Mirsha said I required a magician and the guide we are going to get and where to get him. She also said it would be dangerous."

"The Council directed me to get knights and I'm now convinced we were sent to Norseland on purpose," Kate said bitterly. "You are free to leave Leoshus."

Hestal coughed. "The High Priest might think differently and the Council certainly will."

That gave Kate pause. Was Bear and his brother enough to meet Haervan's expectations? It was a question she couldn't answer until she could write him again.

"What makes you believe you were sent to us under false pretenses, my lady?" Leoshus inquired.

Kate gave him her best little girl smile, "Is Nordsvard on the way to Chryselles? No? Well that's the destination Holy Mirsha instructed us to, so why am I here?"

There was no answer from Leoshus. He removed his gauntlets and accepted a bowl of food from Bernard without comment.

That spurred Kate on, "And the place I'm sent for knights is possibly the one place in the world where the priests of Val are close to wresting control from a duke."

"That's a scandalous suggestion, my lady," Leoshus said nearly dropping his food. "You defame the honor of my Duke and your brother priests."

"Really?" Kate nodded thoughtfully, "Maybe, but it is suspicious. I could have caught a barge in Theopolis and been in Chryselles by now. There are knights in Chryselles."

"And they aren't bad," Bear interjected.

That drew him a venomous glare from Leoshus, but Bear seemed unfazed by the older knight.

Leoshus got louder, "Are you suggesting the priests of Val are working against Mirsha?"

Leoshus sounded outraged, but he didn't look it.

"No. Not at all," Kate placated him a bit. "They are very clear they aren't against the quest. They are against me leading it, certainly, and you are also against me leading it."

"That's not true," Leoshus again seemed outraged. "I'm merely trying to follow the Book of Warfare on the movement of troops. We cannot be tired when brought to battle. You'd know this if you had martial skills."

"This isn't an army, Leoshus," Kate said as she spotted Leoshus' wagons cresting the hill behind them. "Well maybe you have an army, but I do not. I'm directed to Chryselles by a god and I've been delayed two weeks already. I won't be held up longer."

Kate led Zhost back to the stream while Leoshus fumed.

The horses weren't the only ones ready to go by the time Leoshus' caravan pulled up to a stop. There seemed to be men missing. Kate hadn't counted them before, but she felt there were fewer.

Kate eyed Leoshus with a silent question.

"I sent word back about our progress and I am now sending a man forward, Holy Priestess," Leoshus said sarcastically.

Leoshus handed one of the mounted men something and the attendant galloped away to the east.

Kate didn't know what was exchanged.

Leoshus turned back to her, "Do you expect me to leave my retinue here, Holy Priestess? Having knights on your campaign has advantages, but requires more effort and support - traditionally."

Kate walked away from the stream and thought of Hestal's warning, "Just this once Leoshus. Just this once, we'll wait for you - more for your horses than anything else."

Kate walked to the wagons and looked them over with Leoshus following behind her. "You might consider packing lighter, like Sir Berigral."

Leoshus found humor in her statement.

"Pack like a young knight? One who's obviously on the run from his family," he sneered. "He is inexperienced and doesn't know what he should bring. He hasn't even brought his plate mail. What good will he be in battle?"

"What makes you think that?" Kate asked him when they got to the back of his wagons.

"Think? I don't think, I know." Leoshus was chafing under what he must have felt was undue questioning. "His family is rich, but he only has a few men. Not enough to suit him in his plate and not enough horses to carry it all." He handed his dirty dishes to an attendant.

"No," Leoshus turned to look over his wagons. "His father is not behind him. He can't afford his own armor and he has no renown to attract men to his banner on his own. I also know he was denied a writ of leadership last summer. He is battle fodder – nothing more."

Leoshus walked up his row of men, "You have only one knight, me, and one pup who wants to be."

"I'll be honest with you Leoshus," Kate tired of the pompous man. "I find his style much more agreeable. This may be a long trip."

Leoshus kept walking.

Kate got them all going about an hour later. The pace was still slow, but she drove them on until the sun started to set.

Leoshus' men set up his camp and it was huge. The knight's tent was large and was well furnished for his comfort. Two men helped him out of his armor and he disappeared into his tent.

Leoshus' banner flew at the doorway and one of his men stood guard at all times. The rest hacked a space behind his tent out of the woods and lined up their own little shelters.

Bear and his group selected a couple of trees near the fire and slung a tarp. Kate had slept under the stars the few nights on the way to Nordsvard that they hadn't found shelter from the rain.

She expected to sleep on the ground many more nights before this was over.

Whatever reason T'az had for not purchasing tents, was good enough for Kate. She trusted T'az implicitly.

Leoshus joined them for dinner in an exquisite robe and afterwards, exempted himself and his men from the watch list. Kate didn't really mind, since apparently one of them would be awake all night guarding his door.

"Where are we?" Kate asked Foester - who was perusing the map near the light of the fire.

"Well ma'am, were about here." He said pointing a big gnarled finger to a spot on the map.

He pointed behind her, "The cliffs that separate us from the plains are just a few miles that way. We ride along them for a few days. Good weather, and a decent pace, we should ride down a gentler slope here."

He showed her the map again. "Day after that, we'll ride into the port city of Nordrigen."

"So six days then?" She asked.

He smiled at her, "I suspect it will be much closer to seven. No way we'll keep the pace that high." He looked meaningfully over at the tent, where men were rushing in and out with water.

"You seem to enjoy not having that relationship with your knight," Kate observed.

Foester nodded as he watched the men scurrying in and out of the tent.

"I've done it," he said. "Fetch and carry, bow and scrape. Bear's father is like that, you know. I was never popular as a squire there."

Foester rolled up the map. "I was glad to be demoted to the boys and was fortunate to get the youngest."

Kate smiled and stood up and Foester held up his hand to stop her.

"You're going to hear a lot of crap from that windbag, and I don't know when he'll get a chance to prove it, but I wouldn't bet against the Bear. If you know what I mean." He winked a green eye at her.

"I do," Kate smiled conspiratorially towards Foester as Bear walked up. "Thank you."

"Looks all quiet out there," Bear reported.

"Great, let's get some sleep." Kate left them and headed over to the spot T'az had selected for her.

She heard Bear ask, "what was that about?"

Kate didn't hear Foester's response - she was in turmoil. She stood and observed Leoshus' men at work. They seemed to do random things, just to do them. Idleness seemed to be their enemy.

She had no experience with armies, but it reminded her of the Temples. Rank and closeness to power was all that mattered. The flock was kept busy and distracted. Idleness was a sin.

The Code didn't cover rank or position in the priesthood or in the military. All of this was created by men through some drive Kate couldn't understand.

It was puzzling how the soldiers recreated the world they were used to. Hacking into the forest so that lines were straight - order maintained.

Hestal interrupted her musing, "Anything wrong?"

"I'm watching them work and it reminds me of the Council," Kate sighed. "They seem focused on maintaining the structure they created and everyone else tries to be closer to power."

"Well, you've been there," Hestal said. "Aren't you part of the structure -- positioning yourself? Isn't this quest going to advance you?"

"I guess, maybe, I don't really know," Kate replied. "I'm supposed to believe and advocate those beliefs. The Code is clear on my role, but not on the quest - we are outside of the boundaries."

"Maybe Mirsha wants to you to move up," Hestal smiled.

"That feels wrong," Kate admitted. "It just feels wrong to push myself and my ambitions ahead. I don't think that's why I was picked."

Hestal rubbed his beard as he thought. "You're not going to be a winner in the bigger political battle if you don't advance yourself."

Doubt was creeping into Kate's beliefs. "I don't want to win in this political battle you speak of. I'm supposed to serve the gods and advance the cause of the people, bringing them purity, purpose, and ultimate spiritual reward."

Even that common refrain felt hollow to her ears.

Kate pointed at the soldiers. "But this is how it works. It's about structure and control."

"You're just seeing that?" Hestal seemed surprised, "Everyone knows that."

"I didn't," Kate slumped. Everyone knew how the world worked except her. "I always loved our priest, and Haervan. They aren't like this."

"This is what everybody else sees," Hestal said fiercely. "Why do you think so many people stay on the edges?"

"I didn't know they did," Kate admitted. "I thought people were just not honoring the gods - I thought it was sin or our failure to show them the true way."

"No, I think it's a heavy yoke," Hestal said. "People like me run to something that isn't covered in the Code to avoid it."

Kate felt Hestal had gotten too close to the core of her life. She hoped Mirsha would make it clear to her, but something wasn't right.

Kate changed the subject.

"Leoshus is going to be a problem," Kate admitted.

"Get some sleep," Hestal smiled at her. "Tomorrow is another day. Who knows what will happen?"

Kate tried to sleep for at least an hour, but she wasn't tired. She got up and snuck down to the horses. They whinnied nervously at her approach.

"What is it?" She asked them. Their minds seemed blocked to her now. Zhost was straining against the rope tied to his bridle as he tried to unhook himself.

Kate reached out to him, "Zhost what is it?"

She never got to touch him.

CHAPTER 7

Kate woke in pain. Her head hurt and she was face down and blindfolded, over the back of a horse. The leather of the saddle was biting into her stomach.

Kate tried to move, but her arms and legs were tied. She couldn't move to relieve the pressure on her stomach. Her head throbbed and felt swollen from being carried head down.

Kate could hear a second horse and she reached out to both horses with her mind. They were curious about her, but dutifully doing what their riders wanted. She was merely a curiosity.

Her captors didn't speak.

She knew they weren't on the road, because branches were brushing her head and feet.. Kate could feel the horses' pleasure at leaving the thick undergrowth, but they soon became fearful.

Falling was the only impression she got from them, and they were terrified of it.

The man on the other horse spoke first in a whiney, high pitched voice.

"Over here I think. Yeah, this is it," he said.

Her captor had a gravelly voice. "Careful, it's a half mile drop around here. Let's toss her and be gone."

"Not yet," Whiney said. "We gotta wait for the priest or we don't get paid. He'll make you climb down there to prove it was her. You want that?"

Gravel replied angrily, "I don't like it. That horse woulda killed us if it had gotten the chance. I'm sure its awaked the rest of them by now."

"You're an idiot," whiney laughed. "They think they're safe riding around like lords and it was just a horse. It probably didn't like the way you smell."

"Screw you. I been around horses my whole life, ain't seen nothing like that," her captor argued. "I don't care if I get paid. We got to get gone, I'm telling you, they're right behind us."

Kate was pushed off his saddle. It was a short but painful drop to the ground. She could smell the thin grass outside the burlap that covered her head.

"Not possible," Whiney countered. "I was careful. Besides, the soldier we met yesterday was clear. We have to present the girl to get our reward. If I'd known you were such a chicken, I would've hired someone else."

Kate heard the man above her draw steel out of leather.

Whiney changed to a tone of reason, "Listen, it'll take the knights an hour just to get in armor."

A third voice spoke for the first time and it was a loud and commanding voice. Kate had heard voices like that from behind the pulpit.

"They aren't far behind you. How could you mess this up? I was assured that you are professionals," the loud voice said. "It was a simple job."

"Ain't that simple," said the man above her in his gravelly drawl.

"Fine it isn't," Loud said angrily. "Quickly now, bring her over. I need to be sure you've got the right one." Coins clinked. "And then you get paid."

"As you say," Whiney agreed, "show him."

Kate had to think, her head was pounding. She could feel blood running down her scalp and she ached. The cloth in her mouth muffled her attempts at shouting.

It also prevented her from intoning a prayer to Mirsha. She needed help. No ritual could help her, she was blind, immobile, and alone. Fear knotted her stomach.

Kate did the only thing she could think of and reached out to the horses. She sent them the scariest images she could think of and laced it with her pain.

"God's Blood, you stupid animal," Loud yelled. "Hold still, HOLD STILL!"

The horse above her thrashed about as it dealt with the pain and fear it felt.

There was a scream that descended horribly as someone was thrown over a cliff, just to Kate's left. The scream seemed to last a long time. Kate decided to forget ritual and beg Mirsha. She didn't want to be thrown over.

Kate told the horses to run and they did with relief.

"No!" Loud yelled as his horse plunged off into the trees. "Stop damn you!" were the last words Kate heard from him.

There was a thump nearby as she heard the other horses running away. Apparently, her captor hadn't stayed on his horse. Rough hands grabbed her.

"Now little girl, I ain't figured how you did that, and I'm real sorry, but you gots to go over," he said. "I ain't hanging for this."

He picked her up and there was a solid, wet, thunk sound and Kate felt her captor weaken.

"Nrgblssss…. shnr…" Gravel gurgled as he dropped her again. He fell next to her in the grass. He made a sound, "nnnn…", and was quiet.

Kate started to cry when she heard T'az's voice, "Where is she?"

"Over here!" It was Thervan. "I got one of them. I think there are more."

The crashing in the brush nearby grew louder and thundered in her throbbing head. Someone picked her up and pulled her blindfold off. It was T'az and she pulled the cloth from Kate's mouth.

Kate took a quick look and confirmed how close she was to the black abyss of the cliff while T'az cut her bonds.

"Oh, Mirsha! Thank you, they were going to throw me over," Kate cried while T'az checked her bleeding scalp in the dark.

"They aren't anymore," T'az said solemnly.

There was a clash of steel somewhere off in the dark trees, but it only lasted a moment. Thervan was staring that way, bow ready to draw. T'az helped her to her feet and picked up her sword.

"How many were there?" Thervan asked Kate.

"There were two that brought me here to meet a third - they called him a priest," Kate sobbed. "His horse took him off that way through the trees and the second one was thrown over the cliff."

Even though, the man was trying to kill her, she was deeply upset that she had caused his death. She had killed, it was a stain on her soul that would need to be purged.

"Bear went that way with Foester," Thervan said hastily. "Let's get her on her horse and get her back to camp. If the third one is out there, that's the safest place."

"Agreed," T'az replied.

T'az yanked the arrow out of the captor, stood, and kicked the dead body over the edge.

"How did you find me so quickly?" Kate asked as she stumbled away from that awful cliff. The scratchy, grey, leafless scrub was a relief.

Zhost loomed up out of the dark once they got into the trees.

T'az grabbed the rope connected to his bridle. "We just followed him. After he came storming into camp leaping and stamping on the fire. We just followed."

"Thank you, Zhost," Kate said as T'az helped her on him bareback. "He tried to warn me, but I was so caught up with my problems."

Zhost turned and carefully picked his way through the trees and broke into a gallop once they hit the road leaving T'az and Thervan behind.

Their camp came quickly into sight. Brendan, Bernard, and Hestal were armed and relieved to see her. The guard was still at Leoshus' door, but no one else was visible.

"Where?" was all Bernard said as he helped her off her horse.

"I was ambushed, back in the trees by the horses," Kate said as Bernard helped her off her horse.

"Thank Gaia, you're alright," Bernard said as T'az galloped into camp.

"Here, I'll make something for your head," Bernard started mixing smelly things from his bag. He hummed as he worked and Kate found it soothing.

A few minutes later, Bear thundered up, bare chested, on his charger. Blood dimmed the glint of his sword in the firelight.

"Ah so you've found her," Leoshus said.

Kate hadn't heard him join the group. He was still in his robe and didn't seem relieved at all. He took a drink of wine and never looked at her.

T'az yelled at him, "With no help from you. Some protector."

Leoshus ignored her and spoke to Bear. "You see, Sir Berigral, maybe now she'll understand the need for security. Report please, Sir Berigral, and know that I will report your unpreparedness. Have you no decency young man?"

"No decency? Unpreparedness?" Bear stood before him in just a pair of leather pants. There was blood on his bare chest. "We saw a robed man ride out of the woods, two men tried to defend him."

T'az interrupted, "She was ambushed behind your tent, Leoshus. They were going to throw her over the cliff. Five men total. I'd think your guard might have noticed five men lurking around you."

"Where are these men now? We must question them closely." Leoshus said calmly as he ignored any insinuation.

"One of them was thrown from his horse over the cliff, Thervan shot the second at the cliff," T'az reported.

Bear reported to T'az, "I killed the two on the road, Foester and Thervan are searching the woods for the guy in the robe."

Leoshus looked shocked. "Thervan! Your brother is the man under the cowl? Great Val, what were you thinking bringing that reject."

Leoshus howled and laughed. "I bet your father is beside himself. The court must be laughing up their sleeves particularly after his recent success. He may lose his seat over this!"

The group around the fire just stared at him. Bear recovered first.

"Why would that be the first thing you thought of?" Bear took a step towards the older knight. "The person you volunteered to support was nearly killed. Val's blood! You've stained your oath!"

Leoshus stopped laughing, "You will withdraw that charge! I'm not the one skulking and hiding. I am doing this properly and now hope the priestess will agree that it is necessary."

"I do not withdraw my charge," Bear shouted. "I'm ready for your challenge whenever you are, sir."

"This will be reported. All of it!" The big eyed Leoshus shouted, "We have rules for a reason. You may not be punished now, but your father surely will be for your insolence and the behavior unbecoming a knight that is your brother."

T'az stepped up and joined Bear, "Hard not to notice you aren't challenging him though."

Leoshus snapped, "You watch your mouth, servant. The motivations of Southerns are always in question."

Hestal interjected, "The only person whose motivations I'm curious about are yours, Sir Leoshus. You don't seem too upset that they had to kill four men to keep Kate alive. I'd say Thervan has already proven himself useful."

"I don't like your tone, magician," Leoshus said flatly.

"Yeah," Bernard chimed in as he bandaged a barely conscious Kate. "What were you going to do in your fluffy fine robe?"

"Enough!" Leoshus shouted. "My armor is being prepared. I'll not be badgered by the servants."

He stormed back to his tent.

"Servants?" Asked Bernard.

Hestal just shrugged and smiled.

T'az handed Bear a rag for the blood, "You should know, Thervan shot one through the heart - in the dark, at twenty or thirty paces, in high brush. It was a good shot."

Bear nodded, "I told you he was good. Knights don't lie. Well, most don't anyway. Leoshus will pay for this."

T'az held up her hand, "It may not have been him."

Hestal seemed surprised, "You're defending him?"

"No," T'az snapped, "It could have been him. I'm just saying she's angered others. One tried to kill her in the temple complex - this could be related to that instead."

That led to more discussion. Kate wanted to stay in control. It wasn't provable at this point that Leoshus was behind the attack. Kate also wanted to stifle that kind of talk and keep conflict out of her group, but whatever Bernard had given her kept her down.

Kate couldn't think of how to keep the peace at this moment anyway and drifted to a dreamless sleep.

CHAPTER 8

Bear stood in full armor near the fire. He had his shield over his back and coif on. If there was another attack, they'd have to go through him. His oath demanded it.

T'az woke before dawn. She looked tired as she walked up to Bear. "You didn't wake the next person on watch?"

"No," Bear said. "I got it. I was too wound up to sleep anyway."

"First kill will do that," T'az smiled. "You know, a fall off that giant horse of yours is going to hurt."

"Breyier is a steady, well-trained, mount—he'll let me drowse most of the day," Bear said. "When do you think we'll leave?"

"I don't know," T'az said. "Let's let her sleep as long as she will. As far as I know, we don't have to be anywhere."

"Good," Thervan said.

The other two hadn't heard him approach.

"I'll get up in those hills and watch the road," Thervan said, shifting his gear. "If Leoshus is involved, maybe I'll catch him at it - if not - I'll see if we're being followed."

"Good idea," Bear nodded. "Make sure no one can see you, we won't know to ride back if you need help."

Thervan smacked the bigger man on his armored shoulder, "Okay, little brother, I can handle it."

Thervan unhitched his horse, saddled it, and walked it into the forest.

The shouts of the sergeants caught Bear's attention and he headed over to where he could see around Leoshus' tent. He passed Bernard, who was checking on Kate. She seemed to still be asleep.

Hestal was grumpy as Bear got to him, "Do they have to shout?" Hestal rubbed water on his face.

"They're sergeants," Bear shrugged. "That's what they do."

Foester walked over to Bear with the folded tarp that was their shelter. "They've slipped since I left the army, that's sloppy work. As was you staying up all night, you'll be weaker today. Next time wake the watch."

Bear nodded. He couldn't argue. He didn't feel he needed the sleep, but Foester was probably right. He usually was.

Hestal looked at the tent, "You think his lordship is up?"

Foester nodded, "I'm sure. He'll show up in a few minutes all dressed up."

The soldiers were busy as ants for a while and as soon as Leoshus exited his tent, the ants tore it down and packed it all back in the wagons.

In a few short minutes the soldiers had the wagons back on the road as Leoshus stood by and watched. He waved at them and the wagons headed east under guard.

Leoshus walked over to the fire, "I see our leader is not up yet. I shall take initiative then and start now at a normal pace. Be so good as to inform the holy priestess when she deigns to wake."

He dumped his cup in the fire and clanked to his charger. Once he was mounted, his entire group rode away.

Bear watched them go. It was hard for him to believe that as little as eight months ago, that could have been him. So much had changed in his life. Hestal handed him bread and cheese.

"Thanks," Bear grunted.

Hestal followed his gaze, "Missing the good life?"

"You know I thought I would, but not really," Bear replied. "The rigidity is difficult and it's very competitive, but it's not quite so obvious when you're in it."

Foester soaked his bread in broth, "You were never really like that."

"Really? I'd think I'd know, I was there," Bear said sarcastically. "I remember trying to memorize it all with Daerval whipping me at every wrong answer."

"Nope," Foester smiled. "I wouldn't be here if you had been."

He left them and gave Brendan some packing instruction.

Their camp was mostly packed when Kate woke up. She seemed terribly upset and immediately set out a candle and sang. There was some tossing of what looked like seeds and wine was wasted.

Bear could only watch. He didn't have any idea what she was doing, but she was serious about it. She appeared to be crying as she sang sadly.

"She does that every morning," Bernard shrugged. "You get used to it. Usually, it's at dawn - this is late."

"It's her priestly ritual, and doesn't take very long," Hestal said. "She only does the one every day. I haven't asked her about that. I thought most priests did at least three."

"You don't have to make excuses to me. We've got time for whatever she wants to do," Bear looked down the road. He could still just make out the dust cloud of Leoshus' group. "It will take less than an hour to ride down Leoshus and all of his stuff."

T'az helped Kate over to the fire and got her some food.

"How do you feel?" Hestal asked.

"Sore. Thank you all. I'm sorry I walked out by myself last night. I just wanted to see the horses," Kate said as she accepted the bread.

"Don't do it again," T'az ordered. "Take anyone with you, but not alone."

Bear nodded, "That's a good idea. We were lucky your horse warned us in time."

Hestal nodded. "Someone made a bold move on the first night after we leave the protection of the duke."

"Did you see the third man, the one they called the priest?" Kate asked Bear.

Bear didn't correct her count by adding in the two he'd killed, he just shook his head, "Just the dark robe. Could've been a black robe of Val, but I couldn't say that for sure. Foester and Thervan looked but never found him."

Brendan let Zhost go from the line of hitched horses and Kate walked over to him and thanked him.

"I can eat while we ride," she said.

"There's no rush," Bear said. "Leoshus just left. It won't take us long to catch up."

"You could use some rest," Bernard said. "That's a nasty bump."

"No," Kate declared. "I don't want to wait."

There was no sense arguing with the strong willed little priestess. Bear was sure that her horse would take care of her - it was a very committed animal.

Bear rubbed Breyier's neck before he mounted. Breyier seemed particularly pleased this morning, but the knight couldn't fathom why. Bear let Kate lead, but rode with T'az right behind her.

"You were a bit wild eyed last night," T'az said to Bear conversationally.

"Yes," Bear admitted. "I've beaten a lot of men, but those were the first two I've killed."

T'az smiled at him, "The first are the hardest. They won't be the last."

Bear switched to a whisper, "Not the way she's angering them."

T'az laughed. "Yeah, Kate can get under some people's skin."

"Where'd you learn to fight?" Bear asked. He was curious. Women didn't fight in Nordsvard.

T'az rubbed her sword hilt, "Vistula. My father trained me and I fought the jungle men south of the river for five years on and off with Dallon's Southern Brigade."

T'az looked distant for a moment. "I wish I could put that crew back together; they were tough fighters."

"Why didn't you?" Bear asked.

"I came north alone after taking a spear in the lung," T'az smiled. "I don't think those boys would go as far north as Chryselles. If we head south from there, I may look them up."

"Wow," Bear was impressed. "I've injured a lot of people, but I've never been seriously hurt. Do a lot of women fight down south?"

"No, I'm rare even there," T'az grinned at him.

Kate interrupted. "Where's Thervan?"

"He's hiding behind us," Bear reported. "Keeping an eye out for the robed man, or to see if anyone is following us."

"That's a good idea," Kate said. "Wish I'd thought of it."

Kate sagged and put her hand to her head.

"Your head hurting? We don't have to be anywhere today," T'az said.

Kate shook her head, "No, Bernard has skill. I think the bandage is bothering me, but I don't want to stop. We can get it off when we stop for midday."

She turned to Bear, "Do we know who those men were?"

"No." He replied. There was no other answer. They had searched. "There were no markings on their clothes and they didn't have anything written down. The one on the cliff had no armor and the two on the road had black leather armor." Bear shrugged, "Maybe the one that went over the cliff was the ring-leader."

"I don't want to talk about him. I'm ashamed I caused his death," Kate sighed.

Bear was confused. "He was trying to kill you. You shouldn't feel bad about that."

"It was such a long scream," Kate shuddered.

"What? You had a vision?" T'az asked.

"No. Just that scream last night. It wasn't like the man in my dream," Kate smiled sadly. "My mind is filling with horrible screams."

Bear didn't know about the dreams, so T'az filled him in.

"She may do something that seems completely random," T'az told him. "Just understand she's reacting to something you can't see."

Bear was at a loss, "What do you do about it?"

T'az chuckled, "I haven't figured that out yet. Let me know if you do."

Bear started watching Kate closely. He hoped he'd see whatever mysterious thing she saw. He was tired though and his focus wandered after nothing happened.

There was no friendly banter to keep him awake. Everyone was tired after last night's excitement. Even the horses seemed droopy.

In an hour they caught up to Leoshus. He picked up the pace to stay alongside Kate with his attendant and squire. He had apparently gotten some books out of his luggage this morning and had them ready when Kate reached him.

Leoshus started to use the books as references to argue with Kate about the order of military expeditions. She was short tempered and attacked all his assertions with the Code. As far as Bear was concerned, the Code was an impenetrable pile of books that Kate seemed to have memorized.

It was too much for Bear's tired brain.

"You got this?" Bear asked T'az. "I'm going to drop back and check on the gear and, you know, Thervan."

"Yeah," T'az waved to him as he pulled up his charger.

Bear waited for the group to pass and pulled in beside Foester at the back of the line of pack animals.

Foester smiled knowingly at the tired knight, "You come back to enjoy the dust of your betters'?"

"No," Bear yawned. "He's lecturing her on the Book of Warfare and the Right of Command. I don't think he understands what he's doing. She's not interested in any of it."

"There's an understatement," Hestal threw back from a few horses in front of them.

Foester shrugged, "Or you could say he doesn't know what he's getting himself into."

They all chuckled. Leoshus did look back - even though he couldn't have heard them over the distance, the pounding hooves, and the full helmet he insisted on wearing. Bear waved at him.

Thervan caught up a few hours later, with nothing to report. He'd seen no one. Bear was a little disappointed, tired as he was, he was eager to test himself again.

The group rode east as fast as Kate could prod Leoshus, and Leoshus slowed them down as much as he could. It was a long week in beautiful weather amongst the rolling forested hills.

Kate and Leoshus' arguments got on everyone's nerves. Leoshus wouldn't move from his position on his books and his traditions and Kate wouldn't bend on the Code — which trumped everything, except when it didn't. In those instances Kate fell back on the directions from Mirsha.

Bear noticed anytime Kate tried to end the arguments, Leoshus took that as victory, which antagonized Kate and spurred her on. Bear rotated up to the front often and stayed as long as he could keep silent. He had memorized everything Leoshus was arguing years ago, but Kate's arguments made more sense and at times Bear found himself torn between what he knew and what was right for this situation.

On one trip back to the pack horses, Foester said. "Breyier is going twice as far as the rest of the horses."

"I'd love to tell them to stop arguing," Bear said bitterly.

"Sure, but you can't tell your military commander to shut up," Foester chuckled.

"And," Bear added with a smile, "you can't tell a priest to shut up either."

It was a great relief on the morning of the seventh day when Leoshus stayed behind with his wagons. One of them had broken a wheel coming down the steep road to the plain, stranding half of his gear.

Kate took the rest of the group forward. She had been excitedly retelling them everything she'd read about the sea. No one in the group had ever seen the sea and it was getting close.

Bear was ambivalent about it. The sea was just something else to deal with, so it almost made him laugh when they were surrounded by fog on the first day they should have seen it.

The humor in it faded as the grey fog got so thick he couldn't see more than a few paces away. He actually pulled his shield off his back. It would be the only way to stop an arrow - there would be no warning.

Bear and T'az had developed a bit of a routine around Kate. When she saw the shield, she nodded and pulled up on the other side of Kate. It wasn't perfect, but it sandwiched the tiny priestess between them.

The group crept forward in the fog. They couldn't see it, but they could smell the ocean - the salt, fish, and other unrecognizable odors that heralded the salty sea.

The fog just got thicker the farther they went. The group dismounted after Bear couldn't see the road in front Breyier. You could break a horse's leg and never know you'd gone off the road in this thick soup.

As they walked their mounts forward, a gate loomed up out of the fog.

"The gates are closed," Kate said to no one in particular. "What day is it?"

"It's Gaiaday," Bernard responded. "Day for healing and health, thanks to my goddess Gaia."

"Yeah," T'az said, "but not a holiday or anything."

"No it isn't," Bear said as he walked forward. There were two skinny, leather armored men huddled against the damp wooden gate.

They stood as he approached and leaned on their spears. "Halt! Gate's closed 'cause of the fog!"

"Sir," Kate said as she strode forward. "Please take this letter to your commander." She handed the guard the Duke's sealed letter.

Bear watched everything he could see closely. He trusted Thervan and Foester were watching behind. The guards took a good look at the seal on the envelope and one of them darted off.

Bear couldn't see a sally port, but it must exist. In only a couple of minutes, the gate swung open, and the remaining guard waved them ahead.

A portly man in breast plate waited for them inside the gate. A broad smile shown under his heavily bearded face, but his eyes were quite sharp looking.

"Holy Priestess, I'm Captain Dohn. Welcome to Nordrigen," he said in a booming voice. He returned the Duke's open letter to Kate. "The mayor and town council will be headed this way sharp quick I expect, but I won't hold you here for them."

Kate smiled at him, "Thank you."

"What do seek here? This is the limit of the Duke's authority," the Captain inquired.

"Not much. At least a night's lodging, and a ship to Chryselles?" Kate asked hopefully.

"Ship?" The captain said with a sly look. "I can't help you with that, but lodging - well the best in town is the Golden Sheaf. It's not too far from the docks. You might be able to book passage there."

"Again, thank you Captain," Kate bowed her head to him. "You've been very helpful."

"Your blessing priestess, and may your quest be successful," he put his hand over his heart and bowed as Bear expected.

They mounted and rode slowly into town. The fog limited their vision to the street they were on, but the road they were riding was busy with people and wagons.

The shops on either side of the road were made of wood and had porches large enough to park wagons. The broad porches seemed to be where most people gathered and most business was conducted.

Everything was damp and splashed with mud from the road, but the residents didn't seem to mind. There was lively trade happening on the porches and Bear saw a lot of bearded men with axes. Everyone seemed busy and no one noticed them ride past.

"Huh," said Kate.

"What?" Asked T'az.

Kate pointed up. "It's the flags. As it's Gaiaday, you might expect to see Gaia flags or some other tribute to Holy Gaia, but these flags are the ones you put out during celebrations and there's something wrong about them."

"Like what?" Bear asked.

"Well, like that flag there to Mirsha — it is wrong. The dawn is too small and it's missing the plow," Kate said. "The next one down the street has the tree and the sheaf swapped and why would they all be out today? It's odd.".

Foester had gotten directions and led them through the crowd, while T'az and Bear rode next to Kate. The others surrounded their pack animals and discouraged pilfering.

Foester eventually turned them towards a gated compound surrounded by a wooden fence. The gate had the icon of the Golden Sheaf of wheat on it. The yard was green and there was gravel instead of mud. Inside the gate it was clean and tidy.

"I was worried we were going to spend a damp night in cramped quarters," Hestal said flicking water out of his hair.

"It actually looks pretty good, but I'll hold judgement until we sample the beer," Bernard quipped.

A well-dressed gentleman came down the stairs as they dismounted. He walked up to Foester, but Foester pointed in Kate's direction. The gentleman went next to Bear.

"May I inquire, about your needs, Sir?" The man asked Bear.

Bear smiled, "You may, but she's in charge."

He pointed the gentleman to Kate. Bear thought the man hid his surprise well, as he turned to face the diminutive priestess.

"My Lady," he said.

"I'm Katelarin, Priestess of Mirsha," she said as she handed him Duke Comerant's letter. "I have a letter here from the Duke of Nordsvard about our purpose. We will need rooms and accommodations for our horses while we seek ship passage to Chryselles."

"Um," he said looking at the letter. "I'm Crader, the owner of this establishment. May I inquire how you will..."

Kate raised an eyebrow.

"...pay?" Crader completed his sentence with some hesitance.

Kate rolled her eyes, "Don't worry Crader, you'll be compensated."

"Financially?" he asked tentatively.

T'az stepped in angrily, "What did the lady tell you? Now go and get rooms ready. Food. Move it."

Crader scurried off.

Foester said, "You may want some of us to put up in the barn. This place'll probably cost a fortune."

"No I wouldn't," Kate replied. "Do you have a short trip left in you, Foester?"

"Sure," he replied, gathering up his reins. "What do you need?"

Kate looked at him thoughtfully, "I need the local priest of Mirsha at his earliest convenience, and I need somebody to see what's happened to Leoshus. We may want to start seeing what's available on the docks too."

"I'll go with him," Bear said. "That way if we need to split up or Leoshus is a pain, we should still get all of it done."

Foester snorted, "Think I can't handle it, sire?"

"Well you are getting old," Bear replied as he mounted.

Bear let Foester lead as they headed back out into the fog.

CHAPTER 9

Kate sat up in her bed. Sleep failed her when her mind was this active. The nights this far north were so long.

T'az was asleep in a cot on the other side of the room.

Kate rubbed her hand on the wood paneled walls. It reminded her of home. Everything was made of wood in her childhood.

This was different wood - pine or some other evergreen tree. The smell was different, but they were warm, solid, and comforting in appearance and feel.

The wood calmed Kate after an oddly disturbing day.

The local priest of Mirsha had been a fanatic who saw Kate's coming as an opportunity to burn this town for paganism.

"Most people here are dirty pagans," the priest said loudly. "They resist the true faith. I have reported them, but they cover themselves."

"How do they do that?" Kate asked.

"False devotion," he whispered conspiratorially, "The investigators who have come, failed to catch them. The town is now hostile to us."

Kate hid her outrage behind her auburn hair, "We'll be careful."

"They only pray to the god of money," he said as Kate escorted him off of the Inn's porch.

Kate had been arguing for a week with Leoshus and instead of reinforcing her beliefs, it had opened the door to doubt. Not in Mirsha, but in the Code. It was so rigid and even someone as legitimate as a knight tried to subvert it.

The priest was like Leoshus in other ways. He was inflexible in his belief and completely lacking in compassion or charity. He also had no doubts. To him, Kate was bringing the fire of truth into the wilderness.

Kate was just trying to get to Chryselles.

The priest saw the mayor and others coming in the gate and he turned at the bottom of the stairs so quickly, T'az half drew her sword.

The priest wasn't attacking.

He whispered quickly, "I'll do anything to be part of the cleansing. Please let Mirsha know I'm devoted. I want to be part of it - when you bring fire to this place."

Kate couldn't believe what she was hearing. She had seen nothing that deserved such punishment and was appalled that this man thought she had that kind of access to the Goddess.

T'az finally shooed him away.

The meeting with the Lord Mayor had been short. He verified the Letter of Mark and ordered a ship's captain to be made available, but the man that appeared didn't give Kate any confidence he knew where they were going.

Foester reported that the pickings in the harbor were slim. It had only unfrozen enough for ships two weeks ago. Cargo was piled up waiting for the influx of sea traffic.

Kate lay in bed and worried about hiring such a questionable ship.

She was going to have to get up. She needed to pace as she thought and snuck out of the room without waking T'az so she could pace in the hall.

Thervan was at the end of the hallway on guard duty and he waved as Kate paced. Kate approved her friends' watchfulness. The horror on the cliff was still too close.

The ship problem was a conundrum. They needed a ship big enough to carry horses, but they would need a lot of ships to support Leoshus and all of his stuff.

Kate paused in her pacing, she was being watched.

There was a burly spirit in the hall that looked familiar. It was a grey shadow of an ancient warrior with a big axe. He stood respectfully to the side, but he was attentive to her words and actions.

"I'm getting a lot more resistance than I expected," she admitted to the shadow. "I don't think I expected a parade of roses, but the mayor, the ship's captain, Leoshus, and the priest that only wants to burn people, are not actually helping."

The spirit didn't move.

"Sir Leoshus," Kate whispered sarcastically. "He is so inflexible, and so sure he is right. It's different, but he's like the priest of Mirsha today - they are zealots."

The spirit didn't blink as his face followed Kate back and forth.

"Some people on the Council think I'm dreaming this visitation, as do others. I know I'm not, but Mirsha hasn't chosen to show herself to them," Kate told the spirit. "They see the quest as some personal advantage, as it's outside the Code."

"I believe with all my heart, but I don't want to be inflexible or un-compassionate," Kate pleaded with the spirit. "I don't want to flaunt power like Leoshus, or be blindingly ideological like that priest. What does that mean? What am I?"

The spirit picked up its axe and pointed to the other end of the hall where Thervan sat near the stairs. It re-appeared on the stairs motioning her to follow.

Kate grabbed a candle and hurried after the spirit and she went back to the great room on the first floor.

The fire had burned low. The spirit stood in front of great curtains. The curtains fluttered open as Kate approached. The wall was covered in wooden carvings. The spirit touched the carvings and disappeared.

Kate studied them in the candle light. She knew she was looking at a pagan religious text. But these gods weren't horrid or evil. They were warriors, strong and just, but they preached compassion - even love - if she was interpreting the carvings correctly.

Mirsha brought her here, there could be no other explanation for why she had been directed to this inn over the others. Mirsha had never said what was to be changed, only that Kate would do it.

This had to be part of the plan.

Kate moved a chair around so she could sit and contemplate the carvings. The stories were allegories. Graphical teachings on how to live.

Just a few weeks ago, she might have thought this was wrong, but Haervan had a lot of books that could be called wrong. The vision of bringing the torch to this place, also torched Haervan's home and Hestal's.

It was the same and equally wrong.

She wasn't like Leoshus or Vestral. She was supposed to be, but she wasn't. No teaching confirmed that, it was a feeling that came from her heart.

"Oh Grom," said a voice in the doorway.

Kate looked over to see Crader. He looked very worried and obviously he wished he hadn't come to investigate the noise he'd heard in his inn.

"Crader? Would you come here please?" Kate asked him. She was aware Thervan had moved down the stairs. She didn't want Crader to come by force.

"May I help you Holy Priestess?" he was only an inch from groveling.

"Oh Crader, don't worry," Kate tried to ease his fear. "Please pull up a chair, if you have a moment. I want to learn more about these stories."

"Ancient stories, nothing more, I assure you," he said as he went pale and start sweating.

T'az had kidded her about the power of her position, but for the first time she was really seeing it. It didn't make her feel good or powerful. It made her sad. No one but the gods should cause such fear in a man.

"Anything else," Crader whispered, "Holy Priestess?"

"Call me Kate, Crader. All of my friends do," Kate smiled at him. "I'm fascinated by these carvings. Where did they come from?"

Crader was still afraid - his answer was tentative.

"My great, great, great, grandfather carved those when he built this place," he said. "This is one of the few buildings that survived the Eorsian raids - you'd call them pirates - when I was a little boy."

"I've done a little carving and I think he had great skill," Kate said. "They are magnificent. They remind me of the stone carvings in the Temples at Theopolis."

Crader actually smiled. It was the first time she'd seen him do that.

"I'm not following the whole story though," Kate pointed her candle to a part she was stuck on. "In these panels the god crushes the beast, but then it skips and now he doesn't appear to be helping the people."

"Yes, Kate," Crader hesitated. "The building survived, but not all the panels did. My father and I put them back up the best we could."

That made Kate sad. War had already destroyed part of the amazing carvings.

Kate sighed, "You've done a wonderful job. If I hadn't been reading all of them, I wouldn't have noticed at all."

"Very kind of you to say, Priestess of Mirsha," Crader said flatly.

"Oh Crader, I'm not going to report you or try and change you," Kate chuckled. "I'm supposed to, but I'm not going to."

She got thoughtful for a moment. "I'm not sure why I was brought to this inn. It felt like random chance, but now I don't think so."

Kate sat back in her chair.

"There has to be a reason Mirsha picked me," Kate thought out loud. "If the gods know our every thought, she must already be aware of my feelings."

Kate looked at Crader. "Look at me, do I look like an adventurer?"

Crader obviously didn't know how to answer. He struggled for a moment.

Kate laughed at his indecision, "You can say it. I'm small, weak and a woman. Mirsha should have at least picked a man, but she didn't. There has to be a reason."

Crader started to shuffle his feet nervously.

Kate looked at the carvings again, "I've always had solid convictions, but the quest is changing my beliefs. It felt like it was testing them, but now it feels more right to say growing them?"

She looked at the nervous innkeeper. "Does that make any sense?"

"Not really," he said honestly, but he looked more comfortable than he had since she arrived.

Kate was starting to feel tired. "Were you raised in this religion?"

"Yes," he said simply.

She pried a little deeper. "And you were taught to fear us?"

"Yes." Crader deflated a bit. "Many people here have died to keep their beliefs."

Kate stood up. "But you kept them. That's not in the official history, you know."

"I guess that's why it's the official history," Crader said as he got up.

Kate walked along the carvings again with her candle. "They are magnificent. It would be a shame if this disappeared."

Crader was still standing by the chairs in the dim light.

"May I ask how you found them?" Crader inquired.

"The spirit of an ancient warrior led me here. He wants me to do something," Kate said as she moved to the stairs.

"A tall warrior, bald with a great beard and axe?" Crader asked seriously.

"He had a helm, but otherwise your description is accurate." Kate turned around, "What does it mean?"

"He had a helm," Crader repeated. "It is a warning of danger or war. Grom sends Lekni as a warning." Crader bowed. "Thank you, you may have saved us, Priestess of Mirsha."

"From what?" Kate asked. "It seems peaceful enough."

"You do not always know when the storm is coming," Crader smiled. "I need to make inquiries and talk to some people. Sleep well."

Crader left her at the stairs.

"What's going on?" Thervan asked.

"I don't know, but it sounds like trouble," Kate said wearily.

Kate slept well after talking to Crader. In fact, she felt better than she could remember. She knelt by the window after her morning ritual and thought about her conversation the night before.

She had no doubt about her belief in Mirsha. That was real, it was solid. Her doubts about the Code were becoming real too. The morning ritual felt trite - insufficient.

"There's more to this," Kate said to the morning sun. She felt it replied in the affirmative as it reflected off the small bay in front of her. The sea proper was still hazy and distant.

Kate sat at the window for a few minutes. This small harbor town had survived - forever in constant fear of people like her. But it wasn't the people like her - it was the rules and laws they carried.

Maybe, that was the change she was supposed to bring. Remove the oppressiveness in the Code.

The idea was exciting, but heretical. She would be burned if she mentioned this in Theopolis. The idea was good but not quite right. She'd have to work out the rest of it before taking any risks.

Kate joined the rest of the team at breakfast. Kate sat in an open chair and dished herself some eggs as she thought about replacing the Code.

"I hear you had an interesting conversation with the innkeeper last night," T'az said seriously.

"I did," Kate said. "It was about the carvings in the other room. It got me thinking."

T'az snorted, "I'm a little surprised we aren't burning the place down. You do know what they are about, right?"

"Yes. It's quite clear," Kate replied. "It doesn't seem like I have any right to change it and I'd hate to see them destroyed. They're beautiful."

"You have every right," Bear said. "A word from you and Vestral would bring the entire muster of the Norseland Knights and an Army of Churlars here."

"They would, by force, convert or burn this whole town," Bear finished while everyone stared at him. "Not saying you should, just that it is within your rights, by Code."

"I know, but that's horrible." Kate waved a fork at him while she thought for a second.

"And you know what? I don't think it would change anything," Kate said. She was sure. "People would die, they would still hate us, and they would be more likely to keep their beliefs than they were before."

"Very wise," Foester added.

"But the Code..." Bear started.

"Hush boy," Foester remonstrated Bear, "learn something about people."

Kate swallowed a bite of food. "I don't know about wise, but I feel Mirsha agrees with me. I haven't awakened this calm and clear of purpose since the morning Mirsha granted me this quest."

"Knights are a bit hard headed, ma'am," Foester said.

Bear blurted a "Hey!" but Thervan laughed.

"...but he's not as dense as most, he'll come around," Foester finished looking at the knight.

"Val's Blood," Bear swore. "Not like I was quoting the law or anything."

Kate smiled at him. He really was a big man and powerfully built. Haervan had been right about needing knights. She was comforted by the sheer military force of his presence. It wasn't the mail or the weapons. It was the quiet confidence - the will to face anything.

Kate smiled at Bear, "I haven't gotten it all figured out. We'll have time to discuss and argue these issues back and forth for months as we ride."

He looked at her as she finished her thought. "But, I have a feeling that where we come down on this argument is going to be important in the future."

"No argument from me," T'az said. "Southerns have all kinds of religions and some pretty weird ones too. Unless the official rituals are hiding all the headless chickens somewhere they don't let the rest of us read."

"Headless chickens?" Hestal asked suspiciously. "Are you making fun of us now?"

"Nope. I'm serious," T'az said. "You can hardly cross a market south of the Niepper River without having someone babble at you while waving a headless chicken."

The visual of someone waving a headless chicken made Kate giggle.

T'az looked at the giggling priestess for a moment. "Wouldn't happen with you around though. They know what gets their feet heated."

Kate drooped and her humor dried up. There it was. The cold hard fact that at a word she could burn people, and the horror that she was expected to. She was an extension of a system that demanded conformity.

"That's why I was always telling you to watch your words." T'az poked her with a fork, "A word from you and people fry. It's just the way it is."

"That's not why I became a priest," Kate said. "I don't want to burn people."

"And that's why I like you." T'az gave her a big smile as she got up.

Kate lingered over breakfast. She watched Bear and Foester get ready to leave - they were going to make arrangements to board the ship.

Bernard and Hestal were discussing going to the local market.

Kate had to find out what Leoshus' plans were, but she had another idea - a much more dangerous idea than ecumenism. Kate got up and walked over to Hestal.

"Hestal, I want to bounce something off of you." Kate led him to the chairs in front of the carvings.

"What if, when Mirsha said, 'All things that existed, still exist,' she really meant everything?" Kate asked.

Hestal raised an eyebrow, "What do you mean?"

"Well, magic exists but only a few people know. Old religions still exist," Kate whispered. "What if everything still exists, but we are blinded by the Code."

"Whoa," Hestal took a quick look around. "That's dangerous talk, particularly coming from a priest."

"I know, but I think I'm on to something," Kate said. "Maybe that's why we're here. Where else could we even consider such a thing. Look at you and T'az, both of you operate outside of the Code all of the time."

"A pagan town seems like the best place." Hestal looked around again, "But what is the key?"

"I'm sure you already know," Kate said. "What's on the Tablets?"

"The laws of the gods," Hestal smiled at her. "Before the Code."

"Exactly," Kate said.

"So maybe they weren't stolen," Hestal suggested.

"Sent away possibly?" Kate shrugged. "We don't know yet, but I think this is bigger than anyone thinks."

"Agreed," Hestal nodded.

Kate put her fingers to her lips, left Hestal, and walked out of the inn. T'az was going with her to see Leoshus. She had to find out what he was up to and see if he was actually going to participate further.

This wasn't something she wanted to do, but this thorn needed to be plucked and T'az led the way. Kate let Zhost take control and thought as they rode.

Between two buildings, a normal shadow turned into the other kind and Kate nearly screamed as the busy street she was on changed horribly.

She was still on horseback, but the town in front of her was in flames. Black smoke billowed out of the wooden buildings and it was blotting out the sun. Men in burnished steel were herding a large group of bearded men across the street.

Screaming came from all directions, clawing at her brain.

To her left, armored men were executing people as they kneeled at the end of the alley. There was a priest in the black robes of Val in attendance. The eyes of the men on their knees burned her soul.

Kate looked away from that, but the vision only got worse. A woman, already in flames, was throwing bundles out of a third floor window. Kate watched a bundle fall. When it hit the muddy street, arms and legs came out of the cloth.

Oh, Dear Mirsha, she's throwing her children, Kate thought to herself as tears flowed.

Men in red leather armor ran past her. The grins on their faces made the whole scene ten times worse for Kate. This wasn't a duty. They were enjoying it. Kate didn't want to see anymore and closed her eyes.

Zhost never stopped and he walked out of the shadow. Kate felt the sun and opened her eyes. It was a beautiful day again. The town seemed bright and happy.

Zhost must have sensed something was wrong with her. She could feel him in her head. He whinnied loudly and that got T'az' attention.

T'az rode back to Kate as Zhost stopped. "What happened? Why are you crying?"

Kate pointed at the shadow behind them. "I saw the town burning. Churlars and knights were killing everyone. It was awful."

T'az rode into the shadow, stopped, and rode back.

"Nothing," T'az said. "Kate we don't know if you're seeing the future or the past."

"It was exactly the same as now, but horrible," Kate sniffed. "I think it's the future."

"A warning maybe," T'az guessed.

"We have to see what Leoshus is up to and stop this from happening." Kate nudged Zhost and he quickly cantered forward. T'az followed and overtook them to put herself back in front.

They had to hold up, as the gate was closed again today. The Captain walked out to meet her.

"What trouble today, Captain?" Kate sniffed and wiped her eyes. "There's no fog."

"Trouble is right," he said, "Mayor and others are out there trying to put a stop to it."

"To what?" Kate asked.

"That knight," the Captain said.

"Oh for the love of…," Kate wanted to swear like her father did. Her tears dried instantly. "Please open the gate. I think I can control him. He supposed to be bound to my purpose."

"Hope so." Captain turned and bellowed, "Open the gate."

Kate and T'az thundered out and charged for the tent flying Leoshus' banner. As she approached, she had a tinge of doubt. Leoshus had more men than ever before. Perhaps a hundred or more. She could only guess where they came from.

Kate rode past the guard and right up to Leoshus' tent. He seemed pleased at their arrival, which was disconcerting.

"Ah, just the person I needed," Leoshus said cooly. "Someone much more learned in the Code than I."

He took her hand and led her to the group in front of the tent. "This man is a pagan heretic. He was conducting some obscene ritual right over there."

Kate found Leoshus exasperating. "From the point of view of the Council, you can't be a pagan and a heretic, Leoshus. One or the other."

The Lord Mayor was obviously angry and he had brought a small crowd. They stood around a small man dressed in furs who had been tied hand and foot.

"Either way Holy Priestess," Leoshus continued, "you of all people must understand the necessity of following the law. With you here, we need only the wood to burn him."

"What!" The Lord Mayor screamed. "Trial?"

"Ah, you are mistaken, Lord Mayor," Leoshus shouted. "The word of a knight and the blessing of a priest, or in this case a priestess, is all that is required."

Leoshus was right. She couldn't argue with him, challenging him at all would only result in certain death for Nordrigen. Kate decided to try a new tack.

"I'm sorry, Sir Leoshus." She batted her eyelashes at him. "I converted the whole town to the Temple of Mirsha this morning. This man must not yet be aware of it."

She put her hand on his armored arm, "I apologize for not getting word to you sooner."

Kate tried to look genuinely sad.

He was confused. "Converted? The whole town?"

"Oh yes, Sir Leoshus. They were hungry for learning of the Holy Goddess." She gave him her most winsome smile - she'd do anything to prevent that vision. "Our priests are moving through town instructing everyone on how to honor Her."

Kate looked back over the town. Fortunately, smoke was rising from somewhere. "You see; they are already burning their old idols now."

"But.." Leoshus was looking around.

"But... But...," The Lord Mayor's eyes were bulging out of his head and Kate threw him a very stern look.

Fortunately, the man in furs wasn't so slow to catch on.

"Oh thank you. I have longed to know the righteous ways of the Goddess Mirsha," he said in a very convincing manner.

"But, by Code, he can still burn for his acts prior to conversion," Leoshus argued.

Kate knew the Code backward and forward. "But why Sir Leoshus, don't you want to bring them into the fold? Shouldn't we demonstrate our willingness to grant the mercy of the gods to anyone willing to change and see the errors of their ways?"

Kate knew she had him. "Besides, we have more important things to discuss about our holy quest."

"Oh very well, but keep him in the city," Leoshus sounded uncertain.

He had no choice really. Now that she was here, any burning required her support. Which he wasn't going to get.

Leoshus waved his hand and the crowd grabbed up the furred man and ran for the gates. Kate watched them go and let out a long breath.

Leoshus' face reddened. "You're not telling me the truth."

"Now, Sir Leoshus - remember you volunteered to be bound to my purpose." Kate smiled at him, he couldn't actually say she was lying. It was against the rules.

"I will be bringing this up with the Grand Priest," Leoshus snarled.

"Of Val," Kate said. "I won't tell you how to use your sword Leoshus, don't challenge me in areas of religion - it's lose-lose for you."

Kate stood in front of the knight, "And I'm not the only one holding things back. You said you had a broken wheel two days ago, and now you have five times as many men."

"There was a broken wheel, and fortunately reinforcements found me." He spat the last word at her as he sat down with an awkward clunk. His armor didn't allow for grace.

Kate grabbed his greying blonde beard and pulled his head around to face her. Power surged down her arm. She had no idea where it came from, but Leoshus acted like he was being shocked.

"Why are you here?" Kate yelled.

"W...Wh...Why," Leoshus stammered. "Here to support... quest..."

"I wonder," Kate let him go and walked to where she could survey his camp.

He was shaken and rubbing his chin. "Why would you wonder? I bring the strength you need to face the challenges ahead."

"Mirsha gives me the strength Leoshus, not you." Kate walked back to him, "How are you planning to get this host to Chryselles?"

"I have been given funds," he said. He was still a little wide eyed. "Ships are coming to embark the men and horses."

"Who arranged for that, and when?" T'az asked.

She was ignored by Leoshus until Kate reached for his beard again.

"The Grand Priest," he said hastily. "The Temple of Val is behind your quest."

"Uh-huh," Kate said and walked back to Zhost with T'az following her. "We will embark today. When do you plan to leave?"

"Today or tomorrow at the latest," Leoshus replied as he struggled to rise.

Kate mounted her horse, "The sooner, the better."

With that she and T'az rode towards the open gate. Kate thought she heard Leoshus yelling over the pounding of Zhost's hooves. "Damn her! Get me a messenger."

Kate intended to ride past any group at the gate, but she had an inspiration and pulled Zhost up where they had seen the guard captain in the past.

"I don't think that worked," Kate said to T'az as she scanned the crowded gate square.

"At least he doesn't have a lot of men. Even as as weak as this town wall is, they can keep Leoshus and his hundred out," T'az said confidently.

"I don't know," Kate replied as she searched. "Something is not right."

Kate saw the Lord Mayor talking to other men on one of the large porches. Kate dismounted and led Zhost through the crowd. T'az tried to catch up to her as she threaded through the groups of people.

A hand grabbed her and pulled her to the side of a small shed. Kate spun on her captor as she heard a sword drawn. The heavily cowled man was pulled away from her and thrown behind the shed and his hood fell back.

The local priest of Mirsha was pinned to the wall by T'az's sword. He'd been disguised in commoner's clothes instead of a robe, that's why Kate hadn't noticed him.

He was blubbering as he eyed the three feet of steel pointing at his heart.

"What was your name again?" Kate asked him.

"Faisson, Most Holy Priestess," he stammered.

Kate gestured for T'az to lower her sword, "What do you want?"

"Holy Mirsha help me, I risked coming into town to get you," Faisson sighed as T'az stopped threatening him.

Kate was pressed for time. "Why?"

"To get you out. You've brought the light." His eyes burned. "Holy Fire is going to cleanse this place. I've seen it. The soldiers of the gods have finally come."

"Oh Mirsha. Faisson, what did you do?" Kate pushed him back against the wall without touching him.

"When I got the message from the Revered High Priest that you were coming. I saw it as a sign," Faisson grinned. "I sent my assistants to the towns south of here for help and they came back this morning, the Holy Defenders of the Faith will be here today!"

Kate was stunned, her vision was becoming reality before her very eyes.

Faisson continued, "And the gods shine their light on this venture. Knights have shown up to block everyone in the city, until the Churlars arrive."

He was literally shaking with glee. "They're all going to burn! That's why I came, we have to get you out. This is no place for the holiest of priestesses. Gods be praised, we are going to burn these pagans as proof of their sin."

T'az poked her sword back into his chest. "How many?"

He looked at her like she was crazy. "Thousands."

T'az turned to Kate, "He's lying, but it wouldn't take much more than what Leoshus already has to take this town and Leoshus knows. That's why he wanted the heretic back in town."

Kate turned and ran up the porch where she had seen the Lord Mayor. He wasn't there. Kate spun around trying to see him until T'az walked up behind her alone.

"We have to get these people out of here," Kate said. "What happened to Faisson?"

"He had an accident," T'az said flatly.

"You didn't!" Kate was shocked at her friend.

T'az seemed unaffected by the killing or Kate's surprise, "Kate, we can't save these people. I have to get you out of here."

T'az pulled her back down the porch to the horses.

"But why kill him?" Kate spluttered.

T'az looked grim. "We couldn't have him telling anyone you weren't eager to see this town burn."

"But," Kat said as she mounted.

"No Kate, we get the others and we get on that ship now," T'az said fiercely.

Zhost seemed to agree with T'az. Without prompting, he charged through the crowd and back up the street to the Golden Sheaf. Kate ran in the inn and found Crader talking to Hestal and Bernard.

Kate grabbed Crader. "We have to get all of this down." She waved at the carved wall panels. "Hide them."

Crader seemed shocked, "Why?"

"Oh Crader, they're coming," Kate pleaded. "We have to evacuate and it needs to start now."

"You're serious," Hestal said.

"Yes, very," Kate said. "The priest of Mirsha sent for Churlars. They'll be here by tomorrow morning at the latest. Leoshus already has the town bottled up."

Crader ran out of the inn.

"Thervan, everybody, help me get these panels off the wall," Kate sobbed.

No one moved as the information they just heard soaked in.

Kate slumped against the wall. "It's all my fault. I brought this."

Before anyone could move to comfort her. Bear and Foester burst into the inn.

"There are ships blockading the harbor," Bear shouted.

"Our ship?" Hestal asked.

"I don't know," Bear said.

Bernard picked Kate up. "You go with Bear and T'az. See about our ship. We'll get the panels off."

Kate nodded and she and T'az followed Bear back out of the inn. Not long after, they sat on their horses on the empty docks. Kate finally got to see the harbor and it was horrible.

A few small ships had anchored away from shore, and one big ship was ablaze. It was probably a mile away, but Kate was pretty sure she knew what she was looking at.

"Our ship?" Kate asked and Bear nodded.

"They must've tried to run the blockade or Leoshus burned it on purpose," T'az said. "Why did we come north? We should have just told them we were going north."

T'az turned her horse and rode away and Bear sighed as he watched her go.

"She didn't mean it personally Bear," Kate gave the knight a sad smile.

"I know," he said, and they too headed back to the inn.

Crader had returned with a metal tool that allowed him to get behind the panels. Kate couldn't see how it worked, but it worked.

"Crader, I'm sorry, can they be saved?" Kate asked him.

Crader gave a sad smile, "Yes, we have planned for this day."

Foester hurried over, "Our ship?"

"Burning," Bear said.

"Crader, the people," Kate said.

"Don't worry, Kate," he said. "Not many believed me last night, but the tunnels were opened, and most of the ships got out."

He was sad, but determined, "If the warning bells ring, people know what to do and everything will be ready for them. Even an hour head start will save a lot of people."

"Tunnels?" Foester asked.

"Yes. Dug out into the forests," Crader answered.

T'az caught his arm. "We can't get the horses out through tunnels. I have to get her out of here."

"The north wall, where it meets the sea--it's rocky, but you could lead your horses through if you're careful," he replied. "It will be the only way to get horses out. Not many will try it, one slip and you're in the sea."

"That's our path then," T'az said. "Everybody pack it up!"

"Bear, help me stock up our supplies," Foester said and they both left for the kitchens.

Crader was unhooking the last two panels. Kate tried to help.

As the last panel slid down the wall, Kate asked, "will they survive?"

Crader smiled. "I think so. They'll be buried in the basement. Even if the inn burns, they should be fine."

Kate smiled at his glimmer of hope. Bells began to ring and everyone stopped working. There was a moment of silence and then the screaming began.

"They're in sight," Crader said quietly. Kate could tell he was afraid.

The next hour was a blur. T'az had dragged Kate out and sat her on Zhost. The rest of the team ran back and forth readying the horses and filling the panniers with anything they could find. Kate sat in the middle of the chaos and cried.

Crader walked out to her. "Everything is buried," he said.

Kate sniffed and gave him money for their lodgings. She didn't know how much and Crader didn't count it.

"Come with us," Kate said.

"No, Grom will protect us. He sent us you, and you warned us in advance. Many will survive because of it." His fear was palpable. "Go north, along the coast about a day's ride. There is rumored to be a pirate enclave for illegal trade. They are your only hope to get south now."

T'az yelled at her. "Kate! Come on!"

The rest had mounted and were riding out of the inn and into the warehouse district. Zhost followed them without being nudged. Kate knew she needed to leave. Her mind told her there was nothing she could do for these people, but her heart was broken, and it felt like her fault.

Dusk found Kate leaning against a rock, exhausted. The climb up the cliff trail had been torturously slow and dangerous with waves violently crashing in the rocks below. The team had to make the trip several times to carry all their supplies to the top in an effort to make it easier for the horses to negotiate the tiny, slick, and rocky trail.

Foester was the hero. His care and patience had gotten the blindfolded and unburdened horses up the climb, one at a time. Kate felt it was a minor miracle that everyone had made it safely.

Kate stared back over the town. The ship in the harbor had stopped burning, but fires now ringed Nordrigen as the Churlars positioned themselves to block all avenues of escape.

From here she could see the places where the forest reached in close to the walls. Kate knew people were escaping through those long fingers of trees. Kate begged Mirsha to protect the fleeing people. No ritual would fit this situation.

CHAPTER 10

Kate shivered awake on the cold and hard ground. She remembered little of their dark escape through the forest the night before through the haze of her exhaustion.

T'az was asleep next to her and Kate threw her blanket over her friend. Bear was sitting on a rock, staring at the forest behind them.

Kate got up quietly and found a water jug. She eased her thirst, but she was still dry and hungry. It had been a full day since she'd eaten anything. She put the water jug down and walked over to Bear.

The cold light of dawn glimmered on the eastern horizon. Kate shivered. Bear reached out and pulled her under the blanket he was wearing and she was grateful for the warmth. It smelled of oiled metal and leather.

Bear didn't look at her, he never stopped scanning the forest.

"No fire?" Kate asked.

"No, if they are doing this right, they'll have patrols out looking for fires," Bear said.

How long can the town hold?"

Bear sighed, "Not long. Most of the walls are wood and not even twenty feet high. They have no ditch or moat. The wall will only last a few hours before it's breached."

"But they can escape in the tunnels."

"Yes, most of them," he agreed. "I don't know how big the tunnels are, or how long before the troops outside find the exits in the trees. Even if it works, someone will have to stay and buy them the hours it will take to get everyone out."

Kate saw the men in her vision, "Why?"

"If there's no defense, Leoshus will scour the forests for them," Bear said. "He'll find some and they'll lead him to more or he'll chase them down the tunnels and be hot on their heels."

Bear shook his head. "No, some of them will have to stay behind and fight knowing they will lose to protect and close the tunnels. It is an honorable end; those few hours may save thousands."

Kate felt the burning eyes she saw in the vision. That was the fate of the men she saw. Her vision had happened in spite of her efforts.

"Grim morning," Foester said as he sat down. "See anything?"

"No, nothing from that direction," Bear reported. "Crader may be right though, it looked like there were some lights farther up the coast earlier."

"Good. We should get everybody up and head that way," Foester suggested. "We need to get there before there's a rush on boats."

Kate didn't want to take passage away from the people she saw in her vision, but she was on a mission. Mirsha had laid a burden on her and Kate wondered what sacrifice was too great. At what point was recovering the tablets less important than people's lives.

Kate performed her ceremony while Foester woke the rest of the team. There was no candle. It felt like an act of defiance to light it, but Kate wouldn't risk it. In spite of her feelings about Nordrigen, she had to obey her god and it broke her heart.

Midday found a tired and depressed group standing outside a roughly hewn, wooden palisade. It was built in a semi-circle at the edge of a calm bay and surrounded by giant pine trees.

There were ships in the bay and that meant sailors were on the other side of the wall, but no one had seen them. The idea of sailing with pirates made Kate fidget.

"Why are you nervous?" T'az asked Kate.

"I don't like it. It's not the pirates really, it's that I've been counting on the Letter of Mark, the Council, and the power of our faith. All of that will be meaningless in there," Kate sighed. "We'll be at their mercy."

Bear grunted as he dismounted, "What else can we do?"

"Nothing else I can think of," Kate smiled at him. "We have no idea what to expect. They were outlawed, fought against us, and lost. Now we stand at their outpost like beggars."

Foester chuckled, "Maybe, as the working man in the group, I should talk to them?"

T'az nodded. "I'll go with you, in case they hold a grudge."

The pair walked to the palisade without waiting for approval and they were let in the gate. Kate may not have seen anyone, but they had seen her team.

There was nothing Kate could do but wait.

It wasn't a long wait and the pair returned.

T'az shrugged in response to the obvious question, "Well that wasn't what I expected. They're quite civil."

Foester rubbed his chin, "There's a captain who will take us close to Chryselles. He's a sharp one. It'll cost us more than the other ship. How much money do we have?"

Kate pulled out the money Haervan had sent to Nordrigen and gave the bag to Foester. "I hope that's enough. I've never counted it."

Foester counted out coins. He took a small pile of platinum and gold and gave her the bag back. He waved at T'az and they both returned to the compound.

Kate led Zhost through the gate after the bargain was struck. It was just a camp; the wall wasn't sturdy. Bear said it was just to slow down an attack. The pirates could just sail away.

A couple of small fires burned around two small tents. Most of the sailors were waiting on flat bottomed barges tied to the rickety dock. They apparently lived on the ships in hostile territory.

The camp was just a place to trade.

The only person standing in the sand was a tall, deeply tanned man. Bald and beardless, he cut rakish figure as he smiled at their approach. His large gold earrings swayed as he watched them all carefully.

Kate walked straight for him. This man wasn't as dark as T'az, and he wasn't quite as tall as Bear, but he was close. He appeared ultimately confident and it made Kate feel small.

"Captain Jarusco," he boomed in a deep baritone. "I am the Captain of the Magdelaine-she's the three-master there in the harbor. We are ready for you to board."

Kate wasn't so sure about him. His easy confidence in an unusual situation made Kate uncomfortable.

"Captain, how do I know you won't take us out to sea and kill us?" Kate asked.

"You don't," Jarusco laughed. "But, I don't believe I'm any more likely to do that than anyone else."

"That's not very comforting," Kate frowned at him.

"You can always ride your excellent horses to Chryselles," Jarusco offered, "It is a long way, and I don't do refunds."

"Fine," Kate felt manipulated again. "How long will it take to get there by sea?"

Jarusco rubbed his bare chin as he thought. "I'd say two weeks. Since your people outlawed us, I've never been there. But we have charted all of these waters."

"I'm sorry," Kate said sincerely. "I wasn't a good student of history and I don't know why your people were outlawed."

Jarusco laughed again. "You're sorry! Don't worry, we are better off. Now will you board?"

Kate walked Zhost to the flat bottomed barge and boarded it. Jarusco was still laughing and Kate felt he was laughing at her. This was her only choice and yet she felt ignorant.

She knew nothing of sailing. She knew nothing of pirates or why they were pirates. It had all been a story at her father's fireside. Childhood stories were becoming real around her.

Boarding the horses onto the to the Magdelaine took the better part of an hour. They could only row two horses out at a time and the crew loaded each horse in the hold carefully and individually.

Kate spent her time easing the worries of the horses. They were treated well, but the new surroundings had them nervous.

Jarusco strolled up the decks as the last horse was lowered into the hold. "We'll have to stop to re-supply with water and fodder for the horses, but that won't delay us. If you have them packed in, we can start."

Kate nodded nervously.

The Captain started barking orders and the crew responded. Some went up the masts and others ran to the front of the ship. Kate couldn't keep track of what was happening. There were too many ropes and other moving parts. It was a bewildering display.

Sailors moved her out of the way as she tried to understand what was happening.

Kate forgot about her worries for a moment. It was such chaos watching the crew turn the ship into a living thing. The ship turned the small breeze into motion and they glided out of the bay. That's when Kate really saw the sea for the first time.

It was deep blue and ran from horizon to horizon. She just stared at the waves in front of her. It was mesmerizing to watch them roll to the ship and disappear beneath her. The white sails billowed overhead.

The ship laid over on its side as it took the wind and Kate watched the woods they had ridden through last night slip away on the windward side.

Kate tried to walk over to Jarusco by the wheel, but something had gone terribly wrong with her legs. They had turned to jelly. She struggled to get to the wheel.

The crew quietly laughed at her.

"Keep your knees bent," the Captain advised. "Feel the rhythm of the ship and move with it."

A black cloud over the disappearing land rose like malice incarnate to stain the skyline and Kate saw her vision of horror again.

"Nordrigen burns," Jarusco rumbled. "I had friends there."

"I did too," Kate said, feeling cold all over. "I can only pray they are unharmed."

A sailor led the rest of her team came up from below deck forward to a sheltered spot up front. Kate stumbled after them.

She sat down next to Foester. "Where's Bear?"

"Fell asleep in his hammock the minute the ship started moving," Foester replied. "The great oaf will probably sleep all the way to Chryselles."

"Unless he gets hungry," Thervan chuckled.

Hestal and T'az didn't laugh. They both looked a little green and Bernard was violently sick. He leaned over the side of the ship and threw up.

"Stop talking about food!" Bernard howled.

Kate felt for him. She had moments of uneasiness, but she only had to look out at the waves and feel the wonder of the sea for her stomach to calm down.

Thervan nodded towards the ship's wheel. "What do you make of the Captain?"

"I don't know," Kate replied. "He's doing this for his own reasons, besides the money, and I don't know what they are."

"Well it cost enough," Foester grumbled. "I think we might have owned the other ship for this much money."

He looked around carefully, "And do you see how many men he has on his crew?"

"It does seem like a lot," Thervan said as he watched the crew work.

"Five times as many as the cargo ships in Nordrigen," added Foester.

"And no cargo space," Thervan pointed out. "Our horses and gear nearly fills what they call a hold."

"Yeah, if this is a cargo ship, I'll eat my boots," Foester agreed.

Kate looked over the Magdelaine, it was a mass of wood covered in rope. Dark hulled with a light colored flush deck, a large black flag with a white cross was the only ornamentation.

"Maybe they carry cargo up here," Kate said poking one of the bundles lashed to the deck.

Foester chuckled. "No, I don't think so. The bundles are too small and I'm pretty sure we're looking at disassembled weapons-ballistae maybe or catapults. I've built a few siege weapons in training-years ago."

He pointed around the deck. "Notice the evenly spaced metal plates on the deck? One per bundle. I bet they attach to them. It's the only thing that makes sense."

Foester seemed unsure of himself.

"Please tell me you know how all of this works, Foester," Kate implored. "I need someone I trust who understands all of these ropes."

Foester shook his head, "I'm not your man and I don't know anyone who does."

"That's disappointing," Kate frowned. "I've been relying on you for everything practical."

That made Foester laugh, "I'm just an old man, carrying the bags."

The days that followed didn't make Kate feel any easier about Jarusco. She had no idea where they were going. Her initial enchantment with the sea had turned into frustration. There was no way to tell what was happening-they were just constantly surrounded by blue salty water.

Kate spent hours staring at the water. There were things in there, but she didn't know if they were real or vision. Once a large fish swam nearby and then disappeared.

She couldn't say anything. She was afraid of being ridiculed by the crew for her ignorance of the sea.

They couldn't discern any progress at all. Kate had observed the Captain and others taking measurements with some sort of metal contraption, but no matter how often she asked, he refused to explain what they were doing or how they knew where they were.

Kate kept a suspicious eye on the captain and tried to keep her mind calm. The horses in the hold needed her to be confident, as they couldn't see and could barely move. They were trusting her.

The crew was nice to the strangers onboard. They made a space on the dawn facing side of the ship every morning for Kate to set up her altar and Kate was puzzled why dawn wasn't always on the same side of the ship, but she was afraid to ask.

The team had taken to eating with Bernard on deck. He was the only one still suffering. No one wanted to leave him alone with his seasickness.

The morning of the sixth day, after Kate had completed her morning ritual, a man posted in the tall middle mast yelled - "Land! Two points forward of the beam."

Kate was starting to pick up the lingo and that meant some distance in front of the middle of the ship. Kate didn't know which side and she spun her head side to side to see the land.

"You won't see it yet," Jarusco said behind her.

"But he said land. We aren't to Chryselles yet?" Kate asked hopefully as she stared at the sea.

Jarusco laughed, "No priestess, not by half. He can see a lot farther up there, which is why he is up there."

Kate slung her ritual bag over her shoulder and followed him.

She felt most uncomfortable by the wheel. There were always men posted here-day and night. They steered the ship and monitored the wind. Kate felt like an ignorant school girl among them.

It was time for answers, "So where are we Captain?"

"Eorsia, priestess. We'll make landfall in the harbor of Pulu, in about an hour," he replied with his big smile. "I told you we'd have to take on supplies before completing our trip."

"Yes. Yes, you did," Kate admitted. It's not like she knew where they would have picked up supplies, but these were the Pirate Islands in her history. "You just weren't clear where."

Jarusco was still smiling. "And you didn't ask. Does landing in the Pirate Islands worry you?"

"I. I don't know, Captain," Kate drooped. She realized that technically, if Jarusco was hostile, she was captured and there was nothing she could do about it.

"Don't worry. Some of our people still have hard feelings, but we are actually better off," Jarusco laughed. "Because of your people, we found the other side of the sea."

"Other side of the sea?" Kate asked. "What other side of the sea? I mean we were never taught about it."

Kate berated herself for not asking more questions, of course there would be another side of the sea. Her naiveté was a danger.

"Doesn't mean it doesn't exist." Jarusco gave some orders to his men and turned back to Kate. "Let me tell you. There are wondrous things to the east. Great cities of men who want what the islands have to trade."

"Do they call you pirates there?" Kate asked.

"We call ourselves pirates!" Jarusco belly laughed. "What your council thought was an insult has turned into a great asset for us."

That made Kate curious, "Then why do you do anything at all along our coast?"

"We do some trade," he said evasively, "but mostly we just patrol these waters. We are a prosperous people and we have to keep you Theosians away."

Jarusco smiled at her. "Shame really, if history is right, we'd have been even more prosperous in the middle of two kingdoms."

"Patrolling," Kate wasn't a warrior, but that sounded military. "So this isn't a cargo vessel?"

Jarusco chuckled, "I said that I do some trade with your people."

Kate couldn't find the right word. "So it's a ship for fighting?"

"The Magdelaine is a warship and an excellent one at that." Jarusco surveyed his ship with obvious pride.

"So, we are your prisoners," Kate said quietly. Her need had driven her into the arms of an old enemy. Her quest ended here.

"No. Why would you think such a thing?" Jarusco laughed. "You paid us to take you on our normal patrols. Your destination is difficult, but we'll pick up supplies and everything will be fine."

He started to walk away but stopped and turned. "You will need to stay on the ship. Old hatreds die hard and I won't lose you in the dark alleys of Pulu. My crew will exercise your horses before we leave with the tide tonight."

Kate went below and informed her friends of their predicament. Surprisingly everyone was more curious than worried and the whole group hurried on deck to watch the Magdelaine make landfall.

Pulu was at least three times as big as Nordrigen. It had permanent piers running out into the bay. The seagulls chattered and the crew cheered as the Magdelaine was tied up with other ships like her, some of which were much larger.

Other piers held ships that were more obviously cargo ships with bulging bellies and large hatches. It was the warships that drew Kate's attention though. Their low hulls and clean lines made her think of the seabirds overhead. She wondered if they were as sleek and fast as the birds.

Kate continued to worry as she joined her friends on deck.

"We fought wars with these people and according to our history, we won," Kate said.

T'az was leaning on the rail next to Kate. "From here, it looks like it is good to lose to you. That's a rich city and look at all the trade coming and going in this port."

Bear sat on the deck in a sailor's shirt and pants with his feet dangling over the edge. "That's money. A lot of money."

Jarusco came back on board with even more sailors. "Boson! Find berths for these men."

"Aye aye," was the response.

Jarusco strolled over to them. "Tide's right, we'll be back at sea as soon as the water casks are loaded."

"Thank you, Captain." It was all Kate could think to say.

T'az shot Kate a questioning look, "you seem sad?"

"My world is getting smaller," Kate said. "I never used our country's name because I was taught that it was the whole world. But look at this." Kate waved her arms at the busy piers. "There's more out here. A lot more and they don't need us."

T'az smiled. "That's no reason to be sad. We just have more to explore."

Kate was a priestess, the spiritual and political center of her world. She had spent twelve years in study to get to this point and nothing prepared her for a world that didn't need or revolve around those beliefs.

Kate wondered if Haervan knew. If the books he read while locked in his study would have prepared him to see a world that was just fine without him.

Jarusco was right and in an hour after he had come on board, they were pushing away from the pier.

New crew meant a disruption in the order of the ship. Kate and her team stayed out of the way while the senior crew members yelled and drilled the new men.

In spite of the yelling, the crew seemed eager.

Kate finally asked, "Why are they so eager, Captain?"

"We are going somewhere our people haven't been in two hundred years," he said, "against possibly hostile forces-it's enough to make any adventurous soul itch."

Jarusco flashed his nearly ever present smile.

That did nothing to calm Kate. She may very well be letting the wolves in to eat her sheep.

CHAPTER 11

Twelve days at sea, with just the one stop and he hadn't been allowed off the boat. Bear was bored. He had taken to sitting at the rail and staring out at the water and scratching his new beard.

At least today there was a coastline to stare at.

The plan was to land on the coast north of Chryselles. If they rode diagonally across the land it would be less than a day's ride to the city. Jarusco was bold, but he wasn't about to sail right into a big port like Chryselles.

Landing *anywhere* would have been fine for Bear. He missed the land. He missed being in some control over where he was going. Being on this ship was a lot like living in his father's house. No options, just go where everybody else was going.

"Bored hero?" T'az sat next to him. "You should shave."

Without her armor the white shirt she wore was loose and blew steadily in the wind. She kept it mostly buttoned, but Bear found it distracting.

"You don't like it?" Bear ran his fingers through his beard.

T'az smiled. Bear liked that smile.

"It doesn't fit your image as heroic knight. Bernard shaved his," T'az said.

"Yeah, but his was crusty with vomit," Bear laughed.

She turned to look at the shoreline. "You won't be bored soon. I suspect you'll be back to bashing heads by this time tomorrow."

"Can't wait," Bear sighed, feeling the uncomfortable truth. "What's the plan?"

"We find the hidden cove, ride to Chryselles, and split up to find the thief," T'az shrugged. "No, I don't have any idea how we'll find him."

"I guess you'll be with Kate," Bear said.

T'az nodded. "Yep. She's my responsibility."

Bear smiled at the beautiful warrior. "I could say that too."

"But you won't," T'az smiled back. "You'll go with Foester. Maybe we should split up Bernard and Hestal."

"Why?" Bear chuckled. "Hestal and Bernard get along. Besides, no one will be able to get Bernard out of the first pub they come to. He hasn't eaten enough to keep a mouse alive the last two weeks. I bet he's starving."

They both looked up as orders were shouted. The ship slowed.

"Sailing master! I want the topmasts down! Lower our visibility." Jarusco roared.

"Aye aye," was the reply as always.

Bear watched the Captain for a bit. "Have you ever seen him not smiling?"

"Nope," T'az replied. "There's a man that truly loves his job."

"This is going to sound stupid," Bear admitted, "but I thought pirates would be meaner. It's like they're normal people."

Foester was walking across the scrubbed deck to Bear.

"Watch who you're calling normal," T'az said as she got up.

Foester put out his hand. "Come on your lordship, time to get you in your party costume!"

"You're one to talk, old man," Bear let Foester pull him to his feet.

Foester grunted. "Whoosh! We got to start feeding you less."

"Ha ha." It was an old joke. Bear followed Foester down to the room near the hold that held all of their gear. He decided to shave.

It didn't take long to shave and get armored. He really didn't need help with his fighting armor. He tossed the sailor's garb he'd been wearing into his pack.

Foester put his chain and gambeson on as well.

They returned to deck to find the ship slowly sliding into a deep cove with only a small beach and a trail up the steep hill. The cove was surrounded by dark stone cliffs, with what appeared to be forest all around the lip of the cove.

The water was light blue and clear enough to see the bottom.

"Won't get much of a breeze in here," Jarusco growled.

"Land breeze is actually pretty good," The one-eyed man they picked up in Pulu said. "And more importantly, no one will see you here."

"Drop anchor. Lower the boats!" Jarusco yelled.

Kate looked the same as always-small, alert, and calm in her light grey robe and brown riding clothes. The blue trim on her robe was fading.

She seemed eager in spite of her calm demeanor as she paced back and forth.

"Should we prepare to disembark Captain?" Kate asked.

He smiled at her. "Not yet priestess. Safety of the ship comes first."

"Sergeant-at-arms!" Jarusco yelled. "Issue two boat crews with weapons." Jarusco swept his arm around the bay. "I want that whole lip cleared, and I want to know what's nearby. Start immediately!"

The man yelled, "Aye aye," and turned to the ship before bellowing. "Port watch to the lockers! Man the boats! Move it!"

Men lifted the two large row boats stored along the ship's center between the masts and lowered them into the water. Forty men went over the side armed with cutlasses and bows. Bear walked over to the rail to watch them.

They rowed madly towards the small beach in overcrowded boats, and stormed up the trail when they got there. It looked like four or five men stayed behind to monitor the boats. The rest disappeared into the trees.

There was nothing to do but wait.

Bear paced the deck while they waited. The ship's bell rang four times before the answer came back. It was all clear. The horses were brought up and shuttled to shore one at a time.

Finally, it was their turn.

"You will be here when we get back, Captain?" Kate asked Jarusco.

"Yes, ma'am," Jarusco smiled. "Unless I'm attacked. Then look for me farther north on the coast."

"Thank you," Kate said. "It would be a great relief to have a ship available. We don't know where we're going from here."

"Relief or not, if I don't hear from you by the day after tomorrow, we pull out," Jarusco winked at her. "No refunds."

Bear got in one of the boats, wobbling as he tried to walk to a seat. He didn't really care what arrangements Kate made. Not now anyway. All he could think about was getting to dry land.

Bear hopped out as soon as they struck sand and he stomped on the sand gratefully. He was only too happy to walk his charger up the trail to the lip of the cliffs. It felt good to walk again.

At the top Bear waited for everyone else. The pirates had hidden themselves in the trees. It was a minimal defense, but it would warn the ship in plenty of time for them to escape.

The land rose a bit and he itched to ride to the top of the next hill just to see what was there.

That itch was soon scratched as everyone except Brendan and Thervan joined him. Those two were staying with the group's gear on the beach.

Bear led the group through the dappled light in the forest. It wasn't a long ride before they found a road and by evening, they were on the edge of town.

Chryselles was big.

The walled part of town and the castle stood above everything else on a hill to the south, but the sprawl of Chryselles started only a mile or so in front of them. The trees around them had been logged to support the city. They had a clear view in every direction.

"Should we camp here or ride into town?" Kate asked them.

"I say we go on in," Hestal replied. "We can hit some pubs tonight and the markets in the morning. Meet here in the afternoon?"

"That sounds good. Everybody got money?" Kate asked and they all nodded.

Foester and Bear were soon riding alone, the others having gone different directions.

"Where to?" Foester asked.

"Like I know," Bear grunted. "I've never liked Chryselles, it's big, hot, and always stinks." Bear pulled up to the first pub he saw. "We're supposed to be looking in pubs. No reason not to start here."

Foester dismounted and they both entered the pub.

Four hours and five pubs later, they had accomplished nothing. There was one small exception-Bear had beaten a room full of armed men bare handed and Foester was counting the winnings from betting on his knight.

"That was some good exercise," Bear stretched. It was a comfort to hear his armor creaking in all the ways it should.

"Except that's not what we're here for," Foester frowned, "but it was profitable."

"If you know a better way to find a thief that knows the way to magical treasure or holy relics, be sure to let me know." Bear undid Breyier's reins. "Let's find a room for the night."

"Sounds good, we can troll the market in the morning." Foester mounted his horse, "I saw an inn back that way that seemed suitable."

"Right, lead on." Bear said as he mounted.

The next morning found Bear and Foester walking around the market place and the impossibility of their task started to sink in as hundreds of people wandered the market around him.

"Only Kate is going to know if the thief is the real thing," he said. Bear paused in the shade to escape the heat for a moment watching people walk by. "You think she's got us riding around to keep us busy?"

"I don't think she thinks like that," Foester tossed Bear an apple. "I think she's told us everything she knows and is hoping that three pairs of eyes are better than one."

"I wonder," Bear said as someone shouted his name. He turned to see two knights riding up to them.

"Berigral Danagor? It is you."

Bear struggled for a moment as he stared at them, "Keenen, isn't it?"

The knight dismounted. "Damn right! I don't doubt my memory of our encounter is better than yours. Last time I saw you I received a broken shoulder and a broken leg for my trouble."

The new knight walked up quickly with his hand out.

"I remember, that was a tough fight." Bear took his proffered hand. "You seem to have recovered well."

The other man laughed. "I've won a few since then, and landed a rich wife."

"Congratulations," Bear shook his hand warmly. "This is my squire, Foester."

Foester bowed.

"What are you doing in Chryselles with no banner? Tourneys are five months away," Keenen said with a sly smile. "You aren't spying on us are you?"

"I'm on a quest. Priestess of Mirsha, sent to find the lost tablets." Bear wasn't sure what to say, they hadn't talked about what was public knowledge and what wasn't. "Father doesn't approve, so no banners."

"I'd heard that, but I didn't know he didn't approve," Keenen smiled. "Seems popular with the people. How did you get here? The last his lordship heard, the quest was up north somewhere."

"Pirates," Bear grinned.

Keenen's face looked shocked. "Pirates, really? Tell me everything."

The other knight coughed, "Sir Keenen, his lordship?"

"Right. Berigral come with us. You can tell Lord Saban all about it." Keenen mounted the waiting charger.

Bear knew it wasn't really a request.

"Right, let's go." Bear nodded at Foester and the two of them mounted and followed.

Bear was curious and asked, "How did you find us in the market, Sir Keenen?"

"Simple," Keenen answered. "We got a report of a giant claiming to be a northern knight who beat a roomful of armed men last night. I told his lordship it had to be you. As I might be the only person who could recognize you, he sent me out this morning to look for you."

"Oh, well I guess I got myself into trouble," Bear sighed.

"No trouble," Keenen said. "We knew that the quest had to come here from the Grand Priest of Mirsha. We just didn't know when. We've had men watching the harbor."

Keenen slowed as they rode up towards the gate. "I envy you this chance to go on a quest. Even if it is led by a woman."

"Wait 'til you meet her before you pass judgement." Bear smiled to himself as they rode through the gates into the castle. "She's feisty."

Foester brushed up Bear's armor and handed him his helmet and shield after they had dismounted and followed a discreet distance behind the two knights. Bear left him at the door as they entered the presence chamber.

A great booming voice answered after Bear's name had been announced. "So it's true?"

This was a big room, but years of training had taught Bear what to do. He entered and walked to the end of the carpet and bowed deeply. When he rose from his bow, he found Lord Saban standing in front of him.

"This is great news. I only received a messenger yesterday that you were leaving Nordsvard and heading this way." The Lord shook his hand. "You've made great time. Where is everyone else?"

"The Holy Priestess is in town with the others. They are searching for our guide, my lord," Bear said.

"How, in the gods' names did you get here?" Lord Saban asked. "It can't have been three weeks since you left Nordsvard."

"Closer to four, my lord," Bear answered.

Keenen leaned in, "He came by pirate ship."

"Pirates! You came by pirate ship!" Lord Saban was smiling. "That was bold, boy," he said approvingly. "I like my knights bold. Is the ship in the harbor?"

"No, my lord, we disembarked north of Chryselles and rode into town last night." Bear answered truthfully.

"That's a shame, I'd love to meet them." Lord Saban offered wine from the sideboard. "My grandfather told the best stories about pirates."

"Aren't they illegal here?" Bear asked tentatively.

"Pah! Council rules." Lord Saban waved them over to large chairs. "There's a fair amount of trade with the islands that I don't know anything about, too."

They all sat in firm but comfortable chairs made for men in armor.

"Comerant's letter said there was another knight." Lord Saban took a drink of wine, "What's his name?"

"Leoshus and my brother Thervan, my lord," Bear frowned. "We last saw Leoshus surrounding the town of Nordrigen and putting it to the torch for paganism. I don't know if he's coming here or not. Sir Thervan is with the ship and our supplies."

"Leoshus, I know the man. Paganism is grim business." Lord Saban nodded and dropped the subject. "What do you need here, how can we help?"

"We are looking for our guide, my lord," Bear answered. "Mirsha gave instructions that someone in Chryselles knows where the Tablets of Markinet are."

"Historian, sage?" The Lord of Chryselles finished his wine and a servant took his cup.

"No, my lord, a thief." Bear shrugged, "That's why we were in the market and the pubs."

"Thief! Gods! Good luck with that, you'll be here all summer," Saban laughed. "I hope you don't have to interview them all."

"I hope not, sir," Bear smiled.

A musical voice interrupted them, "Where is the priestess staying?"

A beautiful brunette woman in red brocade appeared silently behind them and they all stood in a clatter of steel.

"Sir Berigral, my lovely wife, Lady Athella." Saban bowed her into a chair.

"My lady," Bear bowed. "I have no doubt she stayed at an inn in town last night and will probably stay on the ship otherwise."

He stayed standing as Lord Saban had not sat back down.

"A pirate ship, Athella! They sailed on a pirate ship," Lord Saban repeated excitedly. "I really want to meet this bold priestess."

"I'd like to offer her the comforts of the castle," Lady Athella said calmly, contrasting Lord Saban's enthusiasm.

"I'm to rejoin the group this afternoon, my lady. I will be happy to make your offer." Bear bowed again.

"It will be an official reception. I want Chryselles to celebrate her arrival. It is historic. Sir Keenen, make our request formal if you would, please," Athella smiled.

Sir Keenen bowed to her. Lady Athella stood up, graced Bear with a smile and left. The ladies followed her at a few made bold stares at Bear.

"So you still have access to the pirates?" Lord Saban asked as they sat back down.

Bear nodded. "Yes, my lord. We don't know where we go from here. It only made sense to have a ship waiting."

"Where does he anchor?" Keenen asked.

"I don't think he does," Bear lied. "He's afraid of being attacked and won't stay in to shore long."

Lord Saban leaned back in his chair. The dark, silver trimmed armor he wore creaked as he shifted position.

"Do you think he would accept the assurances of the Lord of Chryselles?" Lord Saban asked.

Bear worried. He wasn't really in charge and didn't know what latitude he had to make decisions. Jarusco would do whatever he felt profited him most.

"I don't know, my lord," he said. "I can only ask him. Be aware, he and his crew are ready for a fight. I get the feeling he isn't very trusting."

Keenen laughed, "I wouldn't be either if I were in his position."

Luncheon was served to the men in the chairs. Bear waited until the servants had left and Lord Saban was spooning out a plate of the noodles that were so popular in the South.

Bear had only known Lord Saban as a judge in the tournaments. He had never had so much personal interaction with any of the royalty.

His experience with Duke Comerant last summer left him tentative, but he knew the questions he would be asked when he got back to the ship. He had to try.

Bear spoke as Keenen served himself. "My lord, if I may be so forward, why would you allow the Eorsians back in the port? The Council may not approve."

"Excellent question." Lord Saban dabbed his mouth with a napkin for a moment. "I'm not used to explaining my motivations, but in this case it may be necessary. The expedition is led by a priest."

The lord put his food down. "Without going into details, I've been hearing that something dangerous was coming from various sources. The Council has its own concerns and ignores mine. This city is my responsibility and I want all options available for my people."

Lord Saban seemed satisfied with his answer but he added, "I think this might be a rare opportunity. To be first to hold out my hand to people who were once our friends may provide a valuable ally in the East. Even if it doesn't play out or takes decades to evolve, I won't miss an opportunity to do the best for Chryselles."

"Thank you for your confidence, my lord," Bear bowed his head.

"It's strange to be discussing such things with the knight in charge of a quest, but not to be speaking to the leader, Berigral." Lord Saban said between bites.

"I know, my lord," Bear nodded. "It's the reason my father wouldn't support the quest, but Holy Mirsha is in charge. I'm here to make sure the priestess lives, not to lead."

"A noble goal for a young man," Lord Saban smiled. "I can't wait to meet her."

"It will be arranged as soon as possible," Bear assured him.

Lord Saban left them after luncheon and Bear spent the next few hours trying to get more information out of Keenen. Bear felt Keenen must be in the duke's confidence to be so available to him, but Keenen wasn't speaking. He was genial, but tight lipped.

Frustrated, Bear reconnected with Foester. They led Keenen and an official contingent of men with banners and the flags of the city back to the rendezvous point in the logged timber outside of the city.

The rest of the team were already gathered and sitting on piles of logs.

Bear stopped his group short-a dozen yards away. "Sir Keenen, may I have a moment to fill everyone in before announcing you?"

Keenen nodded, "Absolutely."

Bear and Foester broke from the armored group and rode up to the logs.

"You get arrested?" T'az asked as they dismounted.

"No," Bear said flatly. "His lordship's men found us in the market, and I had an interesting lunch with the Lord of Chryselles."

Kate eyed the armored men suspiciously. "They aren't here for us are they?"

"No. Why would they be?" Bear asked with curiosity.

T'az interrupted Kate. "We'll tell you about that later. Hestal heard that anyone seeking old lore or knowledge, outside of the official Council versions, should speak to the gypsies. What did you find out?"

Bear turned to Kate, "Nothing on the thief. His lordship is interested in opening communication with the pirates and wants to meet you. The duchess sent Sir Keenen with an official request."

"But he's not after us or trying to stop us?" Kate asked nervously. It was the first time Bear had seen her appear nervous. She was pale and her calm demeanor had slipped. She seemed young and frightened.

Bear was concerned, "No. He finds it unusual like the other knights, but he doesn't oppose us. He thinks something bigger is going on-that's why he wants to talk to the pirates. What happened to you?"

"We'll tell you later," Kate said and her appearance changed like she had pulled on a mask. She took a deep breath. "Bring him over."

Bear waved and Keenen and company rode up in perfect order, their shiny armor reflecting the late afternoon sun. Keenen dismounted and strode up to the group.

Bear introduced him. "Priestess, this is Sir Keenen, Aide to Lord Saban, with messages from his lordship."

Keenen bowed. "Holy Priestess, we have been eager to meet you."

"Thank you, Sir Keenen, well met." Kate offered her hand and Keenen kissed it. "What messages have you brought for me?"

"I have several, my lady," Keenen handed her a packet. "First, the Lord and Lady of Chryselles wish to meet you at your earliest convenience. Her Ladyship, Athella, has also commanded that I offer you the comforts of the castle during your stay in Chryselles."

Keenen pointed at the paper in her hand. "In that packet, I am also authorized to offer your ship and the Eorsian sailors on board, free passage in the port of Chryselles," Keenen finished with another bow.

"That's extraordinarily kind, Sir Keenen." Kate blushed. "We will come immediately to the Lord and Lady, but I'm not sure our ship's captain will want to take advantage of this offer."

"There are official papers in the packet. Assurances from his lordship and an official amnesty for the limit of your visit." He waved at one of the men who dismounted and ran over with a folded flag.

Keened gave it to Kate. "If he chooses to, he should fly this flag and there are instructions in the packet. He won't have to worry about the dock men. Violating the amnesty is against the law."

Bear watched Kate make her decision. "Foester would you take Bernard and ride back to Captain Jarusco with the offer?"

"How will I inform you of his answer?" Foester asked politely.

"If he accepts, we'll see you in the harbor tomorrow," Kate said. "If we don't see you in the harbor, we'll meet you here tomorrow afternoon."

"Yes ma'am," Foester waved at a visibly disappointed Bernard, and they both mounted and rode back to the north.

Kate turned back to Keenen. "Sir Keenen, if it pleases you, we'll ride back to the castle with you now."

"That would be excellent." Sir Keenen bowed. "I'd hoped you would feel that way."

T'az was staring at Bear as everyone mounted. She seemed to be accusing him of something.

He stared back, "What?"

She shook her head and Bear mounted and rode next to her. One of Keenen's troop tore off at a full gallop as the rest rode at a walk.

"Where's he going?" T'az asked.

Bear shrugged and made his armor creak. "To the castle. It's polite to give them notice that Kate's on her way."

Kate rode with Keenen at the front. The men with flags rode behind them. Bear, T'az, and Hestal brought up the rear.

"Aren't you going to ride up front?" T'az asked.

"I could, but I want to know what's going on." Bear didn't like being outside the circle of knowledge.

"Kate killed someone last night," Hestal whispered.

"What?" Bear was shocked. How could the tiny priestess physically overcome someone? "How?"

"We were attacked last night," T'az said flatly. "I got three of them, but one grabbed her with a knife at her throat. She just touched him and it was over."

Bear was confused. "What do you mean, 'touched him'? And why were you attacked?"

"I don't know. I don't even think she knows-she just touched his face and he died," T'az sighed. "We were given the option of dying or being raped to death by some thugs. Not really a choice."

"That's not even the weirdest part," Hestal said. "Tell him the rest."

T'az sighed again. She looked worried as she glanced around. "Kate healed one of the guys I'd speared in the chest. I think it might have been her guilty conscience-but I saw the wound close and the color return to his face."

"Val's Blood!" Bear exclaimed.

"Shh," T'az hissed at him. "We don't want this getting out."

"Was it a spell?" Bear whispered to Hestal.

"I don't think so." Hestal shrugged. "From what was described, it's not like any magic I've heard of and there are no healing spells."

Bear was shocked. He'd never heard of such a thing. In his world the biggest, boldest, and best trained always won. He was nervous about Hestal's magic, but somehow that seemed real-it had limitations.

Spells had to be spoken, books read, and memorized. This sounded like something different. It wouldn't matter how strong you were, or how well trained, if someone could just touch you and kill you.

Bear wondered how important a knight was on a quest where the smallest and weakest could kill with less effort. What would he do in a world where his skills weren't needed? He looked at Kate in a new light. She was waving for them to join her.

CHAPTER 12

Kate rode into the castle to significant fanfare. Men lined the gatehouse. Trumpets sounded. It all made Kate feel small and dirty. Her normally unruly hair had been tied back for the last two days and all of her robes were dirty.

As they rode to the castle's main entrance there was a man in silver lined armor and black hair waiting for her, but the man was over shadowed by the regal woman standing next to him.

Kate felt frumpy as she compared herself to the tall dark haired woman in her beautiful red dress and the silver woven into her dark hair.

She wished she hadn't agreed to come immediately. She wished she had at least had a bath. There was only one thing that surprised her as she dismounted: the priest attending the royal couple wasn't from the Temple of Val.

"Holy Priestess!" The lord of the city called out. "Welcome to Chryselles."

"The honor is mine, my lord," Kate said as she made a perfunctory bow.

There was some question whether priests were supposed to bow to lay people. It was a long running argument, but Kate didn't want to be arrogant. A bow wasn't important. The duke's support might be.

The duke turned to the lady in red, "My wife, Lady Athella."

Kate bowed to her also.

"Holy Priestess, we are so excited to welcome you and your quest into our home. The market speaks of little other than your visitation and quest." Lady Athella's voice was perfect too; smooth and musical.

"Please call me Kate, my lady," Kate said, "all my friends do."

161

Athella looked like she had something else to say, but the duke turned Kate to the priest. Grand Priest Darrin was grinning impishly.

"I believe you know the Grand Priest?" The duke said.

"Yes, my lord," Kate smiled happily, "Grand Priest Darrin was my selector at seminary. He taught me everything I know."

The older man stepped forward and hugged her.

"My dear," Darrin said, "I knew you were destined for something great."

Kate blushed and turned to Athella. "I apologize for my appearance. I wish I had the ability to appear appropriately dressed for the occasion, but the exigencies of travel have made that difficult. I never expected to be received so grandly."

"Why wouldn't you be received grandly?" The duchess said, "You're on a holy quest. I can't think of anything more important. Please bring your friends in-there will be time before dinner to bathe."

"Thank you," Kate bowed again.

The duke led the group into the presence chamber and waved them to chairs. Bear seemed distracted by their reception, but Kate could tell there were a lot of women interested in him. She wrote off his distraction to that.

"We'll wait here a few minutes priestess," Lady Athella said, "as your rooms are being prepared."

Kate introduced the others as they entered, "Bear you know already, this is Hestal, our mage, and T'azula, my bodyguard and friend."

"T'azula? You're southern aren't you?" The duke asked conversationally. "I didn't expect a southern to take on a holy quest."

"No, my lord," T'az shook her head.

"But you are her personal guard." The duke offered them wine. "I guess that it's important for her guard to be a woman."

"Yes, my lord," T'az answered moving behind Kate's chair. "As recently as last night, men attempted to harm her. I'm here to prevent that from happening."

Kate tried to hush her even though she knew it was futile. She was still worried about the man she killed. They didn't need legal troubles.

Athella gasped. "Last night? In town?"

"I apologize and I won't pretend there aren't evil men here," the duke acknowledged, "but I hope there were no serious injuries."

T'az crossed her arms. "Not to us. Three of them won't do it again."

"Ah! Well done." The duke laughed. "Priestess, Kate, we are at your service, what can Chryselles do for you? I can gather more men. In spite of the unusual circumstances, I'm sure some would volunteer."

He turned to Bear. "Don't be offended Sir Berigral, but Nordsvard did not over-provide her."

"No, my lord," Kate said. "I believe I have enough men at the moment, thank you. Holy Mirsha directed us here for our guide. We will not know what we need until we find him."

"I heard about the guide. A thief?" the duke inquired. "How do you hope to find him?"

"We have a lead, my lord," Hestal interjected. "The gypsies may know more. We ride out to them in the morning."

"Gypsies, how mysterious. It's like an old fable," The duke said as he watched a servant talk to Lady Athella. "I believe your rooms are ready and I apologize for the delay. We will continue the discussion over dinner. I want to hear the whole story."

They all stood. Servants were to guide them, but Kate addressed the priest. "Grand Priest, would you escort me to my room?"

"Certainly, my dear," Darrin said as he stood.

As they followed the servant, Kate made a confession. "Grand Priest, I must confess that I've been lax in my ritual. I wish to be cleansed in the Temple of my sins."

Darrin chuckled.

"I should admonish you about that," he said. "It seems you're in a bad position to lose Holy Mirsha's favor. I have some doubt though, about the necessity of any cleansing."

Kate was taken aback and paused in shock. Darrin was a stickler for the details. She wondered if he could know her doubts.

"From what the High Priest has written," Darrin continued, "you are in direct communication with Her Holiness. I'll do what I can, but I'm just a man and priest. We can go to the temple after dinner."

The servant had stopped in front of a door and Darrin stopped with him. Kate bowed her head to him and entered.

As expected, T'az was right behind her.

"Nice room." T'az surveyed the room as she closed the door.

Kate smiled at her. "You know they have a room for you."

T'az flopped on a couch next to the unlit fireplace. "Last night was close, Kate. This will do fine."

Kate bathed and put on her cleanest clothes. She sat at the dressing table and stared at herself in the mirror. Her face and neck had browned from nearly two weeks at sea.

Kate liked the color better than her normal pale skin, but her hair was unruly as ever. Kate started brushing while T'az bathed.

T'az took over when she was ready. "I'm not a hair dresser, Kate. I think we should just braid it back out of the way like mine."

"Okay," Kate sighed, "I just feel like frumpy country mouse around all those beautiful women."

"Not unusual," T'az said as she braided. "Just remember, that's what they do-hair and dresses. They are hunting for a man. Which is why they are all trying to catch Bear's eye."

Kate laughed, "Jealous?"

T'az gave her hair a tug. "No. You are a priestess on a holy mission and I'm a warrior-we don't worry about hair. Our quarry is much more dangerous than some court boob."

T'az nodded at Kate in the mirror to emphasize her point.

"You're right," Kate smiled. "It helps to be reminded of our purpose."

It was a wonderful evening. Athella and Saban were attentive hosts and they kept an active conversation right through dinner. Kate apologized when she saw Darrin was ready to leave.

"I must attend to my holy orders, my lord," Kate bowed to him.

"Of course," Lord Saban said. "You will be accompanied. Jarvis!"

A man ran out from a side room and men were detailed to attend the trip to the temple after dark. In just a few minutes, they clattered out of the gate surrounded by castle guards. It was not a long ride.

There were parishioners in the temple, even at this late hour. They seemed to be waiting for Kate and she was embarrassed by their attention. They all wanted to touch her and T'az used the castle guards to keep most of them back.

Priests and the guards moved the ecstatic parishioners out of the sanctuary and left Kate in peace. T'az stood by for the cleansing, but no one else was visible.

Kate told Darrin everything. The powers, the questions, the people of Nordrigen, and the death of the man the night before.

"Healing." Darrin's breath whooshed out after the ritual cleansing was over. "Are you certain?"

"Yes," Kate said from her knees. "It scares me Darrin, I don't want anyone to know, but I need your advice."

"It can only be the will of Mirsha," he said confidently. "Only the gods have those powers."

Darrin performed the ritual blessing and Kate stood to receive it.

"When I was a boy," Darrin said as he walked her up to the altar. "I chose to serve Mirsha. I looked at all of the gods, but I felt love and compassion from only one."

Kate got back on her knees at the altar.

"I don't feel I'm your superior anymore," Darrin smiled gently. "I have no punishments for you. Please pray at the altar for Holy Mirsha to pass judgement."

Kate was surprised. She turned to the altar with her head bowed.

Uncharacteristically, Kate couldn't remember the penitent's prayer. She was alone, no one would know, but Kate struggled to remember it. Mirsha deserved better from Kate.

"Don't worry," said a voice behind her. "You've done well."

Kate spun her head. The lady from the library sat in the first pew. Her dead eyes seemed full of mirth and there was a smile on her cracked lips. The blood and the blouse were the same.

Kate could see T'az farther down the aisle. T'az hadn't reacted. It could only mean T'az couldn't see the woman.

"But...," Kate started, but the woman held up her hand.

"You are doing well. It will get much harder from here." The woman dissolved and Kate sat back on her feet staring at the pew.

T'az walked up the few rows to where Kate was. "What did you see?"

"I'm confused." Kate shook her head. "I saw the dead woman from the library. The one that scared me. She said everything is fine, but things will get more difficult."

"I think she's right," T'az said. "Let's go. It wouldn't hurt to get a good night's sleep."

Darrin walked up with Kate's case. He had refilled its contents.

"Finished, my dear? Here's your traveling case," Darrin said.

"She interrupted me," Kate said, troubled. "The penitent's prayer wasn't necessary. She told me things were going to get harder."

"Don't be troubled, my dear," Darrin said as he handed Kate her ritual case. "It is the will of Mirsha."

T'az helped Kate push through the crowd of parishioners to the guard protected horses.

Kate hugged the Grand Priest. "Darrin, please write to Haervan and tell him everything. I don't know what's going to happen, but I feel we are headed into danger."

"You know I wouldn't normally share the contents of a cleansing with anyone," he said, "but I will."

The next day dawned with Kate kneeling on the balcony. She hadn't said her ritual. She was just watching the sun rise and mused over her vision in the temple.

How everything could be fine? Kate had missed rituals, she had failed to follow the Code in Nordrigen, and she had killed. She had cleansed herself of these sins and been shriven, but it didn't seem to matter—she didn't feel any different.

Kate felt her love for Mirsha as the sun shone on her face. The goddess wasn't as particular as Darrin had taught her. This quest had opened Kate's eyes to many new things, but the most surprising were the faults in her own faith.

The sun reflected in the waves in the harbor. A ship was rounding the lighthouse and sailing into port. The new ship looked like a sleek wolf in the middle of a pack of round sheep.

Even at this distance, Kate knew it was the Magdelaine. It made Kate smile. Somehow she knew Jarusco would make the bolder choice.

Kate woke T'az up. They hurriedly got dressed and gathered their things. Kate wanted to visit the docks before going out to the gypsies and if she was right, Lord Saban would want to go too.

She was right. Lord Saban could barely contain his enthusiasm. There was a maddening delay while they waited for him. Two hours after Kate saw the Magdelaine slide into the harbor, they finally arrived at the pier.

Introductions were made and Lord Saban immediately began negotiations, but Jarusco held up his hand.

"My lord," Jarusco bowed, "I must point out that I'm in no position to negotiate anything."

"That's alright Captain," the duke laughed, "I'm probably not in a position to negotiate anything either. The Council will rule, I just want to discuss possibilities and I brought documents for you to take home. No time like now, to start talking."

Kate left them to talk. The Magdelaine felt more like home than any other place-even after such a short time. Kate felt the finish on the wood railing under her hand. She felt the ship was alive.

The crew was unloading the horses and everything seemed right in Kate's world. She wandered back over to the group of men, who stopped talking as she approached.

"We'll be going across the river to talk to the gypsies this morning," Kate said to Jarusco.

Jarusco looked across the bay. "Long ride, we could row you over there. That would be quicker."

"My lord, are we allowed to row to the far side of the bay?'" Kate asked Lord Saban for permission.

"Go ahead," he followed their gaze. "They probably won't be open yet."

"I'll take my chances," Kate replied. "I'm eager to get started."

The crew of the boat were in high spirits as they rowed Kate, T'az and Bear across the bay. They were getting the chance to explore the forbidden port and their enthusiasm was infectious.

There were no docks on this side of the river. Barges and a few small craft were beached in the dark mud. The buildings they could see were all cheap and flimsy looking.

"Attractive," said Bear.

"I'm not even sure this is part of Chryselles," Kate said. "No map shows the city crossing the river. There are no bridges that I know of."

"That would be a big bridge," Captain Jarusco laughed. "That river is over a mile wide."

The crew leapt out of the boat as they floated close to shore and tugged it through the mud to the grass. There was some cursing involved, but Kate was able to step off on dry land.

Jarusco gave quiet orders, and as they walked away Kate said, "You have a lot of faith in your crew."

"Of course," Jarusco smiled. "This voyage is going to be yarned for years around the fleet. And they're going to end up with more money than any of them has ever seen. I think the only thing I could do to make it better would be to find them a good fight."

The gypsy camp was quite large and filled several acres of farmland, positioned to maximize availability to the ferry crossings from the city.

They wandered through corridors lined with colorful, solid sided wagons, but no people were visible.

It was deathly quiet.

Kate picked one of the temporary buildings at random and walked inside. Although dimly lit, she could see several small tables and a stage at the far end.

The only person they'd seen in the camp was stocking shelves.

"We don't start serving 'til midday," he said dismissively. "Come back later-the girls will be here. We have the best drinks. If you got somethin' ta sell, you should go across the plaza."

"I'm not here for drinks or girls," Kate said walking forward. "And I'm not selling. I'm looking."

"If you the authorities, there ain't nothing illegal goin' on here." He had gotten wary. "And we don't need priests either. We have our own."

"I'm looking for information. Nothing more," Kate said. "Information on the Tablets of Markinet. I've been told the gypsies might know what happened to them."

"We don't know tablets," he feigned indifference. "We didn't steal nothing."

"Certainly not, you'd be hundreds of years old. They disappeared mysteriously from the Council Chamber in Theopolis," Kate explained. "We've heard rumors that demons were involved."

"Demons," he said, and spat twice. "We have no truck with them."

"Ok. But is there someone here who might know more?" Kate was running out of patience. "I was told I'd find a guide here."

An old man Kate hadn't noticed got up from a table in the corner.

"Where'd you hear that?" The old man asked.

Kate turned to address him. "Holy Mirsha told me during a visitation."

He moved over to the counter where the other man had stopped working. They spoke briefly in a different language. Kate did recognize the tone of command.

The young man acquiesced.

Smiling he came around the counter and waved them to the door. "Follow me."

The group crossed the open area and down another corridor of wagons. The new area had a dozen large multicolored tents. The young man led them to the dark red striped tent.

"You wait here," the man bowed. "I'll tell her she has visitors."

He opened the flap and entered. In a minute, stepped back out and held the flap open.

The interior was dark. Kate saw an older woman was sitting at a table behind a veil. There was only one chair in front of her.

"Not all of you. No," she waved at them. "Just the priestess."

Kate nodded and sat down. Bear and Jarusco left. The woman raised an eyebrow to T'az, but T'az just shook her head.

"Too many people have tried to kill her," T'az said as she crossed her arms. "She doesn't go anywhere without me."

"Very well, but if I'd wanted you dead, you'd already be dead." The woman relented. "What is it you seek priestess of Mirsha?"

Kate was uncomfortable in her gaze. "The Tablets of Markinet. Mirsha said I'd need a guide, someone knows where they are, and she told me I would find that person here."

One very mobile eyebrow shot up on the older woman's face. "Here in this camp?"

"Not specifically, no." Kate knew she was going to ask that question. "In Chryselles, but I need help. I can feel time running out and there are too many people to interview them all."

"We can help," the woman smiled thinly. "For a fee."

"How much?" Kate asked.

"Ten," The seer put her hand under the veil. "In gold."

It was a lot of money. Kate didn't even blink, she open her sack and paid the ten gold coins.

The woman leaned forward. "The Tablets you have spoken of were stolen by the Black Mages. They probably had demons to help them. The Black Mages are powerful and evil. This is not something for little girls to get involved in."

She waved wrinkled hands around Kate's head. "Particularly little girls with little or no magic about them. Knights and pirates will be of little use."

"Exactly," Kate said. "The Goddess told me I needed a thief and that he knew how to get them already."

The woman's eyes flashed fire for a moment. "Really? That is very interesting."

She stood and waved them to the flap. "Come back in two hours. I will have more information for you then."

"We won't be paying again," T'az said. "You know who this is. A hundred knights and their men land today and they are going to escort her wherever we go."

T'az held the flap for Kate, "You wouldn't want that destination to be wherever you're going."

The woman's suspicious eyes narrowed at T'az. "I'll not run. I know someone who knows more, I'm going to see him. He is in this camp."

T'az smiled. "That'll be fine then. We'll wait outside."

They went outside and filled in Bear. Jarusco was outside another tent probably making a deal. Kate didn't really care. Bear looked frustrated.

"So we wait," he said.

"T'az implied we'd follow them to the ends of the earth to get this information," Kate said. "I don't think any of that will be necessary though. Mirsha said the thief would come with us because he has his own purpose."

"So they won't run because he already wants to go?" Bear said scratching his head.

Kate looked around. "That's the way I interpret what I was told."

Bear pulled some empty crates over from another tent and they all sat.

They sat for a long time. There was no way to tell if two hours had passed. The crowd was building around them and brisk trade was already underway.

Women showing a lot of leg were hawking wares to everyone that passed. Groups wandered the area singing, while Kate's group waited silently.

The young man appeared again from out of the crowd. He waved at them. "She is ready."

They all piled in the tent. Kate sat but couldn't make out who was behind the veil until the flap closed. It wasn't an old woman; it was a man.

"What do you want with the Tablets?" He asked.

"The Goddess Mirsha has directed me to recover them," Kate said. "I need a guide."

"Sounds like it," he sneered. "Do you even know where they are?"

"No. Obviously that is why we are here," Kate said primly.

He leaned closer. He was older than her, but younger than Foester. Scruffy looking, but the details of his gear and clothing were meticulous.

"Don't get smart with me, girl," he said. "They're in the Black Tower. The place itself is hell on earth. Horrors abound there and that doesn't take into account the mages."

"How is it you know so much?" Bear asked.

"The gypsies have dealings all over. As it happens, I've been there." He kept his eyes on Kate. "I've seen them."

"Yeah? How did you know what they were? The writing is indecipherable without the Codex," Kate asked.

"They're labeled," he smiled. "So what was your grand plan? Are you going to lay siege to the place?"

"If necessary," Kate replied. "I have the full authority of the Council."

"You really have no idea what you're talking about." The man leaned back and the veil made him fuzzy again. "The building isn't made of stone. It was ripped out of the bones of the world by magic. The mages themselves are thousands of years old. The original thief is probably still there. They aren't afraid of anything."

"That's impossible," Bear said.

"I hope you're not what we call brains on this expedition," the man said sarcastically. "Try to use your head for thinking. These men have defeated death. They are powerful, old, evil, and greedy. Siege is impossible."

"Mirsha told me I needed a thief and that he would already know how to get them," Kate appealed to the thief.

The man leaned forward and stared at empty space next to him for a moment. Kate sensed a presence there, but she couldn't see the spirit.

"Are you prepared to turn your wondrous quest over to the control of a thief?" He leaned back again. "Wouldn't it be easier to tell the Council you couldn't find them?"

"I'll do what I have to do to get them." Kate leaned in. "I didn't dream this trip up. Mirsha herself laid this burden on me."

"Then, at least some of you will die," the thief said confidently.

"So be it," Kate crossed her arms. "But Mirsha imbued me with power to prevent that."

"What power?" The man glanced significantly at the empty space. What Kate had said was important to him.

"True healing," Kate said.

The man's face was expressionless, but the presence moved to stand next to him and he seemed to listen to it.

"You'll have to prove it," he said as he got up. "Follow me."

He headed out the back flap and Kate and the others followed him.

They passed the old woman sitting by the back of the tent and crossed the line of wagons. There was another world behind the wagons. This one was for the gypsies and they seemed shocked to see outsiders.

The man didn't slow or hesitate. He walked straight through to a wagon sitting by itself. A wrinkled, white haired woman sat on the steps of the wagon. She seemed very sad.

"Is he still alive?" The man asked.

"He is," she croaked. "Do not contaminate his last hours with outsiders."

"This woman says she has true healing," the man told her.

"She lies," the old woman spat. "The Gods haven't seen fit to heal him, do not fill him with the false hope of charlatans."

Kate walked past them both and up the stairs, she felt the power already buzzing in her head. This was important. Inside, a woman and a man cried by the small bed of a child.

Kate felt the child's forehead. His skin burned and he had small bumps under the skin of his face. It was the pox and it was nearly always fatal.

Kate sighed to herself. "It couldn't have been something easy."

The child himself was barely breathing and past caring.

Kate prayed to Mirsha. *Holy Mirsha, you've brought us here. You allowed me to heal. I believe this man knows where we are going, or at very least, knows who knows.* She again laid her hand on the child's forehead. "Please Mirsha, please heal this child."

Kate closed her eyes and felt the power surge down her arm again. She kept her eyes closed as she prayed. She was confident it would work. She kept it up until she heard the little boy cry.

Kate opened her eyes. The parents weren't crying; they weren't doing anything. They just stared at Kate. The little boy howled and cried for someone to comfort him.

"We'll see," the old woman hissed as she pushed past Kate. Kate got out of the way as best she could in the small space of the wagon.

The old healer physically groped the boy and put him back down. "It's a miracle. The pox is gone."

"It's not a miracle," Kate said tiredly. "Holy Mirsha wants me to succeed. She healed this child."

Kate turned to the thief.

He was looking at her cooly with narrow eyes. He seemed to be pondering his options.

"Name's Verig," he said. "I've been to the tower before. If your team is any good, I'll take you there. Just remember, I wasn't lying. More than likely, we'll all die."

He turned and left the wagon and Kate followed him.

"Which way do we go from here?" she asked him.

"West," he said as he continued walking. "It will take me a couple of days to put my affairs in order. I'll meet you on his ship." Verig pointed at Captain Jarusco as he passed him.

"Why?" Jarusco asked.

"Cause I don't like to walk," he snarled. "We can take ship to Cromere and head west from there."

Verig never stopped walking and was very quickly out of sight. The old seer was standing near where he disappeared. She was crying. She said something to the young man and then she too disappeared.

"Come," the young man said, "I'll take you back to the seaside."

Soon they were back in the boat and being rowed briskly across the bay to the Magdelaine. Jarusco was excited about the possibility of heading deep inland.

Word of their destination was whispered around the boat and the crew seemed even more excited as they pulled hard to get back to the ship.

"Well that was worth ten pieces of gold," Kate said to T'az.

"No kidding," T'az smiled in the sun. "After all the delay, we finally get to start."

When they boarded the ship, everyone was waiting to hear the news.

"We've found him, and we are going west," Kate said. "If Lord Saban approves, we're taking the ship upriver to Cromere."

Kate held the remaining money out to Foester. "Foester, would you start gathering our supplies? I want to be ready to leave when Verig joins us."

Foester took the bag. "We've already started the lists. Going inland will make it easier. Water and fodder will be readily available."

"Great," she said. "Bear would you accompany me to the castle? I think we should keep his lordship current on our progress. We can also stop at the temple on the way back. Would you like to go too, captain?"

Bear nodded but Jarusco declined."No. I have to find knowledge of the river before I'll take the Magdelaine up it," Jarusco smiled. "Someone will tell us."

"Good then." Kate turned back to Bear, "Let's go."

CHAPTER 13

Kate entered the castle without fanfare, which suited her just fine. They were still welcomed by the castle guard, who took their horses and led them in to the inner ward.

"It's your fault," Bear smiled at her, "you should have sent a runner to announce you."

Kate shook her head. "This is better."

Kate was in high spirits until the last turn to the presence chamber. Someone was already in there and Kate recognized the voice.

It was Leoshus.

Leoshus stood on a wider bit of carpet and Lord Saban was sitting on the throne with a bored expression on his face. Kate decided to walk in and interrupt their conversation and walked through the crowd to the front of the carpet.

Lord Saban brightened as she was announced and Kate took that as a good sign. She walked past Leoshus to the end of the carpet.

"Your Lordship, I have wonderful news," she said crisply.

"His Lordship and I were just discussing you, priestess," Leoshus monotoned, from behind her.

Kate refused to look at him. She kept her eyes on Lord Saban. "It is very good of you to join us, Leoshus. Did you enjoy cleaning up Nordrigen?"

"Sadly, most of the populace escaped. We think they may have tortured the priest of Mirsha and were forewarned. We found his body." Leoshus informed her coldly. "I thought you'd want to know."

Kate ignored him. She already knew how the priest died and she wasn't sorry. She was still haunted by her vision of the demise of Nordrigen.

She spoke loud enough for all to hear. "Your Lordship will be pleased, we found our guide."

"By Val, that's wonderful," Lord Saban said. "I had no hope that you would ever single out a person. Was he with the gypsies?"

Leoshus ignored the lord. "Priestess. Did you test this man? Do you know he doesn't lie to get your coin?"

Kate didn't ignore Lord Saban.

"Yes, my lord," she said stiffly, "he was with the gypsies. Mirsha led us to him and I didn't have to test him, Leoshus. Holy Mirsha tested him and he needs no coin from me to get him to go."

"That's pretty good proof in and of itself, Priestess. Well done," Lord Saban said. "Where are the tablets now?"

"West, your Lordship," Kate replied. "With your permission, we'd like to take our ship up to Cromere, and strike out west from there."

"West," Leoshus sneered. "Is that all he has to say?"

"West from Cromere is nothing but the Wall," Lord Saban whistled. "You're headed into the wilds."

"Yes m'Lord. It was expected," Kate answered him, but Leoshus' insult demanded a response. "And no that is not all he had to say. They were stolen by the Black Mages. They are in the treasure room of their tower and he said-and I quote-'inside it is like hell on earth.'"

Lord Saban whistled again.

The Duke jumped down off his throne and smacked Bear on his shoulder. "Wish I was a younger knight, eh Berigral? This is what legends are made of!"

He stamped over to a sideboard and drew wine. Servants brought wine to the rest of them.

The Duke saluted Bear, "Escorting beautiful women into danger at the request of the gods. Verily, I say, I envy you this chance."

Bear smiled. He might even have been blushing. It was hard for Kate to tell as she accepted her glass of wine without facing Leoshus.

It was possible that Leoshus couldn't help himself. "That would be led, my lord, not escorted. We are here to lead her safely to the tablets."

A shadow passed over Lord Saban's face. "I've read your letters, Leoshus. Is there really a need to quibble over this again?"

"My lord," Leoshus started, but Lord Saban cut him off with a wave of his hand.

"No. We'll discuss it at a later time. Right now, I propose a toast!" He stood in front of them. "First, to congratulate you on your success, second—and most of all—to honor you in hopes of future successes."

He bowed to Kate as courtiers and others cheered the toast.

Kate blushed, "Thank you, my lord."

Grinning hugely, Lord Saban hopped back up on the throne, but didn't sit.

"My Lady, I'm so glad you could join us. I should have held the toast, that was ungallant of me. I apologize." He bowed deeply to Lady Athella.

"Thank you, but I only interrupted you to insist that her holiness join us for dinner." Lady Athella smiled at Kate.

"Of course, my lady, I couldn't possibly refuse," Kate spluttered.

Lady Athella smiled and sat in her chair near the throne. Kate caught a glimpse of Leoshus, he seemed expectant, but Lady Athella just raised an eyebrow to him.

Lord Saban sat. "Would you care to continue, Sir Leoshus?"

Leoshus coughed for a moment. "This is not a delicate conversation, my lord, but I think the news of the quest's destination only fortifies my point and the point of the High Priest of Val-this quest is no place for women."

"Why ever not?" Lady Athella asked him sharply.

Leoshus coughed again. "My lady, if the tower is as awful as described, there will be killing and possibly a siege-that is no place for tender sensibilities."

Lady Athella sat forward in her chair. "I have four children, Sir Leoshus, do you think a woman is unaccustomed to blood and pain?"

Leoshus coughed and Bear shuffled his feet in discomfort. Leoshus recovered first.

"You can't compare childbirth to the brutality of combat or the tedious horror of a siege," he said awkwardly.

Bear chimed in for the first time. "Neither of which you've seen."

Leoshus turned on him, but it was Kate that spoke.

"Our guide has assured us that a siege is impossible," Kate explained. "The tower itself is magic-ripped from the bones of the earth. Impenetrable to assault."

Leoshus dismissed her with a wave. "You cannot know that. I laid siege to Nordrigen, Sir Berigral, which I noticed you were absent from."

Kate finally turned to Leoshus.

"The only person I've found who has been there says so and Sir Berigral has been doing his duty," Kate snapped. "You remember the mission the two of you volunteered for in Nordsvard."

Kate watched Leoshus' beard bristle as he stared at her. Kate held his gaze. She would not be afraid of this man. She had been picked by a god.

"Enough," Lord Saban said. "It's nearly time for dinner and I have many things left to take care of today."

The three questers bowed. As Kate turned to leave, Lady Athella caught her arm.

"Would you care to join me, Holy Priestess," the duchess smiled, "while we wait for dinner?"

"Thank you, my lady. I would." Kate followed the duchess out a side door.

Lady Athella led Kate to a sitting room and dismissed her ladies. A servant held the door open for Kate.

"What a lovely room, my lady." Kate said as she entered.

The duchess's private room had none of the rigidness of the castle. This room had large windows overlooking the city, soft and fragile furniture, and dark wood tones and lovely red floral coverings.

"Thank you, but call me Athella in private," Athella smiled as she took her chair. "Saban had it made for me. I love this room."

A vase of roses adorned the table and Kate breathed the lovely aroma. "Flowers. I've smelled nothing but horses and sweaty men for too long."

A chambermaid brought refreshments and Kate settled in to the view of the city.

"Leoshus is awful," Athella said after the chambermaid left. "Saban hates him."

"I'm relieved to hear it. I've been trying to figure out how to shed him for a month," Kate admitted. "I've had a terrible time keeping him in line."

"How did you manage it at all?" Athella asked.

"Literally, Mirsha has interceded on my behalf," Kate replied, "but since he's so dense-or I should say, so fixated on his goal-he doesn't see the hand of a god directing him."

"That's awful," Athella frowned.

"I hope Bear, I mean Sir Berigral, doesn't kill him. I need Bear." Kate took a big drink to cover her embarrassment.

"Do you need more knights? Saban could get some, I'm sure."

Kate bowed her head. "I appreciate the offer, but I think I need to keep this party as small as possible."

"Are the mages that terrible?" Athella said with concern.

Kate shrugged. "I'm told that these mages have defeated death and call demons to do their bidding."

Athella's look of concern deepened. "Aren't you afraid?"

Kate slumped. "Honestly, I'm scared. I have to trust Mirsha, She picked me."

Kate didn't want to admit it. She hoped that this wasn't a ploy to remove her from the quest. Kate liked Athella, but she didn't really know her.

"You've done a magnificent job so far and you've impressed my husband." Athella said as she stood and walked to the window. "I think the next generation of girls will have a new hero, whatever the outcome. I think you have the strength to do this."

"Thank you," Kate blushed. "I don't know about being a hero. I'm just a shopkeeper's daughter heading into the unknown with a few friends and the love of a wonderful goddess."

"You shouldn't be so modest," Athella laughed. "Commanding men and taming pirates-you are no longer just a shopkeeper's daughter. Girls will follow your example."

"But--" Kate said.

"No buts," Athella smiled at her. "Look at me. I'm the epitome of what women strive for-a powerful family, a castle, and a knight who is also a lord.

That is what girls are told to dream of. There are quite a few dreaming of emulating me and they are after Sir Berigral."

Kate smiled as she thought of the times she'd seen Bear with T'az. Those ladies had fierce competition.

Athella continued, "But what have I done? The boldest thing I may have ever done is risk embarrassing my husband by inviting only you to dinner."

Kate smiled and blushed, "You have achieved what every little girl dreams of, you should be proud of that."

"Yes, I have been blessed," Athella smiled sadly. "I have a wonderful life and four children. I have secured the succession and done everything I am supposed to do." She turned back to the window. "But sometimes, just sometimes, I would like to mount a horse and see what is beyond the horizon."

Kate didn't know what to say to that and fortunately she was saved by a servant announcing dinner.

Dinner was an intimate occasion, as there were no other guests. Kate spent most of her time answering questions for the children. She found them to be smart and delightful.

As the dinner was taken away and the children returned to their activities, Kate was left with just the lord and lady of the city.

"Kate, do you know what is actually happening with Leoshus and these letters?" Lord Saban asked her.

"I do not, my lord," Kate admitted. "I think it may actually have very little to do with me. I think there is a political agenda with certain priests playing politics."

"To what purpose? What more power could they want?" Lord Saban asked.

Kate didn't like speculating. "I don't have any facts, my lord, but it was suggested that some priests would like more control over the knights."

"You may be right. Be wary. Leoshus has powerful backers." Lord Saban stood up from the table. "He will limit the amount of help you will receive as long as you don't bow to him."

"I'm directed by my god. I'll not bow or unburden myself without Her permission." Kate moved to the door, "I must go."

"Kate please, you must stay here," Athella offered.

"No, I'm sorry. Your hospitality has been wonderful and I hate to abuse it," Kate said. "But, it will not benefit you to clearly take sides, and really if I'm on the ship, we can leave as soon as our guide arrives."

Lord Saban smiled. "You are right. Politically, there is nothing we can do for you."

Athella gasped, "But Saban, I've told you how popular she is in the market. They talk of nothing else and the rumors are rampant."

Lord Saban nodded. "Yes, I understand, but they talk of nothing else in the halls of power, too."

Kate thanked them again and took her leave. She hurried down to the castle grounds. As she expected, Bear was waiting for her. He looked jubilant, but that changed as she walked up to Zhost.

Kate felt a dark cloud form over them.

'What's wrong?" he asked warily.

"I don't know, but I have a feeling I need to get on the ship," Kate said and they rode quickly out of the castle.

When they passed the Temple of Mirsha, T'az was standing by the door, leaning against the building.

"Why are you here?" Kate asked her.

Before T'az could answer, Grand Priest Darrin exited the temple and spoke. "I sent to the ship for someone. At first, just to take the donated monies, but something else is happening."

"What, Darrin?" Kate asked.

"A knight stopped at the temple of Val." He pointed across the broad avenue. "Shortly afterwords priests of Val were seen leaving in groups. I don't know what they are up to, but it has to be about you."

T'az mounted her horse.

Kate turned Zhost. Spirits had gathered around her. They were everywhere. She could feel their fear and impatience.

Grand Priest Darrin stepped up to her. "It's so unusual and difficult for me to say, but Kate, do not be afraid. Holy Mirsha is guiding us all."

"You can see them too?" Kate asked in a whisper.

"I can." Darrin looked away from the gathering spirits. "I can't tell you what they've shown me. It's too horrible, but be brave. I'm so proud."

He choked up as he turned into the temple.

The trio charged towards the docks with Bear in the lead. Everyone moved for a giant on giant horse and they made good time.

Something was happening.

The spirits were no longer hiding in the shadows. She'd seen them every day since Mirsha's visit, but never in this quantity. Spirits of men and women lined the roads. An army of them followed her. These spirits weren't guides.

They were angry.

Darkness was falling as they turned on the avenue down to the docks. The spirits were bunched at the edge of the dockyard and as Kate approached she saw priests of Val blocking the road. They had brought their relics and were chanting in unison.

Bear didn't even slow down. He pushed Breyier through the line of priests. Kate and T'az followed him, but what Kate saw was the dam breaking as an army of shadows followed her through the hole.

Leoshus had formed a large troop of men facing the dock where the Magdelaine was moored. Jarusco had rigged nets across his ship and a party of sailors was manning a blockade of stacked cargo.

Kate headed for the ship, but Leoshus intercepted her and they all stopped a few yards from the sailor's barricade.

As Leoshus' mounted men formed a semi-circle around them, the wave of shadows broke over his formation. Dark shapes filled every space. The men didn't seem to notice, but Kate couldn't stop watching the rush of darkness as it filled the docks all around them.

Kate turned her attention to Leoshus. Apparently, he'd been speaking while Kate was distracted.

"What have you done, Leoshus?" Kate asked in soft voice.

He was clearly upset she hadn't been listening. "I said. By the authorization of the Council, as directed by the Speaker, I'm putting an end to this farce." Leoshus was shouting, so his words carried as far as it could.

"The Speaker doesn't have the power to do that. Not by Code," Kate said.

"He can and does," Leoshus spat.

Leoshus threw some papers to the ground in front of her. "The Council is no longer influenced by your dreams and the ramblings of an old man. There is no evidence other than your word and Haervan's delusions, that the gods have dictated anything."

"I have provided them with the evidence that you are doing this for your own grandiose dreams," he yelled. "You have overstepped your place and are violating the Code. You are providing comfort and support to pagans, and this ship is evidence."

"Violating the Code?" Kate screamed. "I have not! The Code allows a priest to perform the duties directed of them by the gods. It also says that priests under such instructions are not to be hindered."

"Oh yes, it does," Leoshus grinned evilly. "Those passages have been re-argued and it clearly, as you just acknowledged, says priest - not priestess."

Kate was speechless. This was all about her being a woman.

"It also says, that the Council may grant their right hand whatever powers he deems necessary to enforce the will of the Council," Leoshus laughed. "And as their right hand, I'm putting a stop to this."

"There hasn't been a hand of the Council since the rebellions against the Code," Kate said.

"What is he talking about?" T'az asked.

"The Council has apparently activated an ancient warrior position called the Right Hand," Kate explained. "The hand took control of civilian and local forces to suppress resistance to the authority of the Council."

Leoshus was enjoying his victory. "You and the criminals you have assembled will submit. You will turn over your guide to my person, and this ship will be burned with all of the pagans on board. I will reconstitute this quest appropriately and continue forward as the Council wills."

"You'll never find him Leoshus," Kate laughed at the thought of Verig submitting. Verig would more likely slit Leoshus' throat.

"If you found him, then I can find him," Leoshus sneered. "Mighty Val will prevail and he will come willingly or not. This will no longer be done on the whim of a little girl."

"You're wrong Leoshus," Kate said. "Leave."

"You're not in charge here!" Leoshus shouted. "You have no right of command. Your resistance to rightful authority though, is noted. I hope your dreams are some comfort during your imprisonment-it will be short and I assure you, I'll be there to watch you burn."

If he had been expecting Kate to anger, he was wrong. Kate only felt pity for him. "Leoshus, I don't know all, maybe this is as far as I am to go, but I don't think so."

"It is if I say so," Leoshus rode forward, but Bear cut him off and T'az drew her sword.

"Good, my men will crush you," Leoshus said to Bear. "Do you know your father has already lost his seat because of you and your pathetic brother? What prospects do your sisters have now? If you surrender, you may not hang."

A laugh came from the ship. Thervan was armed with his bow. "My sisters are stronger than you imagine, Leoshus. That is no threat."

"You'll die as soon as I get my hands on you Thervan!" Leoshus yelled. "Val won't accept you, you miserable runt! You should have done the honorable thing and killed yourself."

Bear, Thervan, and Leoshus started shouting at each other. Leoshus' men drew their swords. The sailors leveled their pikes. Someone on the ship yelled, "load!" T'az moved to block Kate from the initial blows that seemed imminent.

Kate could only see the dark shadows.

They crept up on the horses of Leoshus and his warriors. Although faceless, their intent was clear. Kate had no idea what they could do, but she was sure a lot of men were about to die.

Kate heard Bear say, "I'll die on this dock before I surrender to an oath breaker."

"So be it! As the Hand of the Council, I will crush all resistance." Leoshus turned and raised a hand but he never got a word out.

"ENOUGH!" Kate's shout hit like a shock wave. Power rippled out like rings on a pond and all the way back into the crowd of peasants and dock workers behind Leoshus' formation.

"Enough," she said again. Men were frozen in place. They blinked but otherwise didn't move. Even the spirits seemed frozen.

"You do what you feel is necessary, Leoshus," Kate said, "but I will not allow harm to come to these people."

Kate rode away from him toward the barricade. "Take your men away now, or the power of the gods will destroy you here."

The whole scene unfroze and the spirits started tormenting the dismounted men. The soldiers capered like bees had been released among them. All order was lost and they ceased to be fearsome.

The sailors laughed at the dancing soldiers.

Kate was very tired. She shouted at the spirits. "Let them leave!"

The men stopped dancing about, but they remained wild eyed as they searched for their invisible tormentors.

"Go Leoshus. Do not hinder me again," Kate sighed, and let Zhost carry her to the ship.

What happened hadn't been lost on Leoshus. He turned from watching his men reform. "This isn't over priestess. Raising the devil will not help you."

"There are no devils, only men," Kate called back. "Mirsha's power moves through me for this quest. I believe it is meant for the Black Mages, but if you continue on this path, I will be forced to use it now."

Kate was barely conscious she was so tired. She heard Leoshus' men turn away. The sailors made way for her. It was all Kate could do to board the ship and get to her hammock.

Her dreams were grim. She saw the ghosts individually and heard their stories until sleep took her.

CHAPTER 14

Bear stayed awake that night. He suspected there would be another attack, but there wasn't. Jarusco had played this game before.

The crew sweated and toiled with the anchors to move the ship out of bow shot, against the wind.

The Magdelaine crept out into the bay, one anchor movement at a time. One boat crew would row an anchor farther ahead and then drop it into the sea. The crew on the deck manned a giant windlass and pulled the ship to that anchor. Then the process repeated.

It was slow going.

Sometime after midnight the ship was secured to Jarusco's satisfaction and the crew went below. Bear walked up to the Captain as he oversaw the last actions.

"How will the guide get to us, or the Lord of the City?" Bear asked him.

Jarusco just shrugged. "They'll have to row. I won't risk my ship and crew."

Watches were set and soon it was just Bear and a couple of sailors on deck. The sailors were nice enough to leave him some empty space near the rear of the ship and Bear just stared at the lights of Chryselles until dawn.

Kate came on deck just before dawn, performed a ritual, and walked over to him.

"Did you sleep?" She asked him.

"No," Bear responded, "did you?"

"Not much no." Kate sat down on the deck. "Bad dreams."

"What happened last night?" Bear asked.

"The ghosts of the past were not going to allow Leoshus to stop us," Kate laughed tiredly. "Leoshus will never know it, but I may actually have saved their lives."

"Ghosts?" Bear was confused. "I didn't see anything."

"A large group of spirits followed us from the temples. Everyone of Leoshus' men had dozens of spirits crawling all over them." Kate shook her head. "I don't know what they can do, but it had to be stopped."

"Do you control them?" He asked. This was a lot for Bear.

"No, Kate sighed. "If I could, I wouldn't have spent most of the night listening to them."

"They're here?" Bear looked around alarmed.

Kate laughed at him. "They're everywhere, Bear."

"It would be easier if I could see them," he lamented.

Kate laughed. "Be careful what you wish for. I'm going back below."

Bear leaned on the railing and drowsed in the warming sun until T'az kicked him awake for breakfast. The crew had rigged canvas to cover a large portion of the ship and the team ate in the shade.

There were odd gyrations on the dock. Lord Saban's troops took up positions protecting the now empty berth. Civilians gathered there too. The group really didn't speak, everyone was waiting on Kate.

Kate came back on deck before midday and plopped into a canvas chair next to T'az.

"How do you feel?" T'az asked the diminutive priestess.

"Fine, just tired," Kate said. "Drained maybe."

She looked particularly small and drawn to Bear. Like someone who had been sick a long time.

"I should think so," Hestal said. "The amount of energy required to freeze that fight was enormous."

"It wasn't a spell," Kate said. "It was Mirsha."

"Interesting, but there was something else there," Hestal probed. "What else was on the dock?"

"Ghosts," Bear said.

"Something like that," Kate smiled at him.

"Can't you heal yourself like you did with that poxed kid?" T'az asked.

"I don't think it works like that," Kate sighed, but Bernard perked up.

"Great Gaia!" he exclaimed. "You cured the pox?"

"More like Mirsha did it through me, Bernard," Kate said. "Yours is the goddess of healing and health, you should talk to Her. You're an amazing healer already."

"That's a big deal," Thervan said.

"We've been trying to keep it quiet," T'az said. "You just don't know how people are going to react."

"It's not quiet now," Hestal said pointing at the dock they had abandoned and the people gathered there. "I suspect we'll hear from Lord Saban sometime today."

Everyone watched the activity on shore, with little to do but wait. Verig would show up when he was ready.

Just as Hestal had predicted, a group of armored men rode onto the docks under the flag of the city. Bear thought he recognized Keenen and asked Jarusco to send one of the ships boats to the dock for him.

Bear helped Keenen to the deck.

Kate smiled weakly, "Sir Keenen."

"Holy Priestess," he bowed. "Forgive me, you look very tired."

Kate sighed, "It's hard to hide. I'm drained from last night. What can I do for his Lordship?"

"He and Lady Athella hope you will allow me to escort you to the castle," Sir Keenen said hopefully.

"They are most kind, is there an emergency?" Kate asked.

"None that I'm aware of. We have plenty of men to contain Leoshus," Keenen said with disdain. "Even if he has been elevated to the Hand, there are legal precedents."

Keenen continued, "I believe his Lordship has already sent official complaints to Nordsvard and Theopolis. I know he spent the morning berating the Grand Priest."

"He berated the Grand Priest of Val?" Kate asked.

"Oh yes. There was a large crowd demanding the Grand Priest's head this morning outside the gates," Sir Keenen laughed. "I think his lordship

191

settled for berating him and closing the Temple of Val for the moment-if for no other reason than to keep the mob from burning it."

"That's awful. I didn't want this," Kate fumed. "There is no reason for any of this."

"I disagree," Sir Keenen said seriously. "Leoshus has no right to land forces and disturb the peace in Chryselles and the temples shouldn't be supporting the invasion-these are secular matters. Laws were put in place to prevent the actions of the Hand after the rebellions were suppressed."

"Oh, Sir Keenen," Kate smiled at him. "Of course you are right about that. I meant the whole thing, the quest. There is an illogical need for power and control in some people, and it's tearing us all apart. We should be uniting against the actual evils that exist."

"Evils?" Sir Keenen asked curiously.

Bear explained. "Our guide has been there and says the mages are evil and the tower itself is hell on earth. There will be monsters and probably demons."

Kate shook her head. "We should be joining together to fight such things or at least limit them, not bicker about who's in charge."

"That's wonderful, no one told us that," Sir Keenen said as he smiled at Bear. Then turned to Kate, "My wife will hate me, but I volunteer to go in Leoshus' place."

"That's very kind," Kate said as she held up her hand. "I've been directed by Mirsha to keep this expedition small. Siege is impossible, we will literally be stealing our property back from them."

Bear didn't see Keenen turn to him, Kate seemed wobbly.

Keenen said, "Berigral, you lucky bastard. Please priestess..."

Bear saw Kate's eyes roll back and she started to collapse. He moved as fast as he could, but only just caught her. It may have been an immodest way to catch a lady, but at least she didn't hit the deck.

T'az and Bernard ran over.

"Good Gods!" Sir Keenen exclaimed. "Is she alright?"

"She'll be fine," Bear said as T'az took her and laid her on the deck.

Kate sort of woke up. "I'm fine... just hot."

"You just lay there, Kate," Bernard said calmly. He then turned and yelled at some sailors. "I need help getting her below."

As the men trotted over, Bernard turned to T'az. "Run below and get the two blue bottles out of my bag!"

T'az darted off and was back in a flash. Bernard took the bottles from T'az and mixed some of each bottle together. He put the mixture under each of her arms before allowing sailors to lower her down the hatch.

"Tha's cold. . ." Kate slurred.

Bear was concerned but he still had Keenen to deal with and it was important that he and others didn't get the impression that Kate wasn't capable.

He knew Keenen and he suspected he knew Lord Saban well enough too. He let vent his frustration.

"Damn Leoshus," Bear spat. "He pushed her too hard last night. I'm going to call that coward out. Doing that to a woman is unseemly."

He turned to Keenen. "Keenen, you can tell his Lordship whatever you like, but I need your oath that this won't go any farther. It's just what Leoshus would want. He wants her to appear weak."

"I agree and you have my oath on it," Sir Keenen swore. "Berigral, I admire her passion and I am determined to convince her to let me come, but she does appear weak."

"Weak, my lily white ass," Bear snarled. "What is she, five foot nothing, and maybe a hundred pounds? She stopped Leoshus and his whole band last night single handed."

"I'd heard that," Sir Keenen said carefully. "You wouldn't believe the rumors flying about. The court mage said it was impossible. There are also rumors of miracle healing."

"I've only heard she heals, but last night I was there," Bear said. "Frozen like everyone else. I'll swear it on my sword."

"Can I ask what she said about it?" Keenen asked.

"She thinks Mirsha is taking an active role to ensure this goes the way She wants it to," Bear lied. "But now it looks exactly like what Leoshus wants it to look like."

"Don't worry about him. You can't challenge him here, at least not without Lord Saban's permission." Keenen put his hand on Bear's spaulder. "An Order of Restriction has been enacted around you and Leoshus. I'll go back to the castle, hopefully he'll send me back to be your second."

"I hope he does." Bear stepped back from the ladder. "She thinks Thervan and I are enough, but I wouldn't mind a few more good men."

"You lucky bastard, I'd give my left hand to go." Sir Keenen waved at him. "I'm off, you'll have word soon!"

Bear waved to him as he descended to the boat, then started pacing the deck. It wouldn't do to take his bulk below and crowd the tiny room. He would just be in the way.

He paced over to the hatch and listened. It was quiet. Which meant that there probably was no emergency.

Bear wasn't settled. If he wasn't allowed to challenge Leoshus today, he'd try again tomorrow. He only stopped pacing to get water from a pitcher when he saw T'az coming up the ladder.

"How is she?" Bear asked.

"Bernard says she'll be fine. She's sleeping." T'az took a seat under the awning. "Bernard would like the death's watch stomping above the cabin to stop."

"Sorry," Bear sat down. "I'm just so mad at Leoshus. I was going to call him out and break him into little pieces, but we've been restricted by law. I can't leave without permission."

"And they aren't going to give you permission for that," T'az smiled at him. Bear felt warm all over when she smiled at him.

"I sent a formal request anyway," Bear said.

"You would," T'az laughed. "Why are you putting this on Leoshus?"

"Seems obvious to me," Bear shrugged. "He had no reason to be here last night. We weren't going anywhere."

He took out his sword and a polishing cloth and started working it.

Bear talked as he rubbed. "I don't think he knew what he was going to get, but if he's been made the Hand of the Council, he should have pressed that with his lordship-not on the dock last night."

Bear kept working on his sword. "We could have done nothing, if the entire city was lined up against us. And, he didn't mention it yesterday in court-he already held the papers. Why didn't he bring it up legally."

"You think that knight is going to side with Leoshus?" T'az asked.

"Keenen? No way. He's on our side and sworn to only tell Lord Saban," Bear said. "Besides, he's volunteered to take Leoshus' place."

"Do you trust him?" T'az asked.

"Yeah. I do. I don't know a lot of people, but I know him from tournaments." Bear kept polishing. "He's a tough fighter and seems to be an honorable man."

"Good," T'az nodded and took a sharpening stone from Foester.

Bear, T'az, Foester, Thervan, and Brendan spread all of their gear out and started cleaning and checking everything. It was the perfect time to get everything prepped for the future.

The group stopped when Bernard came back on deck.

"She's sleeping. She'll be fine," Bernard sighed. "We should try and keep it quiet around here today."

"What makes you think she'll be fine?" Hestal asked.

"Her heart sounds good. She's had a bite to eat and she drank a lot of water," Bernard shrugged. "In anyone else, I'd just say she was dehydrated and over worked. But, last night, I don't know what a drain that could be."

"We'll take shifts," Hestal said. "I think someone ought to stay close." Hestal eyed the pile of equipment the warriors had out and got up. "I'll go now."

Hestal disappeared below.

"It's warm down there," Bernard said. "She's got the cooling balm on her skin, so she's not feeling the heat, but we shouldn't leave anyone down there a long time."

"Maybe we should bring her up here?" Foester said. "It's warm, but there's a good breeze."

"Let her sleep a couple hours," Bernard said. "We'll see how she feels then."

Bear took the next watch. He sat in the doorway, leaning on the frame-half in and half out. Sweat rolled down his face as he drowsed in the heat.

Kate seemed to be sleeping peacefully.

Bear thought about praying for her. He hadn't prayed to Val since he learned the knight's trials were a sham. The statues in the temple weren't scary and the heroes were just stone.

He had won his spurs without prayer.

The tournaments were just a game. Rules prevented physical damage. They were run by odds makers and did nothing to prepare him for a quest or warfare.

Now, he would face magic, and magic was scary.

He had to trust it would be alright, but he didn't know whom to trust. Bear didn't see any advantage to returning the Tablets.

They'd been missing forever and it hadn't bothered anyone. People he knew and people he cared about would be hurt. His family may already be ruined.

Bear admitted to himself it was selfishness that led him to defy his father-that and pride. But now, he felt the quest was important, but Bear couldn't put his finger on why when the goals were so minor.

Bear rubbed his chin and felt the stubble of his beard.

A voice in his head said. *"This isn't about the Tablets. You will learn our true purpose. You are important to its success."*

Bear's eyes shot open and his skin crawled. He looked around for the ghost, but he couldn't see them.

Someone kicked his leg and Bear looked up.

T'az was kneeling in front of him. "Didn't you hear me talking to you?"

"No. Sorry. I was distracted." Bear blinked a few times.

"More like napping." T'az said as she moved in to check on Kate.

Bear stayed seated at the door. He liked watching T'az. Her every motion was graceful and fluid like the great hunting cats in the forests north of Nordsvard.

Bear had never met a Southern woman before. He had never met a physically strong woman before either. He stared at her legs and imagined them without the leather pants.

"It's not polite to stare." T'az half whispered and she kicked him again.

"Sorry." He moved his leg so she could sit down opposite him.

Her eyebrow shot up. "What's wrong with you?"

"Nothing," he said as he looked over at Kate. "I was thinking about why I'm doing this."

"Why are you doing this?" T'az asked. "You're rich. You could find a nice wife, have kids, and put your armor on for a Holy day. Glide right through life"

Bear nodded. "That's the plan for every knight. Except me and maybe Thervan. At first, it was my chance to get away from my father. A chance to prove myself and, I don't know, do something important."

He didn't want to admit to T'az that he had come for purely selfish reasons.

Bear looked over at Kate. "Now I know I'm doing the right thing. Not sure what it is yet, but it's right."

"You're a good egg, for a rich boy," she smiled at him.

"Oh yeah? Why are you here?" He asked her.

"Seen any woman fighters around?" T'az asked him. "Not much work in the only thing I know how to do."

"Ok, I'll give you that, but you're no mercenary." Bear probed. "Why her?"

"At first it was free lunch," T'az said flatly. "She'd come down to the market and find me and she just talked and talked. It was boring, but I wanted out of that shitty job, and I thought she might hire me. Then I got to know her."

Her face clouded for a few moments. "My dad used to say something about really good fighters we'd see. He'd say, 'that's a once in a generation sword that is.'"

She looked at Bear. "I think she's a once in a generation priest. She's so innocent, everything is shocking to her. I'd do anything to see her unhurt."

"But you can't," Bear said. "All these ghosts and things only she can see-you can see it weighs on her."

"Maybe," T'az said. "I'd kill them if I could figure out how to."

Bear nodded, "Me too."

T'az kicked him. "It's my watch. Go up, get some water, and cool off. If you pass out, no one is catching you."

Bear grunted as he tried to quietly get up off the floor-not easy to do with his armor and sword. He completed the maneuver and smiled at T'az before heading to the ladder.

T'az grabbed his hand. "Thanks for catching her."

Bear squeezed her hand and headed to the ladder. The rest of the day passed uneventfully. Sir Keenen never returned. Bear expected that meant his request to face Leoshus in combat had been denied.

The next morning, Kate was already on deck when Bear climbed the ladder. That wasn't unusual, as she conducted a dawn ritual every day. What was unusual was that the sailors on deck were armed and everyone was staring out into the bay.

"What's happening? Bear asked as he walked up.

"Three ships have moved into the bay. They are flying Leoshus' banner," Kate said. "I just can't figure out what he's doing."

Jarusco was standing nearby. "You may be taking to horses sooner than you thought."

"Why?" Kate asked.

"If he takes those heavily laden tubs upstream he'll run aground and we won't be able to get by," Jarusco said. "No refunds. Remember?"

"Yes, of course." Kate watched the ships move slowly towards the mouth of the river. "What purpose could he gain in slowing us down?"

Jarusco wasn't smiling. "He could land his force and raid the gypsies."

"He wouldn't find Verig though," Kate frowned. "That can't be it. Besides, it would take so long to off load, the gypsies would just disappear."

"It's what I'd do," Jarusco said. "If he doesn't want you to be successful, then all he has to do is prevent you from getting your guide."

Bear gave his opinion. "Those wagons are so slow. Maybe he does just want to slow us down."

Kate was still frowning. "To what end? We'd still go and pass him within a day or so."

"There's a lot of empty space out there and he has a large force," Bear shrugged.

No one had an answer and each argument was re-hashed every time someone new joined the discussion. All the while, Leoshus' ships slowly moved towards the river entrance.

Foester watched for only a moment and then asked Jarusco, "The Magdelaine is smaller, but if he can't sail up the river, how can we?"

"Pirate trick," Jarusco laughed. "We can adjust the depth of our keel. From almost nothing to extremely deep. That deep bite is what keeps the Magdelaine from rolling over at high speed."

"I suppose the opposite will be true on the river," Foester said.

"Quite right," Jarusco responded. "We won't be able to carry as much sail, but we'll get there."

"They're dropping anchor!" A man in the mast called.

"That's interesting," Jarusco said. "Boson, rig in the nets and dismiss the watch!"

"Aye aye sir."

"What does it mean?" Kate asked.

Jarusco was measuring Leoshus' ships with his eye while his crew scurried to their new tasks.

"It means he wants a fight," Jarusco said loudly. "If that's what he wants, we'll give it to him."

The crew cheered.

"We can't leave yet," Bear said.

"No and we don't even want to," Jarusco replied. "He has staked his position, I can wait until wind and tide are right. Those men have never fought at sea."

They had lunch on deck. The weather was gorgeous, clear, and not too hot. The group sat quiet. They had to wait for Verig and then the Captain would pick his time to leave.

Not long after lunch a note was delivered in a small boat. It was for Kate. It was addressed formally and it was from Leoshus.

"What's it say?" Hestal asked her.

Kate read out loud. "He says that Val has blessed his Right of Command. As the Hand, he is formally taking charge of this quest. He has blockaded the river entrance and any attempt to move forward without submitting will be met with justified and righteous force."

Kate shook her head as she read on, "Let's see, he has a party ashore searching for the guide. Once he secures the guide he will continue with or without us."

That struck Bear as odd. "He's really out there. How could he go without Kate? Kate's the one Mirsha picked."

Kate pointed to the end of the note. "We are welcome to participate, well not everyone. Bear you are under arrest for mutiny and Thervan you are condemned to death, but it doesn't say what for."

"Oh well," Thervan chuckled. "I always guessed I'd come to a bad end."

"The whole last paragraph is about the glory of Val and how his humble servant only wishes to serve." Kate folded the paper back up.

"I think that's a nice way to say he's ready for a fight," Bear said surveying the ship. The crew were mounting weapons to the deck and new, thicker, black sails were being rigged. "Guess we're ready too."

Foester drew Kate's attention to a boat with Sir Keenen and Grand Priest Darrin. Kate rose to greet them as the sailors allowed them onboard.

"Holy Priestess, it is good to see you on your feet," Keenen said as he surveyed the ship's preparations.

"Thank you Sir Keenen," she replied. "Good to see you again, before we leave."

"I've brought you a letter, priestess," he smiled. "I believe it is from His Lordship."

"Thank you." She turned to the Grand Priest. "Darrin? What brings you down to the docks?"

"Ah, Kate. Things are in turmoil," he said. "First, there was a collection and these are the funds from that." He handed her a hefty bag. "Second, a letter from Haervan, which will probably explain why these are the last funds you may receive."

She handed the funds to Foester and took both letters. "Tell me Darrin. What's going on?"

"I'm not sure." Darrin scratched his beard. "It sounds like the Council has been passing a lot of new rules, not the least of which elevated Leoshus.

It appears to be mess. A lot of the Council walked out over the power grab. I could probably be burned for talking to you."

"Why?" Bear asked.

"It's all about Kate," Darrin said. "You've upset their very carefully constructed apple cart. Fortunately, as that bag of money shows, the populace is behind you." He shook his head. "To keep the peace, they cover their moves in secrecy."

"Tell me Darrin." Kate took his hands. "Should I give up this quest to Leoshus? Would that be better?"

He laughed. "Poor girl, you know the answer to that. I don't think you could if you wanted to. Nor, do I think, will they let you. Let an old man sit for a moment and you read your mail."

Kate ripped open the first letter and read it. She looked up at Bear, "Have you ever heard of the secret writings of Val?"

Bear shook his head. "Never. I didn't even know Val could write."

Kate turned to Thervan. "You?"

"No, and while I won't blaspheme Val-it does sound suspicious." Thervan added.

"It's how they justified reincarnating the Hand of the Council position and revoked the Letter of Mark." Kate went back to reading.

"Good thing we hired a pirate ship then," T'az said.

Kate nodded and read another minute. "We haven't done any of that."

"What?" asked Hestal.

"Apparently, the stories about us are wild and we've been rescuing villages from demons and burning corrupt priests." Kate said derisively.

"That's more interesting than the trip we're on," Thervan laughed. "Is it too late to change?"

"The tales are spreading from market to market," Kate said. "We've only been gone a couple of weeks."

Kate opened Lord Saban's letter and read it.

"That really didn't say anything. His lordship won't interfere with us as long as we stay offshore in Chryselles," Kate summarized.

Sir Keenen smiled knowingly, betraying that he already knew what was in the letter. "He won't stop you or hold you. That's not nothing."

He handed her another note.

"It's from Lady Athella." Kate read the note quickly and tears welled up in her eyes.

"Please thank them for me Sir Keenen. They have been the most gracious hosts," Kate said. "I'm sorry I don't have time to respond."

"I'll relay every word, Holy Priestess," Keenen replied. "My wife was very angry that I volunteered to go with you, but I'll still risk it if you need me."

"You are too kind, Sir Keenen," Kate smiled at him. "Please make sure Darrin gets back safely, he's an old friend. Oh, here, give this to Lord Saban." Kate handed him Leoshus' note.

"Any response for Haervan?" Darrin asked.

"Tell him to hang on and I appreciate all of his help. I'll write him soon," Kate said. "We are headed out into the wilds, which will remove us as a thorn for the Council."

"Good," Darrin said.

"We just need our guide, and we're ready to leave," Kate said.

"Well stop waiting. Let's go," Verig said.

Bear jumped a little. He hadn't seen another boat.

Kate had also jumped. "Verig how? I didn't hear or see you board?"

"If you could hear and see me coming," Verig said, "I wouldn't be very good at my job now would I?"

Verig moved over to the far rail.

"Hard to argue with that," Bear said.

Bear escorted the Grand Priest and Keenen to the waiting boat. Jarusco yelled orders and men climbed the masts-turning the Magdelaine into a living thing. Bear waved to Keenen and followed Kate and T'az back to where Jarusco stood.

"Lord Saban would like it if we didn't start the coming trouble," Kate told him.

"No problem," Jarusco said. "I guarantee they'll shoot first."

When the tide and wind suited him, he yelled "hands to braces."

The crew jumped into action and turned the ship towards the blockade. They closed the distance quickly. Bear could see archers lining the other ships sides.

Jarusco turned the ship to run along the line of the other three ships. It was a long bow shot, but a lot of archers over there tried to reach the pirate ship. The Magdelaine must have made an enticing target as she crept along in front of them.

"See, priestess?" the Captain smiled his trademark big smile, "They fired first."

"Is that why you did that?" She asked.

"No. The men are casting the lead," he said. "Hopefully we only need one pass to confirm the charts I purchased."

"The lead?" Kate asked.

"Measuring the depth of the bay here," he explained. "It would not do to make a dashing maneuver and end up aground under fire."

"That would be bad," Bear agreed.

The Magdelaine slid past the blockade and gently back out into the South side of the bay. The crew brought the information to the Captain.

"Excellent," he said. "Give me two more feet on the keel, but be ready to bring it back up quick after we pass them."

"Aye aye," They chimed.

"Now wet down these decks!" Jarusco roared.

He went back to guiding the ship. The crew dumped bucket after bucket of water over the decks and all the equipment on it. They were soaking everything. The Captain had guided them back out towards the sea.

"Hands to braces!" He yelled and something else Bear didn't catch, as he had put his helmet on. The Magdelaine turned in a wide arc. She was picking up speed and was soon racing towards the center ship of the blockade.

Jarusco looked over at them. "Here we go!" And then he yelled, "All hands arm for battle!"

The crew poured up on deck. Every one of them was armed. They brought up large boxes and hooked them to the decks. Buckets of water were hung everywhere. The chaos had purpose as the graceful ship turned into a monster of war.

"Bring in the forward sails and lower the forward booms!" Jarusco roared.

The crew raced up the front mast and bundled the front sails. They also seemed to remove many of the ropes up front. The ship slowed. The tide was racing in and it countered the flow of the river.

That was exactly what Jarusco had been waiting for. The Magdelaine plowed forward pushed by the incoming tide and light breeze.

"Load!" He shouted and then to the steersman. "Two points to starboard."

"Aye aye!"

"Don't get any of that on the deck or I'll launch you at them," Jarusco hollered. The crew giggled, like men dealing with fear.

Jarusco turned to Kate. "Go below with the healer, priestess. There will be men who need you soon."

"I'm not sure I can, Captain." Kate said as she stood and shook visibly. "If it's truly all about me, I need them to see me."

"Your decision." Jarusco turned to the steersman. "Steady on."

"Aye aye," was the automatic reply.

T'az ran up to Kate. "Kate, get below."

Kate swallowed hard. "No. This is because of me. Those men have to see me."

Bear hefted his large shield. "When I tell you, make sure you're under my shield."

"Ok," Kate's lip trembled.

"Fire!" Jarusco howled.

The small catapults started launching black pots out of the big chests. The crews worked fast and kept adjusting the range so more and more of the pots were hitting. Bear had never seen catapults used in this manner.

Someone up front yelled "close" and the big chests slammed shut.

"Light 'em." the man yelled. Grinning crewmen lit the ballistae and they were launched as fast as the crews could reload them.

Arrows and iron bolts filled the air. Men screamed on both sides of the Magdelaine. Fire flashed back and forth. The broad bladed bolts the pirates shot ripped flesh and rope as they tore across Leoshus' ships.

Bear could see men missing limbs. Those iron bolts were taking a heavy toll.

A loud grunt brought Bear's attention back to this ship. The Magdelaine was also taking damage. One of the steersman went down with an arrow in his side. Another sailor quickly took his place.

The steersman dragged himself to the hatch below deck. There was no time for anyone to help the wounded. Blood flowed and pooled on the Magdelaine.

Bear could see the damage was worse on the other two ships.

More pots were launched. The cycle repeated two more times, all the while arrows rained down on both sides.

Bear kept his shield over Kate and blocked all the incoming arrows he could see.

The pirate crew was incredibly efficient. It didn't take very long before the center ship whooshed into a towering inferno as all the ropes and masts went up in flames.

Men were jumping in the water. The armored ones disappeared immediately. Terribly wounded men crawled to the railing and hurled themselves into the water. Men begged for help.

Tears rolled down Kate's face. T'az grabbed her shoulder and Bear kept covering them with his giant shield and watched for the next volley of arrows.

"This is horrible, they're drowning right in front of me," Kate sobbed.

The Magdelaine passed silently through the horror streaming off the middle ship. Burning men continued to jump in the water. Bear could hear the horses screaming over the crackle of the flames. The heat coming off the burning center ship was intense.

Bear noticed the crew had focused their attention on the ship to his left, but they didn't get much chance to do additional damage as the wind pushed them upstream.

When they got to the far side Jarusco asked Kate, "Should we go back and finish them?"

"No Captain," she sobbed. "It may be the smart thing to do, but I can't take it."

He nodded and gave the orders. The crew cheered. Behind them two ships were alight. One was hopelessly burning. Bear could see men still struggling to contain the fires on the other one.

The far ship that hadn't been engaged was lowering boats and barges were coming from shore. Horses plunged off the deck of the not yet doomed ship.

Kate had turned away from the damage and looked over the Magdelaine.

The crew were hot, sweaty, and covered in oil, but they grinned impishly back at her. There were pools of blood on the deck.

Kate thanked them with a small smile and went below. T'az followed her.

Foester walked over and helped Bear pluck a couple of arrows he'd caught with his shield.

"Leoshus wasn't ready for that," Foester said.

Bear grunted. "I don't think anyone was ready for that."

Bear watched the crew work. They packed everything away, cleaned the deck, and started bringing in sails to mend the holes and burns. They were restoring the Magdelaine to her pre-battle beauty.

Bear observed the very efficient work and marveled that the captain didn't have to order anything. His crew knew their jobs and impressed Bear. He thought he could conquer the world with a crew like this.

One of the older sailors came up and saluted Jarusco. "Butcher's bill, sir."

"Right." Jarusco steeled himself and then took the paper. "Twelve dead and only fourteen wounded? That's wonderfully low."

"It's cause of her holiness, sir. She healed lots of 'em." the old man offered.

Jarusco smiled at the man. "We may have to offer a refund-for services rendered."

"Yessir." The old man saluted and left.

Bear could only stare at the column of smoke that was still rising behind them. He was aboard a vessel owned by people his government had declared pirates. There was a better than even chance he was now an outlaw himself.

CHAPTER 15

After doing her best to heal the injured, Kate hid in the canvas walled room that she and T'az shared. She knew the men would want to talk about the battle and Kate didn't want to hear it. It was horrible.

Jarusco and his crew were trained and prepared for that, but the men on the other ships had probably never even imagined it. Kate hadn't.

She couldn't get the image of the men choosing between drowning and burning out of her mind. And the screams-particularly the piteous screams of the horses in the hold-would haunt her forever.

Kate didn't know how long she cried, but there came a moment when she knew she wasn't alone.

"What do you want, Verig?" Kate asked.

Verig sniffed. "Just seeing how you handle it."

"You like to watch women cry?" Kate sniffed angrily. "Does it give you pleasure?"

"Doesn't affect me one way or the other," Verig said. "You need to prepare yourself, this will get worse."

"Thanks. Now go away," Kate said, but there was no one there.

There was no ritual Kate knew to perform and she didn't really know if there were rules to prayers. Kate settled on just asking Mirsha for mercy on the souls of the killed. It was all so unnecessary.

The cabin was dark when T'az brought food in. "Hungry?"

"No," Kate said.

"Please eat it anyway," T'az said. "You need to stay strong."

T'az left her alone. Kate took the food and ate what she could. Kate pulled her blanket off of her hammock and curled up in a dark corner. The looming shadow enveloped her and she slipped into sleep.

She saw the grey spirit apparition again in her dream. Kate hadn't seen him since her night in prison. He wasn't a scary or horrible ghost and he didn't seem to know she was watching.

Kate found she was interested in what the grey man was doing. He knew something she needed to know, but he never went anywhere Kate could recognize. She didn't know how to find him.

Kate woke to see the dead woman from the library smiling sadly at her. The spirit was still pale and blood covered her chest.

"I'm sorry," was all Kate could think to say to the spirit of the murdered woman.

"It's almost dawn," the spirit whispered.

"Thank you," Kate groaned as she got up. She was sore and thirsty, but she grabbed her bag and headed up on deck.

The strong breeze blowing up river was refreshing. Kate just closed her eyes and breathed it in. It smelled like a spring morning. The world had moved on from the horror of yesterday.

Kate walked silently back to the stern rail and set up her altar. She didn't really feel the ceremony was necessary, but after yesterday, she felt she should do something formal.

Kate needed to be grateful for their success and honor the dead. The short ceremony felt awkward, and when she turned around, the Boson was standing respectfully behind her.

"Your holiness, we know you was upset by the violence and we're sorry for it," he said in his gravelly voice.

"Boson, you all have nothing to apologize for." Kate gave him a weak smile. "The battle was just so senseless."

"Yes ma'am," the Boson nodded. "They always are."

"How do you deal with it?" Kate asked him.

"You do what you gotta do. Then you count your fingers and toes and try not to forget to breathe," the Boson gave her a gapped tooth smile.

"Thank you, Boson." Kate actually did feel better.

"Yes ma'am. Ma'am?" The Boson hadn't left. "We bury our dead this morning. The crew would be grateful if you was there."

"It would be an honor," Kate said sadly.

The ceremony was brief. Only the crew not necessary to keep the ship out of trouble formed up and Jarusco spoke about the sailors and home. Kate didn't want to cry but tears welled up anyway.

There was a prayer to their god, Nautilus, and then the bodies tied into their hammocks and weighed down were slid overboard. As the formation broke up, Kate moved to the rail and thanked the souls of the sailors for their sacrifice.

She stayed there a long time watching the river slide away behind the ship. The crew went back to work.

The ten-day on the river was busy. Jarusco was very careful with his ship and he kept men posted to measure depth and warn of floating dangers.

In spite of his caution, they made very good time. Kate and her team had little to do but watch the forests and fields slide slowly by as the wind stayed fair for all but two days of the trip.

Those days, the crew unloaded the horses and rigged harness to the anchor cables. The horses labored up the shore-tugging the Magdelaine upstream. Kate worried about them, but when the wind changed and they were loaded back onboard, they seemed happy.

Zhost actually enjoyed the work. It was preferable to be in the hold. He liked the feeling of progress.

"Not much longer, Zhost," Kate said as she brushed him while he drank his fill. "A few days and there'll be no more ships."

They stopped once and filled their supplies at a barge town. The locals didn't seem to have any idea who they were, and didn't seem to care either. It was nice to be anonymous again.

Kate bought everything the team would need and filled the Magdelaine's larders too. Jarusco would need supplies for the trip back.

Kate had sent a letter to Haervan explaining everything. She had included an accounting of all the money she'd spent. Her old habits died hard and Kate hoped someone was keeping up with the records.

One morning, when Kate finished her ritual, Jarusco was standing behind her.

"I'm sorry, Kate, but this is as far as we're going to be able to go," he said.

"Why? What happened?" Kate asked concerned the Magdelaine had sprung a leak.

"Nature happened," Jarusco smiled. "It's just shallowing too much, and the channel isn't very wide."

"Oh, well we were expecting that eventually," Kate said sadly. It wasn't his fault. "How far do you think we are from Cromere?"

Jarusco thought for a moment. "I'd say just over a hundred miles by river - maybe two to three days in the saddle in a straight line - south of the town."

"Thank you, Captain," Kate said sincerely.

"We're edging as close as we can to the western shore." Jarusco pointed to a place that looked deeper. "We should be able to start unloading soon."

Some of the crew was rigging the anchor cable to deploy off the back of the ship while the rest of them worked the sails and the river current to get them closer to shore.

Kate looked at Jarusco and asked, "what are they doing?"

"Boson's idea," Jarusco admitted. "Drop the anchor aft and let the current turn the bow downstream. It's a genius idea - if it works."

It did. The current wasn't fast and the Magdelaine slowly turned and stopped as the anchor bit behind the ship.

Jarusco tested the tension of the cable with his foot. He smiled and pulled a gold coin out of his pocket, "That's a bonus for you, Boson, good work."

The Boson took the coin proudly. "Thank you, sir."

Verig stormed up to them and the Boson excused himself.

"Why have we stopped?" Verig demanded.

"We're getting off," Kate said. "It's too shallow to continue."

"No it isn't," Verig snarled.

"The sailors say it is and I'd believe them over you," Kate crossed her arms.

"Why?" Verig asked.

"Because you wouldn't care if they grounded the Magdelaine and were put in prison as pirates or burned as heretics," Kate said flatly.

"You're right, but you listen." Verig wagged his finger at Kate. "We're on a time table and we'll have to hurry now. Missing the only day we can be successful is death."

"When do we have to be there then?" She was curious and wanted all the information she could get.

"I'll only tell you later, after I'm sure about you," Verig said. "I've been watching, the pirates don't count, 'cause they ain't going with us. You get this circus moving."

Verig stormed back forward. The crew was busy unloading the boats and Verig quickly disappeared behind the action.

Verig had stayed very quiet during the trip. They had hardly seen him. He kept all his stuff with him and always looked exactly the same.

It was a curiosity that they often discussed, but no one brought it up to Verig. He was the key. They had to have him. So they overlooked his eccentricities.

It took the crew about an hour to off load all of their horses and supplies. Kate waited on the ship. Now that she was here, she really didn't want to leave it.

Kate walked over to Jarusco as he supervised the last load going ashore.

"I once thought I was your prisoner. Now I can't thank you enough, Captain," Kate said to him and gave him the small bag that was left from Nordrigen.

"You're welcome," Jarusco was all smiles. "What's this for?"

"Crew bonus," Kate smiled sadly. "I'll miss this ship."

Verig walked up behind them. "Well, let's go," he snarled at Kate.

"Where have you been?" Kate was confused by his sudden appearance.

"None of your business," Verig said as he climbed down the ladder into the waiting boat.

Kate turned to Jarusco. She was sad and didn't know what to say. Her initial trepidation was gone. She was going to miss Jarusco and his crew's quiet confidence.

Jarusco picked the reluctant priestess up and lowered her to the waiting boat crew and they put her in the back of the boat.

Jarusco waved. "Good luck, priestess! Fair winds and following seas!"

Kate was quickly on shore. She waved to the Magdelaine. The crew were lashing the boats back on the deck and cranking up the anchor. In a few minutes it was over. The Magdelaine disappeared around a bend in the river.

Everyone was packing panniers from the piles of supplies on the shore. Foester had thought to pick up more panniers at their last stop and he supervised the loading.

Thervan had ridden off earlier to patrol the road to Cromere.

Kate took her bags to Zhost and tied them to his saddle. Zhost was ready and his enthusiasm buoyed her flagging spirit.

Verig mounted one of the extra horses and sat waiting.

Foester smiled as he walked by Kate. "All packed. One more stop and then to the Wall."

Kate's team rode through the deep loam of the forest. Thervan and T'az rotated the scouting duties so one of them was always out front. Leoshus knew where they were going.

No one believed he could have gotten in front of them, but caution seemed prudent. Thervan had received verification that they would reach Cromere the next day from a hunter. They weren't making great time, it rained on and off for two days.

These roads weren't as well maintained as ones they had ridden north to Nordsvard and Kate was silently cursing the mud.

The mud stuck to their boots and the horses hooves splattered it on all of their gear. The rain was never strong enough to wash it away.

So, on the third morning Kate shortened her ritual to spend time cleaning the caked mud off her boots with a stick before putting them back on.

This morning, the sun shone and the heavy clouds moved off to the north. Kate put her boots on and soaked in the morning sun.

Hestal had stirred early and stood by the fire drying his robes.

"Maybe we should have a late start today," Kate said to him. "Just dry everything and get cleaned up before we ride into Cromere."

"Not a bad idea," Hestal said as he rotated in front of the fire.

"It is a bad idea," Verig said as he walked into camp. "I told you we're on a time table - with you going soft on the boat - we've lost three days."

He wasn't wet or muddy, and his dryness irritated Kate. "Well, you won't tell us when the deadline is, so it's hard to worry about it. How do you stay dry?"

"I told you, what I do is none of your business," Verig snarled. "You don't pay me. I come and go as I please. I'm not taking any weaklings into that tower. So pick it up, or I'm gone."

"Fine," Kate said sarcastically. "Go back to whatever you were doing, we'll be in Cromere in a few hours."

The team got up reluctantly and packed up the camp after a cold breakfast of dried meat and water. They were mounting their horses when a flash of light followed by a loud bang came from ahead of them on the road.

"That's Thervan," Bear said as he mounted with his armor jingling.

T'az leapt on her horse and the two of them galloped to the disturbance. Verig rode up to Kate.

"Turn west here," he said and then surprisingly, followed after Bear and T'az.

"That's a strange command," Hestal said.

"What if they need help?" Bernard asked. "Or if they're injured?"

"I don't know," Kate replied.

Kate didn't want to split the group, but if it was a large force T'az and Bear would be back soon. They would have to trust that Thervan could escape on his own and meet up with them later.

"He might be right," Kate said. "We don't know what's up there. We have to trust they can handle it."

She turned Zhost off the road and with a quick look at the compass nudged him into the woods. It was going to be much slower going across country. If Verig's time table was that important, she hoped this wasn't going to the decision that made them late.

CHAPTER 16

Bear and T'az had ridden to the road and turned North to where a small stream of smoke marked Thervan's warning. They hurried because Thervan was going to need cover to escape.

Bear considered it a good idea to show force. He wanted to deter people pursuing them. The creak of his well-oiled mail comforted him as he set his makeshift lance that Foester had fashion out of a sailor's spike.

Bear was ready for a fight.

They hadn't spoken or coordinated as they rode. Bear wished T'az hadn't come. She would be facing trained soldiers, not criminals. He may not be able to help her if she got into trouble.

There was also no way he could stop her.

The top of the next rise revealed four armored men on horseback at the edge of the road, yelling at men in the woods. They heard the sound of fighting back in the trees.

Bear glanced at T'az. She was watching the men on the road with her sword drawn.

"Can you take the ones on the road?" she asked. "I'll head into the trees and find Thervan."

"Let's go," Bear grinned and lowered his visor.

It was, at most, barely a hundred yards of road to cover and the men on the road weren't paying any attention.

"Their mistake," Bear lowered his lance.

One man did look, but he must not understand the cruel speed at which a well-trained horse could close the distance between them because he did nothing.

Bear spurred Breyier into a full gallop as the man watching him yelled. Bear heard T'az break for the trees as Breyier thundered forward.

Too late, Bear thought as he aimed at the yelling man.

Bear ran the shouting man through with his spear. The other three had been surprised by his appearance. Breyier kept going forward as Bear released the lance and drew his sword.

Breyier plowed into the confused second horse, knocking the mare over, and throwing the rider. Breyier and Bear wheeled as a team. The other men had now drawn their swords and Bear charged into them. He blocked the blow from the man on his left with his shield pushed his sword under the other man's defense.

His sword bit into a gap in-between the breast plate and the back plate. On foot, Bear's sword might have been bound, but Bear used Breyier's forward momentum to wrench his sword free.

His foe coughed blood and fell to the ground - leaving a confused horse standing in the muddy road.

These aren't knights, Bear thought to himself.

They wheeled again, but the last rider had had enough, and was headed back to town at a full gallop. Bear let him go, as there was no time for a chase.

Bear focused on the dismounted man.

The shieldless man tried to mount the recently vacated horse, but Breyier charged them and the horse bolted.

The dismounted man swung his sword in desperation. Bear let the weak blow glance off his armor. As Bear passed the man, he swung backwards once and connected with the dismounted man's head.

Foe number three fell into the mud facedown with blood filling his shattered helmet. Bear turned Breyier to the trees. There was still fighting nearby.

The pair headed up the hill into the thick woods. Breyier snorted as he carefully climbed the damp hillside.

They rode towards the smoke and Bear was surprised by Churlars running at him. They didn't seem to notice Bear at all. Some of them didn't have weapons anymore and only their red leather identified them as they ran past the giant grey horse.

They hit the road and ran for Cromere.

Bear let them go as he cautiously moved forward. He passed dead church soldiers, some with arrows sticking out of them. A few were wounded and trying to crawl away.

Breyier reached the point the flash had been set off and paused. A burn mark on the ground, but except for the dead, there was no one else there.

Bear lifted his visor. "Thervan! T'az!"

"We're over here!" he heard off to his left.

Bear let Breyier pick his own way over the dead and down the hill again. The horse knew better than he how to do it safely. They moved past the last of the dead before Bear saw the other two leading T'az' horse.

"Sorry, I jumped off and into the fight. We had to catch my horse," T'az smiled at him. She saw him looking her over. "None of the blood is mine."

T'az began searching the enemy dead and wounded.

Bear saw the blood running down Thervan's face, "How about you brother?"

"Nicked, but nothing serious," Thervan said. "I think they may have known I was here. I barely got the signal lit before they were on me."

"Good thing you did. Better a fight out here than amongst the pack horses," Bear sighed with relief. "We'll get you patched up."

"I'm good." Thervan looked Bear in the eyes. "Thanks, it was getting busy here." He untied his horse and headed for the road and Bear followed him.

Verig waited for them on the road.

"Did we lose anybody?" he asked cheerfully.

"No," Bear said.

T'az came out of the forest after collecting as many arrows as she could find. She handed them to Thervan and showed them the books and papers she'd found.

"I think one of them was a mage," she said as she turned the book over. "We'll see what Hestal has to say about these."

Verig's cheer seemed to vanish. Verig muttered, "adequate."

"Adequate?" Bear asked him. "Three on twenty or more?"

"Don't get a big head, boy." Verig turned his horse and galloped back down the road.

"Don't listen to him," Thervan said as they all followed at a canter. "Even if it does get worse. I think we did alright, particularly since I was caught by surprise."

"Might have been the mage," T'az said. "I don't really know what they are capable of."

"Yeah. I have no idea," Bear said removing his helmet. "How'd he die?"

"Thervan popped him right between the eyes," T'az said.

"That's one way of keeping them quiet," Bear laughed.

"I wish I could say I did it on purpose," Thervan admitted. "I shot a dozen or so times at the group and then retreated into the trees."

"Still, well done," T'az said. "And now we know more than we did before."

Verig was waiting at the side of the road. "They went this way. They'll stay on this heading until we link back up. So quit congratulating yourselves on your luck and get back with the others."

"Yes sir!" Bear saluted him as he turned to follow the trail.

The fighters quickly caught up to the group. Bear went right to the front. Which, of course, was where Kate was. Having her in the lead didn't make a lot of sense to Bear, but he wasn't going to start telling her what to do.

Kate eyed them all. "Was there fighting?"

"Yes," Bear replied. "They'd surprised Thervan like they knew he was there. They may have had a mage to help them."

T'az rode up to the front.

"Hestal's looking over the stuff I found," T'az said simply. "It makes sense though. There were also four knights and bunch of Churlars."

"They weren't knights," Bear said dismissively.

"Really? They looked like knights," T'az said. "About a dozen or so Churlars hoofed it once we reinforced Thervan."

"I guess it was necessary, but I hate these stupid fights," Kate said bitterly.

'I think it's important that they know we shouldn't be followed," Bear said. "We can't race to the Wall and fight our way over it."

"We shouldn't be fighting at all," Kate said. "It's ridiculous that we are fighting for the opportunity to face these horrible mages - a fight that may very well kill all of us. It's just dumb."

"Well, you put it that way...," Bear conceded.

Bear knew Kate was against any fighting. The team wasn't starting these fights and as long as someone wanted to stop them, there would be fighting.

Kate was the right choice as far as he was concerned—a good leader. He wouldn't follow Leoshus to the gallows.

T'az was still telling the rest of the group that the four he faced on the road were knights. If those four were what it was like to face the other orders of knights, the other orders were in trouble.

Bear remembered Verig mocking him.

Don't let your ego run away with you, he told himself. Spending a dozen years in daily training with the weapons master was probably the difference. That man had trained him well.

Breyier was well trained too. Bear took off his gauntlets and rubbed Breyier's neck. He silently thanked his horse.

"Is Thervan hurt bad?" Kate asked him.

"No, it's just a nick." Bear glanced back at his brother. "I wish father had seen that fight."

"Why?" Kate asked.

"Father is like Leoshus - formal and stiff. Fights in their world are all formal," Bear explained. "I wish he'd seen Thervan in just his mail holding that hill. We killed a few, but Thervan did most of it on his own with only a slim hope we'd come in time."

"Would your father have been impressed?" Kate asked.

Bear shook his head. "No, probably not. I am though. I'm glad I brought him."

Verig pushed them hard, growling, and cursing all the time. The group pushed on and didn't stop until well after dark. Fortunately, the weather was getting warmer and the days longer.

Four days after the battle, they finally reached the road west of Cromere. Bear turned on to it with relief. Breyier would be able to shake the mud off and they could start making up lost time.

That night they found a dry place to camp. Bear took the middle watch and tried to sleep right after dinner, but Kate was asking Hestal about the books they found at the ambush and Bear listened.

"Are you getting anything from those?" Kate asked about the books.

"They're spell books," Hestal said. "I've never seen a lot of these spells. I'm only a senior apprentice, remember?"

He pulled out one of the parchments. "This appears to be some kind of location spell. That explains how they knew Thervan was there."

"I don't really know what to say about this," Kate said hesitantly. "What's it mean?"

"It means that Thervan shot a Master or Grand Master Mage between the eyes," Hestal shrugged. "Good thing too. I wouldn't have been able to do much against him."

"Would the Mage Guild be arrayed against us?" Kate asked with concern in her voice.

"I don't see how or why," Hestal replied. "I suspect they were paid, nothing more."

"That's a relief. The rest of us have no idea what magic can do," Kate admitted. "Can you use these?"

"I'm not supposed to, but yes I can," Hestal seemed eager. "Although it will take some practice."

"When does a senior apprentice become a mage?" Kate asked.

Hestal snorted. "Only once his teacher is done with and replaced his services. Which can mean never."

"That's awful. So you don't have a spell book?" She asked.

"Yes," he looked embarrassed. "They gave me a few spells the night before we left, but nothing like this. This would have been more useful."

Bear was shocked.

"You want to ask what I was going to be able to do for you," Hestal smiled the thin smile that meant he was upset. "I don't think I was supposed to do anything for you. I'm beginning to think I was a sacrifice."

"I'm sorry," Kate said. "I didn't want to offend you and they didn't know about the Black Mages at that time."

"I'm pretty sure they did." Hestal set to eating but he never stopped reading the books.

Kate left him to read. Bear laid back on the ground and stared at the deep reds of the sunset and fell asleep.

Foester woke him for his watch. They both quietly walked out of camp to the rock they were using as a watch station.

"You heard what Hestal said?" Bear asked the older man.

"Yep," Foester smiled in the moonlight. "Kind of seems like the team was made of cast offs."

"Yeah, they were wrong though." Bear settled in.

"The way Hestal's studying, he'll be the master soon," Foester said. "And Bernard isn't the useless lump he looked like when we met him."

"And," Bear interjected. "T'az and Thervan have both proven better than anyone expected."

"Don't forget Kate either." Foester turned around. "She'll be handy in tight spot."

"Get some sleep, Foester," Bear said. "We should be able to see the Wall tomorrow."

The sun rose and Verig appeared again out of the trees. No one asked him where he went, but every morning he looked the same. He really irritated Bear. Verig acted superior to the others and treated everyone like dirt. When he spoke it was almost always followed with an insult.

Kate told him to wait. Everyone was getting up slow and it was nice not to be rushed for once.

"Need I remind you...," he started to say.

Kate cut him off.

"No you don't. The mysterious time table you won't tell me about," she spat back at him. "We can make up a few hours lost by using the roads to the Wall."

"Roads," Verig chuckled. "You won't be so fond of them soon and after that it'll be nothing but animal trails."

"Great, go ahead, we'll be along soon." Kate was still determined.

"You…" Verig started, but Kate cut him off again.

"Enough Verig," she said sharply. "You don't like us. I got it. You think we don't know anything. You're right. I don't even know how we'll eat now that we've left everything I know. I don't care. We are still going."

That pleased Bear. Everyone had treated Verig with kid gloves or ignored him altogether. Kate had backed him up, but he didn't bend.

"We need you, Verig. Tell us where we are going, or at least tell us the time table," she pleaded. "It will be easier for us to comply with your directions."

Verig finally bent to her will.

"Summer Solstice. We have to be in and ready to get out by that night," Verig said darkly. "It's the only day they are all distracted. After that there'll be Black Mages and worse all over us like fleas. We all die at that point."

Bear didn't think Verig was planning on dying. It almost felt like he was leading them into a trap. There was something completely wrong about his participation.

"What day is it?" Kate asked.

Foester spoke up from behind them, "Planting day."

"That gives us just over six weeks," Verig said. "If you can keep a decent pace we can make it."

"Thank you Verig. We will," Kate smiled at him.

"We'll see," he spat and went to the back of the line of horses.

The roads were ruined and didn't help them speed up. It took two more days to reach the Wall. The sheer enormous size of the Wall impressed, disappearing in the distance in both directions.

Even though they were still miles away, it was easily visible in front of them as they faced the setting sun.

Bear had thought someone would have maintained the roads to the Wall. Verig, it turns out, was right. Bear was annoyed about how often Verig was right.

"Only gypsies use these roads," Verig smiled at Thervan who was looking for tracks. "No one follows you out here."

They made camp for the night near a little brook. Kate stood on the broken road and stared at the distant fortifications.

Bear walked up to her. "Know much about the Wall?"

"Not much," she said. "I know it was built a long time ago, after the rebellions against the Code. I know it was to protect us from the monsters and whatever else lives out in the wild."

"It was more like a myth to me. No one really talks about it," Bear said wistfully.

"Really?" Kate seemed surprised. "I had a book with all of these drawings of it and portraits of the men. A whole army stalwartly manning our defenses, way out here."

"Something's not right about it," Bear said. "You'd think we'd see a light or something."

"On the Wall?" Verig laughed. Bear hadn't heard him approach. "Nothing but gypsies out here."

Kate turned on him. "If no one but gypsies come this way, how do the soldiers on the Wall get supplied?"

Verig nearly collapsed with laughing. "Soldiers on the Wall? Not for hundreds of years missy. Nothing there but ghosts now."

"What?" Kate was shocked. "What protects us from the… from the… well… whatever is out there?"

Verig was still laughing. "What do you think is out there?"

"Monsters," Kate responded. "That's what the history says."

"You mean the 'official' history," he smiled evilly. "They leave a lot out. I'll tell you what protects your precious kingdom. Ignorance. That's it."

He cut a leg off the big bird Thervan was roasting over the fire. "If the other peoples had any idea, they'd take over this pathetic country."

"Other peoples?" Kate asked.

"God you are stupid," he sneered at her around hunks of meat. "You think the rest of the land in this world is uninhabited? I guess you do know about the pirate people you've outlawed out in the east sea."

"Is there a west sea?" asked Foester curiously.

"There is. Don't worry old man, we don't have to cross it." Verig was enjoying his triumph over them all. "This is like leading a horse bound circus of school girls."

"How many people?" Kate asked annoyed.

Verig raised his hands. "Thousands upon thousands. I don't know." Verig's eyes narrowed. "They don't like your pathetic gods. We'll avoid them."

He leaned in and pointed at her with his drum stick. "Some of them make tribute to the Black Mages you know. Those groups won't like our intentions."

"How do you avoid that many people?" Bear asked.

"You are the thickest one of the lot." Verig turned on him. "You think this country is big? It's tiny. There is a lot of land out there. A hundred times this little place."

"Well, that's not what we learn in school," Bear snarled. It wasn't his fault he didn't know.

Kate laughed at him. "It wouldn't have mattered. I've done almost nothing but school and I didn't know any of this."

"This next part is going to be fun!" Verig mocked the group and disappeared back into the trees.

There was a lot of discussion about this revelation, but Bear didn't take part. He had had middle watch last night, and he had last watch tonight. Thervan or Foester would be waking him in the small hours of the morning. He needed to get some sleep.

The night passed quietly. It was still pretty cool, even though it was spring now. They had slowly been climbing into the foothills of the mountains to reach the Wall.

Bear hugged his blanket around him. He spent most of his watch staring in the direction of the Wall. He willed a light to show, anything that would prove Verig wrong, but nothing happened.

Kate walked up to him after her morning ritual.

"It's hard to imagine that it's abandoned. It's so big. So much effort was expended to make it." She shook her head.

"It's like that up north too," Bear said. "They built all these watch towers on hilltops so they could have warning if we were being attacked." Bear kicked the dirt at his feet. "No one even goes out there anymore."

"Was that the boon you asked from the Duke?" Kate asked.

"Yes, it made my father angry. He didn't talk to me for six months," Bear admitted. "There are rumors that evil things have taken over those towers. I wonder if there is any truth in Verig's talk of ghosts on the wall?"

"I doubt it," Kate said confidently. "I think he just likes keeping us afraid."

"It's because you aren't afraid enough. Either of you." Verig was right behind them.

"Are you afraid Verig?" Kate was nonplussed by his sudden appearances.

Verig turned his head to her. "I'm not scared. I'm smart." Verig spat at the Wall and walked away.

"I hate it when he does that," Bear snarled.

"Does what?" Kate asked.

"How he pops in and insults everyone," Bear said.

"It is annoying," Kate agreed. "But we need him."

The group mounted and headed the last few miles to the Wall. Verig seemed surprised by their location once they actually reached the Wall. He halted them a short distance from the gate and went up to look.

Bear was in awe. The Wall stood at least fifty feet high and thirty feet thick. The gatehouse protruded from both sides, making the road through the Wall look like a tunnel. Most of the tunnel was dark, eerie even. A tunnel made of moss and crumbling stone.

The Wall ran as far as the eye could see north and south. The stairs to the top were worn from time and weather. Bear daydreamed about the men manning the Wall and running up all those stairs to their posts.

Verig came back. He looked disturbed and vented his frustration on his horse as he mounted.

"We go this way," Verig said turning them north.

Bear raised his hand. "There's a gate right here!"

"No!" Verig yelled. "That one's cursed. We go north to the next one. Nothing living passes through that gate!"

"Nothing?" Kate said peering into the darkness. "What could be in there?"

Thervan had gotten the closest. "There are no wagon ruts and no animal tracks. I say we do what he says."

No one else even got close to the gatehouse. They all turned north after Verig.

"Won't this hurt our time table?" Kate asked.

"Unlike the roads, everything on this side of the wall is fairly level and even," Verig snarled at her. "We're not losing any time by trying to die early. Go back and try it if you want."

"Why doesn't anyone talk about the Wall?" Kate pressed him. "What happened here?"

"Only the ghosts know and so far, they haven't shared anything with me." Verig trotted ahead, which meant he wanted to be alone.

Bear grunted in irritation. Verig was right again.

Behind the Wall lay about a hundred yards of cleared space, with a ditch between the clear space and the encroaching trees. The flat space was full of grass and weeds, but level as a parade ground, making travel easier.

Bear stared at the Wall all day. An impressive feat of engineering, it was constructed of large and heavy grey stones. Moving even a single stone would be difficult, and there were thousands upon thousands of them.

The whole thing felt solid. There were regular block houses that probably housed soldiers at one time. Everything was dark and empty now.

Bear itched to poke around and see if anything survived. There could be old swords or anything in those block houses. The fanciful idea faded quickly as the cool shadow of the Wall crept into his mind.

There was nothing inviting about it. It was hollow and eerily quiet. The Wall didn't want to be explored.

"This just makes my skin crawl," said Bernard.

"No kidding," T'az echoed. "It's like we're being watched."

The horses didn't seem to like it either. They were nervous and antsy. Breyier pulled to the right, towards the ditch, Bear kept turning his head to keep him in line.

Foester echoed their feelings. "I think the horses would run away if they had the chance."

It was probably why there were no wildlife tracks. Only Kate and Zhost seemed unconcerned. She stared at the wall all day and her horse acted like he was on parade - prancing at the front.

Bear got as close as Breyier would go and he looked and looked, but he only saw empty stone all day. There were moments that he thought he saw something, but whatever it was didn't survive his direct gaze and no amount of staring revealed it.

"Do you see the shadow people here?" T'az asked Kate.

"No. It's odd, there's nothing here," Kate replied.

Verig held them up. "The next gatehouse is fifteen miles ahead. We'll make camp in the forest. No one crosses the Wall at night."

He turned his horse towards the trees.

Bear thought he was fear mongering. It did feel odd, but there was nothing here. What troubled Bear was the part where Verig was always right.

They set up camp less than a mile from the Wall - well back into the trees. Everyone was hushed. It was an oppressive feeling, like the Wall was looming over you all the time.

Verig didn't wander off that night, and he helped gather a lot of wood. The unusualness of Verig helping or working added to the feeling of doom.

"We'll keep this fire burning high all night tonight," he said. "Nothing living will bother us this close to the Wall." Then he pulled out a blanket and curled up on the ground.

Bear worried about Verig's warning. What would harm them if it wasn't living?

CHAPTER 17

Kate woke up much later. Something had been shaking her shoulder, but no one was there. She tried to go back to sleep until she heard a voice say, "get up."

She had been dreaming of the gray man again. He challenged her every belief and it frustrated her. No matter how wrong he was, Kate couldn't answer him in the dream.

Kate sat up and looked around, but no one was near her. It had to be close to her shift for watch. The night air was chilly, but the team had maintained the blaze burning behind her. Kate pulled her boots on and tightened her robe around her.

She moved over to the fire to warm up.

"You're not supposed to be up yet," Bernard whispered. "Well, not quite yet."

"I know, but something really wanted me up," Kate sniffed. "Anything happening?"

"Not really. Except for that creepy wall staring at us." Bernard shivered. "I swear I hear things over there. Hestal thinks it's my imagination."

There was a sound like a hollow scream back towards the Wall. Kate and Bernard both turned to look that way. The scream took several minutes to die into silence

Hestal, who had stepped out of the trees, stopped in his tracks.

"Now I heard that one," Hestal said. "What do you think that was?"

"I don't know." Bernard turned back to the fire. "I think horrible things have happened on this Wall. There were armies out here. Does anybody know any stories about what happened to all the soldiers?"

"No," Hestal said quietly.

"I didn't even know there weren't soldiers on the Wall until yesterday," Kate said. It was like the shadows in Nordsvard. Something about it was different. "I'm going to take a look."

"What?" Bernard leapt to his feet. "No way we let you go over there."

"Oh come on," she whispered dismissively, "the dead can't hurt you."

At least nothing had actually hurt her yet. The shadows had only been filled with visions. Often unexplainable and terrible, but not dangerous.

Kate walked towards the Wall, following the little trail they had made moving back into the trees. Hestal hurried up behind her - snapping twigs and basically making a lot of noise.

"Bernard is waking T'az," he said.

"She'll be happier if she's kept informed," Kate said.

T'az was her partner for guard duty. She would need to be up soon anyway.

Kate stopped at the little ditch between the woods and the cleared area before the Wall. She looked in both directions. There was nothing to see, even in the moonlight. Nothing but empty stone.

There was a breeze blowing down the long open area and the grass and shrubs rustled as it passed.

Kate took a deep breath. She was a little scared, but there didn't seem to be anything to be afraid of. It was just a wall.

Kate crossed the ditch and everything changed. It was still night, the Wall was still a ruin, but she could see them. The soldiers who once stood the Wall were still there.

There were faint outlines of soldiers up on the Wall. Grey faces stared at her from the windows of the guard house in front of her. They all paused to look at the intruder in their midst.

There was no sound and Kate felt a chill trickle down her back.

Kate turned, but couldn't see Hestal anymore. There were no trees. It was like she had stepped into a different reality.

Wispy grey soldiers marched from the guard house towards her. They leveled their spears as they approached. Kate wondered what ghosts did with captives.

She raised her hands as they surrounded her.

"You got me," Kate said, but it didn't sound like her voice.

She felt the gentle poke of a spear in her back. They wanted her to go to the guard house.

"Okay," she said out loud. "You don't need the spears. I'll go."

One of them poked her again anyway, so she started walking. While they slowly walked towards the dark building, Kate tried to get a good look at the ghosts.

They were dead, or remembered themselves as dead.

She really didn't know why they would look so horrible. There were no eyes, just holes. Skin seemed to hang off of them. Skulls and other bones peaked out of tattered hair and tattered armor.

Kate knew she should be more afraid, but the glow of Mirsha was in her heart. This was important. Everything that had existed was still here. That also applied to the men of the Wall.

There were things happening along the Wall. She saw flimsy grey visions of men being burned along the cleared area. Something bad had happened here.

The visions cleared and faceless maniacs pulled intestines out of men tied to boards. Flames leapt back and forth through the buildings. A forest of men impaled on spears sprung up to her left.

Kate gagged at the horrible display and prayed to Mirsha for these spirits. They may be trapped here, forced to stay in this nightmare forever. Kate felt for them - nothing deserved to exist like this.

The ghosts stopped as she prayed and Kate stopped with them. It hadn't been a ritual, just a free form prayer asking for the grace and forgiveness of Mirsha, but she saw a spear pierce her from the back and felt nothing.

Kate had become immune.

The ghosts seemed quite upset about the turn of events. A large spirit stormed out of the guard house. Blacker than night, with grey and white tendrils reaching out towards her.

The face appeared to be screaming, but there was still no sound. Which was odd. No wind, no crickets - nothing here made any sound.

Then there was a noise. What she heard was a very loud "No!" from behind her. The voice was unrecognizable to Kate.

T'az was there, sword out, and eyes wild. Kate could hear her sword clanking on the spears. She kept praying and included T'az. The clanking stopped.

The screaming spirit advanced to Kate and he swung a black slice of darkness at her and she watched it happen. It was so unreal and silent as the terrible shard plunged down over her head.

Kate felt the black darkness of his sword cross her heart. It knocked her down and she fell on T'az. She didn't know why T'az was on the ground. It was very confusing.

The sword was coming back, Kate started to fear it. The shadow crossing her heart had been real. As it came down on her, Kate cringed.

The sword bounced off the second time. The spirit came unhinged and attacked her ferociously. He raised the sword and it started to glow red. T'az scrambled out from under Kate and got back on her feet, but Kate couldn't take her eyes off the glowing sword.

It didn't sweep back down. The spirit appeared frozen.

T'az had engaged the ghosts' spears as they tried to subdue the women. Bear ran past Kate as she stood, and attacked the screaming spirit.

Hestal appeared next to her and he was chanting, but it sounded like a crow squawking to Kate. Whatever Hestal was doing had kept the sword from touching her heart again.

Metal clanged on metal with a very hollow sound. The dark spirit's image had coalesced into armor and he drove Bear back.

Bear was over matched. He fought valiantly to keep the glowing black sword away, but step by step he was falling back.

This was a fight they couldn't win. Their enemy was already dead. Power buzzed in her head. This had to stop. Kate shook off Foester's hand- she hadn't seen him join the fight.

This was up to Kate. She had to intervene. This is why she was here. Even though she didn't know the ultimate purpose, she would bring the light of Mirsha, and through that light, Kate was bringing change.

The armored spirit had driven Bear to the ground and Kate stepped between them. She stared right into the black eyes and raised her hand.

"No," she said.

The ghost had no intention of being commanded, but his sword was immobile. The power in Kate's head was now physically palpable and it spread out from her hand to engulf the others.

Fighting stopped. The ghosts stopped.

"Everyone get back. Now," Kate ordered them.

Reluctantly Bear and T'az dropped behind her. Hestal was sweating.

"Hestal, stop whatever you are doing," Kate said and he did.

The spirits moved forward after Hestal's magic subsided. Kate held up her hand.

"No. I told you. Stay! I bring the power of the Goddess Mirsha." Every dead eye was on her. The godstone glowed brightly.

The ghosts on the Wall had turned to face her. Every window in the guardhouse was full. Even more were coming from other directions. A great host gathered around her.

"Kate, we have to go," T'az said in the odd way sound worked here.

"No. Get everyone back behind the ditch," she yelled at T'az, while she kept staring at the horrible spirit's face in front of her. It was angry. It was incensed. The tendrils reappeared and reached around her.

Kate took one glance to make sure her friends had reached safety and then turned back to the angry ghost. Kate could feel the feathery touch of the spirit's tendrils as they searched her for weakness.

"I don't know what happened to you," Kate said to the spirit. "I'm sorry, but you can't have us. We have greater purpose. We will pass the night in peace and we will cross the Wall tomorrow in peace. I'm sorry, but you will have to seek your revenge elsewhere."

The dark spirit howled loud enough Kate could hear it. The sound emanated from the ground below her - like it was coming out of a grave. She shuddered. She didn't want to cause them pain.

Kate turned away and walked to the ditch, assaulted with images of what had happened to these men as she walked. It was awful. It hurt her to see how the Guard of the Wall had ended.

As the story became clear, Kate felt they were justified in their hate.

Kate turned around at the ditch, tears streaming down her cheeks. These were echoes of real people. People who volunteered to be out here. Now they were murdered and their souls doomed to haunt the Wall forever.

Except for the screaming spirit, the rest just looked very sad.

"I am very sorry," Kate said and she jumped the ditch.

The world went back to normal. An owl hooted in the dark trees. Normal forest noises returned. The whole team was there.

Kate was crying, but managed to say. "Is everyone alright?"

"Yes," T'az replied.

"One day, you'll actually believe me," Verig said as he stood back in the trees. He turned and walked back to the fire.

"That was insane," Bear exhaled explosively. "I've never even heard stories about such things. Is that what you see all the time?"

Kate didn't get a chance to answer.

"What were you thinking?" T'az asked Kate. She had tears in her clothing, but where there should have been wounds, there were just white scars on her skin. They appeared to be slowly fading.

"Something woke me," Kate sobbed. "I think I was supposed to see that. I think it's going to be important."

"That's crazy," T'az shouted. "You keep walking off like that, you're going to get killed."

T'az was angry and scared. Kate took her hands. She looked with her sad eyes at T'az's wide and scared eyes. "I was supposed to see that. I don't know why."

"How can you know that?" T'az asked as she calmed. "You scared me to death. I couldn't really do anything." She turned to Bear. "How did you manage to engage the big one with the black sword?"

"I don't know." He was looking at his sword. There were nicks from the combat. "That was some fight though. Glad it didn't last very long."

"Let's get some rest. Nothing will bother us for the rest of the night," Kate said as she wiped her eyes.

She led the group back to the fire. Kate and T'az took a seat near the fire. It was still their watch.

Amazingly, everyone seemed to drop off into sleep. It was possible that Mirsha was intervening and Kate offered a quick prayer of thanks. She didn't think anyone was going to be able to sleep after what they'd seen.

"None of you should have followed me," Kate whispered to T'az. "I was the only one who had to see that."

"None of us are going to let you do this alone," T'az said. "Well, maybe Verig would, but the rest of us won't."

Kate smiled and turned to stare at the fire. She kept seeing the horrible story of death and torture repeated over and over. She was glad she didn't have to sleep.

T'az looked around and whispered to Kate. "I've never been so scared in my whole life."

"Me either," Kate admitted. "I think we are going to see more things like that at the Black Tower." She shook her head and looked back at the Wall. "Those spirits are trapped by awful events."

"What did you see?" T'az asked.

"I can't. I can't talk about it yet." Kate started to cry again. "They were all betrayed and murdered-just leave it at that."

"Okay," T'az said soothingly.

The rest of the night passed without incident.

When dawn neared, Kate decided to hold her morning prayers on the Wall. Kate packed her saddle bag and pulled out her ritual bag. Zhost followed her down the little trail to the ditch.

Kate kept a book of special rituals in her bag. She pulled it out and opened it to burials. It was the only thing she had to honor the dead.

Zhost was game and his ears perked forward as she mounted.

"Let's go to the guardhouse," she said and Zhost leapt forward and pranced across the parade ground.

Zhost poked his head in the empty doorway as Kate dismounted.

"Show off," Kate smiled at him and he whinnied.

Even though it was still dark, no spirits appeared. Kate pushed past Zhost and entered the building. She wandered the dark halls until she found the stairs and began the long climb to the top.

Out of breath, Kate exited onto the wall and looked east. The sun was just about to breech the horizon. She lit her candles and laid out her sacrifices of meat and bread.

Kate sang the death ritual with her eyes closed. The sun broke the horizon, and she could feel it on her face. Kate didn't rush, she did the entire ritual that she had learned in seminary. She followed it with an earnest prayer to Mirsha to grant these souls peace.

When she finished, the ritual still felt inadequate. Kate whispered quietly, "I'll do more, we all will. You deserve more."

Light spread out below her and Kate gasped. The wilds were in front of her as the land sloped away from the Wall. The forest was endless - from the mountains in the north, to as far as she could see south.

An amazing view.

Bear walked up to her. "This is incredible." He said as he crunched through the leaves, nests, and other debris on top of the wall.

"What brought you up here?" Kate was pleased he came.

Bear bowed his head. "I don't know. I thought I might honor my opponent. That was the toughest fight I've ever been in. I would have lost eventually if you hadn't put a stop to it."

Kate smiled at him. "Did you?"

"Yes," Bear sighed. "Feels inadequate." He echoed her thoughts without knowing it. "I hope he knows I respect him and that he's the better fighter."

"I think he knows," Kate smiled as she put her things away.

"Nice view." Bear looked around. "No one's seen this for hundreds of years."

"I know. It's beyond words. I never thought it would look like this, it's wild and powerful." Kate felt her world shrink again, just like it had in Pulu, with that vast unknown forest before her.

"And endless. I never knew the world was this big," Bear said. "Are you ready?"

Kate nodded.

He picked up her bag. "That's a lot of stairs."

The halls didn't feel so scary on the way down. They were still empty but light streamed in.

Her team was mounted and waiting.

"Can we leave now?" Verig asked without looking.

"Yes," Kate replied.

Verig led them at a quick walk to the north. Kate didn't need to look at the Wall today. She understood what scared the others and it just made her more determined to bring justice to these souls.

Kate whispered, "Your sacrifice won't be in vain," as they passed each guardhouse.

She didn't know when, but she knew it would happen. She was certain that their suffering wasn't forever.

The quick pace on the even ground meant that they really chewed up the miles. They reached the next gate just after midday. This gate had been used recently and Verig turned into it. The tension in the group rose at the entrance to the tunnel through the Wall.

Kate didn't share that feeling. She thought it was a momentous occasion. She could imagine the grand scene with the soldiers, the banners, the trumpets, and drums hailing their passage.

It felt good that possibly someone was acknowledging that they were leaving civilization.

"Thank you for your vigilance, I'll be back." Kate waved at the towering bastions above her.

Verig led them west from the Wall most of the day. Kate couldn't help looking back at it. Everything she knew was back there. In spite of the troubles and her doubts, that was home.

The forest around her felt ominous. It wasn't managed like the forests of her childhood. The undergrowth was thick, even under the tall trees. Birds fluttered overhead and the sound of breaking brush surrounded her.

The forest was alive.

"It's creepy dark in there," Bernard whispered. "I hope those sounds are only small animals watching us.."

Foester nodded. "I wouldn't be so sure. This is like the old forests of legend. It's alive and it doesn't have time for us. We're just passing through."

Very late in the day, Verig turned them northwest on an animal track that headed back into the trees, and towards the mountains.

Kate paused and looked back one last time. She thought she could make out the Wall in the distance.

"Homesick already?" Verig sneered at her.

"No." Kate lied. Dirty and scared, Kate nudged Zhost up the trail. All she could think about was her carved desk in the distant library. That life was gone, and Kate mourned it as the Wall disappeared from view.

CHAPTER 18

Bear walked next to Breyier. He did it several hours a day to give his horse a break from carrying his mass. Breyier seemed to appreciate it.

Bear asked his horse, "Who knew we'd be wandering in these foothills for a month?"

Breyier didn't answer.

Everything and everyone was worn down. Foester's skills were pushed to the limit caring for the horses' hooves and repairing their worn out boots. Bear felt tattered. He was covered in a layer of dust and he could smell the rust in his mail.

They had followed a series of trails that kept them in the hills.

At night Bear had seen lights down in the valleys, and during the day he'd seen land that looked plowed. Most of the trails had led eventually downhill, but Verig had always found another trail to take them back away from the lowlands.

Their supplies had not lasted and hunting was a full time occupation. Everyone except Verig and Kate took turns riding out to find food.

Foester walked up next to him, "Solstice is getting close if my calculations are correct. Can't be long now."

"That's good to hear," Bear chuckled. "But you said the same thing yesterday."

"Did I?" Foester chuckled. "Turns out I'm not that creative. Breyier looks in good shape."

"He is," Bear rubbed Breyier's neck. "He's just tired like the rest of us."

"Except Kate's horse." Foester nodded at Kate ahead of them. "Nothing gets it down."

"That's because he isn't carrying anything," Bear said. "We've all lost weight and she didn't start out with much.".

"Making fun of the priestess? Be wary of her stick," Bernard quipped loudly behind them.

Kate groaned in front of Bear. "That joke was old two weeks ago."

Bear smiled. Bernard was talking about the little doll creatures that had swarmed out of the ground. They carried something like a long needle to fight with. The needle might even have been deadly.

The group had been surprised at night by the swarm and Kate had defended herself from one of the porcelain white creatures with a stick.

It was a comical image. The little, foot high creature was so angry and so serious. To see the tiny non-violent priestess poking it with a stick every time it charged-still made him laugh.

"We've been attacked quite a bit," Foester said. "It adds to the weariness of it."

"So far," Bear sighed, "no casualties."

There had been injuries, but nothing Bernard or Kate couldn't handle.

Bear, Thervan, Foester, and T'az had met every challenge. Hestal had stepped in at key moments, and Bear liked having the magic on his side.

It was Brendan that had saved Kate from her doll attacker.

Verig was never involved in the fights. Wherever he went, he was absent for all the action. He continued to show up each day looking the same.

Bear was getting tired of it.

"I'm starting to dream about a life without Verig," Bear said quietly to Foester.

"You and everyone else," Foester whispered. "It seems like this is all planned, but I can't put my finger on how."

Bear watched Verig as he rode in front of the group. He refused to walk for his horse. Everything about him was suspicious, but Kate had warned Bear not to challenge the thief.

Verig stopped and looked back at them. "Why don't you mount? Hasn't it been an hour yet?"

"Relax Verig, are we late?" Kate asked him.

"No," Verig responded. "Maybe."

Bear just shook his head. They had ridden over a month into the wild on the word of that annoying man.

At least he'd seemed excited to see the trail they were on now. It led into the hills after a week of dusty and dry plains. Bear was looking forward to cooler temperatures and the shade of the forest ahead.

They had crossed a road two days past the Wall, but Verig had shot down all of Bear's attempts to investigate it. Mostly because Bear couldn't justify why he needed to follow that road.

Bear never stopped thinking about it. There was something up that road and it was important. Verig said it was only an abandoned and haunted city from the days of the Empire.

Whatever it was captured his imagination and Bear dreamed about what might be up that road.

Thervan rode up. "Brendan got two deer."

"Deer?" Bernard said hopefully.

"Yes, the hills ahead are full of wildlife," Thervan replied. "Fresh meat."

Foester dropped back to congratulate his son.

Bear saw Kate and T'az mounting. He pulled Breyier's head over.

"Are you ready for more, buddy?" Bear asked.

Breyier nudged him with his nose. Bear took that as a yes and mounted.

"How long?" Kate asked Verig.

"How long... how long..," he mocked her voice. "Just suck it up, priestess. You're almost there."

As they climbed into the hills, Bear looked back over the dusty plain. There appeared to be a well fashioned road farther out. It was more evidence that there was civilization here and Verig was avoiding it.

Bear didn't know why.

Kate was watching him, so Bear pointed the road out to her.

"Why aren't we using the road?" she asked Verig.

"Roads! Roads! When are you going to give up your infatuation with roads?" Verig snarled. "You don't know what's out there, and up here, no one knows you're here."

"We've run into plenty of things," Kate said to him. "Are you saying we'd see more?"

"No, I'm saying this is the best way," Verig snarled. "Do it or don't."

Kate shrugged as she looked at Bear.

Verig led them from one ridge to the next. Each ridge was successively lower. Until they stopped to camp on a rocky promontory above a river.

Even though the light wasn't right, Bear was sure there was a road along the river too. There were a lot of people out here. Roads built by the Emperor would be three thousand years old and Bear doubted they would be that recognizable.

"Why are we stopping early?" Bear asked Verig.

"Change of direction," was all Verig said before he disappeared into the trees.

Bear shook his head.

"Ignore him. Let's get cleaned up," T'az said.

A pool above the small waterfall that drained down into the darkened valley to the north was the perfect place to wash off a month of weary travel.

They bathed in the pool in shifts. Bear took off his armor with relief. He hadn't had it completely off for weeks and it stank.

Bear gratefully dipped himself in the cold pool. The water removed the dust and weeks of weariness. His muscles relaxed as the cold water washed over him, the knots in his neck released, and the fire in his thighs was quenched.

The group took advantage of the time to clean their clothes and gear. It had been more than a week since they could use water so extravagantly. The dry plain was gratefully behind them.

Bear hung his wet underthings on a shrub. Even with the dying light, there was a good breeze. It would be pretty dry when he had to put it back on.

T'az and Kate were cleaning their clothes at the far end and they wore almost nothing. Bear stared at the scars on T'az' back for a moment.

When Bear turned away, Thervan was standing there.

"Good thing we didn't bring any proper women," Thervan whispered.

"Not proper women?" Bear whispered back harshly.

Thervan held up a hand. "Wait, I meant women like we were raised with. These are a different type of woman."

"Yeah, I guess you may be right about that." Bear glanced back down at the ladies' end of the pool.

"T'az doesn't seem to mind," Thervan chuckled.

"What does that mean?" Thervan was making him mad. "She's a fighter not a whore."

"Whoa there brother." Thervan held his hand up again. "I'm not questioning her morality. Can you imagine mother stripping and getting into that pool?"

Anger drained out of Bear and he chuckled. "No. You're right. We would have all died first."

Thervan was right, but their mother would never be this far from comfort. These were different women. He was raised to want the other kind, but, in spite of his mother's efforts, Bear had never met a girl he liked.

He was undeniably attracted to T'az. She could melt him like butter with her smile. Bear not only didn't mind, it was an idea he really liked.

"I think I like this kind of woman better," Bear said.

To distract himself, Bear picked up his stinking armor and started cleaning it. Thervan pulled out his mail and joined in. Foester brought out the wire brushes and oil and soon the stink was gone. Bear's armor only smelled like oil.

"Just like it is supposed to," Bear said as he sniffed it.

Bear was the last one dressed, and Hestal and Bernard joined him at the pool while he got his gear on. Hestal got naked and jumped in, but Bernard went in fully clothed.

Bear smiled as Bernard resurfaced. "It's easier to clean if you take it off."

"I'm hoping it shrinks to fit," Bernard laughed. He had lost more weight than anyone. His clothes hung off of him.

Bear laughed. "I hope it works. We'll have supper on the fire when you finish."

"Mmmm. Venison." Bernard laid back and floated with his eyes closed.

Bear walked back up to camp. It was a clear evening and he looked west following the river with his eye. For a moment, there was a black thorn rising up out of the plain.

When he blinked it was gone.

Bear checked his shield and then sharpened and polished his sword. These were his rituals, as important as Kate's prayers.

It also passed the time, so he worked harder and sharpened the sword again.

There was a crack back in the trees. It was followed by another. Bear turned to the noise but didn't see anything. He could hear an odd noise, like chainmail rubbing on leather.

Bear still had his sword out and he grabbed his shield.

"To arms!" Bear yelled and large, bull headed creatures charged into camp bellowing a deafening challenge.

Bear leapt at the leader to blunt their charge.

These new creatures stood a head taller than Bear and were heavier. Their armor was a mix of leather and patches of chain and they carried large axes.

Bear deflected the leader's ax with his shield. The creature rotated as he swung the big ax through to attack again. Bear was quicker and stabbed his sword through the exposed armpit of the creature's armor. It was a mortal blow.

There was no time to think, he spun back to his left in time to catch another ax on his shield. The creature bore down on his shield and it was strong.

Bear didn't back up. He stepped into and under the blow. Using his legs he pushed up hard and stabbed the exposed groin of the second bull creature.

"T'az!" Kate yelled over the screaming and bellowing around him.

A third creature stepped up as the second stumbled away holding his groin. Bear didn't have time for Kate's scream.

He dodged right as the third ax missed his shield, and spinning back to his left-chopped at the beast's arm. Blood spewed from the deep gash and the unarmored creature dropped its ax.

Bear turned and slashed downward with all of his weight. That blow tore the beast open from right shoulder to left hip. It bellowed as it fell.

The scream seemed very human to Bear.

The beast rolled to the side trying to keep its innards inside, but it was bleeding to death. Bear thrust once to finish it, and ended the beast's pain.

The beast Bear had stabbed in the groin hobbled into the trees and was no longer a threat.

Bear spun around, finding no more attackers, Bear looked over his team.

Bernard worked on a wounded Foester next to another grievously wounded beast. Thervan was standing over a fifth dead creature on the far side of the fire.

Kate was holding a bloody T'az, while Hestal and Brendan stood by the fire.

Bear started moving in slow motion. T'az couldn't be dead. Not T'az.

Kate was panicking and she was hiccupping as she cried. Tears streamed down her face and her hands didn't seem to have purpose. They moved from T'az's face to her wound and back furtively.

Bear looked at T'az. She was still alive. Her armor was crushed on her right side. Blood frothed at her mouth. Bear had an awful sinking feeling, people didn't survive wounds like that. She would bleed out or choke to death on her own blood.

"Heal her Kate. She's still alive," Bear shouted.

Kate gulped air. "It's all my fault."

Brendan yelled. "More behind us!"

Six more enemy charged up from the stream. It was up to him to engage them, but it was as if he was stuck in the mud. He couldn't move fast enough. He wanted Kate to heal T'az, but he couldn't let the new threat approach. His heart was frozen in place.

A flash and a loud bang broke Bear's indecision. The beasts disappeared in a ball of flame. The front ones died instantly, but the ones in the back thrashed and crawled for a full minute before becoming still.

Bear's shocked mind watched them burn as he blinked to clear the flash from his eyes.

The journey had gone from perfect to catastrophic in only the space between two breaths. The sounds of the forest returned as the flames died.

"Hey!" Bernard yelled. "This one isn't dead. Kate, you can save him!"

"No," Kate said as she continued to hold T'az.

Bear knelt and T'az looked at him. "Don't die," Bear whispered.

He could see T'az' lips moving.

Foester put his hand on Kate's shoulder. "She's saying 'calm down'."

T'az nodded and tried to smile.

Kate calmed like she'd been given a tonic. Her hand glowed and right before his eyes, T'az' blood stopped flowing. Her color became less ashy, and she tried to take a deep breath but winced.

"Get her armor off, it's dented," Bear yelled as he frantically felt for the buckles of her armor.

Bear worked feverishly to unhook the tiny buckles with his big hands. T'az' armor was only metal plates sewn into leather, but it bent away from her body with each buckle undone.

"That's done it," Foester said, "thank the Gods, I thought we lost you T'az."

T'az coughed, "Thanks. I think I'll lay here for a minute."

There was more coughing behind the group and when Bear looked, the creature next to Bernard was sitting up.

"What did you do?" Bear asked Bernard.

"I healed it. It worked," Bernard said, "I've never done that before. I prayed to Gaia. I put my hand on him and he healed. It's a miracle!"

Bear moved over to the coughing beast and covered it with his bloody sword.

The beast coughed again and opened its eyes.

"Oh dear," Bernard said. "I didn't think about that."

"How did you heal me?" The beast said in a croaking voice.

"You speak our language?" Bernard was shocked.

"Yes," the beast replied. "How did you heal me?"

"I'm a healer. It's what I do," Bernard shrugged. "It seemed like the right thing."

Thervan walked over. "Why did you heal it? It nearly got Foester and T'az."

Bernard shrugged again. "I don't know."

The beast raised its hands as Thervan and Bear pointed their swords at it.

"No more," it said as its voice grew stronger.

Kate angrily charged it, "Why did you attack us?"

Before the beast could answer, Verig returned.

"Yes! Finally," he shouted as he walked up to Hestal.

Hestal was in shock at his own success. "It worked. That was the first spell I tried out of the master's book."

"Really?" Verig snarled. "Go down there and practice some more of them and stop being the book keeper and start acting like a mage."

Verig joined the rest of the group. "Drorsis' ear! Always telling people the obvious, it's a curse."

The beast nodded at Verig. "That one said you were here to burn our village. I now suspect subterfuge."

"What?" Bear was angry and confused now. "Verig?"

"Yes, that one there," he said pointing at Verig.

Recognition crossed Kate's face. She turned on Verig.

"Anything you want to say to that, Verig?" Kate asked angrily.

Verig smiled. "No. Did I prod these beasts into attacking you? Sure. Did I rile up the wild men? Did I put our camp on the doll creatures' burial ground? Did I pay a master magician to attack us? Yes, I did all of those things."

"T'az could have died!" Kate yelled at him.

"So what?" he spat back. "We go to the Black Tower! I'm not walking into death without knowing if you can handle it."

Hestal stepped into the light. "You hired the Master?"

"Yes, I've already admitted it," Verig growled at Hestal. "You weren't worth taking anywhere. I thought it would be a good challenge to test you, but the damn ranger shot him dead."

Verig moved to stay on the edge of the light. "Waste of good money, at least you got the books, now go practice."

"Verig," Kate seemed confused. "Why would you do that? All of these people didn't have to die."

"They did. I told you why. You want to go into hell and you want me to lead you." He spat in the fire. "You think you're going to face rainbows and sunshine?"

"But," Kate started.

"No buts! No questions. You wanted to pass and do what your goddess told you to do." Verig turned on her. "Fine, you passed. Let's wrap this up. It's not far now, you'll actually see it in the morning."

With that, he walked out of the fire light.

Lightning crackled over the edge of the ridge where Hestal practiced. The rest stood there stunned. Bear recovered first.

He turned to the beast on the ground. "I'm sorry. We didn't know he was doing that. We weren't going to attack your village."

"You've won," the beast said, "I am your prisoner. Answer this before you kill me - why are you off the road, if not to attack us?"

"He told us that was the best way to get to the Tower," Bear replied.

"There's a road." The beast sat up. "Did no one question him?"

"Not really," Bear felt stupid. Of course Verig ran them around by the nose. "None of us has been beyond the Wall."

The beast looked shocked. "You're God Wailers? I didn't think they ever came west."

Kate walked up to the beast, even seated he was almost taller than she was. "God wailers?"

"That's what our lore calls the people east of the mountains." He shook his big head. "You have proved part of our lore. We warn our young, God Wailers are dangerous."

He looked sadly over his dead friends. "Please make my death quick. I don't want to burn."

"We aren't going to kill you," Bear said. "I wish we hadn't killed any of you. Bernard, there's another wounded one that way."

Bear pointed at the blood trail of the beast he had stabbed in the groin. "He might still be alive."

Bernard got up and Thervan went with him.

"It doesn't mean anything now, but, I'm sorry, we never should have fought," Bear said, he stuck out his hand and pulled the beast to his feet. "You are not a prisoner. My name is Berigral."

"Roark." The beast looked at Bear closely. "Berigral? As in the emperor?"

Bear shrugged, "I don't know about an emperor, I was told that I was named after a northern hero."

"Yes, the last emperor was named Berigral. It is a strong name," Roark said.

Kate, now just over waist high on Roark spoke, "Please tell your people how sorry we are. We were both deceived."

"Will you punish him?" Roark asked. "My elder will want to know. My people will want vengeance."

"I'm sorry. I need him. He's the only one who's been in the Black Tower," Kate apologized. "I can't complete my mission without him."

Roark nodded. "You go in the Black Tower? Then we will take comfort in that. You will all die there. Everyone does."

Roark paused to watch Thervan helping the other beast back to the fire. "The villagers will want to come and collect their families. Will they be allowed?"

"Yes. We will pack up now and move west," Kate said. "We cede this ground to you."

The group did as Kate directed. They packed quickly, leaving Roark and the other beast the fire. Thervan led them down the hill and around the next. Foester rebuilt the fire and guards were posted.

Kate made sure T'az was comfortable.

They could hear the mournful sounds of Roark's village collecting their dead and Bear felt bad about it. The silence was heavy around the new fire.

"I shouldn't have burned them," Hestal said.

"No, don't second guess yourself Hestal. You did the right thing. You may have saved all our lives," Kate said as she sat with him. "This was Verig's fault."

No one saw Verig the next morning and Bear was secretly happy, even if it was temporary. Kate on the other hand was worried.

"He's our guide." Kate fretted over breakfast. "Sure we can find the tower now, but how do we get in, get the tablets, and get out?"

There was no answer and there was no going back now. Verig had been right again. The morning sun revealed the black thorn. It stuck up out of the landscape in the distance, not far from the river.

"At least there's a road," Thervan said. "Shouldn't take more than two days to get there."

The group delayed leaving long enough for Foester to pound T'az' armor into something like it used to look. Bear inspected it and was disappointed.

"It's not great," he said.

"It's what I have," T'az said. "Not like we'll find better out here. Help me get it on."

"You feeling okay?" Bear asked as he held the armor up for her to climb into.

"Yeah," she said. "A little sore, but I'm fine. I just wanted you to dress me."

"I thought un-dressing is what you'd want," Bear replied hastily.

"Not a bad response." T'az smiled at him as she held his hand and boldly looked into his eyes. "If we live through this, we'll see about trying it that way."

Bear blushed as he helped T'az buckle the damaged armor over the dirty white shirt she always wore. She left him to watch her walk away to where Kate was waiting.

"Here put this on," Foester tossed Bear his helmet.

"Why?" Bear asked, he didn't see any danger.

Foester chuckled as he led his horse down to the road. "To cover the foolish grin on your face."

She likes me too. Bear thought to himself as he watched the rest of the group descend.

They rode the entire day without seeing Verig and camped by the river. The next day they followed the river all day and camped amongst the small and unnatural vine and shrub covered hillocks by the river.

The tower grew larger and larger each day. Its malevolent presence seemed to hush even the noises of nature. The river grew flatter and calmer the closer they got to the tower.

Verig's disappearance was a mystery. They had his horse and he couldn't travel as fast on foot. Bear didn't want to say it, but he felt Verig had abandoned them at the critical point.

"So now what?" Foester asked.

"We go on," Bear said. "I always figured he was a liar. It fits that he was a coward too."

"I don't know," Foester looked around in the rapidly gathering dark. "I don't think he's gone."

Bear left Foester to muse and walked up to Kate as she stared at the shadows.

"Are there ghosts in the shadows?" he asked.

Kate's gaze never left the shadows, "No. It's like the Wall, cold and empty."

To Bear's surprise, one of the shadows birthed Verig. His smile was as offensive as his insults to Bear, and Bear watched him carefully as he walked into the firelight.

"'Bout time you got here," Verig said sarcastically.

"Where have you been?" Kate asked him hotly.

"Scouting," he said nonchalantly.

"Scouting what?" Bear said. "We just had to follow the road."

"Congratulations," Verig mocked him. "Do you know where you are?"

When Bear didn't answer Verig continued. "You're in Karouk, the capitol city of the Empire. These humps aren't hills, they're ruins. Lots of places to hide here. Lots of creepy things. Can't you feel them?"

Kate shook her head, he hadn't changed. "Well what did you find?"

"Nothing. Like every other time I've been here," Verig said as he pulled some food out of the pile the others had gotten out for dinner. "To answer your other question, yes, tomorrow is the day."

There was one thing Kate wanted cleared up. "There were roads here. You had us ride in the hills so we could fight all those people and monsters."

"Yes," Verig said unapologetically around a bite of food. "The roads will make the trip home faster. As long as you don't piss off any of the tribes on the way."

"We could have been here weeks ago," Foester said. "With a lot less risk."

"What good would that have done old man?" Verig asked him. "You still would have waited until tomorrow and you'd have spent weeks in a place that most people and creatures avoid. I know the priestess can feel it. None of the rest of you can? Interesting."

Verig started walking away with his food.

"Where are you going?" Kate asked him.

"Scouting," Verig replied. "Tomorrow is the big day. Get some rest. Don't venture into the ruins."

And just like that, he was gone again.

"Val's Blood! He pisses me off," Bear exhaled. "This whole thing has been a joke to him."

"We now know he isn't telling us everything," Foester said.

"He hasn't said anything," Hestal replied. "Anything useful."

"There's more he isn't saying," Bear nodded. "I wish I knew what it was."

CHAPTER 19

Verig was there before dawn kicking people awake. He harried them until they had everything packed. They walked the horses away from the campsite into the vegetation covered ruins.

He led them through the hillocks for what felt like hours. Kate could see the light of dawn coming. She said a prayer silently, there would be no altar or candle this morning.

"Why are we hurrying?" Kate whispered.

"No one knows we're going to the tower by our bumbling actions so far. We want to be ready to enter before someone starts looking today," Verig hissed.

"Here! In here." Verig led them into the ruins of a big building. The roof was gone and the crumbled walls made a high ring around the central plaza. In the dim light, Kate could see frescos under the vines on the walls.

"We leave the horses here." Verig dropped his reins and walked towards the western wall of the building.

Foester stopped and handed his reins to Brendan. "Stay here with the horses, boy. If we aren't back by tonight, head home."

Brendan nodded and hugged his dad.

Zhost was upset to be left behind. Kate kissed his head and turned to follow Verig. He led them into what looked like a tunnel.

It really wasn't. It was just an ancient alley covered by ruins and vegetation making a dark tunnel with a rubble strewn floor.

T'az pushed past Kate to get behind Verig. Foester had spent hours getting her armor close to the same as it was before, but it wasn't. It never would be.

The sun was just peeking over the mountains behind them when they came out from under cover. There were less than a hundred yards from the tower.

It had an odd base. It almost seemed to grow out of the ground like a tree.

Kate could only stare up at the massive black thing. Nothing about the stone was natural and somewhere up above them were the mythical Black Mages.

"Don't touch anything!" Verig hissed at them as they sat amongst the humps of ancient runes. "Everything here is a trap."

The tower loomed over them. Hundreds of feet high and several hundred feet wide. They moved as a group to the rubble at the base of the tower and Verig disappeared again.

"If everything is a trap, how does anyone get in?" Bear asked.

Kate watched Bear check his armor. It was obvious he was nervous. Everyone else was too. Foester inventoried his supplies. Thervan thumbed his shield, he had left his bow behind.

Hestal may have been more nervous than anyone else. He was repeating something to himself over and over. Probably checking he could remember all of his spells.

T'az was as cool as ever, but Kate knew her better now, she was nervous too.

"Glad we didn't bring the plate," Foester said lightly.

Thervan snorted. "I didn't ever want to wear all of that metal again, but right now I think I'd find it comforting."

"You might, until you had to climb up to one of them windows. Besides you'd ring like a bell around all this rock," he said as he kicked one of the old broken building stones.

"I prefer to be comfortable," Bear said. "I don't miss the plate mail. It tires you quickly and there will be no tourney breaks today."

Verig came back around some rocks and Bear asked again. "If the whole thing is a trap how does anyone get in?"

"The wizards don't use doors, idiot," Verig sneered. "They do have to communicate with the outside world occasionally, so there are openings.

Those openings are heavily protected. The key is to pick the traps you can survive."

Verig was searching the walls carefully. "Now be quiet while I select our route."

He clambered up the rough walls to what looked like a window and carefully poked something under the sill. It was immediately followed by a howling scream that quickly died. Verig popped the window and poked a stick inside. He then slid in after the stick.

The whole group felt a little silly waiting below the window in broad daylight next to a giant black tower, but no one said anything. They just waited.

"What if he's already dead? How would we know?" Hestal asked as he nervously fingered the book that held the spells he'd been practicing.

Kate just shrugged. She was technically in charge of this quest, but she knew they were completely in Verig's hands.

Kate had to have Verig. No one had a clue what they would do if they couldn't get into the tower and no one knew where to go once inside. It didn't matter that he made her angry.

A rope lowered from the window and Verig's head popped out. "This is the way. If you want your tablets little girl, climb the rope into hell."

T'az beat Kate to the rope and swarmed up to the window. Bear followed her and the two of them helped the rest of the group in.

It was dark inside. Light didn't seem to penetrate the window, which didn't even really appear to exist on this side. The godstone glowed, making Kate a very dim torch, but it was enough to see around the room.

Bear and Foester had already moved to the doorway. Hestal and Bernard were catching their breath from the climb. Verig seemed to be listening to the spirit Kate knew stayed near him all the time.

The room itself was horrible. Nearly every surface in the room held stains of dried blood-very old-with areas of crusty pooled blood.

Someone had used this entry before, and made it no further.

Kate walked up to Verig, "What now?"

"Now we find the treasure room and then try and survive long enough to escape," Verig quipped.

He passed Bear and tested the doorway for traps. Not finding any, he stepped into the hall.

"Golems!" Verig yelled.

Two very large guardians lumbered into the room with axes and the team engaged. The sound of steel on steel rang loud in the small room - mixed with the thumps of hitting the Golems.

They were able to block the clumsy Golem swings, but the Golems were magical creatures and felt no pain. They had to change their tactics. Thervan and Bear got behind them and hacked at their thick necks until they were beheaded.

Bernard chuckled at the still moving heads. "Well, that was creepy, but not very hard."

"Don't get cocky boys and girls," Verig sneered.

Kate wondered how Verig could know so much about this place and who was he speaking to. He was getting direction from the spirit. It was the spirit that was leading them.

She decided to ask. "Verig how do you know so much about this place?"

He stopped searching the hallway. "I've told you, I've been here before. You'll see. No thief can resist treasure like they have here."

He pointed at the stained floors she was standing on. "Where do you think all the blood comes from? Thieves who aren't careful enough."

"Do the Black Mages deal with the thieves?" Kate asked, a little scared of the answer.

"No," Verig snarled angrily. "High and Mighty they are. Immortal, if you believe such things."

Verig turned away from her. "No, no mages will come. Maybe not 'til after we've got the tablets." He looked carefully around the next doorway. "The tower alone is more than enough to kill us."

"Cheery thing ta' say," Foester mumbled.

Verig led them carefully down a short hall that connected to a much bigger hallway. He paused to look at it.

"What kind of traps are you looking for?" Hestal asked.

"Anything," Verig carefully touched the wall in front of him and the wall disappeared. It was now an opening to a much larger hallway.

"There are rooms that will fill with water, floors that actually don't exist over pits of spikes, sliding blades, anything you can imagine really," Verig laughed. "The real question is: are they real or are you imagining your own death? No one knows the answer."

There was light in the bigger hall and doors at either end. The walls were lined with statues and art.

The wall closed behind Thervan and a quiet laughing started from the hall to their left. It rose in intensity until it throbbed in Kate's ears as they walked toward the door on the right.

The artwork was gorgeous and at the same time terrifying. There were pictures of people burning, pictures of naked people writhing with horrible creatures, it was hard for Kate to look at them, but she couldn't stop looking. Every time she looked away, the throbbing maniacal laughter got worse.

The figures in the pictures moved, like they were alive. Writhing and watching the group's progress. The figures wanted you to watch them.

"Stop looking at the pictures - just deal with the laughing," Verig hissed. "They'll capture your mind."

Verig hustled them towards the door. "Don't touch anything. It's not real. Keep your minds on your goal."

Verig led the way with T'az and Bear right behind him. Kate followed with Hestal, while Bernard stayed with Thervan and Foester at the back.

The more you didn't look at the paintings, the more they moved to get a watcher's attention. The laughing was quite hysterical. Kate started to wonder where it originated, she could find no source and covering her ears didn't help.

It was in her mind. Her mind was laughing and she couldn't turn it off.

Bernard started to giggle.

Verig touched the door.

The laughing stopped. Kate heard a voice say, "You're going to die in pain."

Everyone else must have heard it too because Bernard was white as a sheet and he staggered back into Thervan, who pushed him forward through the open door.

The next room was brightly lit, until Thervan closed the door behind them.

The lights went out. Only the soft glow of the godstone remained.

Something large thumped in the dark.

Kate held up the stone. "I need to see." The stone grew brighter.

The walls bled corpses. More and more poured out of the walls. The floor was beginning to fill with the stinking dead.

Soulless eyes followed them as they hurried to the next door.

"Run!" Yelled Verig. "Run to the door!"

The mass of dead shambled to their feet and started to pursue them.

They ran with the dead reaching after them and slammed through a doorway into a stairwell. Bear and Thervan held the door closed, while Foester pulled his farrier's hammer and nails out of his pack to spike the door shut.

The dead thumped on the other side.

Verig searched up the stairwell. Kate stayed next to T'az as the men worked to keep the door shut.

A cold breeze blew up from below and the stairwell smelled like the executions outside the prison in Theopolis. It was awful mixture of fear, sweat, blood, and excrement.

Kate tried to breathe through her mouth. She hated this smell.

Even though there was a glow in the stairwell, it was still hard to see how far down the stairs went. Kate could see doors below, but they were all closed.

Verig came back down the stairs. "Come on. This is just the beginning."

The next room was filled with torture machines. Great wheels and racks filled the room with cages and iron coffins. The bloody floor here was sticky like it had been used recently, but there were no footprints other than theirs in the blood.

Kate felt sad spirits all around. Tortured in the dark, they huddled in the corners. She didn't need shadows to tell her what was there anymore. Kate could see them and felt their sadness and terror.

The spirits weren't comforted by her presence. They wanted her to leave.

Verig led them to a door that didn't want to stay open. He held it as Kate entered. T'az followed her. Verig hissed at Bear to hold the door.

Kate stopped, she'd been in this room before.

Kate turned to her right and as she expected she could hear the shuffling feet of the dead. Unlike the vision in Nordsvard, this time she could smell them. They stood just beyond her glow.

"This is the room," Kate said to T'az. "The dead. When we were in Nordsvard." Kate pointed to the dark end of the room.

Bear was holding the door, so Thervan and Foester moved towards the shuffling dead, but they weren't aggressive and didn't fight back. They shuffled from side to side trying to get around the warriors.

Their dead eyes never left Kate. She was their goal.

T'az pointed at the far door. "But now there's only one choice. Let's get out the other door."

"No," Kate said. "The exit is here." Kate pointed at the center of the wall. This was the place T'az had pulled her through in her vision.

"How did you know that?" Verig walked up and eyed her suspiciously.

Kate shrugged. "I've been here before. In a vision."

Verig looked like he wanted to say something, but shrugged and pushed through the wall. The group crowded through behind him, leaving the shuffling dead behind.

The room they entered was brightly lit in a harsh, reddish yellow light. The center area on the far side was dark and the darkness surrounded a throne. The room reeked of sulfur.

Two long tables made a 'V' with the point towards the group. It was some kind of dining chamber and the tables were set for a large party.

Verig hesitated and seemed to confer with his spirit guide.

Kate looked around.

The ends of the tables held odd contraptions with long metal rods over a deep channel in the middle. There were leather cuffs bolted to the tops of the table.

"What are these for?" Bear asked as he poked one of the cuffs.

Verig grabbed his arm. "What did I tell you? Don't touch anything. I'll tell you when I want you to touch something."

"We have to touch the Tablets," Kate said.

"Fine, you're going to touch two things, but only when I tell you." Verig was staring at Bear. "Touch nothing else."

"But what is it for?" Bear pushed.

"Use your imagination, if you have one. Five cuffs per table. One at the end of the table opposite a large metal spike. Two for arms and two for legs. What do you think it's for?" Verig snapped.

"Ew," Hestal said.

"Yes. Ew," Verig mocked him as he looked around. "I've known people who've probably been on these tables. We've come too high."

"And they survived?" Bernard asked shocked.

"No, moron. They are the mangled corpses chasing us now. Stop thinking about it." Verig turned back to the way they came in. "We have to go back."

"Why?" Kate asked.

"We've come too high. This is where they eat. Do you really want to be in the living quarters of the Mages?" Verig whispered. "We skipped from level one to the top."

T'az asked. "Level one?"

Verig moved to the wall and listened to it. "Yes. What people fear - death, madness, torture, the undead. I think things are going to get difficult much quicker this time."

Kate waited while Verig listened. "Who sits on the throne?"

Verig hushed her. "I don't know. Demon lords maybe. We have to move faster. The tower is responding to us."

Kate moved close enough to hear Verig as he held an ear to the door. He was whispering.

"...I know what room we have to get to," Verig said barely audibly. "It's the only thing that will work."

"Who is she?" Kate whispered to him.

Verig jumped a little. "None of your business." He pushed on the door and led them back through the wall, but it wasn't filled with the same shuffling dead.

Two horribly scabrous beasts howled as they entered the room. Taller than Bear, with black hair and hollow eyes. Their exposed skin appeared green in the soft glow of the godstone.

Bear pushed past Verig and Kate - T'az and Thervan followed him in and the fighters went to work. The room filled with the sound of struggle.

The beasts howled, but their injuries healed quickly.

Foester knocked one down and Thervan beheaded it. Bear and T'az repeated the same trick and the sound died out.

"Looks like we have to behead everything," Thervan said.

Verig was checking the door. "You think you killed them? Check again."

Kate held the godstone up. Nubs of greenish flesh were oozing out of the severed necks and heads.

"They're growing," Kate warned.

Verig used an oddly shaped tool on the lock and opened the door he'd been checking. "In a few minutes, there will be four of them. Hurry! Back into this room."

They expected to reenter the torture chamber, but found themselves in a different room, too dark to see. A light fog floated waist high as far as the godstone glow would extend.

Kate was confused. "This should be a torture chamber. Where are we?"

"The tower changed," Verig warned as he hurried across the room.

Hestal pushed past Kate. "Something's coming."

Hestal was right. A gentle lullaby, sung by a beautiful voice emanated from the ceiling. Kate could see the spirit singing. She was gorgeous. The embrace of her song was cold, but strangely comforting.

Kate felt her eyelids get heavy and her fears eased. Bernard and Foester actually slumped to the floor.

Hestal said harsh words of magic and the fog cleared. Kate felt like she was waking from a wonderful dream. The lovely white spirit was right in front of her. Kate smiled at it.

The spirit's face turned angry, then opened her mouth and screamed. Kate grabbed her ears in pain. The warriors stumbled back from the sound and Hestal was driven to his knees.

The spirit reached for Hestal with ghostly white hands and a smile on her dark open mouth.

Kate had to stop her. She stepped in front of Hestal and prayed to Mirsha to remove this spirit. Light burst forth from her raised hand and the spirit recoiled.

The spirit seemed desperate as it tried to float to the ceiling, but a dark point, impossibly far away, pulled the spirit relentlessly back across the room. The spirit's face changed from angry to hurt, and then to fear.

The sound died as it continued to shrink and get farther away, until it was gone. Kate ended her prayer with a moment of gratitude.

The quiet of the now empty room tingled in their ears and lasted a moment, until the team got back on their feet.

Verig stood at a door. "If you're done fooling around, we go this way."

Kate kept staring at that distant point as the rest moved to the door Verig held open.

"What's wrong?" T'az asked her. Sweat was beading on T'az' brow.

"Nothing," Kate said. "I could feel her sadness and terror as she was exorcised. I thought they were trapped or forced to do this. She wanted to be whatever that was. I just don't understand."

"Thankfully," T'az said as she pushed Kate to the door. "I don't want to understand these people."

In the next room, they fought animated skeletons and in the room after that, armored animated skeletons. After all of that, they found themselves in the stairwell again.

Verig let out a great sigh, "At least we found the stairwell again."

Foester had moved down the stairs a short way. "What happened to our spikes? That door should be spiked."

"It's not the same," Verig said as he passed him. "Don't any of you get it yet? It's magic. The whole place is a maze. There is no direct path anywhere and the tower can change anything it wants."

"On a day full of scary things," Bernard sniffed. "That may be the scariest thing I've ever heard."

Kate walked next to Bernard as they followed Verig down the stairs. Bernard cried quietly.

"You won't be able to say you've never done anything interesting again." Kate smiled at him as she reminded him of their first meeting.

Hestal spoke up in front of them. "Hey, what's in the middle of the maze?"

"Cheese!" Thervan said and the group in front of Kate and Bernard laughed.

Bernard tried to chuckle with the rest, "I miss that Bernard. I'm so scared."

Kate touched his arm knowingly. "We're all scared." A small surge of power pushed down her arm as she comforted him and Bernard seemed to relax.

Bernard stepped in front of Kate and down the next flight of stairs. Kate went to follow but something cold touched her shoulder. Kate wanted to scream, but she was so very tired and without a sound-she drifted into the blackness of sleep.

The last thing she saw was the form of a grey man.

Kate woke up in a panic. She'd seen that grey figure before, but couldn't see it now. She was being dragged by two golems that seemed to be made of dirt. At least they smelled like dirt.

Each one of them had one of her arms. The glow of the godstone wasn't enough to show her much else. They drug her through a hall and as far as Kate could tell, there was no one else around.

The two giant things wouldn't let her get her feet under her and their grip tightened every time she moved.

Kate had been separated from the group. She had no idea what was happening to her friends. She thought about being scared for a moment, but couldn't raise it over her anger.

Kate was angry at herself. Everything she'd done to get here, everything they'd been through, and something snuck up behind her without a sound. Now she was a prisoner.

This was intolerable.

Kate prayed to Mirsha. She was not going to be tortured to death. She had killed the rapist in Chryselles and she'd caused the death of the man on the cliff.

Kate concentrated on their hands and willed them to break free. The normal buzzing in her head turned into a roar and there was a quick flash and two loud snaps.

Kate dropped to the ground.

"It worked," Kate said.

The golems weren't dead though. One of them reached down and grabbed her shirt with its unbroken arm.

Kate concentrated again as the thing's face grew closer. There was a great shove, like an invisible hand pushed them apart. Kate heard something rip and she fell to the floor again.

This time she was ready and ran for it.

Kate had only taken a couple of turns when she ran into the grey apparition. He was the ghost in her visions, with indistinct features and unruly white hair. He had black holes for eyes and he floated towards her.

"No more running, young lady," the apparition said in a hollow distant voice.

Kate sucked in her breath and turned to run, but only saw the floor coming up to meet her as the blackness returned.

When her eyes fluttered open again, she was in a darkened room. Braziers burned in the corners, casting an eerie faint orange glow over a cluttered room filled with unexplainable instruments and unmarked boxes.

Kate couldn't move. Her arms and legs were cuffed to a table. Her head was immobilized and her field of vision was limited and she prayed there wasn't a metal spike at the end of this table.

Her robe was gone, and she wasn't sure, but it felt like her shirt had been torn open. Kate struggled against her restraints.

A voice stopped her struggle.

"It's not possible. There are rules!" The voice was loud and commanding.

Kate twisted as far as she could to see across the room. The grey ghost from her vision was standing in front of a featureless and nearly transparent figure. That figure was too thin and too tall, but a crown floated above his nearly invisible head.

"It's not possible," the crowned figure snarled again. "She's no wizard, she's a priest."

"Yes, my lord," Grey spirit agreed hollowly.

"A priest with power!" the dark figure chortled. "Oh that is very good. That pathetic god is giving powers to priests again."

Grey thing seemed to nod. "It appears so." Then the grey thing held out its hand. "Also, she had this, it glowed."

Dark man looked at it. "What is it? There doesn't appear to be any magic in it. Get her to tell you."

"Yes, my lord," Grey thing answered.

"Get it done. Before tonight, I want everything back to normal before the ceremony. Nothing is more important." Dark man ordered and then faded, or left, Kate couldn't tell.

The apparition came over to the table. "I see you're awake again." His voice was deep and hollow, but his mouth-or the place a mouth should have been-never moved.

"I'm Gracar. Now tell me who you are and why you are here." Gracar said as he stood over her.

Kate didn't want to tell him anything, but he was so close and cold that Kate shivered and feared his touch.

"I'm Katelarin, Priestess of Mirsha, we are here-thieving," she said.

"Of course." The smile returned. "But what would a Priestess of Mirsha steal?"

Kate didn't answer. Gracar lowered his hand onto her chest and icy knives burned through her skin. She screamed from the pain.

"You don't like my touch?" Gracar moved around the table. "There was a time, long ago, when young ladies clamored for my touch. Some still do. I believe you met one already-you shouldn't have destroyed her. Beautiful spirit."

Kate coughed. Her throat was rough from the screaming. "Why? Why are you here? This is a choice. I saw it in the screaming woman's spirit."

"Power. Why else?" Gracar had stopped behind her head. "But here, I ask the questions." He placed his hands on her head and Kate screamed and the pain rose to an intolerable level. Kate passed out.

Kate woke up again, her lips parched and her eyes gummy. She could see there was more light in the room than there was before. Her shirt had been completely torn off and her pants were pulled down to her boots.

Strange designs marked her body and whatever they used was causing her skin to tingle.

Dark robed figures moved in and out of her view. Something was bubbling nearby and the odor was a foul combination of rotten eggs and fermented cabbage.

The smell burned her nostrils.

Gracar, his shape even less distinct in the increased light, floated over to her.

"You are awake again. So frail," he said as he slid a finger across her breasts.

Even his lightest touch hurt, but Kate stifled the scream. "I've seen you before in visions. I thought I was shown that to get knowledge from you. Now I know it was a warning that you're going to torture me."

"No. Torture is so mundane. It only works on people who fear death." Gracar moved his face close to Kate. "I don't sense that fear in you. I plan to give you life. Unending life. Then I can educate you."

"No!" Kate yelled at him. "I don't choose to be here. I'm not volunteering,"

Gracar moved away.

"Not all the spirits here are volunteers. Of course, the only ones with power are, and I educate them all." He floated back into her vision with one of the dark robed figures. "Either way, I think you'll be a wonderful addition to my collection."

"You're evil," Kate gasped.

"Evil? How is this any different than your life, your precious Code?" Gracar glided out of view. "Your people are the same as mine, but mine do not die. They enjoy endless purpose and you will too."

"What do you know of the Code?" Kate had to keep him talking, anything to postpone what was happening.

"I was there when it was written," Gracar said wistfully. "Those were the days. Priests with mystical powers were like gods."

"What happened?" Kate asked as she struggled with her bonds.

"The powerful were few at that time," Gracar drifted to the cauldron. "Did you know that in those days, no matter what name you used, it was always one god?"

"What are you talking about, there are seven gods?" Kate resisted the idea even though it rang true and confirmed her own doubts.

"I see a small part of you knows the truth," Gracar drifted back in to view. "It is so interesting to hear what has become of what we started."

Gracar made the black robed servant scoop up dark liquid. "The great Annais himself declared me a witch, when he decided to eliminate those few of us who could challenge him."

Gracar actually seemed sad. "Oh yes, I know all about the Code. It only came to be after the powerful lost their mystical abilities. Those weaklings justified their power with law."

"You lie. The gods dictated the Code," Kate spluttered. In her heart Kate knew he was right, but years of training refused to be released.

Gracar was unmoved. "Why would I lie? You'll find I only speak truth." Gracar brought the dark robed servant with its ladle full of smoking liquid to Kate.

The hot liquid poured out of the ladle on a moon drawn on her belly. It didn't splash, but raced across the interconnecting lines drawn on her skin. Kate's heart started beating very quickly until it felt like it would pound out of her chest.

"We have a few minutes, while that takes full effect. Then we can extract you from that body." Gracar was perfectly calm. "Tell me what this is, it glows when it's near you. Is it the source of your power? I would be greatly disappointed if it was."

Kate couldn't speak. Her heart was racing and her brain screamed as her strength started to fade. The field of her vision collapsed.

Kate stopped watching the writhing goo and tried to focus on resisting. She had to resist. To endlessly roam these horrible halls for eternity was too awful to contemplate.

Death was a better option, but what was left of her vision was going grey. She could feel life slipping from her arms and legs. For a moment she was staring down at her own face.

She saw her struggle from the outside. Being outside her body was so calm and pain free, but Kate dove back in. She had to resist.

"Of course," Gracar said in his hollow drone. "You don't have to tell me. Once I have your soul, and it won't be long now, I'll know everything you know."

The godstone glowed, and as he brought it closer to her it shone even brighter. Kate couldn't scream, she couldn't move. Her heart was fluttering and her limbs were numb.

Only the light of the godstone penetrated her pain. Light washed over her and the terror subsided. Death was better.

"Thank you, Holy Mirsha," Kate whispered through dry lips. Kate was sincerely grateful for the chance to die at peace.

Her heart slowed and she didn't die. The power built in her head and Kate willed it to push ghost and his servants away from her.

It didn't work. Gracar had power too and he resisted. Kate could feel the pressure building between them.

He flung the godstone far from her. "I see," he said. "I'll not make that mistake again."

It was too late. The terror was gone. Kate might die here, but her last act would be to cleanse this room in the name of Holy Mirsha.

She fed the thundering power in her head. It may be her last act, so she poured all of her will and emotion into it.

Gracar continued to resist the buildup of power with his own and his expression never changed. Suddenly, he held up his hand and disappeared. There was a noise like an explosion when he left and Mirsha's power swept through.

Shockwaves rattled the furniture and stacks of boxes fell. The servants evaporated, leaving their robes empty on the floor. The black liquid stopped moving on her skin and the tingling stopped.

Kate gasped. The love of her goddess comforted her as she lay calm and at peace. Feeling returned and with it the pain, but the power stayed and her whole body seemed to hum with it.

She could wiggle her fingers and toes again. It was a huge relief to feel the pain again. It meant she was alive.

Kate knew she had to get off the table. She had to get up. Gracar would be back.

The restraints were broken and Kate rolled off the table to the floor. The stone floor was gritty, dirty, and cold.

Kate grabbed an empty black robe and brushed the liquid off of her chest and face. In the brazier light, Kate could tell it had scarred her. She was branded with evil symbols.

Kate rubbed off everything she could see in the dim light and pulled her pants up. The leather pants were still in good shape. Her shirt, on the other hand, had been torn to shreds.

Kate made a cursory search for something to replace her shirt and to see if the godstone was still in the room. In one dusty old bin she found some moldy clothing that covered her nakedness, but little else.

In the corner, under an overturned brazier, Kate found the godstone. It was broken and she felt guilt at the loss of the gift. The little shards barely gave off a glimmer of light, but Kate collected them anyway.

Grief would have to wait. Her pack was gone. She had no food or water, no candles or ritual supplies, and no idea where she was.

Kate sighed as she leaned against the wall for a moment - her strength was coming back, but part of her life was gone. She'd had doubts, but the rituals had been integral to her life.

It was her love of ritual that had led her to the priesthood. She had studied so hard to master them all-even the obscure ones. Kate had performed thousands of rituals, and now they were gone.

Kate stood with new purpose. She hadn't needed rituals for a long time. She hadn't needed the Code. True or not, she had only needed one god.

Now here, alone in the dark, Kate knew what she needed to change. The freedom to die her way was a choice. Everyone deserved the right to choose for themselves. As she had.

Kate pushed away from the wall. "Nice. Now I know what to do and I can't do anything about it."

The only thing left to do was to escape through one of the doors. Kate opened them all, and they all had identical dark hallways on the other side. She was lost.

"Alright. One is as good as another," Kate said resolutely.

Kate lit her torn shirt in one of the braziers. She was weak physically, but she could still feel Mirsha's power and that drove her forward.

"Let's see what damage I can do by myself," Kate smiled as she stumbled down one of the hallways.

Kate would probably never see her friends again. She suddenly knew what Bear meant in Nordrigen as she forged down the first hallway. There were honorable ways to die. There were sacrifices that mattered.

CHAPTER 20

"Where's Kate?" T'az yelled.

"She was right there," Hestal said.

Bernard gulped. "She was right behind me."

Bear ran back up the stairs. "Where Bernard? Where?"

"Just back there, where we changed flights," Bernard pointed up a few steps.

Bear and T'az started pushing on the walls. For several minutes, they slowly worked their way back up the stairwell.

It was Bear who found it. With a gentle push and a light click a section of wall silently disappeared leaving an opening to a dark hallway.

Verig rushed back up to them. "That's not the way. That will get you nothing but an army of Black Mages."

"I don't care," T'az said. "This is nothing without her. You all get the Tablets, I'll get Kate."

Foester put a hand on her shoulder. "I don't think so T'az. We're all going. No one dies alone in this place." He pulled torches out of his pack and worked for a moment to get them lit.

Bear took one and headed into the new hallway.

Verig got in front of him. "Just keep the light up so I can see."

The group hurried behind Verig. These halls were made of the same black stone as everything else, but they were painfully uniform in size and shape.

Bernard spoke up. "These halls are different. There's no weird art or doors, or anything."

"And they don't seem to change or vibrate with magic like the rest of the place," Hestal said.

Verig didn't stop, but he responded. "I think this is like a very rich person's house. One set of halls for the rich and one set of boring functional halls for the servants."

"I guess it depends on who the servants are," Foester said from the back.

"Yeah, that's no joke," Thervan chimed in. "What serves the Black Mages?"

"Don't ask me, this side venture is going to cost us," Verig snarled. "I never investigated the servants' quarters. There's no money in it."

They came to a four way intersection. There were no markings or differences in any direction. Whomever used these halls didn't need any form of navigation.

There was a loud thunk down the left hallway and the group followed the noise.

As they explored forward, the hall reverberated with a loud scream, back the way they came. T'az ran back down the hall and everyone followed. In moments the whole group was back at the intersection they had just left.

"Which way?" T'az shouted.

"No way to tell." Verig pushed through and took his place at the front. He led them down a different hallway.

This hallway ended in a large round room that disappeared up into the darkness, and down deep below. It was cool and a breeze seemed to flow from the deep, up into the darkness.

Stones floated up and other unidentifiable objects floated down.

The torchlight didn't illuminate very much, but there were thick ropes running up and down the walls and strange statues lined the walkways around the room. Grey wispy shadows floated on the breeze.

"Lifts maybe?" Verig suggested. "But I don't get the statues."

Hestal pushed his way to the front and examined a statue.

"Golems," he declared.

Bear pushed the nearest one with his sword. It moved, but went right back to its original position. "Why don't they attack?"

Hestal shrugged. "I don't know. Golems are pretty simple magic. They probably have no orders to fight or defend."

"Great," T'az said. "Back up the hall - we take the other direction."

Down the final choice from the four-way intersection, they came to another intersection, and continued straight. Another scream rattled throught the hall and was followed by echoes.

The blank walls of this hallway ended in another blank intersection.

"This part of the tower doesn't have to move," Foester groaned. "Everything is exactly the same and it's actually worse."

There was a bang of an explosion farther down the right hallway, so the group followed that noise. At the next intersection they waited. Bear was hoping that another noise would signal which way to go.

"We have to try one of the directions," T'az whispered after several minutes. "We can't just sit here."

"You'd think there would be rooms," Hestal said.

"Probably are rooms," Verig snarled. "We just can't see the doors."

"Look!" Bernard whispered. "A light and it looks like it's coming this way."

"Put the torches over here and get ready," Bear said as they passed the torches to Verig.

Bear and Foester were on one corner of the four-way intersection and T'az was on the other with Thervan. They would ambush whatever came down the hall between them.

The light got stronger and stronger. They could hear the shuffling steps as the thing drew closer. Bear gripped his sword. He would make this quick.

Whatever it was stopped before the intersection. It was now or never.

Bear leapt around the corner and a bright flash of light blinded him. He was frozen in his tracks and he couldn't see. Fear filled him-to be immobile and in danger was his nightmare.

Bear's fear lifted when he heard, "Oh gods! Thank you Mirsha!" He unfroze and started blinking. As his vision cleared, T'az was wrapped around Kate.

Kate had found them on her own.

T'az pulled back. "What is on your neck and where did you get that shirt? It stinks." T'az pulled her finger back and there was some black liquid on it.

"Ugh! Get that off your hand. It's part of the ritual in which they pull your soul out." Kate quickly used the tail of her long shirt to wipe T'az's hand.

Kate quickly told them story in-between guzzling water from Foester's jug and nibbling on some jerky. Her torch had quickly burned out but Kate could make anything glow now.

She was now the bearer of a glowing ladle.

It was a good thing too, as the group's torches had burned out.

Verig interrupted. "Nice reunion and all, but we don't have time. We are now behind schedule, if you want this to happen we've got to hurry."

"I agree," Kate said. "That dark man Gracar called 'my lord' wants everything settled back to normal by tonight. Whatever they are doing is very important to them."

"Then let's go," Bear said taking the lead.

Foester had smartly marked the turns with the soot of his torch and it only took them a few minutes to get back to the stairwell.

Verig hurried them back down the stairs.

At Verig's insistence, the group strove to make up time. Room after room they struggled forward. The fighting was always brief, but each encounter had been a vicious and close quartered knife fight-usually in the dark or the dim light of the glowing ladle.

Verig finally called a halt.

The group seemed relieved by the break and everyone sat down in a little blank room with three doors.

Bear put down his sword and leaned against the wall. He needed a rest. He checked over his armor and was pleased to find it in good shape. He'd lost count of the skeletons and corpses he'd smashed.

He wanted to say killed, but they were already dead. He wasn't really sure what he was doing to them, except making them stop. Foester was breathing hard as he sat, the last fight had been fierce.

"I'm too old for this," he mumbled.

Bear was glad to hear his squire still had his sense of humor. "I've been telling you that for years."

Foester seemed to relax. "Knights. Always supportive."

T'az seemed tired, but she and Bernard kept watch. Bernard had done all he could to heal the wounds. Kate tried to use the rejuvenation prayer, but it wasn't physical ailment holding people down. It was the endless horror.

"How long have we been in here?" Bear whispered.

He could feel Foester shrug. "I don't know for sure. Best guess, six or seven hours. Must be late afternoon."

Bear nodded. "Wish I knew what compass Verig was following."

Verig kept leading them up and down, back and forth. He seemed confident now that they were out of the blank corridors. When they entered certain rooms, he was obviously relieved.

Kate had started to stay close to Verig, but Bear didn't know why.

"Are we getting close?" she asked the thief. "They know we're here."

"We've always been close and they've always known we're here. Nothing is what it seems," Verig responded. "We have to invade this place without looking like we are invading it."

Bear laughed at how illogical it all sounded.

Verig ignored Bear. "The harder you try and force your way in, the more force you meet. I've spent days moving from one room to another."

Bear wondered out loud. "If they know we're here will the Black Mages come down?"

"Don't even think about such things," Verig hissed. "Did you think I'm allowing you a break out of concern? I don't care how tired you are. We need the tower to think we're lost and weak. We need to be on ground of our choosing when they finally send someone."

"Where?" Kate asked.

"Not here," Verig snarled.

Bear ignored Verig and thought about the the mages. They were apparently far above them in the tower and preparing for some momentous event. It was a question, what they knew about Kate, but she said she'd never revealed their purpose, and Bear believed her.

"He's still lying about something," Foester said.

"I know." Bear gave a half smile. "Seems like the wrong time to call him out on it though. Could you get us back the way we came?"

"No," Foester said. "It's like being trapped in a moving prison."

"Except it's full of things that want to kill you. Or worse, capture you alive. You want to go through what Kate went through?" Bear leaned back against the wall again.

"They sure like torture," Foester said as he handed Bear the water jug. "I've never even heard of a place this full of death and hate. I've been thinking of all the stories I know, there is nothing to match this."

That actually made Bear feel better. "Sounds like a good job for a knight then."

"Yeah," Foester agreed. "Pick the hardest thing possible and expect a good outcome. That does sounds like a knight."

They could hear Thervan chuckling in the darkness nearby. Kate had moved to where Verig was and the dim glow of the ladle went with her. No one else said anything for a while. Finally, Verig got up and everyone else did too.

"Come on," Verig said as he worked the door in front of him.

Bear thought he heard Verig say "…I know; we have to do it to bring him." The door opened and a black mist filtered into the room from the open doorway, grabbing Bear's attention from Verig's mysterious conversation with the air around him.

The room beyond the door was pitch black. The darkness seemed velvety soft and suffocating. Kate's light didn't penetrate very far, so Bear poked his sword in front of him, trying to push the darkness back.

Verig grabbed him. "Get back. Back through the door."

A hissing voice said, "INTRUDERS."

The group slammed the door shut behind them and the whole team leaned against the heavy door as Foester hammered spikes into the floor to keep it from opening.

"What was that?" T'az asked.

Verig rubbed his chin. "They moved the dragon. That's not good news."

"Dragons!" Thervan exclaimed. "You're telling me that they have dragons."

"I thought dragons were myth," Bernard said. "No one's seen dragons."

"No one living anyway," Verig smiled. "Of course they have dragons, they can have whatever they want. That only leaves us one choice and it's probably a trap."

"Won't the dragon follow us?" Hestal asked.

"Stop asking questions and come on," Verig snarled. He put his hand on a new door. "When we go in this room, don't look around."

Verig had become sad as he continued. "The souls in this room are trapped. They won't harm us, but you'll feel them."

"Why?" Kate asked.

"What did I say about questions?" Verig snapped. "We have to get through this room quickly."

The whole group followed him in.

Lightning flashed at Bear and it was a near miss. Bear chopped down with his sword cutting a thing in robes covered in mystical designs in two.

Flame shot from behind him and two other robes burst into flames.

Bear was unprepared for what he saw in the light of the flames. He expected more enemies, but bodiless heads floated in clear crystal containers. Hundreds of them.

They all glowed a sickly green and every disembodied eye was watching them. Grey spirits hovered on the far side of the room. They seemed indecisive and reluctant to attack.

Bernard choked as he pointed at the heads. "They're alive."

"Only in the sickest form of the word," Verig stated flatly. "This is how you become a black mage. Capture a soul in its head and keep it for eternity."

He was trying to push the stunned group along. "This is what ambition gets you. Unending life. Ignore those grey things. Keep moving."

There was a spark of light when Verig touched Kate. He reeled back in pain-cursing.

"I'm not leaving them in this room," Kate said. "I know why I've come now. We will not ignore the trapped and defenseless. Mirsha will not have it."

Kate's light brightened as she raised her hands. The white light washed over the group and spread out across the room. The grey shapes in front of Bear fled.

The light was peaceful and calming. Bear was no longer sore. He didn't feel hungry. The light spread and touched each crystal container. As it did, the head inside fell still and the green light faded.

It only took a moment.

"What are you doing!" Verig yelled at Kate as he recovered from his shock. "They will not stand for this!"

"I don't care," Kate said. "I'm bringing the light of the gods to this place. Even if we are unsuccessful, these souls have suffered enough!"

Bear agreed. He didn't care if he died here. This was a death knights dreamed about. To rescue hundreds of trapped souls, facing evil on a scale he never imagined existed-this was why he wanted to be a knight. Not to fight tournaments or argue over money and inheritance.

Bear said a quiet prayer to Val. He thanked Val for this opportunity, no matter how it ended. This is where Bear was supposed to be.

Verig stomped angrily across the room and Bear followed him through the now still rows of dark crystal. Bear grew up wanting to be in a legendary story like the ones Foester mentioned, and now he was.

Verig grumbled, "so much for a perfect plan."

"Let them come," Bear replied and Thervan agreed.

"You're all crazy." Verig was exasperated. "This guarantees we don't all leave here alive."

"Then that's the way it is," Kate said. "It wouldn't be right to walk past this when something could be done. That is just as evil as what Gracar was doing to me."

"Well if you're done saving the world, we need to go out that door over there," Verig said as he stalked to the door.

Bear was ready when Verig opened the next door. Armored skeletons surged into the room from the far door. These did not have the cheap, flimsy armor they'd run into before. It glistened black with spikes. The eyes in the skulls glowed red.

Bear didn't care. He bowled into them like a charging bull. He smashed them with his shield and chopped at them with his sword. This is what he was for.

The skeletons turned out to only be better armored. They were as unskilled and uncoordinated as all the other skeletons Bear had faced today. There were a lot of them and Bear was busy deflecting their clumsy attacks as he crushed them.

The crashing of steel on steel was deafening. There was no time to look around, he could only guess what was going on with the rest of the fight, until he saw the bright flash of lighting over his head.

Bear ducked an axe blow and shattered the skeleton with a powerful blow of his shield.

Bear could hear the explosive exchange of magic over the ringing of the steel. The evil mages were on the far side of the room and more skeletons pushed forward to protect them. Most of the new waves of enemy didn't have armor and that made them much easier to smash.

Bear drove forward and crushed the fallen skeletons under his boots. He was getting close to the mages, in another moment he'd engage them too.

It was in that moment that everything changed.

A large black creature entered from a door to his right. Bear heard someone scream to his rear as he faced the beast. It could have been T'az or Kate, he couldn't tell as he looked at the horrible demon crushing skeletons to get to him.

He saluted the thing and turned to meet it. The dog-like head roared like a lion and the huge bearlike body lumbered forward. The soul-less eyes were locked on the slits in his visor.

It charged Bear and he raised his shield.

The flaming claws were deflected by Bear's shield and Bear countered with the sword, but he missed. Nothing was there.

For a beast that large, it was incredibly fast. Bear felt the searing heat as his back plate turned a blow of the flaming claws. He knew that plate was ruined.

There was more screaming behind him, but he still didn't have time. Bear ducked and spun, avoiding the next blow from the claws.

Bear stood and pushed some unarmed skeletons out of his way. He circled to the beast's left and leapt back as it lunged with flames dripping from its teeth.

The two of them clashed back and forth. Neither made a sound as they struggled.

The only noise Bear heard was the crunching of the bones under their feet.

Bear had turned several savage blows with his shield and the shield was severely damaged. He doubted if it would take another blow as he watched the thing circling to his right.

I have to get past its defense, Bear thought as the great maw lunged at him.

It was so fast, he had little option but to use the shield again.

The great teeth clamped down on the shield and wrenched Bear to his left. Bear didn't resist. He let go of the shield and spun away from it to the beast's right.

Raising his sword over his head he chopped down, behind the beast's head with both hands. A great flaming rent opened in its neck and it howled and tried to back away.

Bear brought his great sword down again like an ax-with all his strength and weight behind it. He hit the flaming gap in the beast's neck again and again. Burning blood leapt from the wound.

The beast finally collapsed, the claw flames died, and the fur smoldered. Its head was nearly severed. Flames licked around the body once and then died.

Bear could hardly believe it. It had been luck or the will of the gods, to be spun in that direction. A breath of relief whooshed out of him as he became aware that no sounds of battle remained.

Bear wearily tried to catch his breath as he turned around. Piles of cinders were heaped by the far door. The mages he'd been trying to engage were gone. Hestal had done his job.

There was another dead beast across the room. In the dim light of the ladle laying on the floor, Bear thought something was in its mouth.

Bear crunched bones as he walked across the room to the second beast.

The light of the ladle laying amongst the skeleton bones revealed Foester in its mouth. One whole side of Foester's body was torn open and all of his blood had poured out to mix with bones and dust.

Kate was leaning over him, her hair covered his face.

"Kate," Bear said.

"No, no, no," Kate shook her head. "It should be me."

"He's dead," Bear said as the sadness hit him.

T'az was trying to put a bandage on Thervan. Blood oozed out between her hands. They already had a tourniquet on his arm. His left hand was gone.

The beast must have crushed it along with his small shield. Thervan was very pale in the dim light.

Bernard was working on Hestal. Hestal looked badly burned and there was a bloody scar across his face. The battle was fiercer than he knew.

"Kate, the living need you," Bear sniffed. He wouldn't cry for Foester in front of his enemies. He wouldn't.

Kate got up and moved to help Thervan. Bear kneeled down to his squire's head and closed his eyes. "I promise; your family will be alright. I'll serve them like you've served me. I swear it."

Bear wrenched the jaws of the beast apart and eased his friend to the ground.

"He saved us," T'az said. "Thervan went down. That thing was just too fast. Foester saved us."

Bear could only nod. He had known all his life that Foester was a hero. This was only confirmation. Bear covered his hero with a blanket from Foester's scattered pack.

Verig hopped cheerfully back into the room and tied a bag full of something to his belt.

"Let's go!" Verig said, "I told you what would happen."

He seemed inordinately happy as he looked over the battered group. Bear thought he looked unusually disheveled. It appeared he'd participated in the fight, but Bear hadn't seen him in the room and he opened the door from the other side.

"Give us a moment," T'az yelled at him.

"No," Verig snarled at her. "We have to get out of this room before everything changes. Come on. Now!"

Bear picked up Foester's body. He'd leave his shield behind; it was mangled anyway. Bear followed Verig into the next room with his sad burden.

This room was quiet. There were four doors on the left wall, a great double door on the right, and a small door stood open straight ahead.

Bear put Foester in the middle of the room.

T'az helped Thervan in and Kate helped Hestal. Bernard slammed the door shut behind them.

Bear sat down next to his dead friend. "What's next?"

"Collect the treasure," Verig laughed. "Ladies, come on-through the little door. The thing you're after is in there. Hurry and get them."

Kate seemed very tired, but she got up and T'az went with her. They both disappeared through the small door in the far wall.

Bear watched Verig. The new bag tied to his belt sounded like it was full of stones, and he paced back and forth in front of the double doors. He was talking to someone. Which seemed crazy, but Bear would believe anything now.

"I know, I know, the old plan isn't going to work," Verig whispered. "We won't get another chance after this debacle and we can't go back. This is the only opportunity. It has to be now."

Bear thought it was an argument. Verig said he didn't care a few times and then he stopped across the room from Bear. His shoulders slumped and he turned to face the knight.

He seemed to say, "...you're right, if it gets him it's worth it," and Verig walked straight over to Bear.

"Knight, you're the only one that can do this." Verig took a knee next to him.

"Do what?" Bear asked.

"What is with you people and the questions? You want to live?" Verig waited until Bear nodded. "Then shut up and listen."

CHAPTER 21

Kate shuddered as she stood up and said a quick prayer. She had loved her village priest as a child. Revered him even, but he would have been useless here.

Today had been so far outside what anyone even imagined, Kate wasn't sure she could take more.

She had used her power to fight. She'd healed and helped. In the last room she'd deflected magic and fought skeletons. They were only halfway through the adventure. They still had to get out.

"It's near the middle. Read the labels," Verig said and Kate walked into the room.

This room was indeed full of treasure. Incalculable wealth lay before her. Trinkets and displays of swords and armor lined the walls. Chests and chests of jewels and gold lay around the floor.

This was the wealth of nations, tithed to Black Tower for millennia.

Kate wasn't interested in the money. She spun her head around and took in the whole room. Kate's vision swept over T'az, who had her dagger out.

"What happened to your sword?" Kate asked. This is the first time she'd seen T'az without a sword.

"It broke killing the beast that got Foester," T'az said grimly.

"Your father's sword." Kate knew that was T'az' last link to her father. It felt like the last straw. "I'm so sorry."

"It's a small sacrifice if we can get out of this place alive." T'az moved forward. "Let's get what we came for."

Kate agreed and they began the search. The light was dim and the writing on the displays was very spidery. Some of it looked like a different language completely.

The murdered woman appeared before Kate again, her cracked lips smiling. She beckoned Kate to follow her, she led Kate to a cabinet in a row of displays.

The woman disappeared.

Kate walked over and stood in front of the display cases. The case on her right held a large leather bag. The writing on the label may have said 'Markinet'.

Kate opened the display case and fished open the leather bag. Inside were a magnificent pair of stone tablets. They were shiny and grey-marbled like polished granite. The gold lettering was inlaid and beautifully crafted even though she couldn't read it.

"T'az! Here they are. Haervan would love this," Kate cried with joy. Months of travel, death, and torture to stand in front of this goal. It was unreal.

"Wow," T'az said, "That's something to see."

Kate touched one of the tablets. They were smooth and warm to the touch. It felt like they were vibrating. "They have power; the story was right."

"What are you going to do with them?" T'az asked.

Kate hefted one. It was fairly large. "They don't weigh anything, but I've lost my pack."

Kate had come to take them but, it was almost as if she hadn't planned to get this far. She had no plan to carry the stones. She had no plan to win.

"Take the bag too," T'az said, "and let's get out of here."

Kate tested the old leather. The bag seemed strong, so she left them in the bag. T'az had moved back to the door and Kate followed.

Passing a display with a single sword in it, Kate heard the sword plead. The case was made for a pair, but the sibling was missing.

Standing in front of the sword was like being outside the prison in Theopolis. The sword seemed to beg to be released and it called to Kate for justice.

T'az did need a sword.

The sword glowed blue as Kate reached for it. There was no time to ask questions, but she felt like she'd seen this sword before. She grabbed it and followed T'az back out of the room.

"Why did you grab the sword?" T'az asked as she closed the door behind them.

"I think it's for you," Kate said as she handed the sword over. "Take it. I'm sure we're still going to need you to fight."

T'az drew the sword from its intricate scabbard and hefted it. She wielded the big sword like it was a feather. The sword seemed to sing it was so happy.

T'az seemed nervous of the sword. "I don't know, but it hardly seems like anything worse can happen."

Kate left T'az and looked over the others. All they had to do now was get out.

Verig was in a huddle with Bear. Hestal, in spite of his burns and obvious weariness, was keeping watch with Bernard. Bernard stood at the door that they had fought so hard to get through with his club and shield.

Thervan seemed asleep but he was holding Foester with his one good arm.

"Got everything?" Verig asked as he left the troubled knight.

Kate was suspicious. "You seem positively giddy Verig, what's going on?"

"Oh, it's going to be a great day, little missy." Verig had a big smile on his face. "Great day."

T'az stopped him. "We still need to get out of here before it's great, Verig. How many rooms like the last one before we escape?"

"Oh, just one more room." Verig moved over to a large set of double doors. "Just one more."

Thervan and Hestal could barely walk, leaving Bear and T'az to fight. Kate and Bernard would have to fill in and help. It was too much to bring Foester with them. He was a big man, even in death.

Kate's eyes filled with tears and she prayed for his soul.

"He wouldn't want us to die to save his body," Bear said as he watched Kate bless his squire. "I know it.

"Besides," Verig offered. "You gonna ride all the way home with a stinking corpse?"

Kate groaned. He was right but, "you're a piece of work Verig. Why the big doors?"

"Check the others if you want," Verig said calmly. "They aren't trapped."

Bernard yanked open all four doors across from the big double doors. There was nothing behind them but wall. He turned back to the others shocked.

"No choices now. Only one place left to go," Verig shrugged.

Verig swung open the double doors and led them down a broad staircase. It ended in another set of double doors.

The doors behind them shut and the sound of creatures filling the room behind them clearly echoed in the stone stairwell.

"Is this the way out?" T'az asked.

"Nope!" Verig answered cheerfully. "There is no way out now."

Confusion was starting to set in. Kate looked around-there were no exits in the stairs. They were made of the same magic rock as the Tower, but the wall at the bottom of the stairs was made out of marble blackened by soot.

Kate put her hand on the very old and rotten doors. She turned and faced Verig. "What do you mean?"

"Thanks to you, there will be no sneaking out." Verig took the vial hanging around his neck off and held it in his hand. "We will have to make them let us leave."

"How do we do that?" Kate was tired of his riddles. The buzz of power in her head had diminished. Her friends probably didn't have the strength for another fight like the one they had just survived.

Verig swept his hands over the door, pushing Kate back. "The last room," he sighed and turned back to them. "This room is the emperor's throne room."

"Yes, that emperor," he said. "All the stories you've heard are true and more. This is the room."

He paused and listened to the door.

"I haven't been in it. The gypsy rumors say it's exactly like it was that day." Verig turned back to them. "The day it was cursed."

"Cursed?" Hestal wheezed.

"Oh yes. Cursed. Don't try any magic here. The last emperor never liked magic," Verig chuckled at Hestal. "This room has seen mages so powerful they made the gods tremble. There is some question how well magic works in here at all now."

He opened the door wide. "Do not touch anything. You are going to see and hear a lot of awful things. Stick together no matter what."

"You said we had to touch two things. The tablets and what else?" Kate asked him.

"The plan has changed," he hissed as he stepped into the dark room. "Touch nothing else."

He led them into the room. Which started to glow brighter and brighter. They could now see the thick coat of dust, that had lain undisturbed for so long. It was fluffing up like a mist around their feet.

The hall was huge. Gold pillars and doors lined the walls. The ceiling, though dirty, was covered in beautiful frescos. The light magically filled the room even though a source for the light couldn't be seen.

The double doors they exited were almost centered on the wall. Far to the right was another set of double doors, but those doors appeared to have been barred by giants. Kate doubted Bear could lift those braces.

"You could fit four or five of the biggest ships I've seen in here-masts and all," T'az said.

Verig was headed in the other direction. There was a dais with steps up to large golden throne. Two smaller thrones sat below it. There was a partition wall behind the thrones with wide hallways on either side.

Kate felt malevolence lurking behind that wall.

"Hmm...," Verig said thoughtfully. "I had no idea it would turn light in here, no one said anything about that. Stay where you are. I'm going down to the thrones."

He walked off with the mist of dust swirling around his feet.

Kate noticed the carpet in the middle wasn't nearly as dusty, at least from a point about halfway down the room to just before the thrones themselves. It reminded her of something.

As she looked around she couldn't help feeling this room was beautiful. The intricacies of the carved stone were amazing. The gold was not overdone and helped bring light to every corner. It was possibly the most beautiful place she had ever been.

The whole room spoke of grandeur long past.

"I've been here before, but it was all dark," Kate said as she thought back to her dreams. "You couldn't see any of this."

"What are the humps in the dust?" Bernard asked. "More bodies?"

"I don't think so. I think there was furniture that has rotted over time. It's been a couple thousand years," Kate shrugged. It would be hard to touch anything here. There was little standing.

"The thrones look fine, shiny even," Bernard pointed out.

"I don't know, Bernard, magic maybe?" Kate was investigating the closest statue.

The craftsmanship was amazing and they were very life like. Some of them were monsters she didn't recognize. Their gemstone eyes gleamed in the light.

They were a little frightening, but gorgeous.

"Beautiful," she said.

"Horrid," T'az disagreed.

Kate turned back to the group. They were huddled together. Obviously, they didn't seem to feel the same as she did. It was like they saw a completely different room.

Verig made his way to the spot where the dust on the carpet wasn't very thick, just in front of the smaller thrones. He laid his amulet on the dais and stood up.

There was a quiet pop and Kate realized they weren't alone. A darkened figure in a long black robe had appeared on the carpet.

"Verig," the new person stated.

"Theris." Verig seemed to know this person. "It's been a very long time."

Theris strolled towards Verig. "Getting a little gray there." He laughed pointing at Verig's hair. "I'm the same and always will be."

"I wouldn't call that an advantage," Verig sneered at the newcomer.

"You've been busy, Verig," Theris said. "I'm not sure what your amulet is made of, but we've had trouble tracking you, and we couldn't see you. I just assumed you were using the carbuncle you stole from me. Don't worry though, I have plenty of time to examine it after you're dead."

"Oh I used it," Verig laughed. "Mother protected me from you, you know. She made that amulet, after you stabbed her, but before you cut off her head."

Verig peered at the dark man. "I always wondered what happened, did you get squeamish after you stabbed your mother in the heart? Do the others know?"

"You know nothing," Theris growled. "Our mother was weak. Peddling cantrips to bumpkins. The stupid gypsy woman couldn't even keep either of our fathers around. I made her immortal."

"I know everything," Verig hissed. "I was there. Hidden in the trick box. I saw it all, you malevolent ass."

Verig started pacing. "After you left, she was still alive. She filled that amulet with her heart blood before she died."

"Big deal. No one cares," Theris mocked Verig. "You stole from me and you became a thief that day. While I became one of the most powerful mages in a select group of powerful mages. I'd say the results prove I was doing what was best. You're nothing but scum, begging and stealing from your betters."

"Really. That's how you feel." Verig stepped up on the dais. "Is that how you feel when you lead some poor fool in here to die?"

Kate gasped. Her vision of this place and the sacrifice had been through Theris' eyes. She knew this man from her dream.

Theris smiled. "Yes. Surprising how many of the gypsy rumors are true. That sacrifice is necessary to save our magic. Mother would have understood."

There was a bright flash. Energy was deflected away from Verig.

Verig laughed at him. "Mother wasn't weak, idiot. She's been protecting me since her death. Mother's power is the reason you couldn't track me in your own tower. She stayed with the gypsies because she loved us more than magic."

There was a furious assault. Terrible creatures, that Kate could only describe as demons, rose from the dust to support Theris as he hammered at Verig, but Verig just stood there and laughed.

"It would work better for you if you came over here and stabbed me. But, I'm better with the knife and you know it." Verig stepped towards Theris and the magical assault continued.

Demons moved to keep Verig from reaching his brother. Verig stopped in the face of the violent demons. "Oh well, we'll do this the other way."

He walked back to the dais.

"What other way?" Theris said glibly. "You say that like there are options."

There was a female figure Kate recognized, standing near the lower thrones. It was the murdered woman with the bloody chest. She now stood clearly between the two. The dead woman only had eyes for Verig.

Theris turned away from her and Verig laughed at him. "You kept her head for all these years and now you won't look at her?"

Kate now knew why he was so distressed in the room of disembodied heads. It made sense why he hadn't really tried to stop her from freeing those souls in spite of the danger. One of them had been his mother.

"Coward," Verig spat. "I knew the Grand Master would send you. I bet he knows all your little secrets."

Theris seemed stung by the words, but he also seemed to notice the group huddled not far from the door for the first time.

"Oh brother. I had no idea the depth of evil you had sunk to," Theris laughed. "All righteous in your indignation over the death of our mother and you led such a merry little band here as your own sacrifices."

He turned back to Verig with an evil smile. "Do the little mice even know why they are here?"

Theris turned back to Kate and the group. Demons swirled in the misting dust as he came closer. Kate didn't know what to do. She prayed, but it felt like her very soul was draining out of her.

Hestal started to mumble, but Bernard silenced him.

"Yes, silence the little magician, healer." Theris stopped but he was not far enough away to suit Kate.

Theris chuckled. "He knows he is nothing. His death will come soon enough. A perfect sacrifice for the pathetic emperor. The rest of you will wish you lived that long."

Theris laughed and his dark eyes flashed fire.

Kate stared at him, poleaxed by fear.

Theris turned to her. "And the little priestess is here too. No little stone to help you now. Gracar was quite upset with your little stunt. I don't think he'll be as nice next time. You won't like the punishment planned for you."

Stinging pain raced along her scarred skin as Theris' eyes bore in on her. Kate could feel power probing out of him. His eyes were like needles.

"He isn't here to help you?" Kate said out loud, but it sounded like a whisper.

"It speaks," Theris smiled. "Here? No one comes here. Do you even know where you are?"

He swelled until he was taller than Bear.

"This is the Throne Room of the Emperor," Theris yelled triumphantly. "In this room the Black Wizard king and his few remaining men faced the Emperor of the world and his priests. Not even gods come here. I volunteered and I will be rewarded for my daring."

He walked to the middle of the room. His robe swooshed around him causing dust to billow up in clouds.

"It was here. Right here," Theris said extravagantly making his point. "The Emperor's armies were destroying all of the Southern kingdoms. The power of the Black Mages was broken. Weak and facing certain death, they tricked the emperor into leaving his armies and coming back here."

He stomped his foot again, making the dust cloud up. "But the mages were already here. They trapped him in this room. He cursed them in this room. Thousands died in this room!"

Kate could feel it. She didn't need shadows to see the echoes of the past. The long dead were still here and cowing her friends. They were all here. Thousands of years of hate and anger.

Theris walked back to the group. "And this room has stayed exactly the same. Nearly three thousand years. Not even the dust moved. Until you came."

Theris pointed at Kate. "You can feel them, can't you priestess? They are beyond your gods." He reached out gingerly to the air around him. "You can almost touch them."

Theris laughed again as he surveyed the fear in their eyes. "He didn't tell you any of that. He didn't tell you that's why the doors won't open."

He pointed at the doors. "All sealed by a powerful curse. Just the one you came through. Just the door the Black Wizard King made. The one that goes back into the tower."

T'az stepped in front of Kate and raised her new sword.

"I know that sword little girl. It may keep me at bay for a moment, but not for long," Theris laughed as demons swarmed up to T'az.

T'az stood her ground and Kate started to worry it was all over. Verig had lied.

"Theris," Verig shouted. "Aren't you forgetting something?"

There was a pop and Theris was back on the carpet, leaving demons to surround the group.

"Forgetting? I don't think so," the black mage said smoothly. "I just want your little mice to know how they are going to die and that it's your fault."

He waved expansively towards them. "Your plan is faulty, Verig. They aren't going to touch something for you, you don't have another way to trap me, and the carbuncle may not save you."

"Who said I'm here to be saved?" Verig asked.

Another assault of magic fire washed over Verig. He seemed stung under the pressure.

Theris laughed. "She weakens Verig. That trinket she gave you won't hold forever and once you're dead, I'll be redeemed. We'll feed on your little friend's souls during our rituals this very night."

Theris turned back to the group which was still surrounded by demons. "He did tell you that's why you are all here. This day in particular. Didn't he make you wait until this day to come?"

He smiled knowingly. "Oh he brought you here, but he has no intention of staying with you," Theris gloated. "The little thief probably even told you not to touch anything until he directed you to."

Theris walked to a golden candelabra.

"No one truly knows what will happen when you do touch something in here." Theris waved a hand around the ancient piece of furniture.

"But it will be awful," he laughed. "Why would he ask you to do it then? Because he has no plans to share your fate. My conniving, thieving, little brother, always looked out for himself."

Kate felt the truth of what he said wash over her. Verig had brought them here on this day. He ordered them to stay huddled together while he separated himself. He controlled the rooms they entered and demanded they wait until he said to touch anything.

Fear gripped Kate's heart. It was her fault. She had never questioned Verig. She had led her friends to their doom.

Verig's laughter broke into Kate's fear. "You're right Theris. That was the plan. It seemed perfect. They mindlessly wanted to come. They were good enough to kill your demons and acolytes. I knew the Grand Master would send you for me. Mother would protect me, and you would die."

Theris swelled. "But you aren't going to do it. There is no way out of this room. Not even a magical one where you are standing, Verig. No magic works near the throne itself, I'm told. No way out and your little friends aren't going to sacrifice themselves for your revenge," Theris laughed, "Which means I win."

Theris looked quickly around for a moment. He was obviously proud of himself, but he seemed curious about the room itself. He didn't talk for a moment as he took it in.

"I am a little surprised your presence at the thrones hasn't already angered the emperor," Theris commented. "No one has seen this room since that day. It's always too dark in here to see anything when we bring the sacrifice. I must question your souls to find out how you made it light."

The demons seemed to sense victory and they danced and howled around the group. Kate couldn't look at them. They were horrid with sharp teeth and claws. Fire dripped from their mouths in anticipation.

Another magical assault drove Verig up to the golden throne. His mother didn't have to protect him now. All the spells seemed to fade as they neared him. Magic didn't work near the emperor's throne.

The ghostly woman seemed to be crying.

"Aww. Mother's crying for you Verig," Theris mocked. "She knows you will soon join her and since she stayed, both of you can enjoy eternity in your very own crystals."

Theris seemed immensely pleased with himself. "You can't stay near that throne for long. What's it feel like? Can you feel his presence?"

Verig looked over and caught Kate's eye.

She couldn't help but feel compassion for this man. Even if he had knowingly led them to their doom. A small boy had been forced to watch his own mother's murder and beheading. The crime committed willingly by his own brother as a way to feed the brother's ambition.

Kate wondered how many times Verig had come here. How many times had he seen his mother's disembodied head floating in green horror? How many times had he tried to get revenge?

She understood the man. He was just a man, facing a brother who had become one of the immortal Black Mages. Power flowed through his brother like blood. A knife, no matter how righteous, could not touch him.

How could any man get revenge against that power? She thought Verig was defeated and no matter what her future held, she couldn't be angry with him.

Kate's heart swelled. She felt the peace of Mirsha. She smiled at Verig and tried to share her peace with him and whispered a prayer for the poor tortured man that led them here.

Verig smiled back. He was not defeated. He stood and stepped up to the Emperor's Throne. "You are wrong on a couple of points, Theris."

"Wrong. Pah!" Theris smiled. "You always were a pathetic little worm. The others are coming, you know. This will be a great night."

"Really? Okay. Now where did I put that carbuncle." Verig rooted through his pockets dramatically. The female ghost seemed very sad, but it moved up to be next to Verig. "Oh yeah, I don't have it anymore."

Bear spoke softly. "Everyone interlock your arms. Hold on tight." The group quickly followed his quiet commands. They didn't know why or what he was doing with the thing in his hands.

This was hope.

Theris was still yelling at Verig. "What do you mean you don't have it? It is priceless! Not even a worm like you would have sold it."

Verig moved to the throne and started to sit.

Theris panicked. "Hold, damn you! That could end the world! YOU WOULDN'T DARE!"

Verig raised an eyebrow to him. The sad ghost put her hand on his shoulder. "Wouldn't I? How little you really know, Theris."

"NO!" Screamed Theris.

"Hold on" said Berigral and he pushed something in his hand.

Kate heard a little pop and they were suddenly standing at the horses. Brendan was shocked by their sudden appearance and quickly realized his father wasn't in the group.

Hestal and Thervan collapsed. Bernard ran to the horses for supplies. T'az seemed stunned but she continued to hold on to Bear and he hugged her close.

Kate could only stare back at the tower. Nothing seemed changed on the outside.

"That poor man," Kate thought.

What horror was he suffering so he could avenge his mother.

Verig let them live.

CHAPTER 22

Back in the throne room Verig sat. The room filled with screams of agony and the dead rose to life. Theris cursed viciously as his demons evaporated before the emperor's army of dead warriors.

Theris fought them. Screaming the whole time and blasting the dead away from him. He killed them in great swaths, but they kept coming-eating away at him and his power.

Verig smiled, the rumor had been right, no one could leave the room, even by magic, after he sat on the throne. It had taken decades of collecting stories and searching the tower for clues, but this was the perfect ending.

It was his brother's turn to suffer. Something large and malevolent stood behind him. He knew what it wanted. He held up his hand. "Wait, just a moment."

The spirit paused.

His brother was being torn apart. He wanted to see it.

Whimpering and crying Theris was finally pulled down. He wailed one last time, "Why won't you help me?" and was forever silent.

Verig put his hand down.

"Thank you," he said sincerely.

There was a swift motion and Verig's head rolled across the dusty carpet. He was still smiling as the light in the room dimmed back to the quiet blackness.

CHAPTER 23

Kate entered a crowded Tabbard's at midday. Tabbard waved from the bar and Kate knew what he was pointing at. He knew they were coming today and had set an area aside for them.

Autumn was upon Theopolis. Four months to the day from their escape from the tower.

The day Foester had died.

The day she was sure Verig had also died.

Even with the magic jewel that had allowed Verig to come and go as he pleased, they had ridden home. The team agreed to leave it with Hestal. He could study it.

It was made by a Black Mage and they were wary of anything that came from that awful place. If it appeared good and easy to use, there had to be a payment.

Hopefully Hestal would figure it out.

Today was not the day to worry about it. Today was the day Kate had made everyone promise to meet. She had wanted that promise because their return had been nearly as traumatic as the quest itself.

The weary travelers had been greeted with celebration. It felt like everyone wanted a piece of their victory. Every member of the party was pulled in different directions and they were quickly separated.

They all faced the aftermath alone.

The Council had been the worst for Kate. After all their machinations, they arranged a moving ceremony to restore the tablets in the Council Chamber and completely ignored the laws they had passed to stop her. The position of the hand was quietly removed and the laws on secret votes—as

299

well as the interpretation that priestesses were inferior—disappeared from the record.

She had been feted and promoted. Kate had been surrounded by talk, but no one listened. Her lone voice and the true account of what happened, was drowned in tub of inaccuracies and lies.

Deoshus had been clear in his speech that it was the Council's responsibility to control the narrative. Information had to be released in a way that supported the Council and the rest of the Council agreed.

The story was dangerous. The sheep must remain sheep.

T'az had gone with Bear to Nordsvard and his family's home. Kate wished them well, but feared their relationship was bound to cause trouble. They had love, but they were from diametrically opposite worlds. Overcoming the chasm between their pasts was going to be difficult.

Kate had hoped that three months was long enough for the fervor to die down. It was long enough in Theopolis. People barely noticed her anymore, but she didn't go out often and stayed covered to avoid the stares her scars attracted.

Here the suppression by the Council was absolute and that frustrated Kate, as she had changes to make. She'd experienced the truth. The Code was the problem and even more radical were her ideas on the nature of the gods.

A small child approached her as she sat alone at the table reserved by Tabbard for the questers' reunion.

The young southern girl was wide-eyed as she stared at the red haired priestess in the light grey robes - trimmed in sky blue. The little girl had a beautiful autumn floral dress and bare feet. Her hair wildly framed a cute little face.

"Come here, little girl," Kate said with a gentle smile, and the girl complied.

Kate picked her up. "Do you like cheese?"

"Yes," she said as she took the cheese. "Why are those funny marks on your face?"

Kate laughed. It was the first question everyone asked. "An evil man attacked me. Even though I won, I was left scarred."

The little girl had moved on to her robe. "You've got a star!"

"I completed a quest given by Holy Mirsha." The child seemed unimpressed as she fingered the trim on Kate's robe and noisily ate cheese.

Kate smiled at her. "It is a symbol of success."

A voice Kate knew all too well spoke behind her. "Was it, then?"

Kate turned to see T'az with another woman. T'az looked the same in her blousy white shirt and leather pants.

The other woman begged Kate's forgiveness and snatched up the cheese eating child. Kate was a little sad to see her go, but smiled at T'az.

"Well was it?" T'az asked again.

"I guess there is some doubt about that," Kate said. "Where's Bear?"

T'az darkened. "I haven't seen them in months."

"Why?" Kate asked. "I thought you two were destined for each other."

T'az laughed. "Maybe, but when we split up, I was about as welcome as a case of the pox in Nordsvard."

"By Bear?" Kate couldn't believe it. He loved T'az, Kate was sure of it.

"No, not him." T'az poured her wine. "He was confused back in his old environment. He was the returning hero. Dukes and Lords wanted his time. I don't know if he knows what he wants."

"I'm sorry," Kate said.

At that moment, Bernard wandered in. He wore stained peasant brown robe and mismatched shoes. He looked terrible.

"What happened to you?" T'az asked.

Bernard had gained a lot of weight and looked sickly. He sat and poured himself a glass of wine and drained it.

"A lot," he said around a mouthful of cheese.

A quiet pop alerted them that Hestal had arrived. He was still scarred from the battle and looked very thin in unmarked grey robes.

Bear and Thervan walked in before Kate could do more than say hello to Hestal. They were tan and looked in good health.

Greetings were shared around and everyone took a seat. Tabbard brought more wine and more cheese.

Bear raised his glass. "To Foester, the bravest and best of men."

The group drank their toast.

Kate raised her glass. "To Verig. Not the bravest or most honest man, but without whom we wouldn't be here."

The group again drank the toast.

"So there's still a question outstanding," T'az said. "Bernard, the story?"

"Well, my wife declared me dead and found another while we were gone. Not a big loss." Bernard emptied another glass and T'az refilled it for him. "I tried healing people when I got back, but the priests of Gaia claimed I was a witch. I got a month in prison, only our recent success kept me from burning."

"That's outrageous!" Kate exclaimed.

"I told you people wouldn't react well," T'az said as she refilled Bernard's glass again.

Bernard nodded to her. "I won't do it again. I've decided to be a drunk."

"That's awful." Kate felt pity for him. He didn't deserve this. "Hestal, what about you? You've gotten better."

"Yes, the book in Verig's bag was a spell book of the Black Tower, but my story is similar to Bernard's." Hestal smiled sadly. "I was thrown out upon my return for not turning everything over to my master and learning things that weren't authorized by my master."

He finished his glass of wine.

"I started my own school, but within a month, it was closed." Hestal paused and T'az filled his wine too. "The guild has been hunting me. I've been in hiding."

"Our story is also similar," Thervan said. "After the parties ended, our place and that of our family was only reluctantly restored. Leoshus and Vestral had their day. History is being rewritten. We no longer resemble the people that went on the quest."

Bear nodded. "People's minds can be manipulated so easily. The truth doesn't matter."

Thervan waved his stump. "I am, on the other hand, learning to shoot with a modified bow. That's something."

Everyone smiled at his little joke, they all knew what he lost.

Kate thought about the pain Thervan had suffered. They had been afraid of pursuit and pushed as hard as he could stand to get home. Weeks of riding in that kind of pain-Kate couldn't imagine it.

"He's still good." Bear clapped his brother on his shoulder. "I'm out of the tournaments as no one will fight me. Mother grieved us as if we died, she's not ready to go back on that, and ignores us. I think the idleness is worse than anything."

"Well we're not idle anymore," Thervan said happily.

"We bought a farm," Bear said. "Like Foester wanted. Far from the cities, near the mountains. That's where Brendan is. He's the man of the house now that his family has moved in."

Thervan smiled. "Hard work in the outdoors and good food. It's not too bad. It's remote, but the view is spectacular."

Bear looked longingly at T'az. "It's different for us now."

T'az pushed the wine at him. "My story is the same. After Nordsvard, I worked a couple of small jobs and wandered back here."

"But you all have money." Kate hadn't taken any of the loot Verig had stolen and given to Bear before the throne room. It had all been in gems and there was quite a lot of it.

Bernard chuckled. "Money hasn't gotten me anything. Who knew I was in as much danger at home as I was when I nearly pissed myself in the tower."

"When was that again?" Hestal asked.

Bernard hung his head, "You all know, when those beasts came out and I screamed."

Bear put his arm on Bernard's shoulder and refilled his wine as everyone had a quiet chuckle.

"You're honest and right to be afraid at times like that," Bear said. "You're alright in my book."

"Mine too." Kate smiled at Bernard and everyone else agreed.

"What about you?" T'az asked Kate.

"I guess I fared the best. I was promoted and serve on the Council," Kate sighed. "I thought I could make change that way - from the inside."

Kate felt the hopelessness creep in. "But it's impossible. I'm blocked. One voice in hundreds. To discuss what I know is heresy."

Kate turned to T'az. "I'm less popular now than I was before in the cloister. People are scared of the stories about what we did, even if the stories are all lies. Then there's the scars..."

Kate uncovered her arms, showing the deep red marks in her pale skin. Kate traced the scars Gracar had given her. They lured her, the power, the unending life, and the knowledge Gracar had.

"They haven't faded. No one wants to be around me. I'm told that people say I'm cursed." Kate covered her arms again. "Maybe I am."

Kate smiled as her friends looked concerned. "I don't participate in rituals anymore. Haervan and a few others still speak to me. I guess stories are easier if you don't meet the subject of them."

They all nodded, lost for a moment in their own thoughts.

"What about the tablets? Those are powerful objects." Hestal asked.

Kate shook her head. "They argued about that for months. Without the Codex, no one can read them. They are going to put them on a statue."

Hestal grimaced. "A statue! Why? They could research the language, they could try."

"I don't think they want to know what those tablets say," Kate sighed. "Gracar said as much and we guessed as much in Nordrigen."

"Why did we go then?" Bernard asked.

It was Bear that replied. "I don't think the tablets were the real goal. I think it just set into motion the gods' bigger plans."

Bernard finished his wine again. "That's depressing. All that suffering."

The mood darkened around the table.

"Anyone hear anything about Jarusco?" Hestal asked to break the tension.

Bear shook his head. "Keenen was at the big celebration, Jarusco passed back through Chryselles without trouble, but nothing other than that."

Tabbard brought everyone food. He had made Kate's favorite dish, pot roast with potatoes and fresh greens. Kate smiled at the brusque man. Scarred as he was, he was very thoughtful.

Kate's parents had seemed frightened of their scarred daughter. She knew from his tone, Haervan wasn't pleased with her Council performance, so more and more Tabbard was filling the role as father for her.

Tabbard nodded and left again.

The group ate, but Kate was troubled. "What will you all do now?"

"Nothing," said Bernard.

"What we need is another adventure." T'az said as she speared a potato.

"What are the odds we survive another one?" Hestal asked.

"You call this surviving?" Bernard asked. "I'm in, I don't care what it is, as long as we don't spend a lot of time at sea."

Bear smiled sadly. "You're probably right. Maybe it is better to go again. Die a legend. The family would like that outcome better."

"I don't know," Kate said. "There is so much trouble here. Can't you feel the undercurrent of anger and dissatisfaction? There are work stoppages, and angry mobs here daily. The Churlars are being pushed to the limit."

"How is staying going to help?" T'az asked. "I'm with Bernard."

"There's nothing here for me," Hestal said. "I'll go."

"I'll go," Thervan agreed. "I don't want to be part of the troubles and I'm afraid they are going to ask us to lead it."

"So Kate, we're going somewhere, are you in?" T'az asked her with a smile.

"You know it's not that easy for me," Kate sighed. "The chains of the Code are more restrictive for priests. I'll have to get permission. I'm not even supposed to be here now."

"Just say you're going to market and don't come back," Bernard suggested.

"They'd hunt me," Kate said. "It's a long ride to the Wall."

Hestal nodded. "They would. They fear you."

"So convince the High Priest," T'az suggested. "Call it missionary work."

"Besides, we don't need funds," Bear said. "You should all come to the farm first. We can work it out there without being troubled."

Kate hesitated. Haervan wasn't happy with her. He may even be relieved if she left. But how could she do missionary work for the Council when she didn't believe in them anymore?

"I think even you are an outcast now, like the rest of us," Hestal smiled at her.

"I will ask," Kate said as she decided to go. It was the best choice for her. "We will figure something out."

Kate knew she wouldn't be able to work in the library again. She still saw the shadow spirits, but now they comforted her instead of scaring her. Mirsha had a plan and Kate had to trust that. She would figure out a way to go.

CPSIA information can be obtained
at www.ICGtesting.com
Printed in the USA
LVOW12s1823170717
541648LV00004B/857/P